AMAZING GRACE

Praise for Book One, *Amelia's Prayer*

"The quality of the writing and the sweetness of the story will carry readers to the poignant conclusion."
—*Kirkus Reviews*

"Will appeal to fans of family saga although it easily transcends the genre."
—*Blue Ink Reviews*

"Elegantly written, a must-read, one that begs to be enjoyed again and again."
—*Clarion Foreword Reviews*

Christiane Banks

AMAZING GRACE

iUniverse

AMAZING GRACE

Copyright © 2020 Christiane Banks.

All rights reserved. No part of this book may be used or reproduced by any means, graphic, electronic, or mechanical, including photocopying, recording, taping or by any information storage retrieval system without the written permission of the author except in the case of brief quotations embodied in critical articles and reviews.

Certain characters in this work are historical figures, and certain events portrayed did take place. However, this is a work of fiction. All the other characters, names, and events as well as all places, incidents, organizations, and dialogue in this novel are either the products of the author's imagination or are used fictitiously.

iUniverse books may be ordered through booksellers or by contacting:

iUniverse
1663 Liberty Drive
Bloomington, IN 47403
www.iuniverse.com
844-349-9409

Because of the dynamic nature of the internet, any web addresses or links contained in this book may have changed since publication and may no longer be valid. The views expressed in this work are solely those of the author and do not necessarily reflect the views of the publisher, and the publisher hereby disclaims any responsibility for them.

Any people depicted in stock imagery provided by Getty Images are models, and such images are being used for illustrative purposes only. Certain stock imagery © Getty Images.

Book cover designed by Katie MacPhail, Victoria Mininni and Christiane Banks

ISBN: 978-1-5320-9196-4 (sc)
ISBN: 978-1-5320-9197-1 (e)

Print information available on the last page.

iUniverse rev. date: 03/24/2021

For all the children,

with love

*"I will walk with you as far as I see.
I will hold your hand with all my might.
And as we stray from our path to love,
It's all I can do to hold on, to you."*

Matthew Banks
Singer-Songwriter

Acknowledgments

I am grateful to so many people who have helped me bring *Amazing Grace* to fruition:

The editors who have collaborated on the manuscript. As Frank McCourt wrote so eloquently, you have worked wonders with my beads, creating an extraordinary necklace.

Margaret Brady for typing, reading, and sharing. Thank you.

Eileen Bell for your constant support and faith in me and also the beautiful, inspiring views.

Kathryn Riddell, my sister-in-law, good friend, and multitalented supporter. I am grateful and will never forget your kindness.

Victoria Mininni for all you give to me. I love how much you care.

Paul and Gill Goule´ for the giving and caring as though this book were your own.

To my family and friends who have shared in this journey, offering me encouragement, and believing in me, I thank you, and I cherish you always.

To my husband, Gary, your unwavering support and belief in me have given us *Amelia's Prayer* and *Amazing Grace*. Gary, you are my grace, and I am indeed blessed.

Prologue

Christmas Day 1975

On Christmas Day, Sebastian Lavalle sat at the large dining room table, surrounded by his family. He was more than grateful to be part of this celebration, which marked the coming together of his children and grandchildren for the first time in six years. Sebastian's daughter Abby Lavalle spoke up.

"I'd like to say the grace," she said softly. "I'm going to recite something very special: Amelia's prayer." Abby touched her angel Gabriel she wore at her neck. "Mother Mary, bless this day. Keep us safe in every way. Guide us to a peaceful place; fill our hearts and souls with grace. Enfold us in your tender care. Mother Mary, this is my prayer."

Sebastian could barely control his tears.

"Good call, Abby." Andre, Sebastian's son, spoke up, standing and tapping his glass. "As I am the eldest, the smartest, and the best looking," he said, laughing, and everyone groaned at him. "Behave yourselves, as I'm about to make the Christmas toast."

As he spoke, the family settled down, and a gentle silence

fell upon everyone, except for the little ones. The scene was perfect as Sebastian looked around the table. The jocularity had left Andre's voice and eyes. Sebastian thought he had a melancholy aura. It was his usual look. He was like Amelia in that way.

"Welcome, everyone. A merry Christmas to you all. As I was thinking about what I'd like to say, it occurred to me Mam would've called this family reunion nothing less than miraculous. As the oldest sibling of the eight siblings, now thirty, I'd like to say that we have, over the years, experienced rather difficult times. It is true, I have discovered, that adversity does make one stronger.

"I'd like you all to know that if you were not a part of my life by birth, I'd seek you out in order that I might call you my friend. Dad, I know this has been difficult for you, and I cannot pass judgment. In becoming a Father, I've learned to understand many things I did not understand before. We all appreciate your commitment to the family and know that Mam would be overjoyed to witness this Christmas celebration. We know how much she loved you, and we thank you for your presence. Let us raise a glass to the family."

They all stood up and said, "Cheers!" Sebastian knew there were not many dry eyes.

Sasha shouted out, "Well done, Andre! Abby, where are you flying off to next? You're lucky. Will you take me in your suitcase?"

"I'd love to," Abby replied. "This new year, we have new flight routes: Chicago, Miami, and Nashville."

"That's in Tennessee, right?" Andre said. "You'll be able to go see Aunt Helen and the family and some of the friends you made."

"I certainly hope to." Abby smiled softly.

At the end of the day, Sebastian sat beside the tree, looking at the manger. On one knee sat his Granddaughter, Amelia, and on the other knee sat his Grandson Malachi. As Andre had said, although Amelia was not physically present, her beauty shone from within the two grandbabies, leaving a legacy of love, strength, and courage for all those who came after her.

— 1 —

France 1978

Sebastian Lavalle moved with precision, winding his way through the cobblestone streets of the medieval village. As he walked, he passed the church of St. Nicholas, with its ancient steeple stretching toward the sky—a silhouette in the early evening. It was as if the steeple were reaching upward in search of some secret mystery.

Sebastian walked past the school, the bakery, and the hardware store. He meandered past the town square and the statue of St. Nicholas, which stood as it always had, sacred and strong. He saw the old town hall and the many beautiful homes winding their way toward the crest of the hill. All the homes were proud owners of window boxes bursting with hollyhocks, barberries, cyclamen, and roses in dusky reds, bright yellows, and soft mauves, all tumbling down from each box. The flowers cascaded like waterfalls full of the myriad shades of autumn and saturated the air with their perfume. Every step and every building triggered within him a memory and the emotion associated with it.

He eventually arrived at a familiar street. As he moved along the winding path toward the front door of the old stone house, he saw the old apple orchard and the mountains that framed the property. The sun was setting behind the mountains, which seemed to protect the village like the arms of the gods, steadfast and familiar.

Standing still to allow the image and the beauty to surround him, he watched the sun slip behind the mountain as it took with it the last light of the day. Breathing in the air and inhaling the perfume of France, he was filled with emotion, a warm sense that he was home, close to his roots and to his parents, his sources of strength. Wiping a tear from his cheek with the back of his hand, Sebastian looked up; he could see the stars shining like candles in the night sky. It seemed to him that the stars had guided him back.

Sebastian, for the first time in forty years, had come home.

Sebastian was not unlike the village he had returned to in that he was the same yet older. He was not as tall, as time had removed some of his height. He was heavier through the middle. However, his hair was still thick and wavy, though now it was pure white. His blue eyes were not quite as sapphire blue but more periwinkle, as they had faded over time. His eyebrows and long eyelashes were as thick but lighter. His jawline was equally as strong. Sebastian was still handsome for a man in his sixties.

After removing the key from his pocket, Sebastian unlocked the door and slowly pushed against it. The house had been vacant for those forty years. He thought to himself it was likely dilapidated and in a state of disrepair. The door creaked, heaved, and groaned as he pushed against the swollen wood.

When Sebastian stepped through the doorway, a flood of memories instantly carried him off to a distant time and place. He could see himself lifting his Amelia in his arms, carrying her over the threshold, and kissing her tenderly.

As long as he lived, he would never forget the first time he'd seen Amelia. He had been in the Free French Navy, when his ship had been torpedoed in the North Sea and badly damaged. The *Jeanne d'Arc* had been redirected to Hadrian's Shipyard in Newcastle upon Tyne to be refurbished.

Since it had been Bastille Day, the Captain had given some of the young sailors shore leave to celebrate at the local tea dance in the city.

Sebastian had been up in the balcony of the Crystal Palace ballroom, looking down on his shipmates as they danced with the beautiful young girls. He'd felt like a soaring bird, free and happy to be in the moment, away from the savage destruction of the war. Then his eyes had found her. He'd watched her gently move from table to table, pouring tea from a giant teapot. She had been tall, with dark curls cascading onto her shoulders, and wearing a golden dress. To Sebastian, she'd looked like a goddess. He'd known he had to dance with her, to hold her in his arms for just one moment.

They'd danced together all afternoon, and six days later, he'd married her. From the moment he first had laid his eyes upon her, Sebastian had understood there was no other woman walking the earth for him.

The chilly damp and darkness brought him back to the present. Every step he took induced another memory. This was the home he'd been born in and lived in during the first fifteen years of his life with his Mother, Father, and sister so long ago. Taking a flashlight from his pocket, he moved around the house, wandering from one dark tiny room to the next.

During World War II, the house had been occupied by the Nazis. His parents, sadly, had died during the occupation, leaving little to remember them by. The few sticks of furniture they'd owned had been destroyed or stolen. He had been filled with anticipation after the war, excited about the future because he and Amelia had had a home, and he'd had a good job with the French diplomatic corps. Sadly, their destiny had not been to settle in France.

Amelia had pined so badly for her home in Newcastle upon Tyne and her family that their doctor had told Sebastian to take her back to England, where she belonged. She would have some family support after giving birth to their first child, he'd said.

As he walked through the old rooms, Sebastian wondered if he had made the right decision to leave France and their little home with Amelia. He had been young and frightened. She had been young, homesick, and unable to speak the language; had not liked the food; and had been isolated day in and day out when he went to the city to work. They'd met and married in haste, and he had not understood the difficulties she'd had in adjusting to her new life. Relocating to England had been the only thing he could do for the good of their marriage and the unborn child.

Now Sebastian turned to the kitchen. Surprisingly, it was still mostly intact. He saw an old black iron sink, an oven, and a fireplace with an iron grate that looked the worse for wear. Smiling to himself, he remembered how his family had used the fire to heat the home and had carried water from the well in from outside. His Mother, and then Amelia, had prepared most of the meals over the fire. Sebastian passed the flashlight over the small space.

The structure of the building had not changed; it looked exactly as it had when he and his Amelia had left it so many years ago. Sebastian had decided to stay in England after Amelia's death in order to be near his children, but several months ago, he'd received a letter, and as a result, he'd made this journey to France. Sebastian stopped wandering and pulled the letter out of his pocket. It was in a thin airmail envelope. Holding the flashlight, Sebastian read.

Dear Sebastian,

I hope you and your family are well.

I am writing to you because it has recently come to my attention that the old stone house and the property and orchard your parents owned may be available to buy. I think there is an opportunity for you at the auction September 18, Saturday morning, at 11:00 a.m., on the property. It's not worth much; however, I believe this is something you will be more than interested in. If you visit, please let me know, and we can have dinner together.

We can meet at the house the morning of the auction.

Warm regards,
Your cousin Louis

The auction was to be held the next morning on the property.

Sebastian arrived early the next morning, as he wanted to look around the property in the daylight. His cousin, waiting for him as promised, greeted him.

"Thank you for bringing this to my attention," Sebastian said after their catch-up talk.

"I think it's a very good opportunity for you," Louis said. "Let's walk around back."

Sebastian was overcome with sadness when he looked at the overgrown chard; mangled, tangled mess of weeds; and long grass. Many of the apple trees were diseased; most had died and fallen to the ground. Sebastian looked around the property with a heavy heart. It was not the beautiful place he remembered.

He noticed one of the apple trees still stood tall and strong. "Look!" he cried out. "One of my favorite trees has miraculously survived."

As it was early autumn, the tree was filled to overflowing with ripe, juicy red apples. Sebastian studied them, plucked the two best-looking apples, and gave one to Louis. Sebastian sat under the apple tree, leaning and relaxing against the strong trunk, taking infinite pleasure in polishing the apple on the sleeve of his jacket until it shone. Biting into it, he allowed the juices to run down his chin. As he ate the apple, the taste, juices, and texture all came together, bringing a flood of memories.

Sebastian spoke, partly to Louis and partly to the tree. "I can hear my Mother calling my name: 'Sebastian, come in for dinner!' I can see my sister giggling as I chase her around the trees as we play hide-and-seek. I remember we used to love coming to the orchard to play among the trees and feast on the apples until we were sick. When Amelia shared the news that she was expecting our first child, I took her in my arms, and we danced around the orchard, filled with joy." Sebastian bent his head as his eyes filled with tears. "I have never known too many memories, Louis. I cannot let them go; they are too precious—a legacy I want to leave for the children."

Louis nodded thoughtfully. "Of course. That makes perfect sense."

After finishing his apple under the tree, Sebastian stood up and walked toward the front of the house with purpose and a feeling of determination. "Let's go, Louis. I'm going to buy this house today."

2

Abby Lavalle stood at the door of the DC-1011 aircraft, which had landed in London Gatwick after an overnight from San Francisco. She repeatedly thanked passengers as they disembarked, looking down the aisle to see how many were left. She sighed under her breath quietly, for it had been a long night. As the last of the passengers were leaving, Abby looked across at her fellow crew member and smiled at Jenny.

"I must get across the terminal this morning, as I am meeting my sister," Abby said excitedly. "We're flying home to Newcastle together. My Father has called a family meeting—for something important, apparently!"

"Why don't you go? I'll finish. You should hurry, as you don't have long to catch that flight," Jenny replied.

"Thank you. I owe you one, Jenny." Abby smiled gratefully. She grabbed her bags, disembarked, and dashed across the terminal to meet Leah.

It was already 8:15 a.m., and they were catching the 9:00 a.m. flight. The last boarding call was 8:45 a.m. Abby looked at her watch, weaving her way in and out of the crowds effortlessly. She cleared crew customs and ran all the way to gate number seven, where Leah was waiting for her.

"I am relieved to see you," Leah said, hugging her warmly.

"Let's get on board. Then we can talk." Abby pulled back, heaving a big sigh.

After they'd settled into their seats and the seat belt sign was off, they enjoyed a light breakfast and coffee. Abby looked at her older sister. Leah's hair was styled in a fashionable shag, and her face was still fresh and didn't reveal her thirty-odd years.

"I am so pleased we could travel home together. I'm rather nervous about this meeting. Did you get the same call from Dad as I did?" asked Abby.

"Yes, we all did. I was talking to Andre and Cammie. Dad put the same call out to all of us. I shouldn't worry too much. Andre told me he saw Dad last week and said he had never looked better."

"I wonder what it's all about. Do you think he might've met someone?"

"I doubt that. You know how he felt and still feels about Mam," Leah said.

They both fell silent for a moment, reflecting.

"I know; I understand what you mean. Still, it has been over ten years now. Maybe Dad's lonely," said Abby.

"I can't imagine Dad marrying anyone! He might go out on a date from time to time. Anyway, stop fretting. We'll find out soon enough."

Abby studied her older sister. She was glowing. Her golden-blonde hair was cut short, framing her beautiful face, and her huge blue eyes were just like their Dad's: a true sapphire blue.

"You can tell you're married to a dentist. You have the most amazing teeth—straight, white, and dazzling! They look like pearls." Abby grinned, and they both giggled. "How is Tristan?" she asked.

"He's okay. He has taken the next few days off to spend time with Malachi."

"My cute nephew—how is he?"

"He's a handful—definitely a curious toddler. He is into everything. He likes to climb up, onto, and over anything and everything whenever and however he can. His new favorite word is *why*," Leah told her.

"You are so lucky. You have a decent husband, a perfect little boy, and a good life. It doesn't get much better."

"You've got to be kidding me," Leah said, interrupting Abby. "I was just thinking the same about you. My God, look at you, flying around the world first class and being paid for it. Let me give you some sisterly advice: enjoy it, pet, while you possibly can. I'm serious; don't rush into anything."

"Oh, you are funny, Leah." Abby smiled and wondered if her sister knew what she was saying.

"I am aware I have a wonderful life. It's just that sometimes I look at you and think maybe I should've stayed single longer," Leah replied, reaching over to briefly squeeze Abby's hand.

Abby didn't respond. It seemed to her enough had been said. The seat belt sign went on, and they both were silent for the rest of the flight.

— 3 —

Sebastian sat at the dining room table, surrounded by most of his children. It had been several years since any of them had come together in Amelia's home in Newcastle upon Tyne. The house was cozy and filled with Amelia's personal touches, which Sasha and Cammie had left in place after she died, including the old-fashioned china cabinet, whose glass, gold inlay, and mirrored shelves enhanced the china and trinkets that lay inside, each of which had its own history. Framed photos showed family members long gone. China vases filled with fresh flowers stood on the sideboard. Sebastian took a sip of his wine, observing his brood quietly, reflecting on how they had matured and developed into fascinating varied adults.

He was proud of his firstborn son, Andre, who was strong and tender, with the dark hair and eyes and melancholy soul of his Mother. He was a husband and the Father of Sebastian's little Granddaughter, Amelia, her grandMother's namesake.

Then Sebastian's gaze moved to his firstborn daughter,

Leah, who was tiny and nymph-like, maternal, and nurturing and was a successful Mother, wife, and nurse. She was Mother to his Grandson Malachi, named after the child he and Amelia had lost more than twenty years ago.

Next was happy-go-lucky Cammie, who was similar to her sister Leah, only with darker coloring. Like him, she had a strong jawline and blue eyes. Unlike him, she did not have the wandering bug he and some of the other siblings had.

His gaze fell upon Abby, and his breath caught—not because of her exotic beauty but because of her likeness to Amelia. He admired her composure and her ability to excel. She was head stewardess for one of the best airlines in the world. Abby was a traveler too.

Sasha, chef extraordinaire, worked hard and was like Sebastian as a young man but was handsomer and taller. With his wavy hair, eyes as blue as the ocean, dimples in his cheeks, and straight white teeth, he had movie-star looks. Sebastian secretly envied him his youth and wished he could have that now with his present knowledge and maturity.

"It's good to be with you," Sebastian said, and everyone stopped chatting to look at him respectfully. "Unfortunately, Eugene is somewhere out in the Atlantic Ocean on reconnaissance with the British navy, and Noah and Nathan are in France together on holiday. We'll miss them; however, they will hear soon enough. Also, I would like to thank your sister and brother Camille and Sasha for hosting this dinner, particularly Sasha for cooking a delicious meal."

Everyone raised his or her glass and cheered.

Sasha spoke up. "I'd like to say let's eat and then talk. However, curiosity moves me to say let's talk first."

Amazing Grace

Sebastian smiled. "Please, let's eat. There is nothing so important that it can't wait."

"Abigail, where did you fly in from?" Sasha asked.

"San Francisco," she replied.

Sebastian observed his youngest daughter.

Abigail touched the golden angel necklace she wore and held it between her fingers, sliding it around the chain. Sebastian knew it meant something special. It seemed it had appeared after she came back from visiting Tennessee several years ago.

Abby flashed a cheeky grin in Sasha's direction. "We spent two days there. It was my first trip to San Francisco. We managed to see the Golden Gate Bridge and Fisherman's Wharf, both huge tourist attractions and with good reason. Next time I fly there, I'd like to visit Chinatown. San Francisco is an amazing place—sunny and cheerful, with a freedom you can feel and an easygoing atmosphere. Very cosmopolitan at the same time. It appears to have many wonderful opportunities to offer young people and immigrants."

"Nice," replied Sasha. "On my way to work yesterday, I crossed the Tyne Bridge and walked along the fish market on the quayside—in the rain, of course."

Everybody laughed.

"We all envy you, Abigail. You have the best life," said Sasha.

"When you become a qualified chef, you'll be able to travel the world also and regale us with your escapades. Be patient; your time will come," said Abby.

"I know you are right, but I can hardly wait!"

Sebastian leaned back in his chair, sipping his wine and

participating in one of his favorite pastimes: observing his adult children as they engaged with one another, laughing and sharing stories. They all got caught up on one another's families, work lives, and hobbies.

"Dad, what is this meeting all about?" Andre finally asked.

"An opportunity has shown itself that I could not resist," said Sebastian. He glanced about the room for a quick moment, wondering briefly if this was the right decision for him and for his family.

"Are you getting married again, Dad?" asked Cammie.

"That's exactly what I thought," said Abby. "With those good looks of yours and that charming French accent, it wouldn't surprise me one little bit!"

"No! Never!" replied Sebastian.

A stunned silence swept across the dining room table.

"I'll have only one wife in my life, and that was your Mother."

"That's exactly what I thought," Leah said.

"Tell us what it is, Dad. What's this opportunity?" Andre asked.

"I've purchased a holiday home in France," Sebastian told them.

"That's amazing news, Dad!" Andre sat up straighter.

Then they all spoke at the same time.

"What is it?"

"Where is it located?"

"Can we visit?"

"Patience, and I'll explain everything to you," Sebastian replied. "It's in the village of Rougemont. Translated to English, that means Red Mountain. It's located in the

Amazing Grace

province of Alsace-Lorraine—a magnificent part of France. It's the home I was born and raised in."

"Dad," said Abby, "this is so nice for you!"

"Merci, Abby. I have some photos to show you of the house and the property. It has been vacant for many years, and it shows. The reality is, it's going to take time, money, and hard work to fix it. However, it's a project very close to my heart. I am excited to start; my motivation is to spend some time back in my homeland and also the desire that I have for my children to know the beauty and history of the area and to bring my grandchildren, young Amelia and Malachi. Eugene and Stephanie can bring Stephan."

"That's fantastic and exciting," said Sasha, who was clearly bubbling with enthusiasm. "You mean we can come anytime and see it?"

"Oui," said Sebastian. "If you bring a toolbox with you! There's enough property for you to bring caravans or tents and camp in the orchard once we get the kitchen and bathroom built."

"What an opportunity. We should all try to organize a trip together," said Andre.

"I am delighted you are all so enthusiastic," said Sebastian. "I have many fond memories of the place, and I simply could not let it go. As some of you may know, your Mother and I lived there for a short time together after the war. It means a lot to me that we'll rebuild it together. This is more than I ever expected—better than I deserve." Sebastian wiped his eyes with his napkin.

Abby stood and walked over to her Father. "I'm so happy for you. Speaking for myself, I was a bit worried about this meeting. I'm thrilled to hear your news. Now I can go back to

London knowing you are fine and looking forward to visiting you in Red Mountain." She kissed him on the cheek.

Abby and Leah flew back to London together the next morning, enjoying a light breakfast. The plane's engines hummed steadily as they sat next to each other, continuing their long chat.

"How do you like living in the room in the house you're renting?" asked Leah.

"I don't. Not much," Abby replied.

"Why not?"

"The landlord is rather strange. Actually, I have to say he is really strange."

"My goodness, Abigail! Are you at risk?" Leah gasped.

"No, nothing like that. It's his beliefs. He is what you call a Scientologist. It's a religious cult from America. He does rather weird things behind closed doors with an odd-looking device that looks like a radio. He explained the process to me. It's supposed to help him discover his past lives, and in doing so, it helps him understand his present life and where he's going wrong. Not only that, but he has a Dalmatian the size of a horse!"

Leah laughed. "You're kidding me."

"No, I'm not. The house is the size of a thimble, which makes the poor animal look even more enormous. The worst of it is, he feeds the poor beast on pigs' heads, with their eyes, brains, and all intact. He brings them home and dumps them into the kitchen sink, and they stare at you. When we are washing the dishes, we can see the hair around the snout and ears."

"Good God," said Leah. "That's the most disgusting thing I ever heard. How do you stand it? Why don't you leave?"

"Because I am not there enough, and the price is right. I also like Sarah, my other roommate. She's an only child, and her parents run a very successful printing business in Harrogate. I think she is homesick and lonely. We get along very well, and we often eat together when I am home.

"Besides, the setup makes for remarkably interesting conversation—the extreme situations. For example, last week I flew to New York, and when we go there, we stay in the luxurious Park Plaza. If we go to the coffee shops in uniform, we get free hot chocolate. It's a wonderful life."

The seat belt sign went on, and the aircraft soon landed.

"You make it sound so exciting," said Leah. "My life seems so boring. Look at me. I am going home to make Malachi his lunch and then put him down for a nap. I do envy you the freedom."

"Don't waste your time. There is nothing to envy. You are the one with the wonderful life. You have what's important: a family. I'd give this up in a heartbeat to be with the man I love," Abby told her.

"Oh?" said Leah. "Do you have one in mind?"

"No, I do not; I'm still looking." They laughed together, hugged one another, and then went their separate ways.

Within the hour, Abby arrived home before lunch, where she was surprised to find Sarah sitting on the couch. She looked cute with her blonde pigtails, big green eyes, and freckled face. Sarah was small in stature and reminded Abby of a doll she'd owned when she was a child, called Lucy.

"What are you doing home?" Abby huffed as she lugged her suitcase inside the door.

"I took the day off." Sarah sniffed as though she had been crying.

"Let me pop the kettle on and make some tea," Abby said. "We can have a chat. I haven't seen you for over a week. Is everything okay?"

"No, it's not. Far from it!" Sarah burst into tears.

"What is going on with you?" Abby put her arms around Sarah.

"My God, my life is in total chaos. It really is," Sarah sobbed. Her face looked grimy, and Abby realized she'd been crying for quite some time.

"Calm down, and tell me—what is it?"

"I'm pregnant!" she blurted out. "My parents can never, ever find out about this! No one can. Do you hear me? Do you?" Sarah was close to hysteria.

"Everything will be all right. Please calm down, and we can discuss this together."

"Discuss it? I have nothing to say about this, except *abortion*!"

Such a drastic word and so final, Abby thought. "Have you really thought about this?" she asked with concern.

"I've thought about nothing else." Sarah broke down crying heaving sobs. "I am such an idiot."

"No, you are not."

"You'll think so when I tell you who the Father is." Sarah looked at Abby and then looked down at the floor.

Abby waited for some time. "Well?"

Amazing Grace

"It's Bob!" she wailed.

"Bob? Our Bob? Landlord Bob?" Abby asked, incredulous. *Good grief, what a surprise.* There had been no hint that Sarah and Bob were involved in that way.

"Yes!" Sarah cried. "Do you remember the party we had a couple of months ago? You were the smart one and went to bed early."

"Yes, I was working the next day."

"Either way, you did the right thing. At the end of the evening, Bob and I finished cleaning up together. We also finished all the wine, one thing led to another, and we made out!" Sarah continued to cry. "It was all over and done with in a flash. Abby, I don't love him. I barely remember doing it. But I do know that I do not want this child."

"Sarah, don't worry; it can all be resolved. I know it seems overwhelming right now, but there are ways around these things."

Sarah's sobbing slowed down to a whimper. "I know. I've considered it from every angle," she said, wiping her nose again. "I'm not going to the national health service—too archaic for me. After all, it's the seventies, and abortion has been legal for a few years. But I hear they still frown on you, treating girls and women like cattle, hoping you don't return. I have the funds to pay, and I found a private clinic in London. But I don't want to be alone. Would you come with me, Abby?"

She did not relish the idea, but Abby's compassion for Sarah overcame her remorseful feelings. "Of course I will. You should get in touch with them as soon as possible, Sarah—today if you can."

"Promise me you will never, ever tell a living soul, Abby," Sarah said.

"I promise," Abby assured her.

Several days later, Abby and Sarah boarded a train into London King's Cross. There they hired a taxi to Harley Street, to a private gynecological clinic. Sarah was registered for a dilation and curettage, a simple procedure. She was admitted, gowned, and placed in bed in a private room. All the doctors and nurses treated Sarah with kindness and respect. She was sedated and taken away for her surgery.

After the procedure, Abby stayed beside Sarah, holding her hand, until she awoke.

"It's all over now, Sarah; you can rest, and I'll come back tomorrow to take you home."

"I don't know how to thank you, Abby." Sarah started crying.

"There is no need to, Sarah. Sleep now. I'll see you tomorrow." Abby placed the blanket over Sarah and then gently kissed her on the forehead. Looking down at her, she could see that Sarah slept peacefully. Abby was grateful to be with her at such a difficult time. No one deserved to be alone in a situation so devastating. After all, she knew from experience, as she had gone through an abortion herself—alone—several years ago.

Memories of the event came tumbling back as Abby walked toward the underground to head home. Weeping, she felt a great sense of regret, sorrow, and guilt—always the guilt. What gender would her little baby have been—a beautiful boy or a sweet girl? What potential had she single-handedly destroyed? What had she done? The only way she felt she could forgive herself was to reach out and help others in any way she could. Sarah was a good opportunity for Abby to offer help without judgment and be there for her after.

With a somber heart, Abby made it home to their gloomy house, feeling as low as she ever had been. She sighed, made herself some tea, and then watched the day disappear into a cloudy, starless gray night in the neighborhood around her.

— 4 —

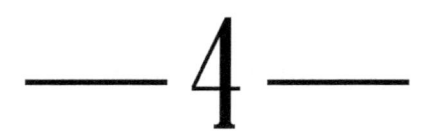

Two weeks after Sarah's procedure, Sarah invited Abby out for a Sunday lunch in London at the top of the Royal Hotel. Their table was nestled in a corner, looking out a window directly over St. James's Park, part of the gardens belonging to Buckingham Palace, Queen Elizabeth II's residence when she was in London. From their seats overlooking the glorious gardens, they could see the famous black swans moving serenely through water lilies on the pond. Flowers bloomed beside every pathway, giving bursts of yellows, pinks, reds, and oranges among the green of the grasses.

Abby thought Sarah appeared to be back to her perky self. Her eyes were bright again, and her hair was clean and neatly styled, with her Farrah Fawcett hairdo tumbling over her shoulders.

"What a treat," Abby said. "I'm delighted to be here sharing Sunday lunch with you. My goodness, what a view. It's like a window into a world not known to us—a secret garden. Look! There's the Horse Guards Parade! And the Houses of Parliament!"

Amazing Grace

Below them, the black horses trotted by. Their riders wore red uniforms, with tall black busbies on their heads.

Sarah smiled. "It's the least you deserve. I'd like to say something to you. Please don't interrupt. Allow me to finish, okay?"

"Of course." Abby leaned forward a bit.

"We haven't known one another exceptionally long, I know. I mean, we weren't childhood friends, and we don't have a history. To put it simply, I am amazed how you helped me, stood beside me, and did not judge me throughout this ordeal." Sarah grimaced and hesitated. "To be honest with you, Abby, under normal circumstances, you're not someone I'd have approached for help with this situation, because you appear somewhat aloof. But it turned out you were the best person to help me."

"It just goes to prove the adage that you should never judge a book by its cover." Abby smiled back at Sarah.

"I realize that now," Sarah said. "It's just that, well, you appear to be a religious, spiritual type of person. I've seen the pictures on your wall of the Virgin Mary and your rosary beads on your bedside table."

Abby laughed out loud. "That doesn't make me the Virgin Mary or indicate that I wouldn't understand. The truth is, though, you remind me very much of myself."

Sarah raised her eyebrows. "Really? In what way?"

"A few years ago, I spent some time in Tennessee in the United States of America. I was visiting my aunt and her family. My aunt had only recently emigrated; my Mother was her youngest sister, and they were very close. Sadly, my Mother and my aunt's husband, my uncle, both died within months of her emigrating."

"I'm so sorry. That is sad. How old were you?"

"I was seventeen."

"You were so young not to have a mum."

Abby nodded, remembering the challenges she'd faced. "I went out there to bring her some comfort. It was a disaster from the beginning as far as bringing comfort to my aunt. It was totally the opposite, for reasons that still aren't truly clear to me."

"Surely it wasn't your fault. Your traveling all that way to help her shows a lot of courage and love, though maybe with the wrong result."

"During my time there, I met a young priest, Father Gabriel. He was newly ordained and was the curate in the parish where my aunt and her family lived. He took me under his wing, as it were, and introduced me to young people within the parish and the youth group, where he and everyone befriended me. I'd never met anyone like him in my entire life. He didn't act like anyone I'd ever met, priest or layman. The first time I heard his voice, I thought it warm, infectious, and soothing like a warm cup of cocoa on a cold winter's night by the fire. He seemed like a gentle bear from the pages of 'Goldilocks,' with curly golden-brown hair and amber-green eyes filled with magic light. His face was covered with freckles, and I was instantly captivated by him. I thought he was wonderful. I fell deeply in love with him, as he did with me."

"Oh my gosh, Abby, this is so romantic. What happened? I can hardly wait to hear."

"Nothing happened. We kissed very tenderly like lovers do. Sadly, we were both too naive. We decided to separate. He stayed a priest, and I came back home to England to help my family with my younger brothers."

Amazing Grace

"What a sad story."

"After that, I was devastated, and I reached out to the wrong person. I was desperately hungry for something—anything that felt like love." Abby paused and looked out the window into the secret garden. She felt vulnerable. Tears gently pricked behind her eyes.

She gazed back at Sarah, who had recently been through so much of her own trauma, and took a deep breath. "I've never spoken to anyone about this story. I became pregnant. It was the most difficult time of my life. My family doctor arranged for me to have an abortion in the local hospital. I stayed at the YWCA for a few days alone while I recovered. I felt alone and guilty, as I had lied to everyone I loved, and I was deeply ashamed. I learned from the experience. I wouldn't wish something like that on my worst enemy, let alone a sweet girl like you."

Sarah, gently weeping, wiped her eyes and sipped her drink. "That's the saddest story I ever heard. Oh my God, Abby, you poor thing."

"I'm a lot stronger for it. As you will be one day. Maybe because of this experience, you'll find you're able to help someone else."

"I don't know about that, Abby. I'm not like you. We don't think the same."

"When you put some time, distance, and healing in the equation, you'll find you do," Abby assured her.

"What happened with the priest? Did you ever hear from him again?"

"I received a letter several months after I came home, telling me he could never see me again."

"Do you think that's true?" asked Sarah.

"I don't know. He may be right. At this point in my life, I consider myself quite fortunate. I have a terrific job; it certainly keeps me busy. I have lots of friends and a great family. I get to see my Dad, my siblings, and my nieces and nephews—life is full."

"Would you like to see him again? What do you think would happen if you did?" Sarah nibbled at some breadsticks, her face aglow with interest.

"Most of the time, I try not to think about it. The reality is, the emotional distance between us is just as great as the size of the ocean that separates us. If I wanted to see him, I could. It's not impossible. I've tried to honor his request and think of him as a good friend who helped me on my way."

"That is so romantic." Sarah sighed. "I think you should go find him."

"And I think I'd like to change the subject," replied Abby.

"Okay, if you like. I do have something else I want to discuss with you. I have a proposition for you."

"That sounds mysterious," said Abby.

"My Father has a cousin. I don't know him very well. He is an engineering specialist; he builds bridges. He lives in an amazing Tudor house nestled in the woods near the village of Fairwinds, minutes from Gatwick. Do you know it?"

"I've definitely heard of it," said Abby. "A very elite area."

"Apparently, he's had a two-year contract job offer in the United Arab Emirates. The upshot of it is, he is looking for a house sitter he can trust. He doesn't want to rent it, and he doesn't want to leave it empty. My Dad suggested me, God bless him. I met with him this week, and he offered the job to me, and I've accepted."

"It sounds amazing," Abby said with a touch of envy. It sounded like a lovely home.

"It has four bedrooms and two bathrooms. I'd like you to come along. It's perfect for you, Abby. Neither of us needs to be staying at Bob's any longer. It's time to get out! It's the right price point. We pay for what we use; the house is free if we look after it. We can move in at the beginning of next month. There's transport from the village every half hour to Gatwick, as a lot of airport personnel live in the village. What do you say, Abby?"

"I can hardly believe it. To live in a real Tudor home in the forest. It sounds like a fairy tale!" Abby jumped up and hugged her friend. "No more Bob or pigs' heads in the kitchen sink!" They both howled with laughter. "You can count me in with a million thanks."

"Let's toast to new beginnings!" Sarah raised her glass.

"New beginnings!" said Abby.

Later that evening, Abby lay still on her bed, thinking of the afternoon out with Sarah. She had enjoyed herself and was delighted to be moving out of that house and into an elegant new area and a fabulous Tudor home—almost for free. Still, Abby felt restless. She'd been somewhat shaken up inside all afternoon since sharing her secrets with Sarah, even though she realized it had been necessary to help her gain Sarah's trust.

She stepped out of bed, put on her housecoat, went downstairs to make herself a cup of tea, brought it back up to her room, and climbed back into her bed.

"Gabriel." Abby breathed his name softly. Whenever she thought of him, she was churned up inside like the North Sea on a stormy night. Sliding her hand under her pillow, Abby pulled out an envelope, and she removed the well-worn letter. She propped herself up to read it.

> My dearest Abigail,
>
> How I have longed to reply to your beautiful poem before now. I must start by offering my heartfelt gratitude for such beauty and grace. It took me several attempts to read it through in its entirety, as tears blurred my vision. Abby, I haven't allowed one single day to pass without reciting it, as it's impossible not to do so.
>
> When I speak, it tumbles from my lips like a prayer. It's inscribed upon my soul. I carry you within me always.
>
> There is so much I want to say to you. After you left, my parish priest approached me. There were some concerns within the parish regarding my relationship with you during your visit. I was most distressed at such a suggestion and expressed to him that we had done nothing to hide, regret, or be ashamed of. He is a good man, and I did confide in him how I felt regarding my vocation and questions about my feelings for you. He has been most understanding, suggesting a change.
>
> Your Kennedy cousins have asked me several times to supper. I went once but

could still feel your presence. I believe you to be my soul mate, yet it is not to be, not now.

I requested a move, and they're sending me to a small parish outside Memphis. I've been counseled to give it some time, maybe a year or two. I can only give you the same advice, and hopefully, in time, Abby, you will feel the freedom to move on and live your life. I hope you always remember me as someone who touched your life as a kind person. I know this is not what you want to hear. I cannot give you my forwarding address; however, I'll be sending you my eternal love. I do not know why our paths crossed, but I do know you have given meaning to the words *life*, *love*, and *laughter*. For this, I shall never forget you.

With you all the way,
Gabriel

He'd written the letter almost three years ago, yet still, his presence stayed with her. She had not heard one word from him or about him since. Abby looked up at the ceiling. *Where are you? How are you? Do you think about me like I think of you?*

Abby placed the letter back in the envelope, slid it under her pillow, switched off the light, and lay down and wept softly. *Maybe it's time for me to return.*

Fitfully, she fell into a deep sleep.

5

A year later, Abby sat in her favorite room, the living room of their elegant Tudor house. Sarah was away for a few days, and Abby had two days off and was relishing the time alone.

Abby looked around the room in wonder. *Three weeks until Christmas*, she thought. The original cathedral ceilings soared above her, with black oak beams supporting them. Turkish rugs were scattered across the polished oak planks, with square nails made by original blacksmiths holding the floor together. Dark paneling adorned the walls, on which framed Constable and Turner prints were strategically placed. The walls were four feet thick. Tartan-print curtains draped the original leaded windows, and matching cushions were on the window seat.

A floor-to-ceiling stone fireplace took up almost one full wall of the room. The stone had been carried in from the local quarry more than five hundred years ago. A fire was roaring and crackling in the grate, sending a welcoming warmth throughout the house. Two wingback chairs on either side of the fire were upholstered in the same tartan as the curtains. Abby sat in the window seat. Although neither of them would be at the house to celebrate Christmas Day, they'd decorated the house in the style that was befitting. They'd had so much fun.

An eight-foot-tall fresh pine tree covered with a hundred lights and every possible ornament imaginable stood in the room. She and Sarah had gone out to antique markets, collecting old glass and new. They even had some homemade novelties from their childhood days. Silver and gold garland cascaded from branch to branch. When the tree lights were switched on, the tree looked like a night of a thousand stars.

Abby had also borrowed the nativity scene that had belonged to her great-great-grandMother. She remembered using the same nativity scene when she and her brothers and sisters were little. It had been their tradition to set up the Christmas nativity scene under the tree, building a stable and mountains with brown paper, and light it from underneath. They all had worked hard to keep it a secret from Mam. Then Andre gleefully had guided Mam into the room with her eyes closed. Everyone had warned her, "Don't peek, Mam," and she always had acted surprised to see the charming decorations. All the kids had loved to please her.

Abby had heard stories from her Mother and aunt about how they'd used the same nativity scene during Christmases through World War I and World War II, the Great Depression in the 1930s, and the Jarrow March, when they'd had little to celebrate. Throughout time, the nativity scene brought with it a feeling of comfort and faith that eventually, in time, all would be well. Abby enjoyed the tradition of ancestors and family bringing out the same nativity scene year after year.

This Christmas, it was her tradition. She placed it beside the tree, underneath the lights. As she gazed around the room, she thought of her Christmases in the past. How many generations had lovingly placed the nativity scene under the Christmas tree? She thought about her ancestors and those who had gone before her. Her own Mother always had made Christmas special, with midnight Mass, Christmas trees, sweet mince pies, Christmas cakes, and turkey dinners. On Christmas Eve, the family had hung their socks on the mantelpiece with the anticipation of what Santa might bring them.

Sipping her wine and listening to songs of the season on the record player, Abby looked about her. Staring through the ancient windows, watching snowflakes gently falling onto the pine trees in the forest, she said aloud, "This is one magical moment."

Abby had received several Christmas cards in the post that day and was looking forward to opening them. One of them was from her cousin Aidan and his wife, Rosella, who lived in Tennessee in the USA.

She continued to sit in the window seat and opened the card. The front artwork was a beautiful painting of the Madonna and Child from the Vatican art series, signed with love from Aidan, Rosella, and the children. Inside was a folded letter.

> Hi, Abby,
>
> I hope my Christmas card and letter find you well. I have so much news to share with you. Everyone here is well. We are all

looking forward to Christmas, especially the children.

The big news is that we are moving from Tennessee in the spring. Aidan has been promoted, and he is being relocated to Virginia Beach, a small town outside Williamsburg. It's so beautiful. You will love it.

Grandma Helen is going to stay with her sister, your aunt Deidre, in Scotland indefinitely, although we'll keep accommodations for her in the new home.

I am busy trying to get ready for Christmas as well as pack and get organized and prepared for the move.

How do you like the new house you're living in? The jet-set lifestyle? I am very happy for you. Certainly, you deserve the best. I imagine all the young men are chasing you!

I have some news for you that I'm not sure if I should tell you. It was announced in our church last Sunday that Father Gabriel is coming back to St. Michael the Archangel as assistant pastor. They are expecting him here in the late spring. We won't see him, as we are moving in April, and he arrives in May.

I don't know what you'll feel about this information. It's the first I've heard of him in several years. At least you have an address now should you wish to communicate with him.

Please come visit Virginia very soon; we all miss you very much.

Lots of love,
Rosella (and Aidan, Greg, Ryan, and Kelly)

Abby placed the letter back in the envelope, gazing out the window as snowflakes continued to fall. There was enough snow to lay a sparkling carpet of white at the entrance to the house.

It was surprising news. At the mere mention of his name, she'd felt a joy, a spark that brought part of her back to life. The letter marked the first words she'd heard about Gabriel in several years, and her Kennedy cousins were moving just days before he arrived back where it all had begun.

Indeed, God works in mysterious ways.

Rosella was correct: she now had an address. Abby wandered over to the wine bottle and poured the last of the wine into her glass. She had three weeks of holiday time coming to her and several free flights she had not yet used.

I think it's time I go visit my cousins in Virginia.

Raising the glass high above her head, she said, "Cheers. Here's to reconnecting!"

— 6 —

Across the Atlantic on a frigid December morning, Father Gabriel had been summoned to the bishop's palace in Nashville, Tennessee, for a meeting. It was the first in several years since Gabriel had requested a new parish after Abigail had returned to England. Bishop James looked at Gabriel across the large oak desk. The bishop had a reputation for being a stern, no-nonsense man but with a touch of kindness. He also had a naturally powerful presence at more than six feet tall, with a strong jawline, a long nose, steel-blue eyes, and a full head of thick white hair.

Gabriel felt out of place and fidgeted in the large high-backed armchair.

"How have you been getting along, Father Gabriel?" the bishop asked him in a rich baritone voice.

"Very well, Your Eminence."

"I am pleased to hear that, my son. I'd like to get on with the business of the day. I'm thinking of bringing you back into the heart of the diocese. You've been out in the sticks long enough. Do you agree?"

"Yes, Your Eminence." Gabriel's hands were clammy, and beads of sweat appeared on his top lip. He could feel sweat running down his back. He crossed and uncrossed his legs several times before deciding to find a place for his feet under the desk.

"Relax, my boy. I'm on your side. You are a gifted minister; we need you out among the people. Do you feel prepared to return, my son, with a stronger faith and a renewed commitment to your vocation and your vows?"

Gabriel was silent, keeping his head down and his hands clasped together as if in prayer.

"Speak up, Father. Now is the time."

"I am, yes, Your Eminence. I am committed to my vocation and ministry. With the grace of God and his guidance, I am willing."

"Very good, my son. I'm posting you to your old parish of St. Michael the Archangel," the bishop told him.

Gabriel gasped, using every ounce of strength in his reserve to prevent himself from fleeing to the freedom of the soft, gentle breeze of the palace gardens, biting down on his lip, knowing he must accept the post. He stayed silent.

"I understand it's not what you expected. Father, you must look at it as a test. You must return. It's how you will heal. You will take up your new position in May, replacing Father Jackson as assistant pastor. Father Damien Brown is the pastor, and Father Sean O'Shea is the curate. He is newly ordained; you have much to share with him, Gabriel, as a dedicated priest. My door is always open. Please remember, we are men first. God understands that well."

Bishop James stood in front of him and offered his hand. Gabriel kissed his ring with reverence.

"Good day, Your Eminence." Gabriel walked away and closed the huge oak door to the office in the bishop's palace. Walking along the corridor toward the entrance, he passed the chapel on the way. Gabriel entered and genuflected, kneeling. He clasped his hands together in prayer, and looking up to Almighty God, he spoke out loud.

"I beg for the strength and courage to return to that place of memories, desires, and my insatiable need for her!"

Several months after his meeting with the bishop, Gabriel stopped his VW Bug and switched off the ignition outside the presbytery. He had a fleeting feeling as though he had never left, even though it had been almost four years. Father Brown greeted him at the front door.

"Welcome, Father Gabriel," Father Brown said as they shook hands warmly.

"Thank you, Father."

"Come in, Gabriel." Father Brown ushered him through the front door as he helped him with his luggage.

Gabriel heard a shriek of delight. He looked up to see Mrs. B., the housekeeper, a short lady with her white hair piled up in a bun on the top of her head and a sweet face. Gabriel remembered her as someone kind and caring, even though she was somewhat of a busybody. She came toward him, drying her hands on the bottom half of her apron.

"Come here, Father Gabriel. You are a sight for sore eyes. Let me give you a big hug."

Gabriel opened his arms, and Mrs. B. hugged him like a long-lost son.

"Thank you, Mrs. B. How have you been?"

"Wonderful, Father. I've been dancing a jig since they announced your return."

"You are too kind, Mrs. B." Gabriel smiled.

"I have your old room all set up for you, Father."

"That is marvelous. Thank you, Mrs. B." He glanced around quickly; the house looked to be the same as he'd left it years ago. The old furniture looked clean but worn, and he saw an assortment of rag rugs on the floors and Mrs. B.'s sparkling kitchen.

"I'll make you some coffee and fresh muffins and bring them up to you."

"Let me help you with your luggage and boxes." Father Brown took some of the cases. "Father Sean will be in for supper tonight, Gabriel. We can all get acquainted."

"I look forward to that," Gabriel replied.

When the last of his belongings were in his rooms, Gabriel thanked Father Brown. He closed the door and leaned up against it for support. He felt drained. He looked about the room to see if anything had changed. Everything appeared the same.

The most beautiful part of the room was the picture window, which faced west, looking out behind the church and overlooking a field with many oak trees. Gabriel's mind cruelly flashed a memory of himself and Abby standing side by side and looking out the window together as the sun went down. He still felt as though he were connected to her in every sense—mind, body, and spirit as one. He watched a horse canter around the field, simply enjoying the moment. A knock on the door broke Gabriel's thoughts.

"Come in," he said.

Mrs. B. stood at the door with a tray of coffee and muffins.

"You are going to spoil me," Gabriel told her.

"That I am, Father," she said with a twinkle in her eye.

"Thank you." Gabriel took the tray.

"It's wonderful to have you back, Father; many of the parishioners feel the same as I do. Mostly the same group are living here in the parish as when you left, although there are some new ones, of course. Some have left for various reasons, passed on or moved. You remember the Kennedys, Father. I know you had a special affection toward them."

Gabriel's heart thumped so loudly he could hear it; he wondered if Mrs. B. could. "Yes, I do, Mrs. B. I must visit them as soon as I get settled. Their children will be grown. And Aunt Helen—how is she? I look forward to seeing her—seeing all of them."

"I'm afraid they've moved, Father. Just last week. You missed them by days."

Gabriel felt his insides do cartwheels. "Mrs. B., I can hardly believe that."

"I knew you would be disappointed, Father. They've gone to Virginia. I don't imagine we'll see them back here in Tennessee, not for a while."

"It's disappointing. I do appreciate the update; it's good to know. As you say, Mrs. B., people do move on. I'd like to enjoy this coffee while it's nice and hot. What time is supper tonight?"

"Seven, Father."

Gabriel ushered Mrs. B. out the door. After pouring himself a cup of coffee, Gabriel sat in the chair, allowing the leather to caress his aching bones. He felt shocked at his own reaction to the news that the Kennedys had gone.

Gabriel could feel Abby's presence in the room. He remembered the day when they'd spent the afternoon together, sharing their hearts and emotions, talking, and laughing. He had watched her sit in that very chair as she poured her heart out to him. He'd studied her golden curls falling forward and the smoothness of her skin where the virginal white blouse had opened slightly at the curve of her chest. The sadness of her story had moved him. His desire had been to go to her, sweep her away, hold her under the stars, and kiss away her sorrow. He had never felt such a strong longing in all his life. It was tormenting and painful.

Tears ran down Gabriel's cheeks. He was back now to where it all had begun—to where it must end.

"I am grateful for the answer to my prayers, although it may not have been what I was searching for. Lord, you have shown me the path I must follow."

— 7 —

As Colleen Grant awoke, she lay in her bed lazily, watching the Virginia sun slowly rise. Over the Atlantic Ocean, the light cast pretty shadows around the bedroom. She sat up, stretched, and slowly maneuvered her enormous pregnant body to the edge of her bed. Looking at the top of her belly, she spoke.

"Good morning, Junior. How are you this morning? It seems to me you are growing so fast; I cannot see the floor to find my slippers." She giggled to herself.

She carefully slid off the bed and then put on her dressing gown and found her slippers. Going about her morning ritual, after tiptoeing from her bedroom to the kitchen, she opened the drapes, placed the kettle on the stove, and went about setting the table for breakfast as she waited for the kettle to boil for her early morning tea. She looked out the window at the Atlantic Ocean, watching the sunrise.

Colleen felt renewed, filled with the wonder of life, every time she witnessed the different versions of the sunrise performed for her most days. The shapes of the clouds would determine the splendor and the color of the Atlantic: angry, kind, or excited. Some mornings, the sun was a huge, hot, fiery ball filled with the energy of a brand-new day. Occasionally, the sun had a cool, lazy essence surrounding it, and the colors were soft blue, indigo, pink, orange, and silvery pewter. From time to time, she did not see the sunrise, as the clouds were too thick; the sky simply changed from dark to light. Spending some quiet time before the day began was her gift to herself.

Her girls were sleeping; Grace was seven, and Aria was four. Patting her tummy, she hoped this one was a little boy. She knew her husband, Byron, would have been thrilled to have a son, although he adored his girls. Byron loved the females in his life, holding them all high on a pedestal.

Colleen was one of the luckiest women in the world; she had married her childhood sweetheart. She had been the prom queen, and Byron had been the Captain of the football team and a typical gorgeous-looking athlete. He was more than six feet tall, with dark hair and dark eyes.

As Colleen looked out over the ocean, she inhaled and exhaled several times. She was enjoying every moment of the privileged life she lived. She loved living on Virginia Beach—what a spectacular place to call home.

Colleen heard a noise and turned. Aria was standing in the doorway, sleepily rubbing her eyes, wearing a pink Sleeping Beauty nightgown, with Mrs. Bunny, her bunny, firmly tucked under her right arm. Her long blonde hair was loose and tousled around her shoulders; she was a precious sight.

"Good morning, Aria. Come sit on Mom's knee." Colleen patted her knees, "Bring Mrs. Bunny. We can watch the sunrise together."

Aria ran to her and wrapped her tiny arms as far around her Mom's waist as possible.

"Would you like a drink of milk?" Colleen asked, and Aria sleepily shook her head. "Okay, let's just cuddle quietly."

Aria snuggled in closely with Mrs. Bunny lying safely between them, softly humming to herself, as she always did. Aria had the gift of a voice like an angel, sweet and pure, which she unconsciously shared, for she sang softly to herself whenever she could, unaware of her gift. Colleen thought singing was like breath to Aria, an essential part of her existence.

Grace arrived on the sunporch, running toward her Mom. Grace had her Father's looks and looked completely different from Aria. Grace was tall for a seven-year-old and slender, and her hair was very dark, long, and straight and hung down her back, reaching her waist. It was a glorious head of hair, like velvet. She had the most beautiful dark brown eyes flecked with gold and long black eyelashes protecting them. Her eyebrows were arched and perfect. Grace had something few were given: a hidden strength, a strong presence, as her Father had. For Byron, it was powerful and a useful and provocative asset in his profession as one of the world's prominent magicians. It gave him a great advantage when he performed.

It was not always such an advantage for Grace, as it sometimes made those around her uncomfortable, both adults and children alike. Grace seemed to be serious, distant, and indifferent. However, she was not; she was anything but. Colleen hoped one day her gift would end up being useful to her.

Grace read constantly; she always had a book in her

hand, by her bed, in her schoolbag or toy box, or on the kitchen table. She was a wonderful conversationalist, filled with imagination and insight far beyond her tender years.

"Good morning, gorgeous," Colleen said.

"Hi, Mom. Can I come in and cuddle too?" Grace asked.

Colleen opened her arms, and the threesome sat together quietly enjoying one another.

Later, after the children had left for school, Colleen was cleaning up the breakfast dishes, when the telephone rang.

"Hello, Byron. It's so good to hear your voice," said Colleen. Her beautiful husband called every morning when he was away from them.

"Hello, Colleen. How are you and our beautiful girls? Oh, and I'm not forgetting Junior."

"Everyone is well. The girls just left for school; you've just missed them. Junior is just getting bigger by the day. Will you be home at the weekend?"

"Yes, it cannot come quickly enough for me. I am happy to report we had a sellout crowd here in Atlantic City all week. Very successful—the new format is a smash success. I'm looking forward to coming home to relax and staying for a while, until after the babe is born. Spending time with all my lovelies. Let's plan on taking the kids somewhere fun for a few days when I come home."

"Not too far. I'm as big as a house." Colleen patted her belly ruefully.

"I can't wait to see you, Colleen. I love you. Especially when you're carrying a baby; it's the greatest magic of all. I must go now; someone is paging me. Goodbye, honey. See you soon!"

Amazing Grace

"I miss you, Byron. We all do. Love you. Kisses from the girls and Junior."

Colleen hung up the telephone and went about her business, cleaning up the kitchen. She had the best designed kitchen in the United States of America, she thought. Byron had made sure of it. She had had the pleasure of working alongside the architect who'd designed the house. Colleen had been involved in the design, particularly of the kitchen and the bathrooms. The kitchen had been designed specifically for entertaining. The architect was female; hence, there was a lot of attention to detail.

Colleen could reach every handmade oak cupboard without stretching or using a stool. Lazy Susans were strategically placed in awkward corners, and there were a multitude of sliding drawers for easy access to kitchen utensils. The centerpiece of the gourmet kitchen was the walkout onto a large cedar deck that looked out onto the Atlantic Ocean.

She went to her bedroom. It was getting late, and she had a meeting downtown with her volunteer group, Women for Women, at eleven o'clock. She and several other women in the local area had brought the group together several years ago in order to assist less fortunate women. At first, there had been only a few members; however, over the years, the group had grown, and it was now a large organization. They raised money through fundraising events during various times of the year.

Colleen was part of the ways and means committee, and they were currently planning the Strawberry Festival for June. It was the biggest fundraiser of the year, providing them with money to afford many essentials and sometimes a few luxuries for the women and their children.

Colleen stepped out of the shower cautiously, moving slowly. She was towel drying under her left breast, as there was little room between the underside of her breast and the top of her belly. Using a small washcloth to dry the area thoroughly, she felt something unfamiliar. Colleen's heart jumped. She stopped drying, trying to see what was there, but she could not.

With panic slowly rising, she moved as quickly as she could and stood in front of the floor-to-ceiling mirror on the bathroom wall. She moved in as close as physically possible under the circumstances. Slowly lifting her left breast, squinting, she scrutinized the area. She saw a sore about the size of a dime. It appeared to be dry, with a crust on top; there was no weeping.

She breathed a sigh of relief. *It must be from the friction of my breast rubbing on top of my tummy.*

After using ointment and a bandage to stop the friction, she finished drying off and getting dressed. As she left the house, Colleen decided to discuss the spot with Andrew Mason, her doctor, on her next visit.

8

Abby sat at a small table in her favorite Italian restaurant, nestled in the village of Fairwinds, affectionately known to the locals as That's Amore. Abby and Sarah had become frequent patrons since moving into the Tudor house two years ago. The restaurant was just down the street from where they lived.

That night was special, as they were celebrating Sarah's graduation from university with a business degree.

As Abby looked around, she had a view of every table, approximately twenty of them, all occupied. Crisp white tablecloths, napkins to match, and purple and yellow pansies arranged around a candle adorned each table.

The tables were filled that night. Abby observed groups celebrating birthdays; secret lovers together by candlelight in the window seats, holding hands; and Italian immigrant Grandmas and Grandpas, all together, eating spaghetti, pizza, and pastas. The aromas of garlic, olive oil, roasted peppers, and baked lasagna collided and touched her feel-good senses.

On the walls was a hand-painted mural of various Italian

landmarks: Trevi Fountain, the Roman Coliseum, Vatican City, and the Leaning Tower of Pisa. The ambience of the restaurant brought back memories of her trip to Rome several years ago with her best friend, Sally.

Abby looked at Sarah across the table.

"I am both happy and sad to be sharing this moment with you, Sarah. Congratulations! It's truly a milestone for you and a tremendous accomplishment. Now you can go join your Father and help run the printing business with him in Harrogate. You will be joining the league of the working class!"

"I know. I cannot believe it. Four years of university—gone just like that." Sarah snapped her fingers. "How am I going to adapt to a working life in Harrogate, living with my parents and not with you in our comfy house? My cousin's returning next month from his travels does not make this any easier for you. I wish things could stay the same. I really do," Sarah replied.

"Unfortunately, they don't stay the same, but it's good to move on. In fact, I found a room in the village. The house is owned by an older lady. Gives me use of the bathroom and kitchen and laundry facilities and, when I'm home, an evening meal. It will work out fine. After all, I'm not around that much."

"That's good news you decided to stay in the village. I hope we can visit each other when we can. We will in time."

The main courses arrived. They had both ordered spaghetti and meatballs, which was the house special, and they both expertly negotiated the spaghetti onto their forks.

Sarah said, "Abby, what happened to … I wondered when you would visit Tennessee. You told me one day you would go back. I think you should."

Amazing Grace

Abby put down her fork, lifted her glass of wine, and swished it about inside the glass, pensively staring into it, before she responded. "Yes, I am hoping to go visit my cousins in Virginia this winter. I have three weeks' holiday and a free flight."

"Good. When you're there, visit Tennessee, and maybe bring home a surprise." Sarah picked up her glass. "To you, Abby, my friend. I'll miss you."

They clinked their glasses, and as Abby sipped her wine, she felt a wave of sadness and a shiver run through her.

Several weeks had gone by since Abby and Sarah's bittersweet celebratory dinner. They had moved out of the Tudor house. Sarah had gone back to Harrogate, and Abby had moved into her new lodgings.

The house belonged to an older lady, Mrs. Smith, a widow. Abby appeared to be the perfect tenant for Mrs. Smith, and the accommodation was ideal. Abby was working more recently; she had been promoted several times in the last two years. Her seniority with Global Airlines was growing. She worked mostly transatlantic long hauls; they often took her away for ten days at a time. She was permanent first class, currently working on the exam that would move her for promotion to being lead flight attendant on a DC-1011 aircraft, which meant more pay and not as much hard work.

The housing arrangement seemed to be working out well, mostly because Abby wasn't around that much. Mrs. Smith clearly liked that.

Abby was preparing to leave for another long-haul transatlantic flight. That day she would fly to Los Angeles and then on to San Francisco. After a layover, she'd go on to Montreal, return to San Francisco, and then fly into New York and, eventually, home to Gatwick. This was one of her favorite flights; she loved it at the best of times, particularly this time of the year.

The Christmas shopping in New York was fantastic, and the crew had discovered dock shopping. The market on the Hudson River was an experience to repeat. One could find endless wonders and bargains galore. The last time Abby had had a chance to shop there, she'd purchased a black-and-white silk maxi dress for just five dollars and three eight-track tapes—one of the Bee Gees, Rod Stewart, and Elton John—for just two dollars each. Furthermore, she'd bought a delectable pair of black platform shoes and a pair of white go-go boots for disco dancing, all real leather. There was always something for everyone in New York City at the right price. She had her Christmas shopping list all ready.

"Mrs. Smith, I'll be home on November 19," she called as she moved toward the front door. "I'll see you when I get back."

"Have a good flight, and safe travels, dear."

The fourteen-hour flight to LA was busy, as it was a full load. It was one of the longest flights the crew could fly without a break.

"Do you have plans for tonight, Abby?" the other first-class attendant asked.

"Yes, I do. I'm looking forward to getting to my hotel room; taking a long, hot bubble bath; and slipping into the crisp, clean white sheets. It's the very best part of my day. Why do you ask? Do you have a better idea?"

"Some of the crew were talking about getting together and going out to see the new *Superman* movie everyone is talking about. What a hunk Christopher Reeve is, and the special effects are unbelievable. It's not released in the UK yet, so we can be some of the first to see it and brag when we get home. What do you think?"

"As I said, a hot bath and crisp sheets await. But I'll have breakfast with you tomorrow."

As Abby slid into her crisp, clean white sheets, she felt almost dizzy. It had been a long day—eighteen hours by the time they'd arrived from Gatwick. As she drifted off into a blissful sleep, she thought about San Francisco, Montreal, and New York City. *Tomorrow, tomorrow,* she thought, and she fell into a deep sleep.

The following morning, Abby joined the crew for breakfast in the hotel restaurant. When they were all finished, they congregated outside and were driven to Los Angeles International Airport in a crew van.

When they arrived at the airport, it appeared there was some sort of altercation or distress going on around the check-in desk. Large crowds seemed to be irate. The Captain suggested that maybe the flight had been canceled. The group arrived at the crew room. As soon as Abby entered, she was aware that something was terribly wrong. Several of the girls were crying, and many of the flight deck crew were pacing the floor and yelling at one another at the tops of their voices.

"What is going on?" Abby's Captain spoke up.

Another Captain responded, "Haven't you heard? It's a goddamn nightmare. Global announced bankruptcy this morning at eight local time. Six thousand passengers and crew stranded on both sides of the Atlantic. Twelve aircraft grounded and twenty-six hundred staff and crew redundant. No jobs—they are all gone just like that." The man snapped his fingers.

Abby's Captain turned visibly gray and spoke with a quiver in his voice. "Good God. Dear God, what are we supposed to do? We have a protocol to follow for every possible scenario but not this. What about the passengers? How are they supposed to get home? How are we supposed to get home?"

"They're bankrupt!" the other Captain snapped. "Don't you understand? We all will be lucky if we manage a fucking ride home!"

Abby watched as everyone went quiet. She placed her hand over her mouth to prevent herself from vomiting. Shaking and feeling helpless, she ran to the bathroom and just managed to reach the toilet before emptying the contents of her stomach. She was in shock. Shaken, looking at her reflection, she splashed her face with cold water. She was as gray as her Captain had been. Inhaling some deep breaths, she went back to the crew room.

Abby poured herself a cup of water and headed out the door toward the airport terminal, hoping to get some fresh air.

"I'd not venture out there if I were you."

Abby turned to see who was talking to her. It was First Officer Butler from her flight. "Why not?" she asked.

"In that uniform, most likely, you will be lynched. They are all after blood out there, and I can't say I blame them."

Abby came back toward Butler. "I daresay you're right. I'll just sit here with you. Let's be scared and miserable together. This is surreal. This morning, I was thrilled, looking forward to a ten-day trip and five hundred dollars in flight pay to go toward Christmas shopping. Beautiful hotels, glorious beds, good wine, fine food, and camaraderie with the crew. And just like that, this morning, no job, no planes, and here we are, stranded."

"That's right," Butler said, and he shook his head. "No job means no pay for mortgage payments, car payments, kids' school fees, and Christmas on its way. There will be well over two thousand staff crew and ground crew looking for work. I'd say it's highly unlikely we'll find a job."

"Oh my God, I'm so sorry, Butler. I wasn't thinking. I at least don't have those kinds of financial responsibilities. You're right. Finding work will be almost impossible." Abby bit down on her lip. She felt like bursting into tears. "This is just terrible. What will we do? Where will we go? How will we manage?" She dropped her head into her hands as she spoke.

Several other employees gathered around them, all looking distraught. Some were weeping; others were silent and shocked. There was no comfort. There were no words of wisdom.

Some hours later, an airport representative came into the crew room with a message. He stood in the middle of the room and, at the top of his voice, called out.

"May I have everyone's attention, please? My name is David Taylor. Your employers express sincere apologies. We at the LA airport are doing our utmost to see all stranded passengers returned to their destinations safely. We'd appreciate your patience. British Air and Pan American have kindly offered to honor the return tickets of all those who had Global tickets. As you are aware, this could take some time. British Air and Pan American have put on extra flights. As soon as all stranded passengers are accounted for and taken care of, we'll then start to look at crew. This is the only information available at this time; I'll keep you informed. The airport will provide you with refreshments. We request you do not leave the crew room. Thank you for your attention."

Abby stayed in the lounge along with all the other crew members for close to fifteen hours that day. They were transported home as passengers, with no rank or pecking order. The list was alphabetical, and Abby, being an *L*, was halfway down the list. Abby hadn't traveled as a passenger for almost six years. She had had the luxury of flying in a uniform and traveling first class wherever she went.

The flight back to Gatwick was like a bad dream. Abby sat in a back seat, squished between two loud men who smelled like beer, garlic, and sweat. She felt nauseated. She left her seat, and after locking herself in the bathroom, she heaved and wretchedly wept until she was spent. Eventually, she returned to her seat, and after anguishing for several hours, Abby knew what she had to do as soon as she arrived in Gatwick: she would call Sasha and Cammie to ask them if she could return home to Newcastle to stay with them in the family home until she found a new job. It was the last place she wanted to return to after the wonderful life she had become accustomed to. Her heart was sick as she looked out past the putrid-smelling man, beyond the window, over the wing, to the vision of a thousand stars blinking at her.

Never mind. I have no alternative.

With a sad sigh, she pushed aside her tumbling thoughts and tried to doze the rest of the way home.

9

In early November, Colleen stepped into the shower cautiously; she felt enormous. Byron came into the bathroom.

"Hey, can I help you?" He chuckled.

"Only if you go away and leave me alone. I'm in a hurry; I need to get ready for an appointment to see Dr. Mason. It's my biweekly prenatal visit," she replied.

"You are the picture of good health. I've never seen you look more beautiful than you do this very moment."

"Get out of here, Byron, before I shower you with this hose!" Colleen was trying to wash her hair.

Byron left, laughing aloud to himself.

Colleen was still concerned regarding the sore she had discovered under her left breast ten days ago. Fortunately, she was so big Byron did not notice it. She wanted to discuss it with Andrew first before she told Byron anything. She was now eight months pregnant, plus a few days.

Last time she'd looked, it had not disappeared, as she had hoped. It appeared to be a little sticky; she felt as though she had knocked the crust off when drying herself. It was still there, no bigger and no smaller. She would be relieved to show Andrew and get his opinion.

Andrew Mason, Byron, and Colleen had gone to high school together. Andrew had left for medical school and greener pastures after graduation. He was gorgeous and dashing; every girl in high school had been in love with him, except for her—she'd had Byron. Though she had been sorry to see him go, she had been delighted when he returned several years later to set up a private practice. Dr. Andrew Mason was a brilliant family doctor and an asset. He was also a fantastic friend to her and Byron.

Byron came back into the bathroom as Colleen was drying herself. "Would you like some help now?"

"Yes, please, you could help me with—" Colleen stopped suddenly. Her water had just broken. "Oh God! Byron! Byron!"

"Stay calm. We have this under control, Colleen." He was by her side instantly.

"I am calm!" she screamed.

Byron grabbed her housecoat, put it on her, and wrapped his arm around her to support her. "Everything is fine, Colleen. Lean on me. We can drive you immediately to the hospital. We can be there in minutes. Do you have contractions?"

"No, I don't. At least I don't think so. Byron, I've had a lower backache for a day or so. I thought it was the size of the baby pushing up against something."

"Let's go, my darling, right now."

The Health Center of Virginia was a new state-of-the-art 250-bed hospital and institution located centrally in Virginia. Byron had donated a significant amount during the fundraising campaign to the maternity obstetrics wing, as his girls had been born in the old hospital.

The hospital auxiliary had decorated one of the rooms on the maternity ward to resemble and feel like a luxury hotel room. To have access to the room, a donation of $200 per day was required. All proceeds went to the wing for premature babies. Byron planned to book the room for three days after the baby was delivered.

Colleen was rushed into a labor and delivery room, where she was prepped and examined by an efficient nurse.

"Excellent. Mrs. Grant, you are nine centimetres dilated; you arrived in the nick of time. Any later, and Mr. Grant would have been delivering your baby on the backseat of the car." She smiled.

Colleen didn't smile back. She felt like screaming instead, and she did. The delivery was fast. Byron was with her every breath.

"One more push, Colleen," her obstetrician said. "The baby is here! What a beauty! Congratulations! You have a big, bouncing baby boy!"

Colleen and Byron both cried out with joy, thrilled at the news they had a son.

After the baby was weighed and measured, he was cleaned, swaddled, and passed over to his proud new parents. He lay between them. Byron looked at the baby. His eyes filled with pride and joy; he was exhilarated.

"Look at him, Colleen. He's spectacular, perfect in every way. What should we name him?"

"I'd like to name him Benedict Byron Grant. *Benedict* means 'blessing.'" Colleen smiled at Byron.

"I love it. Benedict it is. Can we call him Benny for short?"

"I think that suits him; it's such an appropriate name, as we are so blessed."

"I am so proud of the Mother you are. I couldn't love you any more than I do at this moment, Colleen." Byron kissed her gently on her lips. "You need your rest now. I'll go break the news to the world, especially the girls. I cannot wait to tell them they have a beautiful little brother and to bring them in later to meet him. Would you like me to call your Mother and tell her to come sooner?"

"I think you should; we'll need the help."

"I'll be back soon." Byron kissed Colleen and gently placed a kiss on his new son's forehead. "See you later, Benedict Byron Grant." As he said the baby's name, Byron jumped into the air. "I feel like I have a spring inside me that just wants to jump for joy!"

Colleen lay in bed, looking around the room; it felt surreal. Beautiful burgundy velvet drapes hung by the picture window with a view looking out onto a water fountain with weeping willows surrounding it. Inside the room stood a cherrywood armoire, and a writing desk sat against the wall. A bedside table matched them, although her bed was still a hospital bed. There were two burgundy velvet chairs matching the drapes. She was in a room that looked like a five-star hotel, though she was aware she was institutionalized, as someone's voice came across the PA, paging.

"Dr. Johnson, please report to the OR. Dr. Johnson, please report to the OR."

Colleen could hear the babies crying in the nursery and the business and activity of the nurses' station—telephones ringing, a multitude of conversation. The desk sounded like a car engine running.

Amazing Grace

"Take baby Darren to his Mother after that circumcision is finished. He will be ready for a feed and a cuddle," said one nurse.

"Are you going to Mary's jewelry party on Sunday?" asked a nurse.

"No, I am on days," another replied.

"Too bad. It's supposed to be very nice jewelry."

Colleen wished the door to her room was closed. She could then have imagined she was in a faraway place, lost in another world with Byron, the girls, and the new baby, surrounded by love and light, with no weeping sore to worry about. Deep inside her, at the bowels of her soul, she was terrified of what might be. The unknown—that mangled, insidious, distorted view of the fear of fear itself—had a deep hold on her. She prayed out loud to God for courage to deal with it as she gave in to sleep.

Colleen could hear someone calling her name. She awoke to find Andrew beside her bed. He had a smile from one side of his face to the other.

"Colleen, you are a clever girl, presenting Byron with his son, a boy child. I bumped into him when he was on the way out. He's like a spring lamb. Congratulations to you!"

She smiled; she was still waking from her deep sleep.

"I've just come from the nursery. I did the baby's ten-point check; he scored eleven. He's magnificent. I do love the name Benedict."

"Thank you, Andrew. I was on my way to see you this afternoon when my water broke."

"I heard. That's why I dropped by. I wanted to see how you're feeling."

"Very tired," she told him.

"It was a textbook delivery, Colleen; I can discharge you in a couple of days."

"I am expecting my Mother to arrive later today. Byron will bring my Mom and the girls in all together to meet Benedict."

"That's just wonderful. Everything is in order. Unless I can get you anything, I'll go and leave you to rest."

"Andrew, I do have a question. I was going to discuss it with you this afternoon."

"How can I help you? What's the question?" Andrew drew closer to the bed.

"I have a sore on the underside of my left breast." Colleen pulled up her gown, lifted her left breast, and pointed to it.

"Lie back, and relax. Let me look."

She watched Andrew and could feel him lifting her breast carefully. His reaction was immediate and spontaneous. When he looked at the sore, he pulled back from her with eyes enlarging, and his lips tightened. The color drained from his kind, handsome face. Her fears and suspicions were confirmed by his horrific expression.

"When did you first notice this, Colleen?" His voice was slightly raised. She was aware that he was trying not to show alarm.

"Ten days ago," she answered.

"Why didn't you come to me immediately?" he asked.

"I thought—no, I hoped—that it was just friction from rubbing on my belly. I prayed daily that it would disappear, not wanting to do anything to affect my unborn baby before he arrived."

"I understand." Andrew put her gown back in place and sat down beside her bed. Taking her hand in his, he continued. "Colleen, I am concerned. Looking at it, I'd say it needs a biopsy as soon as possible for any of us to decide what to do next. I'm going to contact Dr. Burke; he is the specialist surgeon. I'll suggest that he come by this evening after visitors leave. I'll attend to that right away."

Andrew left the room without looking back at her, and it appeared the smile he had come into the room with did not leave with him.

Colleen had just finished feeding Benedict, and the nurse had taken him back to the nursery. The door to her room opened, and Byron came in with an armful of long-stemmed red roses. Following behind him were her Mother and, on each side of her, Grace and Aria. It seemed everyone rushed over to the bed at the same time.

Colleen's Mom was unique, a bright star. She was four feet eleven inches, with short tinted-red hair, blue eyes, and energy beyond reason. Grandma Viv was a tornado whenever she came into a room, and that day was no exception. She was beside herself. Viv adored her girls, and Colleen was grateful to have her as a Mom.

"My darling girl, Benedict is a true dreamboat!" she exclaimed.

The nurse brought him in and placed him in Colleen's arms.

Viv bubbled on. "He's a double of his Father. I'm so proud of you! How are you? Come along, darlings; come see Mommy. I was astonished when Byron called to tell me you'd had the baby. Fortunately, I was home. Darling, what a day. Oh, he is a gorgeous boy! Girls, meet your new brother."

Grace looked at Colleen, waiting patiently for Viv to take a breath. "Mommy, may I hold Benedict?" she asked.

Byron interrupted. "Of course you can. Sit down in this chair, and I'll put him in your arms."

Aria came up to her Mom. "Can I touch his face? I'd like to sing him a lullaby." She smiled and hummed.

Byron sat on the bed as Viv watched over the three children. "How are you?" he asked Colleen.

"I'm sleepy."

"We won't stay long. Andrew told me this afternoon that he might discharge you tomorrow. That's fantastic news—to get you both home."

Colleen observed her three children together. The girls were so tender with Benedict that she could not contain her feelings. She broke down and started to sob uncontrollably with tears pouring from her eyes. The girls were alarmed, and Aria started to cry too.

"Please don't cry, Mommy. Please."

"Take the girls out, please." Byron looked at Viv.

"Come along, girls. Say good night to Mommy. It's time to go. We'll see her tomorrow. Say good night to Benedict." Viv ushered the girls from the room.

"I don't blame you; you've had quite a day. Postpartum, I suspect. Try to rest now, and I'll come in early tomorrow. We can have breakfast together." Byron held Colleen in his arms.

"I feel overwhelmed," Colleen told him.

Byron kissed her gently on the lips. "I'll take Benny back to the nursery. You rest now," he said as he left.

Amazing Grace

Colleen was relieved, as she felt guilty for not sharing her secret with him. The nurse came back in.

"I'm going to give you a nice bath and change your sheets and gown. I'll get you ready for Dr. Burke to come in to see you; he should be here in half an hour or so. I'll bring you a hot cup of tea when we have finished."

Later, Colleen was just finishing off her tea, when the new doctor came into her room.

"Hello, Colleen. My name's Dr. Burke. Dr. Mason asked me to stop by to see you. I don't want you to be concerned. Andrew has explained everything to me, but I'd like to take a look myself. Just relax and lie down."

"Thank you, Doctor. It's kind of you to come by this late at night."

Dr. Burke gently lifted Colleen's breast. It seemed to Colleen that he looked at it from every angle. She studied his round face and his kind green eyes. His mouth appeared to carry a permanent gentle smile, which was part of his tender bedside manner. Placing her gown back, Dr. Burke sat on the edge of the bed.

"When did you first notice this, Colleen?" he asked.

"Ten days ago," she replied.

"Is there pain or discomfort?"

"No. Sometimes it's itchy from friction. There's very little room between the bottom part of the breast and the top of my tummy." Colleen attempted a smile.

Dr. Burke didn't return her smile. "Colleen, listen to me very carefully. What I'm about to say is very important. I don't wish to alarm you. I understand this will sound rather scary. For me to understand what is going on and how to treat you, I must move very quickly. When a situation like this arises, we always work toward the best result for the patient, and in this case, I'd like to biopsy the lesion tomorrow morning. That's about as much information as I need to give you tonight. We should contact your husband. I'm sure he'd like to be here with you this evening. Does he know anything?"

"No, I didn't tell him. I prayed it would go away."

"I believe Andrew is a close family friend. Is that correct?" Dr. Burke asked.

"Yes, he is," she answered, crying.

"I'd like to call Andrew and ask him to explain to your husband."

"Yes, Doctor, I'd like Byron here with me. It's time he knew everything."

"Colleen, try to rest. As difficult as this is, please try not to worry. Trust the system and allow us to do our job. I promise you I'll take the absolute best care of you, along with my nurses and staff."

"Will this affect my baby?" she asked.

"I have no reason to believe this will affect your baby. I suggest you bottle-feed him now until we understand just what we're dealing with; otherwise, he should be just fine. The nurse will be in shortly; she will put you on an antibiotic IV and some fluids. No food or drink by mouth from now until after the surgery. You won't be discharged tomorrow as expected. Is there someone at home to help with the children?"

"Yes, my Mother."

Amazing Grace

"I'll leave you to rest and see you in the morning," Dr. Burke said as he left.

Later that night, Andrew drove Byron to the hospital in silence. When they arrived at the hospital, Dr. Burke met Byron outside his office.

"I apologize for the urgency and disruption tonight; I'm sure it's the last thing you expected, Byron. Please understand I am here to help in any way I can. You must have many questions; I'd like to explain some of the procedures to you before you go in to see Colleen."

"How is she? I'd like to see her," Byron sputtered.

"Colleen is resting. I gave her a sedative. Our main concern is the lesion; therefore, I'll remove it as soon as possible and take a closer look. Ninety-five percent of these lesions and lumps are benign. However, it does look suspicious," Dr. Burke said solemnly, and he waited for Byron to respond.

Byron only nodded, his mouth falling open.

"It's important that you're prepared."

"How could such a thing appear? How can it happen?"

"It was not in an obvious place. It has been there for some time. We hope for the best outcome and prepare for every possible scenario. When I remove the lesion tomorrow, it will be biopsied immediately. Depending on the results, we may have to remove part of Colleen's breast—a procedure called a lumpectomy. Or we may have to remove the breast and the lymph nodes—a double radical mastectomy. The worst-case scenario would be removal of both breasts, all lymph nodes, and possibly chest wall muscle."

"Dear God!" Byron looked for somewhere to sit. His legs gave out as he fell into the chair beside him. Andrew patted his shoulder.

The doctor continued. "This is very rare. I haven't discussed this with Colleen. I will prior to the procedure. As I said, she is sedated. I've prescribed IV antibiotics and fluids, nil by mouth. It will help her get a good night's rest. Do you have any questions?" Dr. Burke asked.

Byron could barely think straight; it was as though the doctor were talking to someone behind him. Byron wanted to turn around and look to see who it was, as he felt sorry for the poor man and wondered how he would cope with such overwhelming news.

"No, thank you. I think you've covered what I need to know," Byron replied.

"The best thing you can do is be with her, hold her hand, and support her. She's frightened; she does need you."

Byron spent the night and early hours of the morning holding Colleen's hand. She looked peaceful, like one of his daughters, with her breathing flowing in a gentle rhythm. The reflection in the shadows from the early morning light played tricks with his eyes, creating shapes on the walls of the room that looked like angels' wings. The long-stemmed roses he had brought in that afternoon were blooming in a vase beside Colleen's bed. He thought they looked like black velvet and shuddered.

The nurses brought Benedict to him, and he gave him his feeding. Benedict was the most beautiful baby Byron had ever seen. He held Benedict close to him, trying to hold back tears, hoping the dam would not break and wondering when he would wake up from this nightmare.

The five-star room looked more like a hospital room now, with IV bags hanging beside Colleen's bed and equipment beeping at her side. Byron heard the hustle and bustle outside the room—breakfast trays coming up, babies crying, telephones ringing—and the noise inside his head. He knew he had to be strong; Colleen needed him. She stirred in the bed.

"Good morning. You slept well," Byron said as she opened her eyes.

Colleen sat upright, looking at Byron. She opened her arms wide. "Hold me, Byron, please. I'm so scared." She wept.

Byron held Colleen as close as physically possible. He believed the pain he felt inside was his fractured heart. "Please, Colleen, don't cry. We can work through this together. Dr. Burke is brilliant, and he'll take extraspecial care of you." He gently stroked Colleen's hair, holding, calming, and comforting her.

A nurse came in and interrupted them. "We must prep you now for the OR."

"Don't go. Stay. Please stay," Colleen pleaded as she reluctantly released her grip on Byron.

"I'll be here next to you every moment."

"What about Benedict?" Colleen asked.

"The nursery is looking after him. He's in very good hands," Byron assured her.

"Good morning," Andrew said as he came into the room.

"Thanks for coming," Byron said gratefully.

Andrew shook his head, and Byron thought he looked exhausted. "How did you sleep, Colleen?"

Colleen was still crying. "Okay, I guess. Andrew, I am so frightened."

"Dr. Burke has had a sedative set up in the IV bag. It will help you. I can only reassure you this is the best hospital, with the best medical staff waiting to take care of you, Colleen. I know they'll do everything in their power to help you."

After Colleen was taken into the OR, Dr. Burke came and spoke to Byron. "I'll keep you informed throughout the procedure. As we discussed last night, this is a process, and it will take some time to get results from the biopsy. The results will determine how we proceed."

Byron sat in the waiting room, watching the hands on the clock move as if in slow motion, aware that he had to find the strength to be prepared for whatever result came from Dr. Burke. Byron prayed to anyone who might be listening for the courage and help to get through this. Most of all, he prayed for a benign result.

After what felt like an interminable amount of time, as each second felt like hours, Andrew sat with him in silence for a short time. When Andrew was called away, Byron was grateful, for he could not cope with more than his own anguish.

Finally, Dr. Burke approached him with a grim face. Byron didn't need to hear his prognosis; he could see it and feel it in his demeanor. Byron broke down before Dr. Burke spoke. A deluge of tears poured from his eyes, dripping from his chin.

Dr. Burke placed a hand on Byron's shoulder. "I'm afraid it's malignant, and I'm preparing her for a double mastectomy. And all lymph nodes."

Byron wailed. "No! How can this be? Why? How?"

"I realize this is a shock, and performing such a devastating operation the day after the birth of your child seems a radical response. But this is an extremely aggressive cancer, and time is crucial."

Byron continued to sob, nodding.

"I must get back into the OR. I'm sorry, Byron. This will take several hours. Go home and rest; you'll need your strength."

Byron wiped the tears away with his handkerchief. He wasn't going anywhere; he would stay on that chair and wait for each agonizing second to pass for his Colleen to come back to him.

Colleen slowly opened her eyes, hearing a crying baby. She felt as though she were in a tunnel. Lying still for a moment, she remembered that she was home from the hospital and in her own bed, minus both breasts and lymph nodes. Any slight movement reminded her, causing pain.

She'd been home for several weeks and was healing slowly.

The baby stopped crying. Colleen heard her Mom go into his room to pick up Benedict and comfort him.

"There, there, little man. I'm here. Good morning. Now, let's get that diaper off and give you some breakfast." Her Mother fussed with the baby.

Colleen pulled herself up using her elbows, still feeling the searing pain across her chest. She maneuvered herself to the side of the bed, feeling exhausted, dizzy, and nauseated.

She looked down at her pillow and discovered even more hair. Her golden tresses lay in shreds and threads, scattered across the pillow. Her hands flew up to her head, which was already mangled, tangled, and half bald, feeling the deterioration. How she hated all this. Having no hair felt worse than having no breasts.

She slid off the bed, her hands clinging to her head, and moved as fast as her body would allow her to the bathroom. She fell to her knees by the toilet, and her head dropped into the bowl. She heaved and vomited, weeping, clutching her aching chest. Eventually, her body calmed itself long enough for her to move to her washbasin.

After finding a glass, she filled it with water. When she looked into the mirror, she was struck with horror when she saw her reflection. Crying out, Colleen touched her reflection with her hands in disbelief at what she was looking at. Chunks of hair were missing from her head, leaving patches everywhere, and straggles of hair lay upon her shoulders like limp spaghetti. Her skin was a pale yellowish gray, and her sunken eyes stared back at her, surrounded by dark blue circles. She cried out and slid back down onto the bathroom floor.

Grace came into the bathroom. "Mama, please don't cry." Grace sat beside her, taking her Mom's hand and looking at her with wide eyes and an openmouthed expression, as though she had never seen the person in front of her before, yet she managed to speak to her with loving messages. "Come on, Mama. I'll help you back to the bed. Grandma will bring you some tea. Would you like that?"

Colleen felt hopeless and useless. Her body had betrayed

her. Now her eight-year-old daughter was reversing the roles of Mother and child.

"It's okay," Grace said. "Grandma told me the medicines you need to take to help you get better would make you very sick. She also told me it would make your hair fall out. That's very sad. Maybe we can buy you a beautiful wig exactly like your own hair."

Colleen stayed on the floor, holding her amazing Grace's hand, when her Mother came into the room.

"Okay, Gracie, will you help me? Go sit with Ben. He's awake. I'll take care of your mama. Thank you, darling."

Gracie stood up and kissed her Mother on the cheek before she left. "I love you, Mama."

Colleen's Mother looked down at her on the floor. "Oh, my darling girl." Her Mother's expression—shock mixed with tender, loving care—penetrated Colleen's soul. She could do nothing.

Later, after her Mother had brought her back to bed, Colleen sipped herbal tea, as nothing would stay down.

Her Mother tried to comfort her. "The doctors explained to us the chemo effects are sometimes accumulative. This being your third chemo treatment, we'll see more of the effects. Darling, let me buzz your head, and we can find a beautiful turban."

Colleen nodded reluctantly.

"You're halfway there. Three more treatments, and you will be done!"

Colleen attempted a smile as she closed her eyes, blocking out the unbearable world that was now hers.

10

Abby stood outside the front door of the family home for several moments, looking down the street at the familiar sight. It was a bitterly cold day in December, and she had just arrived from London on the overnight bus. No more first-class flights for her! Nothing would be the same for her, or thousands of others, since Global had gone bankrupt.

The realization settled upon her like the piercing, damp, chilled air. She gazed at the row of terraced redbrick single-front Victorian homes with chimney pots releasing soot and smoke that curled and swirled in different directions up toward the miserable, heavy-looking sky. The only spots of white in the bleak sight were the net curtains hanging at the windows.

The houses continued until an unexpected break, an empty piece of land, a gap that looked like an open mouth with missing teeth—spaces where they didn't belong. There were no houses there, and then, once again, the homes reappeared like magic and continued to the end of the street. For Abby and everyone around who had been raised on the street, the sight was a continuous everyday reminder of the bomb that had fallen on the street during World War II in April 1941. It had killed dozens and injured many civilians who'd slept in their beds that fateful night. The youngest had been a nine-week-old boy; the eldest had been a seventy-seven-year-old woman. Through the years, various witnesses had described the incident to her many times over.

Abby felt it was long overdue that someone build something there to fill the void and hide the memories. It was a dark and damp day. The northeast winds howled around her head, burning her ears and eyes, with the wicked chill that only the north winds could bring. Abby pressed the doorbell, and moments later, she heard footsteps. The door swung open, and there was Sasha, tall and splendid, with his blue eyes shining.

"Welcome home! Hell, don't just stand there. Come in," he told her. Sasha took hold of both her hands, pulling her into the vestibule. "Let me get those cases." He placed them inside and closed the front door, shutting out the misery of the day. "Come here," he said as he wrapped his arms around her, giving her a warm hug. "It's really great to see you, Abby. I'm so sorry it's under such rotten circumstances."

Abby shivered.

"Come on into the kitchen; I'll make us a nice hot cuppa!" he said.

Abby followed Sasha along the dark passage, and the unmistakable aroma of Christmas cake slowly baking in the oven—candied fruits, brandy, cinnamon, and nutmeg—permeated the air with a nostalgic scent. Arriving in the kitchen, Abby could feel an immediate warm glow. She stepped into the kitchen, where the fire in the hearth was blazing. The light, warmth, and aroma in the kitchen had a magnetic effect; Abby could feel herself drawn in.

"I'm making the Christmas cake. Better late than never. Mam would've had it done in September." Sasha grinned at her, showing his dimpled cheeks. The moment was reminiscent of their childhood days. "Sit down in front of the fire. I stoked it up for your arrival. Get warm. I'll make some tea."

Abby took off her coat and sat down, staring into the roaring flames and listening to the cracking and popping as the fire burned. The light, warmth, and aroma in the kitchen made her feel as if the presence of her Mother were in the room, keeping a watchful eye over her children. The contrast between the cold, dark December day and the welcoming warmth inside made her feel relieved to be home and somehow close to Amelia.

Sasha brought the tea and some homemade shortbread to her as he sat down beside her. "What a predicament for you," he said softly.

"I'm one of the lucky ones. I have somewhere to go, thanks to you and Camille taking me in," Abby replied.

"Don't be daft!" Sasha sipped his hot mug of tea. "What now?" He stared at her with his deep-set blue eyes and dark arched brows.

"I need to find work, although I may have a problem this time of the year. I'll start looking tomorrow."

"I can't imagine what it must feel like for you, Abby. You had the best job in the world."

"Not anymore. I've cried enough these past few weeks. Some of the staff have families, mortgages, and car payments, not to mention Christmas coming, with little or no hope of finding any work," Abby told him.

"What a bloody crying shame. Don't you get compensated?"

"No, we don't even receive any wages; the company is bankrupt! I'm sure I'll find something; it won't take me too long," she said hopefully. She wasn't sure she would find work though.

Sasha nodded. "I don't know. I hate to say it, but things are very tight, and the economy is really slowing down. It's obvious at the hotel by how many people come out for dinner on Saturday night; the numbers are dropping. I think that's just the tip of the iceberg. Maybe the one thing on your side is that it's Christmas, so you might pick up a part-time job somewhere."

"I think I'll drop in on my old employers at the hairdressing salon and the pub," Abby said.

"That's a great idea! And you know you're welcome to stay here as long as you need to; this is your home," Sasha told her.

"Thanks, Sasha." Abby sipped her tea.

"We can put the Christmas tree up together just like the old days." Sasha smiled. "I'll take your cases upstairs and put them in your room."

Abby looked about her and shuddered at the thought of the adjustment she was going to have to make. Tears tumbled from her eyes. She couldn't help herself; it was all too much to process.

"Please help me, Mam. I don't know what to do," Abby whispered.

Abby had been living back at home for three weeks, and now Christmas was a week away. She'd found employment at her old hairdressing shop, and they wanted someone full-time between Christmas and New Year's. She'd also found work at the Bells, the pub at the end of the street she lived on. She worked there three nights per week between Christmas and New Year's.

The salon Abby worked in was far from beautiful. It was on the ground floor of an old three-story Victorian building, and it needed some tender, loving care. The salon consisted of two large rooms with twelve-foot ceilings, spiders and cobwebs included. Each room had a large picture window that faced a brick wall outside but gave little natural light.

All the walls inside were painted with yellow distemper. Brown linoleum covered the floors and was cracked in most places. Four old-fashioned hooded hair dryers stood against the wall. Two black shampoo basins and two old-fashioned kidney-shaped dressing tables with mirrors with plastic chairs in front of them completed the room.

What Abby noticed most was the stench. The smells of mildew, ammonia, hairspray, and coffee all tangled together, creating an indescribable aroma, making her feel sick. She tolerated it out of necessity; the job paid her reasonably well.

Abby was working on a permanent wave for one of her old clients, Mrs. Whitehouse.

Amazing Grace

"What a wonderful surprise to find you here. I love the way you do my hair. You have a canny knack. It holds well for the whole week. What brings you back home to Newcastle after flying around the world for so long?" Mrs. Whitehouse asked.

Abby felt embarrassed, feeling her face flush, as she wrapped the end paper around Mrs. Whitehouse's hair and wound the hair around the perm roller. Abby had several appointments for permanent waves booked that day. She was fortunate to work full-time because of the busy season. She looked back at Mrs. Whitehouse's reflection in the mirror as the woman awaited Abby's response.

"Global went bankrupt," Abby replied.

"Oh! You poor thing! What an awful experience it must be—like driving a Rolls-Royce and then moving to a Mini. I mean, such a change! Are you living back in the family home?"

"Yes, for the time being."

"I, for one, am thrilled to see you back. You can book my appointments in every week. I love your magic fingers," Mrs. Whitehouse said.

"Thank you so much, Mrs. Whitehouse; I'll be happy to do that." Abby smiled.

At the end of her busy day, Abby and her boss cleaned the salon. Before going home, Abby counted her tips. They were good that time of year; however, the pay was nothing like the money she was used to making.

Abby headed home, fighting the elements. It was one of the shortest days of the year, December 18, and was dark by three thirty. It had been raining all afternoon, and the temperature had dropped, turning the rain into sleet, and there was a heavy fog rolling in. She walked quickly to help stay warm and get home, as she was scheduled to work in the pub that night.

Later, Abby stood behind the bar, cleaning the glasses. The pub was the same as the salon in that it had not changed in years. The walls were painted brown, the carpet was brown, and even the light appeared brown. The aroma was of cigarette smoke, beer, onions, and urine all mingled together. Abby hated the job; it was loud and busy, as it was so close to Christmas. People pushed and shoved to get their pints ordered. She stood behind the bar three nights a week, watching the same men stare into the bottom of their beer or whiskey glasses, looking for answers that were not there. The pub personified hopelessness and misery—no light at the end of the tunnel.

"What are you doing back at this shithole, pet? I thought you was winging ya way around the world. What happened?" It was Fred, one of her neighbors. Abby had been reunited with some old customers at the pub.

"The company went bankrupt, Fred," Abby told him. She was growing weary of explaining herself and her grim situation. She washed a glass with more force than necessary.

"That's a rotten shame. I'm sorry for your troubles. Have one for yourself, bonny lass."

"Thank you, Fred," Abby replied.

"No bother. It's grand to see your bonny face back on the other side of the bar."

Abby smiled at Fred, although inside, she groaned; she wasn't happy to be there.

Sebastian was in the scullery, stirring the fish soup; it was his favorite. He'd invited Abby for her tea that night, as he hadn't seen her since she'd returned. The doorbell rang, and Sebastian turned the soup to simmer and went along the long, dark hallway to answer. Opening the door, Sebastian found Abby looking at him. As always, she took his breath away. Her similarity to Amelia was striking.

Fighting back tears, he said, "Bonjour. *Ça va?*" He kissed her on both cheeks. "I am very happy to see you."

"Me too." Abby hugged her Dad.

Sebastian stepped back. "Let me look at you. You look good—a little tired around the eyes maybe. Come. Follow me. I have the fish soup ready."

"Magnificent! I could smell it from the street. I've been daydreaming about this all day. Thanks for inviting me, Dad."

Sebastian led the way as Abby followed him into the old kitchen.

"Dad, when I arrived at the gate tonight, the old house looked the same, although it seems a little smaller now that I'm bigger. I could barely see it in the night mist and fog, although the silhouette was clear. A thousand memories tumbled past my eyes like a film. I could see the lazy summer days when I played with the boys in the garden, with the trellis almost falling over from the weight of roses cascading to the ground in every color of the rainbow and the perfume floating through the air as we played."

"You make it sound idyllic," Sebastian said.

"Dad, do you remember the house halfway down the street? Like this one but different?" Abby asked.

"The ostentatious one?"

"The owner painted the steps, the front door, and all the window frames white. The front door was turquoise, with brass doorbell, door knocker, and door handle, and the gate was brass. It shone like gold in the sunshine!"

"Oui, yes, you're right. I remember."

"The net curtains hanging at the window were so white and glorious, like clouds. They belonged in the windows at Buckingham Palace, not on our street. I used to stand outside that house for hours, looking into the magnificent garden. It had every possible flower you could imagine—foxgloves, roses, pinks, carnations. I imagined so many wonders happening on the other side of the door. One day I walked the boys down the street to the house. It was past our boundaries; I told them it was our big secret." Abby giggled to herself as she looked off into some far-off place in her memories while she told the story to Sebastian.

"Richard Chamberlain lives in there with his Mother," she had told the boys.

"Who is that?" Sasha had asked.

"You know—Dr. Kildare," Abby had told him.

"Oh, him. The one on the telly?"

"How do you know that?" Noah had asked.

"Look at the house. Somebody rich and famous lives in there!"

The boys all had nodded. "Have you seen him?" Nathan had asked.

"No, I haven't. He only comes out at night, when it's dark. Because he's famous, he doesn't want people to know. When I am sixteen, he'll come out in the daylight and see me. I know that when he does, we'll get married!" Abby had said.

All the boys had giggled. "You are daft, Abby!" Nathan had said.

"If I give you my sweets on Friday, will you all promise to keep it a secret? We can play weddings under the roses and the archway and practice."

"Yes, anything for more sweets!" Nathan had said.

"Cross your heart?" Abby had asked.

"Cross my heart," he had said solemnly.

Sebastian wiped his eyes, laughing and crying as Abby finished her story.

"Dad, you must promise me never to remove the arch over the gate. It holds too many precious memories."

"I promise. Cross my heart," Sebastian replied.

"I do love the changes you've made to the inside," said Abby.

"I only painted it and changed the carpets and some of the furniture."

"I like that it looks the same yet different. I am so happy you kept the fireplace! I think especially of the Christmases we spent around it."

"I agree. Abby, sit down, and we can talk and eat."

Sebastian felt a fleeting sadness in thinking about memories of Christmases past. He carried in the fish soup with croutons and cheese rouille. In his world, this was a ritual almost as sacred as Holy Communion, even more so when sharing it with one of his children.

"Bon appétit." Sebastian looked at Abby. "You've had a difficult time, Abby; I was shocked when I heard the news on the radio."

"It has been devastating for the employees. Many of them are married with families. I'm one of the fortunate ones. I have a home, and I found work," Abby replied.

"I'm very impressed at your finding work so quickly."

"It's really not that difficult this time of the year."

"What are your long-term plans?"

"Quite honestly, I'm not sure. I can tell you that I'm not happy here. I love being at home with the family, but I'm very unhappy in both my jobs; they are so depressing after the job I had."

"I can understand what a difficult adjustment it must be."

"I think I'm still in shock. In January, both jobs will probably let me go or just keep me part-time. I've been thinking that if I can save enough money, I'd like to go back to America. To Aidan and Rosella. Did you know they moved to Virginia from Tennessee?"

"No, I didn't," said Sebastian.

"Aidan was promoted to the head office. They have a beautiful, large home, and they have invited me many times to come visit them."

"What would you do for work?"

"I don't know. I'd find something. It's such a different world out there, filled to overflowing with possibilities. I love it."

"I can tell. But I'd like to ask you a question, Abby. Who

is he?" Sebastian smiled as he looked at Abby's surprised expression.

She dropped her gaze. "Is it so obvious, Dad?"

"I recognize the look of love when I see it. Whenever you discuss your time in America, you shine. The warmth you convey is not created from the place as much as someone. You always go subconsciously to the angel around your neck."

"Oh, Dad." Abby broke down. There were tears upon her cheeks as her face glowed in the firelight.

Sebastian hadn't yet turned on the lights. He could see through the window that there was a full moon, and the night was clear. Silver beams reflected through the glass into the kitchen. Between the warmth of the orange flames from the fire and the light from the silver moon, the moment around him was magical. He felt as though Amelia were sitting in front of him, almost translucent. He was lifted back in time.

Abby shared her story with him and, almost speaking to herself, explained how she'd fallen in love with the young priest Gabriel. They had parted, never exploring their love or its potential. Gabriel had moved, and she hadn't known where to find him or if she would ever see him again. However, a recent letter from Rosella Kennedy had told her Gabriel was back in Tennessee, where she and Gabriel had first met.

"Do you really love him?" asked Sebastian.

"How should I know?" Abby cried out. "If what I am feeling is love, then the answer is yes, with all my heart!"

"I can only tell you this. I felt that way about a woman at your age. We were at war; the situation seemed impossible. Because we did not know if tomorrow would even come, I decided to tell her how I felt. Life is short. She showed me love, and she gave beats to my heart. She brought meaning to my life I had never experienced."

"What happened, Dad? What did she say?" Abby looked at him with tears filling her sad eyes.

"She married me—it was your Mother! Follow your feelings, and don't ever live with regret. Abby, go to him when you can, and tell him how you feel; you owe it to yourself. After he hears your truth, have courage to listen to his. You must allow him to make his own decisions, and you make yours. Let us have a brandy." Sebastian poured brandy into crystal snifters.

"Look! Out the window. The first snow of winter!" Abby cried.

The flakes looked like frozen teardrops in the full moon light. They floated softly and gently down upon the gray-black concrete yard, creating a shimmering crystal blanket under the silver moon.

"True love. Don't let it go," said Sebastian as he raised his glass.

Father and daughter stood together looking out the window on the December eve, each immersed in his or her own thoughts.

— 11 —

On Christmas Eve, Abby sat in a pew inside their town's ancient monastery, listening to the pure voices of the choirboys singing "O Holy Night," sitting side by side with her siblings, as tradition demanded. The Lavalles always returned home for Christmas midnight Mass at the monastery at all costs. Abby loved the tradition; it gave purpose and meaning to the Christmas celebration. It was a memory she felt connected to like an umbilical cord carrying her back to days gone by. Beyond her memories of her Mother, Amelia, it kept her grounded like an anchor.

Christmas seemed to her to have become too materialistic. As much as she adored it, the decorations, music, and frenzy all seemed to begin much earlier than they had in the past. There had been a time when Christmas didn't start until Advent on the first Sunday of December. She'd recently seen the window of a department store in Newcastle fully decorated with trees, lights, and all the bells the day after Remembrance Day on November 12!

Abby shivered. She felt cold, as the old monastery was

enormous, damp, and freezing. She pulled up the collar on her coat and pushed her hands deep into her coat pockets.

Abby stood for communion and walked up the aisle to the high altar, where the nativity scene was displayed in all its splendor. It looked bright, shining, and new compared to the ancient pillars of stone supporting the beloved, historic monastery. Abby always felt close to Amelia on Christmas Eve, as though her Mother had wrapped her in a beautiful, warm blanket and held her close.

Abby glowed from the inside out. Returning to her pew after taking Holy Communion and kneeling, Abby whispered the words from her lips: "Mother Mary, bless this day. Please help me find my way back to America, to Gabriel."

The next day, Abby was grateful and feeling the warm camaraderie of the season. The Christmas table was decked out in its full glory, overflowing with ham, turkey, potatoes, stuffing, many different vegetables, and Christmas pudding. Around the table, her family were dressed up, with suit jackets on the men and dresses on the women. Sebastian sat next to Andre, followed by Andre's wife, Jane, and their little Amelia. Amelia was now going to school and was beautiful like her namesake. She was affectionately known as Millie, and she had long dark curls and big brown eyes. She had inherited the melancholy stare of her Father and grandMother before her.

Abby's sister Camille was three years older than Abby but looked younger, as she was three inches shorter and had a pixie face. She was still single and not even engaged, though she'd been courting John for almost seven years. She looked happy enough. Leah and Tristan, with their son, Malachi, were next. Malachi was going to school and blessed with the good looks of his parents: blond hair and blue eyes. Alas, their brother Eugene, Stephanie, and their little boy, Stephan, could not come home for Christmas, as Eugene was away with the navy.

Nathan and Noah sat side by side at the table. Abby could not tell them apart.

"You two look more alike than ever—same dark hair, broad shoulders, and dimples in your cheeks," Abby said. "You're both so handsome. Nathan, put some tinsel around your head—we need to know who we're talking to!"

Everyone laughed. Malachi jumped off his chair and ran toward his uncles.

"Can I show you my fire truck, uncles? Santa Claus brought it. It's red and big, with a bell that rings loud! We can play with it now." He jumped up and down.

"You can play after dinner. Now, sit down, and behave yourself." Tristan caught Malachi by the hand.

Sasha spoke up. "He's fine. Leave the little bloke alone. Christmas is all for children. It's about them having fun and making good memories."

"It's smashing having most of us home." Abby raised her glass to Sasha. "Well done in preparing such a sumptuous Christmas Day feast. I feel lucky to have a home and be together here with everyone. Everything is so reminiscent of Christmases past—the turkey with all the trimmings, the Christmas trifle, that famous rum pudding! Look at the magnificent Christmas tree dressed in lights, garlands, and vintage glass ornaments. My favorite is the manger underneath the tree, with the star of Bethlehem over the stable, just like when we were kids, with Christmas carols playing on the gramophone and a warm, crackling fire to welcome all!"

Sebastian stood to make a toast. "To Sasha, our talented personal chef, with thanks, and to all a joyous Noel."

"Happy Christmas!" they all said.

As they were eating and enjoying the turkey and trimmings, Andre looked over at Abby with an expression of sympathy. "How are you managing after losing your job with the airline? Unexpected and a shock. Dad told me you already found some work. Good for you."

"I was very lucky," Abby said, even though the topic still made her nervous. "It's December, and both industries I work in need extra help. However, January may be lean. I suspect part-time work at best. Thanks for asking."

"We may all be in the same boat soon," Andre replied. "If the miners walk out like they are talking about. The unions and the management are not coming to agreement; we certainly do not want a repeat of the winter of '72."

"Do you really think they will go on strike again?"

"The talks don't look very promising. The miners are looking for more benefits and better working conditions—the usual thing. Several of the unions are restless. It's not just the miners. The papers have dubbed it the winter of discontent. Don't worry about it right now; there isn't anything we can do. Let's just enjoy being together on Christmas Day. Cheers!"

Later, after the turkey, pudding, and other goodies had been eaten and the dishes had been cleared, as the children played with their toys, Abby sat at the foot of the tree, looking at the manger, grateful for the fact that she had this family—her Father, her siblings, and their lovely children. They were a beacon. Their shining light brought Amelia's presence into all their hearts, especially that day. The children were Amelia's legacy, a reminder of her loving strength and courage, an example to build upon. Abby was bound and determined to forge a better life for herself and hopefully for her own children one day, with less struggle and more freedom and opportunities to develop and discover a finer life with love and laughter.

She had to find more work—several jobs if necessary. She could work as a cleaner and babysit if necessary, she thought. She needed enough money. Desperate to find her way to Virginia no matter what it took, she was convinced the answer was in the USA.

12

Colleen Grant held Benedict in her arms as he slept. It was February 14, Valentine's Day, and her precious darling was growing strong. How she loved the peacefulness, simplicity, and wonder of watching her beautiful boy as he slept. He was a replica of Byron in every way.

She sat in her rocking chair, looking out to sea. She watched the lightning as a storm moved toward the land. The sky was a color with no one name for it. It was dark, and the ocean reflected the same image: green, yellowish, and dark purple. The scene was mesmerizing. There was no sunlight, even though it was three o'clock in the afternoon. Great flashes of forked lightning ricocheted across the ocean, giving a strobe-light effect, as the slow rumble of the thunderclouds moved closer. Colleen loved to sit in the dark and witness every second of the perfect storm.

The gale-force winds churned the ocean waves until they were ten feet high. They crashed against the sandbanks below, spewing foam, seaweed, seashells, and all the natural inhabitants that had been disturbed from the ocean floor.

Amazing Grace

There the debris would lie until the dawn, when the children would go out to collect the treasures left behind. As far as Colleen was concerned, she lived in paradise in Virginia Beach. There was no other place in the world for her to be.

"Look at that boy sleeping. He is spectacular." Viv's voice interrupted the magic silence. Her Mother's quick movements and endless chatter sometimes put Colleen on edge. "Did you feed him? Did he finish it? He is growing like a weed. The bottle is empty—well done."

"Yes, Mom, I did feed him, and he drank it all. I've had a wonderful time sitting here and holding him in my arms, feeling his warm little body blend with mine; it's a wonder to me. We have been watching the storm," Colleen responded.

"Well, everyone is safe and sound. The girls are in the playroom. I have supper prepared: Virginia ham with scalloped potatoes. I thought I'd make a chocolate cake too. Since it's Valentine's Day, we can have pretend champagne—drink ginger ale using champagne glasses. What do you say? Yes? A good idea?" As always, her Mother answered her own questions.

"Thank you, Mom. I don't know how we would have managed these past few weeks without you here and your support."

"My darling, there is nowhere else I'd want to be other than here beside you and my beautiful grandchildren. I should be thanking you for such an opportunity. It's wonderful to feel needed, wanted, and useful," her Mom told her.

"Valentine's Day?" Colleen said with some surprise. "It seems I've lost so much since last February 14: my breasts, my hair, my health, and my strength. The only good thing to come out of this past year is Benedict." Her mood took a dive.

"Colleen, talk to me about what you are feeling. Maybe it will help."

"I'm scared, Mom—on so many levels. Will I ever feel well again? The chemo and nausea are the worst. It seems so pointless to eat or drink anything, when it's only going to come back up again. I hate for the girls to see me then; it frightens them too. I don't feel like a real woman anymore; my chest is concave and full of scars. I can't bear to look at it. I hate that I can't breastfeed Benedict like I did the girls."

A few tears oozed down her cheeks as she continued. "And it sounds vain, but losing my hair has been such a horrible experience, along with having no eyebrows or lashes. I see a stranger when I look in the mirror. Although it also means I don't have to shave my legs." Colleen tried to laugh. "I know I shouldn't feel sorry for myself—I'm lucky in so many ways. I have a loving husband, beautiful children, no worries about money, and a gorgeous house—but without my health. I have so much to live for, but sometimes I don't know how I can keep going."

Her Mother put down the baby in his crib and turned back to her. "Colleen, I know you are frightened, and this has been a harrowing year for you. Please, darling, I know it seems impossible to do, but try not to focus on the bad things. Look at this perfect baby boy. Think about Byron and your girls."

"That's just it. How can Byron find me desirable again when I feel this way about my own body and how it has betrayed me? Will he still love me? And I can't help but worry that I'll never live to see my children grow up. I feel I can't be a real Mother to them. But I am glad you are here. I couldn't cope without you, Mom." Tears fell into Colleen's lap.

"Rest, my darling. You are tired. Rest is what you need to get your strength back. Before you know it, this will all be just a bad memory. Concentrate on the future and your many blessings. You take care of yourself, and I'll take care of everything else until you're well again. I have faith in you and the Lord that day will come and sooner than you think." Her Mom kissed her gently on the top of her head.

"You're right." Colleen nodded and wiped her face.

"Let's have a little party later. We can watch one of Byron's recorded shows—*The Magical World of Byron*—even though he is in Las Vegas. The girls might enjoy that. What do you think?"

"I'm really missing Byron, Mom, especially today. That's a great idea; it'll help us feel he's not so far away. I'll be so relieved when he comes home to us this week."

"Understandable. Maybe when you get a little stronger, we can all go out and stay with him in the desert and enjoy the mountains. We can get tickets for a show to go see old Blue Eyes himself! When you have finished your treatments, my darling, one little step at a time. I'll put Benedict down in his crib. You rest now, and I'll call you for supper."

Colleen watched out the windows again as the monster storm made landfall; it was creating havoc. She was close enough to see the damage—witnessing fallen trees, broken branches, rising water, and power outages—yet somehow apart from it all.

The feeling within her own body was similar. She was close enough to feel and see the damage; her eyes could see it, and her hands could touch it. Yet she felt detached from it all. Much had transpired since the birth of Benedict. It was as though she were observing someone else.

She felt weak, helpless, and tired. She longed to be strong and fearless; she needed to be for her girls and her new baby boy. As Colleen sat alone in the silence, she allowed the tears to spill freely as the rain fell from the sky. The teardrops dripped from her chin. It was cleansing, she told herself.

I must be squeaky clean by now, she thought as she dried her eyes and closed them, searching for some gentle, peaceful sleep.

— 13 —

Byron looked around the sumptuous five-star Las Vegas restaurant. Chandeliers hung in splendor from the ceiling, dripping with thousands of hand-cut Waterford crystals. The marble walls and pillars were adorned with silk drapes. The round table was covered with a white Irish linen tablecloth and napkins folded to perfection. Waterford crystal goblets for wine, water, and cognac were placed strategically in order, and Royal Doulton plates and dishes adorned every table setting. The ice bucket beside his elbow held a large bottle of champagne. The six men around the table, including himself, were enjoying oysters and waiting for their next course: chateaubriand.

Byron leaned back in the velvet chair, allowing himself to relax. He gave in to the effects of the champagne, allowing it to untangle his weary, confused thoughts. This was the deal he'd been working toward most of his life. He liked being wined and dined.

One of the hotel managers leaned his elbows on the table. "Well now, Byron, let's see if we can seal this deal tonight.

We are happy to honor most of your requests: a six-month contract with the biggest hotel and casino in Las Vegas, with a six-month option to renew. Five nights a week, with a nice bonus on sellout evenings. Also included is a large home with a swimming pool and tennis courts a ten-minute drive from the hotel, as well as a permanent suite in the hotel. Most importantly, full medical family coverage. Can we shake on it, Byron, and let the lawyers iron out the details?"

Byron extended his hand to all the managers, nodding and smiling. "I'll say yes to that offer."

The hotel manager shook his hand vigorously. "Welcome aboard. Here's to closing night—may it never arrive."

As Byron sipped his champagne, he wondered how the gods, in their infinite wisdom, could send such good news in one aspect of his life and events of catastrophic magnitude in another. He felt almost detached from the celebration, as though he were watching it from afar. He was overcome with a feeling of guilt. He thought of moving Colleen and the kids, including the hassle and the danger to Colleen's health.

"When will the family join you?" asked the manager, as if reading his mind.

"I'm not too sure." Byron hedged a bit. This was a huge decision. "We have a new baby, and my wife is not yet recovered from the birth. I think we might bring everyone out at the end of the school year in May."

"That's a good idea. We'll arrange for the agent to show you around the home we have rented for you. It's near schools and shops and is ten minutes from the hotel."

Byron smiled. "It all sounds perfect. I am excited to share the news with my wife and family."

"Welcome. I think we are going to accomplish magical achievements together."

Come what may, it was imperative that he, Colleen, and the family be together, especially now. He had to find a way to tell Colleen. He decided he would get the help and support of his good friend and their doctor, Andrew. There was his answer, Byron thought as the waiter poured cognac into the Waterford crystal snifter. Between himself, Andrew, and Dr. Burke, they would convince Colleen that moving to Las Vegas was the best decision for everyone.

— 14 —

In Virginia, Andrew gently closed the door of his office; he was weary. It had been a long day, and he would be more than relieved to arrive home and spend some time with his little daughters. He had missed them more than he realized. He couldn't believe it was January already. He shook his head. *Where did the time go?*

His children were flying back home that day from Killarney, Ireland, where they had spent the Christmas holiday with their Mother, Shannon. She now lived there; she had moved away from Virginia after their divorce one year ago. They had managed to arrange an amicable custody situation. Every other Christmas, the girls went to Ireland. Every summer, Shannon came back to Virginia and rented a cottage. Otherwise, Andrew had full charge of the girls. They managed nicely with the help of his nanny, Heather MacDougall.

Heather should be home from her Christmas holiday today as well, he thought. She had been visiting family in Aberdeen, Scotland.

When he and Shannon had first started experiencing troubles in their marriage, it had been devastating to him. Shannon had just given birth to their second child, Babette. Shannon had hoped to have a son and had displayed obvious disappointment in her new daughter. There had been no bonding with the new baby, and Shannon had suffered from postpartum depression. Andrew had sought the best help for her, and they'd tried everything, including counseling separately, together, and with the family. He had taken her on romantic weekends and family holidays, but it had seemed hopeless; nothing appeared to work.

Eventually, the psychiatrist had suggested they hire a nanny, allowing Shannon to go back to work part-time. The help also had given them more time together as a couple in order to communicate and have more date nights. They both had agreed to explore every avenue and overturn every stone to salvage their marriage. Everyone had much to lose.

After a lot of research into several different agencies, they'd hired a nanny from Scotland. Her name was Heather MacDougall, and she was twenty-six years old and a qualified early childhood education teacher. They had been fortunate to find someone so experienced; she was overqualified for the position. Heather had said she was delighted to be living with a professional family. She was paid a good wage, with the use of the family car and an apartment above the garage. When off duty, she had ample time to discover America, something she had dreamed of all her life. It was a wonderful opportunity for her, and she'd said so at the interview. Shannon had liked her very much right away, as had the rest of the family. Eventually, Shannon had gone back to work part-time. At first, the situation had seemed to be hopeless; there had been little or no improvement.

However, gradually, day by day, Shannon had appeared to be improving. She had become reminiscent of the girl he'd met in Dublin's fair city in spring 1969.

Andrew had attended a medical conference at Trinity College. On the first night of the three-day conference, there had been a meet-and-greet. Andrew had been seated next to Shannon at the dinner table. He'd heard her before he saw her.

"And where do you hail from?" she'd asked, looking at his name tag. "Andrew?"

He had never heard his name spoken so sweetly. "Virginia," he'd answered.

"Virginia is for lovers, they say. Is that true then?"

Andrew had felt an attraction toward her immediately, with her voice, her curiosity, and her steadfast gaze. "It's very true. A beautiful place and very historical. We boast Williamsburg, Jamestown, Youngstown, the Blue Ridge Mountains, and Virginia Beach. That's where I live—on the beach."

"You know, that sounds like it's worth a trip. I might just drop in one day and look for meself. Tell me something—are all the doctors as handsome as you are?"

"Oh yes! Much more so." Andrew had smiled at her. "What brings you to this medical conference?" He'd looked at her name tag. "Shannon—how beautiful. The name suits you," he'd whispered.

"I'm a radiologist. I work in the hospital here in Dublin. Andrew, if you're planning to do a tour of Ireland, it seems to me you won't need to stop and kiss the Blarney Stone." She'd chuckled at him, flashing a dazzling smile with a glint in her perfect, smiling Irish eyes. "Where are you staying?"

"Trinity Hotel. I'll be taking a few days at the end of this conference before I go back to Virginia. I'd like to take in some of the sights. I'm told it's well worth it."

"Well now, Andrew, I'm thinking I could help you there."

Andrew had watched Shannon toss her glorious auburn curls over her shoulder. "I can't wait to hear how," he'd teased.

"I know this land inside out; I can be your guide. It will only cost you the price of a Guinness and maybe a meat pie. What do you say?"

"Just tell me when."

For the next several days, they'd been inseparable. By day, they'd walked the beach hand in hand and toured Ireland. They'd made love under the moon and stars by night. It had been one of the most glorious times of his life. He'd adored every part of her: her long fiery-auburn curls, emerald-green eyes, freckled face, slender build, long legs, and funny and beautiful expressions.

Most of all, he'd loved her Irish accent and her gift of storytelling. Andrew could have listened to her until the end of time. He had fallen in love with the mysticism of her Irish magic. He'd been besotted, and he'd wanted her to be his wife and the Mother of his children. Following his heart, with little or no time to truly discover who she was, he'd brought her back to Virginia.

He reflected now with a heavy heart; they should've spent more time together. Perhaps he should have encouraged Shannon to live and work in Virginia for a time to let them get to know each other better. Driven by his own passion and Shannon's ticking maternal clock, they had rushed into marriage. He now realized it had been a mistake for both of them. However, he would not have changed it for the world, as the result had been his two daughters, Babette and Katerina, the best of himself and Shannon. Sadly, a lot of suffering and sorrow had ensued because of their incompatibility; Shannon's postpartum depression and homesickness; and, finally, her affair.

Andrew arrived home. Opening his front door, he could hear that Heather had arrived back from Aberdeen. He walked into the kitchen. Heather was chopping vegetables. It looked like she was preparing to make soup.

"Well, hello to you, and welcome back. How was your trip?" asked Andrew.

"Ochs, it was grand. I had a fabulous time back home; it was nice to spend time with my family, especially Christmas and Hogmanay. But it's good to be back in Virginia. I missed everyone," Heather answered.

Andrew looked at Heather. She was attractive, with long flaxen-blonde hair flowing to her shapely waist. She was the image of a true lady Godiva, with a tall, slender frame and large blue eyes. After his time alone, she appeared noticeably more attractive to him now. *I guess Scotland was good for her.*

"What's Homagenee?" he asked.

Heather laughed out loud at the way Andrew pronounced *Hogmanay*. "It's our New Year's Eve celebration—a very big deal! It's a time to party, send up fireworks, and parade through the street with torch lights. And the first foot— the first person to enter the house after midnight, ideally a tall, dark male—brings gifts, such as food, coal, cake, and whiskey. The first foot is supposed to predict the household's fortunes for the coming year. I'm never invited to be a first foot." Heather laughed.

"Byron would be popular with his dark, handsome, magical looks," said Andrew.

"Exactly right!"

They laughed together, sharing a nice moment.

"What time are you picking up the girls?" Heather asked.

"Six thirty. In fact, I should be on my way," answered Andrew.

"The girls will be so happy and excited to see you, although, I suspect, very tired, when they land. I'm making some soup just in case they would like something to eat. Or we can get them into bed right away."

"That's a good idea. I'll change and get on my way. See you later."

"Bye-bye just now!"

Two hours later, Andrew was heading home in his car with his girls. Katerina, his firstborn, sat up in the front seat beside him. She was a near duplicate of her Mother, with the same auburn curls and dancing Irish eyes, and was a wonderful storyteller; it was uncanny how similar they looked. Katie—his pet name for Katerina—was a typical firstborn child: a natural leader and responsible, with a passionate desire to achieve. She chatted on, telling him all about their journey back to Virginia from Ireland.

"After Mommy dropped us off at the airport with the lady who was going to look after us, she put us on the plane, and we were in our seats. I helped Babs with her seat belt, and I looked after her. The stewardess kept coming back to see if we were all right or if we wanted something. I was very polite—indeed, on my best manners," she told her Father.

"That's very good, Katie. I'm proud of you, as always." Andrew smiled.

It seemed to Andrew that whenever his girls returned from Ireland, they became a little more Irish and brought a piece of the old country back with them. Katie was seven years old going on fifteen, mature for her tender age.

Babette, his little darling, sat in the back quietly. She was five years old and more like himself. She had short, thick, wavy blonde hair the color of a wheat field in the summer sunshine. Sun-kissed golden highlights framed her beautiful golden-amber eyes and long black eyelashes. He often thought she had the face of an angel, and she was kind and tender. Babs was his pet name for her. He thought if there was such a thing as an old soul, he believed his Babs was one.

"Daddy, I was very well behaved, a good girl. I promised Mommy I'd be a good girl." Babs yawned a giant, wide-mouthed yawn. "And I brought you a present from Ireland. It's in my bag. We had fun with Mommy and Grandma and Grandpa. I missed you, Daddy; please, please come with us next time we go to Ireland."

"One day we'll do that; we'll have so much fun," said Andrew as he smiled at her.

"Oh yes, Daddy! I can't wait. I can show you all the things we see at Mama's house." Babs rubbed her eyes with her little fists and gave another giant yawn.

"Heather's back, and she's making you some soup, although I don't think Babs will be eating any," Andrew told the girls. Babs had closed her eyes and was fast asleep.

Some time later, Andrew settled down in his study after the girls were in bed. Heather had retired to her apartment; she'd said she was tired after her long journey from Aberdeen.

He was happy to have some quiet time; it had been quite a day. After pouring himself a glass of red wine, he picked up the *Virginia Gazette* and sat in his chair to read the news of the day.

Suddenly, the telephone rang and gave him a start. He picked it up.

"Hello. Dr. Mason speaking."

"Andrew, it's Byron."

"Byron, is everything okay?" Andrew asked.

"Yes, thanks. Everything is good. Listen, I wondered if you have some time to chat this evening. I need your advice and possibly a favor," said Byron.

"Of course. Come on over, my friend, and join me for a glass of wine in the study. I picked up the girls today. They're in bed sleeping."

"Great. Be there in fifteen minutes."

Andrew heard a click on the other end of the phone and then silence.

Byron arrived at Andrew's front door fifteen minutes later. Andrew brought him inside and sat him down in the opposite chair with a glass of red wine, more than a bit curious.

"How can I help you, Byron?"

"I've been offered the most amazing job in Las Vegas: a six-month contract with another six-month option at the Sands Hotel and Casino. The contract includes a huge house and a permanent suite at the hotel. Full medical insurance. I tell you, Andrew, it's the job I've been waiting for all my life."

Andrew jumped up from his chair, delighted and excited for his friend. "Congratulations! This is amazing news!" he said, shaking Byron's hand. "Does Colleen know?"

"No, not yet. That's the favor I need to ask you." Byron ran his fingers through his hair, looking concerned. "This is where I need you to help me. I'd like you to talk to her and convince her it would be a safe and sensible decision to move to Las Vegas. You know how strongly she's connected to her home and the beach, especially since having her surgery. I'd also like you to investigate a cancer hospital. Maybe Dr. Burke could assist. We all could present her with the idea together."

"Byron, I am more than happy to help you in any way I can," Andrew replied, his brain racing ahead. Of course he could help. "I know that Dr. Burke will have some excellent suggestions for an oncologist and a hospital. We can prepare and help Colleen with every medical challenge. However, as a longtime family friend, I must advise you on everyone's behalf, especially Colleen. Talk to her as soon as possible. Present her with the suggestion, and give her the options."

Byron shook his head. "For me, there is no alternative; I've signed a contract. I must have my family with me. We cannot be separated at this time. My newborn son is changing every day, and he doesn't know me—my voice, my scent, or my presence. The situation with my darling wife—no one will say this out loud, and I don't even want to think it out loud, but the reality is, none of us know how much time we have left together as a family. It's all a bit fragile. We need to be together!"

Andrew looked more closely at his longtime friend. The past few months, he had seen a change in Byron. Not only had he physically aged, but he realized the stress of his wife's illness was slowly but surely changing Byron, taking him away piece by piece. It was as though parts of Byron were disappearing. A light was going out within him that once had radiated a powerful presence captivating everyone who met him. This situation was a terrible thing to witness. It was hard to see Byron so distraught.

"I understand you feel isolated and alone. Believe me, you're not; you're blessed with a wonderfully supportive, loving family. I must caution you though. It's a mammoth decision for any family under the best of circumstances. With your family situation, I'd say it's asking a lot."

"I can't turn this down; I've signed the contract for six months with a six-month option," Byron told him.

"Why don't you try it yourself for six months and have them visit?" Andrew said.

"No, Andrew, I cannot accept that as an option. I need my family with me. We need to be together."

"Well then, I strongly suggest you have everything prepared and in place before presenting it to her. Be honest with Colleen. Tell her precisely how you feel, and don't underestimate her; she's more aware than anyone of how you feel. Give her the opportunity to make her own decision; it's the kindest option. She might surprise you."

Byron finished his wine, set the glass down, and stood up. "Thank you, Andrew. You're a good friend, and you've given me good options to think about. I think you are correct; I'll present this to Colleen as soon as possible. Would you talk to Dr. Burke? I must move on this within the month. I feel better for sharing this with you." He shook Andrew's hand.

"I'll investigate immediately, of course. I'll be in touch with you as soon as I talk with Dr. Burke."

Andrew showed Byron to the door and watched him walk away. He was slower, and by his posture, Andrew could see his friend was a broken man.

He closed his front door and slowly went back to his office, where he poured himself another glass of wine and sat down in his chair. Andrew had felt sorry for himself that past month without his girls. Living alone was empty and lonely. The divorce had made him feel useless and depressed, as if he had somehow failed and let his family down. Yet when all was said and done, Andrew's life was a gift compared to Byron's. Time was helping his family to recover. Slowly, they all were adapting to their new life and different rules.

But Byron was in turmoil. Andrew resolved to do all he could to help the Grant family. They had so much going for them: the bond of true love they all shared, three beautiful children, and Byron's exceptional new job, which was a fantastic opportunity. They had so much to live for, fight for, and love for, and so much to lose.

15

Abby could feel January's bitter northeast wind and howling gales as she battled against them while making her way home from work for the last time. It was late afternoon and as dark as midnight on the winter solstice.

She'd forgotten how brutal northeastern coastal winters could be, unlike the negative-twenty-degree temperatures of the Canadian winters, where she'd been that time last year. During a flight to Toronto with a two-day layover, she and the crew had visited Niagara Falls. Everyone had wrapped up in warm down-filled jackets, mitts, and hats; it had felt like a warm bed inside. She'd enjoyed the beautiful, crisp, fresh frozen day. The crystal rainbows of magical spray had showered them as they walked past the partially frozen Niagara Falls, one of the natural wonders of the world. Abby had seen why as the mist floated and landed softly upon the trees and branches, freezing in layer upon layer. The effect was like Waterford crystal on the trees, with row upon row flashing and glistening in the sunlight. The memory of the image was pressed between the pages of her mind that day.

But this! Abby pulled her hat down hard toward her freezing ears and pulled her collar up on her coat about her neck. She felt as though the sleet and wind together would penetrate every single layer of her clothing and reach the marrow of her bones. She shivered, glad she was close to home. However, the truth was, it was almost as cold inside the house as it was outside.

The miners were going into the third week of a strike, and the effects were being felt nationwide with shortages of everything: fuel, petrol, and food. People stood in line for hours for daily necessities, such as food, milk, bread, and eggs, when they were available. The schools, shops, and businesses were on a three-day week. There was no money, no heat, no food, and no end in sight.

It was the worst possible time of year for the miners to strike, although it was the best time for the effort to have any real effect. It was becoming more and more difficult to sympathize with the miners, as Abby had at first. She did not anymore. That day, she'd lost her job at the salon, and last week, she had been laid off from the pub. She was unemployed, and she was not alone.

Abby arrived home and let herself in. She could smell homemade soup, and the aroma warmed her. Poor Sasha had been reduced to working two days a week, as Cammie had been.

"Hello! I'm home!" she called out as she took off her wraps. "It smells so good! It was a brutal walk home, so cold and damp. Thanks for making soup."

"Hello there. I managed to grab some scrag ends from the kitchen today. I think it will make half-decent soup for our tea," said Sasha.

"I see we're still in the dark."

Abby looked at the flickering candles. Normally, she loved the soft light and serene effect they gave. She watched the dancing shapes and shadows as they moved across the walls of the freezing kitchen.

Sasha looked at her with sad eyes. "Alas, we'll have no lights until ten tonight and then for three hours only. They're off at one tomorrow morning. We don't have very much coal left. Possibly enough for the next two days—that is, if we put the fire on later in the day. I think we should move our mattresses from the bedrooms and sleep in the kitchen. That way, we'll be able to stay warm for part of the time. We can also heat the water on the gas stove, fill hot water bottles, and drink as much hot soup and tea as we can. Thank goodness we have a gas stove."

Abby shook her head, and droplets of rain fell from her hair and hissed on the stove. "I can't believe this situation; it's getting so bad, Sasha. I was told today no more work in the salon. My boss kept me on as long as she possibly could."

"That's a bloody rotten shame. I heard on the news today they are no closer to a settlement."

"What are we going to do?" asked Abby.

"Who knows?" Sasha heaved a great sigh. "As bad as we feel, we don't realize that we are the lucky ones. At least we don't have bairns to feed and keep warm."

"You're absolutely right, but I still feel helpless and worried. Do you think the government will force them back to work?"

"I don't know. I don't understand the unions, government, or striking," Sasha replied. "None of it makes sense to me. Management at the hotel have put me down to one day per week as of tomorrow. They are discussing closing the hotel down completely until the strike is over."

"Oh, Sasha, what a mess!" Abby felt she was about to burst into tears.

The kitchen door suddenly swung open, and Cammie came rushing in, pulling off her coat and hat. "Thank God I'm home. It's freezing! There were no bloody buses running. They are only running them every two hours to conserve the fuel. I had to walk home, and to top it all, as of today, no more work! The management has regretfully closed the office until further notice!"

As Abby looked at her brother and sister, she could not hold back her tears any longer. "Me too, and poor Sasha is down to one day a week, if they don't close the hotel."

"Oh, come on, Abby. It's nothing to bubble about," Cammie said. "Nobody here is ill or anything! We'll manage together. If worse comes to worst, there is plenty of old furniture upstairs riddled with woodworm. We can chop it up and throw it on the fire. That should keep us cozy and warm."

Abby chuckled faintly, and Sasha put his arm around her. "Have faith, Abby, me pet. Let's put a nice fire on and use some of our coal. We'll warm up the kitchen and bring the mattresses downstairs. We can boil some water and fill the water bottles. When the light and power does come on, we can switch on the immersion heater and have a nice hot bath before we all go to sleep."

"I am sorry; you're both right. Thanks for the pep talk; it's been a long day. Let's get cracking and make the best of things!" Abby smiled and wiped her eyes.

Later that evening, Abby stretched out her aching limbs

in the tepid water of the bathtub. There was only enough hot water for two half-filled bathtubs. She and Cammie shared one, and Sasha had his own. Abby offered to take the last, as she could feel menstrual cramps and knew she was getting her monthly. That was probably why she had cried like a baby that night; she was feeling so miserable.

Abby could hardly believe the difference in her life and the changes from last November, when Global had declared bankruptcy. She felt as though she were in a time machine, trying desperately to find her way back to the life she once had known and loved. The situation was hopeless. She felt as if she were screaming for help, and no one could hear her. She longed for the days of flying and freedom—joyous and carefree days of living life to the maximum.

Currently, she had no control over her life. The miners' union was dictating the simplest necessities of life: light, heat, and work. Abby shivered, feeling the water turn cold. After stepping out of the bathtub, she dried herself as quickly as possible and put on her warm flannel pajamas and candlewick dressing gown.

When Abby arrived downstairs in the kitchen, Cammie and Sasha were both in their beds, sipping tea and holding on to their hot water bottles. The fire was burning, and the lights were already out, as it was after one o'clock.

"You feel better now?" Cammie asked. "We put a hot water bottle in your bed, and there's tea in the pot. You should get into bed while it's warm. This is the best I've felt all day."

"Me too. I feel almost normal," Sasha said.

The transistor radio was playing soft late-night music; the atmosphere was cozy, warm, and inviting.

"Thank you, yes," Abby said softly. "It does feel lovely. Let's try to get some sleep while we're still warm. I'll leave the radio on. We can listen to the music; it may help us drift off. Good night, all!"

The three of them lay quietly, listening to the gentle music playing on the transistor radio. Abby snuggled down into her warm bed, clutching her hot water bottle. She felt safe as she watched the flames from the fire dance in the grate. The coal made a soft noise, almost comforting, as it shifted between orange and red. The embers from the burning coals gave off a bright glow, making the kitchen feel like a safe, inviting haven.

Abby could hear the rhythm of Sasha and Cammie breathing; it seemed they had fallen asleep almost immediately. Abby lay quietly, listening to the melodic, soft sounds of the radio. As she was slipping away into a warm and peaceful sleep, she could hear the radio in the distance— familiar, searching, reaching, aching lyrics.

Simon and Garfunkel, their voices soaring, sang about dreams on their way.

Yes, time for my dreams to shine.

Abby fell into a dream-filled sleep. She could hear herself calling out in the distance, "I am with you all the way, Gabriel!"

— 16 —

Not long after Valentine's Day, Byron stood tall, wearing his white tuxedo and golden cape. He was center stage, looking out at the crowd on their feet at the Sands Casino, the most famous nightclub in Las Vegas, where Frank Sinatra, Dean Martin, and Sammy Davis Jr. all had performed. The orchestra was playing "That Old Black Magic."

Byron stood among the lights and music, feeling the moment. He could smell not only the pungent aromas of cigar smoke, cigarettes, and whiskey but also sweet perfume and perspiration blending together, stinging his eyes and burning his throat and nostrils. He was beginning to feel the essence of the room deep in his lungs. The energy of the crowd and their appreciation were intoxicating to him. Bowing one more time after four curtain calls, Byron was exhilarated with the thunderous applause of the enthusiastic crowd. With the bright lights and the heat, he was beginning to feel light-headed. His new show was a huge success. It was a spectacular event, and everyone who came to see the show could not believe his or her eyes. Although in Byron's mind, the true magic was within the room, not on the stage.

The critics raved that Byron was an outstanding illusionist and magician. He had a gift and a talent beyond comprehension. He was way ahead of his time and was credited with single-handedly reviving the public's interest in magic after a long slump in the 1950s and '60s. He had updated the performance, combining it with music, comedy, beautiful women, and flashy costumes, making it attractive to a new generation.

Besides the usual magic tricks Byron performed, the highlight of the show were several luxury automobiles: Lincolns, Mercedes-Benzes, and Bentleys. He created the illusion of the automobiles disappearing and reappearing, including the lovely showgirls insides the cars.

The illusion wasn't entirely his invention. He had purchased it several years ago from a Canadian magician and illusionist he had met at a magic convention in Toronto. The magician had become ill and been unable to continue in the profession. He'd offered the illusion, including his notes and all the work he had done to that point, at a good price. Byron had continued to work on the illusion for several years until he'd perfected it and made it his own. It was unique, breathtaking to audiences and critics alike. He'd just happened to be in the right place at the right time.

The curtains closed, and Byron indicated to the stage manager that was it. It was his second show of the day, and he was exhausted. After closing the door of his dressing room, Byron removed his makeup and costume and changed into his street clothes as quickly as possible.

He was excited, as that was the first week of Colleen and

the children living with him. Colleen had finally agreed with him regarding moving to Vegas and being together. Andrew and Dr. Burke had convinced her to try moving to Las Vegas at least for three months. If she didn't like it, he would take her back to Virginia and commute and would not ask her to go anymore. Viv, her Mother, had come along to help, and Byron had hired a housekeeper.

Grace and Aria went to a private school during the day. They were collected and returned home on a private school bus, leaving only Benedict at home with Colleen. As Byron thought of his new son, he smiled to himself. A placid child, Benedict never cried.

Coming out of his dressing room, Byron bumped into some of the cast members and stage crew. Ed, the stage manager, stopped him.

"Congratulations, Byron! Another wonderful show and a spectacular, very successful week."

"Thank you, Ed. I don't do it alone." Byron mimicked a sweeping bow to the cast and crew who were present.

"We're all going out to celebrate for an after-show drink. Please come with us," said Gloria, one of the many beautiful showgirls.

Byron smiled at her and the rest of the crew. She was stunningly beautiful. "That's very kind of you and a very nice invitation; however, I have a much more important invite to attend to."

"You do? What could be more important than celebrating with us?"

"I have a late-night date with my five-month-old son, Benedict. I give him his midnight feed, and I can't wait to see him."

Gloria smiled at Byron, showing her perfect white teeth. Moving a little closer to him, she whispered in his ear, "Byron, sir, you are truly unique. Not only are you gorgeous, but you're gracious, polite, and apparently a family man. I didn't believe they made them like you anymore. I believe you're like your show: just an illusion. Mrs. Grant is a very lucky lady!"

Byron dropped his gaze. Smiling softly, he raised his hand and waved. "Have great night. I'll see you all tomorrow."

When he arrived home, it was close to midnight. After entering the house quietly, he tiptoed to the master bedroom, where Colleen and Benedict were sleeping. He moved closer to the bed, where Colleen lay. She appeared serene as she lay softly on her pillow. She was pale; the fragile beauty of her skin was the color of alabaster. She wore a blue silk turban to keep her head warm and hide the sight of her bald head. Through the whole trauma, he knew hair loss was one of the most difficult side effects Colleen was dealing with. As superficial as it seemed, with the loss of her hair, it was as though she had lost herself. Byron's heart ached within his chest. Bending over, he tenderly kissed Colleen on the lips.

"I love you," he whispered. He could hear the baby stirring. Gently, not wanting to wake Colleen, he lifted Ben from the bassinet surrounded by blue and white lace and satin and quilted blankets. The little guy was hard to find within the maze of material, as though he were sleeping under a cloud. Byron's giant hands holding him gave Ben the appearance of a smaller child than his actual twelve pounds and twenty-four inches. Ben did have large hands and feet for a little fellow.

Byron went about his routine of changing Ben's diaper and heating his bottle. He was convinced Ben recognized

Amazing Grace

him now—his voice, the touch of his hands, and his own personal scent. Benedict whimpered, as his diaper was clearly causing him discomfort, and he was hungry.

Benedict was five months old, and Byron had spent little quality time with him because of the circumstances surrounding his birth and their recent move. He was grateful to have these special individual moments with his son.

After changing Ben and preparing his bottle, Byron quietly carried the baby to his favorite room in the house: an octagonal-shaped glass room facing the pool and tennis courts, with cathedral ceilings. The room was well insulated from both the intense heat and the extreme cold of the desert. The design of the room let him look out on the magnificent mountains that surrounded the valley. The night sky was so clear Byron could clearly see the North Star, the planet Venus, and the Big Dipper. A full silver moon hung between two mountain peaks, looking like a giant silver beach ball. The powerful rays showered silver light across the tops of the mountains, illuminating the snow. The snow twinkled and shone, creating a magical illusion far beyond any magic he could have produced. Sitting in the rocking chair with the baby, holding his bottle, Byron was full of a sense of wonder. Holding his beautiful boy, Benedict, he reflected on the sublime perfection of the innocent baby.

Unlike other memories that faded as the years passed, holding his babies stood the test of time. His son was equally as magnificent as his girls, yet there was a different feeling for each one of his children. Somehow, this time, he felt more emotional—maybe because he was older. His past experiences told him that the ordinary was indeed extraordinary. Embracing his son under the stars personified that.

Perhaps the greatest of gifts was the image of Colleen when she held Benedict, instinctively showing a power to love far beyond her own understanding. Byron rejoiced in every moment he was able to observe Benedict grow. He wanted to be a Father—to nurture, protect, teach, and love his son and, indeed, all his children.

Byron and Benedict were both content; the baby lay within the folds of his Father's loving arms, close to his heart. Byron gazed at his boy in awe and then cast his glance toward the top of the majestic mountains. He gazed up toward the open sky; it was a night so clear that Byron believed he could see beyond the distant stars into eternity. His son's breathing was steady, his weary eyes were heavy with sleep, and his dark eyelashes lay softly upon his peach-like skin. His lips were parted slightly, as if to show Byron a tiny smile of gratitude.

Byron released a heavy sigh, breathing out in a whisper, "Almighty God beyond the stars, allow us all to stay awhile. Please hold us all in the palm of your hands." Closing his tear-filled eyes, he gave in to the exhaustion of the day.

— 17 —

Andrew would be home that night for dinner, as it was his birthday. Part of Heather's duty as nanny and housekeeper was to prepare all meals and take care of the two girls' needs. In return, Heather enjoyed her own apartment above the garage, the use of a car, privacy, and an ability to come and go when she wasn't on duty looking after the girls.

She meticulously placed parsley between the Scotch eggs on the platter she had prepared for that night's dinner. The girls loved them: hard-boiled eggs encased in sausage meat, rolled in bread crumbs, and then deep fried until the outside was brown and crispy. More to the point, Andrew had commented on how much he enjoyed them the last time she'd made them for supper.

Heather and the girls had had an exciting day in preparing for a celebration. They had also baked a chocolate birthday cake and decorated it with chocolate candies—although more of those had gone into the girls' mouths than on the cake.

The girls had made a birthday card last week, one

afternoon when it was raining. She had suggested it might be a nice thing to do with their time. Heather had bought some bristol board, and using finger paints, she'd helped the girls make a unique card. It had worked out beautifully.

"Heather, please, can we eat in the dining room?" Katie entered the kitchen, breathless with excitement.

"Of course we can. We are having a wee celebration! Go quickly and fetch Babs. We can work together and set it all up." Heather smiled at her and rustled Katie's gorgeous red curls. Katie disappeared, skipping all the way.

Heather had purchased party hats and favors, along with balloons, paper tablecloths, and all the necessary requirements for a birthday party. She thought it appropriate for her to help the girls participate in a meaningful way for Andrew's birthday. He deserved something special. It seemed to her that he was isolated and rather lonely now that his divorce was final and his ex-wife was living in Ireland. He worked all the hours God sent as a family doctor, delivering babies, pronouncing deaths, and doing everything in between, usually into the wee hours of the morning. His isolation had appeared more evident to her since Byron, Colleen, and the children had moved to Las Vegas. She was keenly aware the girls missed Grace and Aria, though not so much Benedict, as he was just a baby.

Andrew was a good-looking man, tall and slender, with a head full of thick, wavy hair whiter than blond. With his tan skin, blue eyes, and black eyelashes and eyebrows, he was striking. One or two of her other nanny associates had met him and suggested he was gorgeous. He was in his prime— far too young to curl up and hide away from living and all that had to offer him. She was going to help kick-start some activity and fun back into his life that night!

Since that day was going to be special, she had invited Andrew's parents, Mr. and Mrs. Mason. They were delighted to be coming, as they rarely spent time with their son. When they did visit the girls, Andrew was usually working.

As the girls returned, Babette said, "Oh, Heather, Daddy will be so surprised; he will clap his hands and jump up and down!"

"He just might. Ha-ha! I'd like to see that; it would make me laugh!" said Heather.

They all worked together in preparing the dining room. Heather thought the house was perfect for entertaining—a ranch-style home, they called it there in Virginia, with enormous rooms. It had a well-appointed kitchen, all modern equipment, and a dinette, with an open-concept living room and dining room. There was a two-way fireplace between the living room and family room, which fascinated her. One fire for two rooms—how clever. The rooms were painted in gentle tones, with a shaggy pale green carpet throughout. It had such a large backyard that in Aberdeen, they would have called it a park. She thought it luxurious.

When all the work was done, a "Happy Birthday" banner stretched across between the living room and dining room, and balloons of various sizes and colors were strategically hung from various framed prints that adorned the walls. Party hats with pointy ends and pink tassels flowing freely were placed at all the place settings.

As a finale, Heather placed candles on the chocolate birthday cake.

"When my Daddy sees this, he will love you for it," Katerina told Heather.

Heather smiled at the girls. "Come on. Let's go put on our party frocks!"

Andrew arrived home to a wonderful birthday surprise. His family all gathered and enjoyed the Scotch eggs for dinner.

"That was delicious, Heather. Thank you."

Soon after dinner, Heather brought out the birthday cake, and they sang "Happy Birthday."

His parents, Katie, and Babs stood beside Andrew, and on the count of three, they all inhaled, exhaled, and extinguished all the candles on the chocolate cake.

"Make a wish! Cross your fingers, and make a wish, and keep it a secret!" cried Babs.

"You make a wish for me." Andrew smiled at Babs. She was so endearing.

"You know I must keep it a secret, Daddy. If I make a wish for you, I can't tell you."

"You think of something special, and keep it under your hat!" he said.

Babs stood still, crossed her fingers, closed her eyes tightly, and stood still for several seconds. "I made it, Daddy."

The girls stood up excitedly together.

"We have a surprise for you." Katie smiled at her Dad.

Heather gave Andrew a knife to cut the cake. "It's your birthday; therefore, you do the honors." She smiled at him.

Amazing Grace

"You've gone to a lot of effort, my dear," Andrew's Mother told Heather.

"I love those eggy things you gave us. You must give Maude the recipe," said his Dad.

"I'd love to," Heather replied.

Andrew watched everyone around the table. It seemed his Mother was giving Heather the evil eye, but he guessed she was just looking out for him, as Mothers did.

The girls returned, carrying what looked like a piece of bristol board.

"This is for you, Daddy," Babs said. "Katie and I made it for you. Heather helped us a lot, but we made it ourselves."

"Open it, Dad," Katie said, almost in a pleading tone.

Babs jumped up and down with excitement.

"My, you are excited, and that's before the chocolate cake," said Andrew's Mother.

"She's fine, Mom. She's having fun!" Andrew lifted both girls onto his knees so they could read the card together.

Andrew looked at the card and felt somewhat overwhelmed. Written across the top in a half circle was "Happy birthday, Daddy!" Underneath that was "We love you." Directly underneath was a perfect circle made up of various-sized handprints—clearly, some were Katie's, and the others were Babs's—in various bright shades of blue, pink, red, purple, and green. Each handprint had words on it.

"This is amazing, my beautiful girls. You went to all the trouble of making this for me?"

"Yes, we did. Read it, Dad. Read it!" Katie said.

Pulling Katie closer to himself, he tightened his arm around her. "I can't wait to read it, Katie."

"Daddy, can we read it out loud together?" asked Katie.

"I think that's a wonderful idea."

He looked up at his parents and Heather sitting around the table while drinking tea and eating chocolate cake.

"Come on. We are all waiting with bated breath," his Mother said.

Together they started to read—out of synchronization at first. However, Andrew slowed down to keep up with his girls, and they were soon reciting the words in perfect harmony.

"He helps me make my bed," said Babs.

"Helps you make your bed? You mean I make your bed," Andrew said.

"I know!" Babs giggled. "Tucks me into bed and lies down beside me until I go to sleep."

"He usually falls asleep alongside you! I often find him in there when there is a call for him." Heather tossed her long blonde hair over her shoulder.

"Please, Daddy. Would everyone be quiet so we can hear Daddy and let him read our birthday card?" Katie said.

Everyone nodded apologetically.

"I'm sorry, Katie; we're just having so much fun," her Grandpa said.

"This is such a wonderful gift, sweetheart. We are all enjoying it. We don't mean to make fun," Andrew said. He read, "He is the best Dad in the world."

"I wrote that, Daddy, because I think you are." Babette smiled up at him.

"He is a kind doctor. He kisses my toes when we play 'This Little Piggy Goes to Market.' He calls my dog Kitty."

Everyone spontaneously laughed together.

'He sings 'Row, Row, Row Your Boat' when he is in the shower—very loud!"

"Ochs, I can attest to that; I can hear him clean across the yard in my rooms above the garage. It's insane!" cried Heather.

"Oh, it's not that bad, surely," Andrew protested.

"Yes, it is! Sometimes I think we need earplugs." Katie put her hands over her ears, and everyone laughed and copied her.

They started to sing together at the top of their voices: "Row, row, row your boat gently down the stream!" Everyone laughed uncontrollably.

"Stop now, everyone. We have to get control of ourselves. I am just having so much fun. This is a brilliant card, girls—I love it!" He kept reading. "He kisses my cat on the nose until she sneezes! He holds my hand tightly when we go outside. He is a silly Daddy. He is our Dad, and we love him. Love, Katerina and Babette."

"We both wrote that, Dad, and you see? It's in both hands, the big one and the little one," Katie said.

"I can see that. This is the most excellent birthday card I've ever had. I'll keep it forever and ever! I believe this is the best birthday I've ever celebrated. I want to thank everybody, with special thanks to you, Heather, for all your efforts. I think we can all say we've had a terrific evening."

"Och! It was no trouble. I loved it, and we all had a great time, especially the girls!" Heather smiled, and everyone nodded in agreement.

"I have a surprise for the girls, and it would appear this is a perfect time to share it with them," said Andrew. "I was speaking with Byron and Colleen on the phone yesterday.

They all miss us very much, and Grace and Aria especially miss you, girls! We've been invited to visit with them for spring break in March. What do you think?"

The girls jumped off their chairs, leaping into in the air with joy.

"We can't wait! We miss them so much!" Babs said.

"How long can we go for?" Katie asked. "Are we staying in their house?"

"I'll answer all your questions later, girls. I just wanted to know what you thought. I can see by your response that I think I can book the flights."

"That sounds like a wonderful idea, Son. It will give you all the change of scene you need, and I'm sure it will be good for Colleen, Byron, and their family," Andrew's Mom said.

"I'm very happy for you, girls. It's such a great idea, Andrew. I know the girls have been missing their friends," said Heather.

"I'm glad you agree, Heather. I'd like to invite you along if you're interested. I could use the help, and I know Colleen will need the extra pair of hands. You are not obliged to, if you wish to take the week off. Please know, however, I'd appreciate you joining us."

"Ochs! Just watch how fast I can pack me case. I'd love to come with you. Thank you. We'll have a lot of fun with everyone together."

"I can't wait! How many sleeps?" Babs asked.

"We can count them together later," Katie told Babette.

"It's time we were clearing up. It's a school day tomorrow. You girls need to get ready for bed. Say good night to Grandma and Grandpa. I'll come tuck you in later," said Andrew.

They all said their farewells, hugged, and kissed, and the girls ran off. Andrew's Mother thanked Heather for a lovely dinner, and his Dad reminded her not to forget the eggy-thing recipe. Andrew walked his parents out to the car.

"What a smashing night, Andrew! Our Granddaughter are great kids. And Heather—all I can say is wow!" said Andrew's Father, Harold.

Andrew's Mom shot a piercing glance toward his Father. "Hold your tongue!"

"Well, I'm just saying, Maude—"

"Come on, parents. Let's get you in the car." Andrew got them down the driveway.

"Andrew, keep your guard up, Son. That one is out to catch you—mark my words," his Mother said.

"Mother, don't be paranoid. Give me a birthday kiss, and let's get you into the car."

"Don't say I didn't warn you." His Mother kissed him on the cheek.

"Good night, Mom and Dad. Thanks so much for coming."

His parents drove away, and he waved them off. He stood in the driveway, hesitating for a while; he didn't feel like going into the house. He stayed outside for a while, enjoying the cool breeze of the evening, the stillness of the moment, and the sky scattered with twinkling stars. It had been quite a night.

He headed back into the house and toward the girls' room. Heather was coming out of the house to go to her room, and she brushed past him.

"I'm all done for today; I'm heading back to my rooms."

"It was a wonderful party—so well prepared and organized. I appreciate all you do for us," Andrew told her.

"Ochs, it's my pleasure. You're welcome as the sun."

"We can talk more about the trip this weekend. You understand it's a working holiday, and I'll of course pay for your ticket and all other expenses."

"It's a fantastic opportunity. I can hardly believe it. I'm very excited. Thank you, Andrew. Bye just now then." She turned at the door and waved.

Andrew watched her walk away. Her long golden hair glistened like liquid gold beneath the outside lamp.

What had he just done? Shaking his head, he told himself, *It's a good idea!* Colleen would need the help, and the girls would too. Who was he kidding? More and more each day, he was feeling a growing need—and not just for her help. With an uneasy acknowledgment, he realized his growing need was for Heather.

18

The miners' strike was finally over. Abby was both relieved and angry for all the country had suffered. They'd been on strike for almost nine weeks before the unions gave in.

The newspapers were saying the damage was irreversible—to the miners and the mines. The country had been thrown into financial turmoil. The trickle-down effect had touched every individual in one way or another, mostly financially.

Neither Abby nor Sasha nor Cammie had any money. They had used it all up weeks ago during the worst of the strike. Sebastian had moved in with them and brought some food and his small amount of coal. It was a small gesture; however, it made an exceptional difference to all of them. Abby felt they weren't facing the struggle alone; they had come together. There was warmth and comfort in the camaraderie.

Fortunately, two weeks after the miners went back to work, so did Sasha and Cammie—and full-time—which was a relief to the household. The government was helping by infusing money into new jobs; however, it would take some time to get the wheels turning. The electricity was back to full service, and they were once again receiving coal deliveries regularly. The government paid for coal for the first two weeks to help everyone get back on their feet.

Abby had secured part-time work back at the salon and the pub as of yesterday; however, she continued to scour the papers for full-time work.

That evening, she and Cammie finished their supper of homemade beef-and-barley soup with bread that Sasha had brought from the hotel. Management was allowing employees to bring home leftovers, which meant less waste and also helped the staff. Indeed, it was a blessing, as all three of them had lost weight over the past nine weeks, mostly due to having little or no food some days. Some of the weight loss was stress-related as well.

"I'll make a nice cup of tea. Abby, you stoke up the fire," Cammie said. "Let's see those flames leap up the chimney! That will be a real treat. Sasha brought some raisin scones home yesterday. They're a bit stale, but if I warm them up and put some jam on them, they will be nice. Besides, beggars can't be choosers." She chuckled.

Abby stoked up the fire with as much coal as she could. It was a good feeling. The old kitchen never changed; everything was as familiar as it had been when she was a child. She half expected to see her Mother walk through the kitchen door.

"Cammie, do you feel Mam around us sometimes?"

"That's a bit of a queer question. Are you all right?"

"I'm fine. It's more of a feeling in the kitchen, especially on a cold winter night. The aromas of soup and bread, the tea and the biscuits, the warmth of the fire, and shadows of the flames dancing on the kitchen walls. The northeast winds howling around the house and the rain lashing up against the window. I loved coming home to her, especially on those nights."

"That was a long time ago, Abby."

"I know, but don't you feel it?"

"I certainly remember her. I think about her. Of course I miss her. Grief is timeless; it creeps up and grabs you from behind like a black velvet cloak being thrown over you when you least expect it, taking you by surprise. It's hard, I know. We must move on and let her go."

They sat in silence together, looking at the flames leaping up the chimney. Cammie broke the silence.

"Let's move over to the kitchen table and look for jobs in the *Evening Chronicle*."

They opened the newspaper to scour the help-wanted ads. Cammie pointed at the paper. "Hey, look at this!"

> WANTED. Evening job. Cleaners wanted part-time to clean council houses after renovations. Heavy work will pay up to ten pounds per house, depending on size. Call city council Monday through Friday, 9:00 a.m. to 5:00 p.m. Phone 659-5772.

Abby nodded. "We could easily do that together, Cammie. We should jump at the chance. I am so broke, and it's great pay."

"Makes one wonder what you must clean up!"

Abby raised her eyebrows. "At ten pounds a house, I'm happy to wear rubber gloves and a face mask!"

"I'll phone them from the office tomorrow to see how we apply," Cammie said.

"I hope we can get the job. We could make a small fortune together just by using some elbow grease and working hard."

"Slow down though. There are a lot of people looking for work, especially the jobs created by the city council."

"I know, but I'm desperate to save some money. I'm restless; I need to get away. I can't do that until I have a lot of extra money."

"Oh, Abby, you and your itchy feet, always looking over the fence to greener fields. You never know—we might get lucky. I'm off to bed. I'm tired."

"Good night. I'll tidy up."

Cammie left the kitchen, and Abby went about cleaning up. She washed the cups, dried them, and put them back in the cupboard. She decided to put more coal on the fire, as it was a bitter night. Sasha would be coming home from work after the late shift at eleven. He could have a hot tea by the fire if she stoked it up before she went to bed. She filled the kettle and put some tea leaves in the teapot, preparing it for him when he came home. She was just finishing off, when Sasha walked in the kitchen door.

"Sasha, you surprised me. You're early!"

"Nowt going on in the hotel kitchen. The rotten weather keeps people at home, so they cut my shift. Can't say I'm sorry. I'll make up for the time on the weekend," Sasha told her.

"Cammie just went to bed; I was making a cuppa."

"The fire looks canny and inviting."

"You go have a warm."

"I will. It's good to be home on nights like this." Sasha took off his coat, hat, and gloves. He pulled a chair up to sit as close to the flames as possible, holding his hands in front of the fire and rubbing them together.

Abby walked over to him with two cups of tea and a scone for Sasha.

"Thanks, Abby. Nice to be welcomed home with a cup of char and a scone."

"I know exactly how you feel. I was just saying to Cammie that on miserable winter nights like this, I miss Mam even now." Abby smiled at him.

Sasha looked up at Abby from his tea. The steam from it swirled up toward the ceiling. "You know, it's a funny thing. I was thinking as I walked home that I wished Mam was still here. She would have the fire on and a nice cup of tea ready. In many ways, I think she's still here." He winked at Abby and continued sipping his comforting tea.

"We found a great job in the paper tonight." Abby showed Sasha the ad.

"Bloody good money! If you get it, I'd like to help when I could."

"I hope we do get it. I must save some money; I've got to get away from here."

"What is it you are pining for in America? It can't be just our cousins," Sasha said.

"Well, it's just their way of life. Everything is bigger, brighter, and more available—not only the materialistic things. It's the understanding that if you put your head down and work hard, it's an open book. You can achieve anything you want, supported all the way. I love that mentality."

"Oh, is that all? You are starting to sound like an educated, intellectual Yankee, not our little lassie from the Tyne!" Sasha smiled. "Just kidding. Abby, you deserve to go back, and you will. I can tell you're motivated. Where are Aidan and Rosella living now?"

"Virginia. I've never seen it. Rosella waxes poetic in her letters to me about it."

"What does she say?"

"Virginia is for lovers! The beach, the valley, national parks, the Blue Ridge Mountains, history, wine, vistas, bird sanctuaries, and much more!" she told him.

"That sounds beautiful and suggests plenty of employment opportunities. Will you stay with Aidan when you go back?" he asked.

"Yes, they've invited me to stay with them indefinitely."

"That's a fantastic opportunity. I might follow you out there one day!"

He sat silently for a moment and then picked up the poker from the corner of the fireplace and gently poked the red coals in the grate. The fire was calming down and fading softly into the night. Sasha's handsome face flushed from the heat. He placed the poker back and sat down.

"I can tell you're warmer now," Abby said.

"Yes, I am, thanks. Do you think you'll find what you're looking for in Virginia or Tennessee?"

"What do you mean?"

"Abby, you pine day in and day out, especially when you think no one is watching. It's sad watching you sometimes. Now it's become a concern because it's becoming obvious. You're so anxious to return it's almost urgent," Sasha told her.

"We've all suffered with anxiety, thanks to the miners."

"That is not what I mean, and you know it!"

"Yes, I know you're right." Abby chewed on her bottom lip. Her eyes welled to the brim with tears. If she didn't hold it in, she felt it would take hours to stop the flow. "It's where I want to be, Sasha!"

"I don't blame you. Who wouldn't want to be there when you hear the descriptions and compare it to here? You just must work hard and take your time, and one day you will return, I'm sure."

"The problem is, I've lived it. I've tasted the glorious freedom and felt the open, loving arms of the place. I understand every moment I'm away just what I'm missing."

"Whose open arms? That's the question," Sasha said.

Abby broke down in tears. "Does it matter? I'm as far away from it as I can be. Every second, I feel more and more removed from … everything." Abby was about to say *him* but stopped herself.

"Keep your dreams, pet, and move slowly toward your goal. You seem to excel at making the impossible possible. Try not to be sad. So what if it takes a year or two? The point is to have the dream. You have had more opportunities than most of us have in a lifetime." Sasha stood up and patted Abby on the back. The action felt empty to her. Although she knew his intention was to bring her comfort, there was little.

"I'm off to bed. I'm shattered," he said. "Good night."

Sasha went upstairs. There was little light coming from the fire and less warmth. It was dark outside, and the winter storm continued to howl around the house relentlessly. Abby felt as isolated as a little lost girl. Sasha had opened a Pandora's box of emotion within her, and she wasn't sure what to do about it.

After placing the guard against the fire, Abby turned off

the light and walked out of the kitchen. *I'll move forward and find my way back to you, Gabriel!*

Colleen stirred in the early light of the Vegas spring morning. The March sun rose slowly, warming her face. She lay still on the large bed, feeling Byron breathing beside her. For the first time in months, Colleen awoke not feeling nauseated. She had survived her last chemotherapy treatment ten days ago. She lay still, allowing the heat from the early morning sun to wash over her; the feeling was glorious. Realizing this was how normal felt, she was both happy and grateful.

So much had happened in the past six months: she'd given birth to Benedict and endured and survived a radical double mastectomy and chemo treatments, and they had moved from Virginia to Las Vegas. When Byron had first suggested moving, she had been shocked and scared; however, her doctors, Andrew and Dr. Burke, had reassured her it would be beneficial to everyone. She realized it was important for them all to be together.

She missed Virginia Beach; it was home. Yet gradually, she was adjusting to this unexpected new world. Colleen was learning to appreciate the perennial beauty and diversity of the desert. Driving through the desert was a feast for the senses, with a myriad of colors: blazing reds and oranges. The shapes of the rocks, the harmony of the sounds, and the diversity of the plants and cacti were an eternal tapestry of textures and colors. The sun, moon, and stars were brilliant, and the sounds were unique and touched the senses exquisitely. Colleen noticed a serenity in the desert unlike any other she had experienced—a stillness reserved for that place that seemed to reach out and take her to a serene and tranquil space within. She would be forever grateful that her family hadn't missed out on this opportunity.

Colleen slipped from the bed, put on her housecoat, and reached for her blue satin turban. She could tell by the rhythm of Byron's breathing that he was in a deep sleep. She quietly left the bedroom and looked in on Grace and Aria. Her beautiful girls were sleeping. She was proud of them. She quietly closed the bedroom door and moved toward the nursery.

Benedict lay on his back with his arms above his head, breathing softly. He was gradually awakening as the sun came up; he pulled himself from sleep slowly. When his eyes opened, he always greeted Colleen with a beaming smile. He was sunshine to her. In his infant and infinite wisdom, he had carried her through some of the most devastating hurdles of this godforsaken disease. His unconscious need for her, together with her aching desire to love him, fed the growing connection they had for one another. He gave Colleen the strength and courage to carry on when she felt she had reached her limit. She bent over the crib and popped a kiss on his forehead.

Colleen made her way down to the kitchen, the masterpiece of the house. The kitchen was effectively in the middle of an atrium and surrounded by every type of palm tree the desert produced. It was an indoor-outdoor room with a glass roof that allowed for a full view of the top of the mountains and, in the evening, every single star. *Architecture at its very best*, she thought.

"Good morning, my darling. How are you feeling?" Viv entered, looking at her daughter with loving eyes. "You look magnificent!"

"Thanks, Mom. You're so good to me," Colleen said as she kissed her Mother on the cheek.

"The coffee is on, and the morning-glory muffins are freshly baked."

"I smelled them all the way down the stairs and followed my nose to the kitchen. I'm going to miss you when you go home today, Mom. You've been an absolute godsend to me and the kids, as well as Byron." Colleen placed her hands on her Mother's shoulders and looked into her eyes. "You know how much you mean to me; I wouldn't have made it without you and your loving care."

"There's nowhere else on this earth I'd want to be than here with you, my darling. Come now. Let's stop this silly business and enjoy some coffee and muffins," Viv said with tears in her eyes.

They sat together in the atrium, enjoying their breakfast and looking at the mountains.

"This place has such an extraordinary beauty and a peaceful feeling," Colleen said. "I've missed Virginia Beach, but I do find the desert has a powerful effect."

"I am so glad you are enjoying it. We were concerned you might not adapt, but it's having quite the opposite effect. It seems to have invigorated you, and certainly the children are enjoying it. Byron is elated to have his family with him. It was a very good decision, sweetheart."

"I'll miss you and will be counting the days until you come back to Vegas."

"I'll be back in ten days, and besides, you will have enough going on around you without me interfering. It'll be so nice to have Andrew and his family here. I'm pleased he is bringing that nanny of his along to help."

"Her name is Heather, Mom."

"I keep forgetting. I must think of a way to remember. I know—I'll think of a Scottish weed. I only met her once, but I got the impression she's rather pushy, telling the girls what to do and making eyes at Andrew. She's no Mary Poppins. He needs to watch out for her."

"Maybe he has his eye on her, Mom, and anyway, they're single, young, and good looking. If she makes him happy, I don't see the problem. Not everyone is willing to take on a doctor, let alone a divorced man with two children. I say kudos to her if she's willing; it's a big responsibility. She would need a lot of support. It might be good for that family—stabilize the girls."

Her Mom sat silently for a moment and then frowned. "It's just not appropriate to be fraternizing with the nanny. I mean, she's the hired help. There's right and wrong, and in this instance, it's very wrong!"

"Mom, that's a very poor attitude to take."

"All the same, I'd keep tabs on her while she's here. It's very likely she has her own agenda going on. And someone should speak to Andrew about it. I mean, he's like one of the family. I don't want to see him make another mistake like he did with the Irish one. He appears to have a thing for Celtic girls," her Mom said snippily.

"Mom, please, this is none of your business. Let's not discuss it anymore."

"All right, whatever you say. I have more packing to do. I'll go get on with it."

Grace came into the atrium, carrying Benedict, who was gurgling and cooing in her arms. "Mom, I changed Ben's diaper. Can I give him his bottle, please, as it's not a school day?"

"Look at you—almost grown up. Of course you can."

Viv looked at Colleen cautiously. Colleen nodded toward her Mother.

"Sit down in the rocking chair." Colleen patted the seat gently, and Grace moved confidently toward it. Benedict was the happiest baby, never more content than in the presence of his sister Grace. From the moment they first had met, they'd had an extraordinary connection, as if they had been together in a distant lifetime and were now somehow celestially reunited. It was beautiful to watch.

Grace had a natural approach with Ben, and he appeared to sense her presence even before she came into the room. He would kick his arms and legs and shriek with pure delight.

"Mom!" Grace said. "I'm so excited Babs and Katie are coming today with Uncle Andrew. I can't wait for them to see how big Ben is now."

"They certainly will," Colleen said. Her daughter continued to amaze her with her maturity. "I'm looking forward to spending time with everyone. It'll be so much fun to show them Las Vegas. Where shall we take them, Grace?"

"Can we take them to the Grand Canyon? I bet they have never seen anything like that, and I know Katie's and Babs's eyes will pop out of their heads when they see it!" Grace laughed as she held Benedict's morning bottle with the expertise of an experienced nanny. Lifting him onto her shoulder, she gently patted his back, telling him to burp so he could have some more. He did as he was bid immediately, and Grace went back to feeding him without a hitch.

"Can we go to the Hoover Dam? And we must take them to Daddy's magic show. We can swim and play tennis and go for pizza."

Colleen smiled at her amazing Grace—part child, part adult, and part angel. "You have lots of plans for seven days. We'll cram in as much as we can. I promise."

Later that evening, Andrew and Byron sat quietly, each of them sipping a glass of wine, old friends silently listening to one another. Everyone else had turned in, as it was ten o'clock, and it had been a busy day between the traveling and the excitement of seeing one another for the first time in several months.

"This is a spectacular home," Andrew said, motioning with his glass. "I've never seen anything so brilliantly designed. And this location—it's like paradise!"

"It's exactly what we need as a family. Colleen and the kids love it, and that's all I really care about. I feel stronger and more capable, not always yearning to get back to them. It helps me focus on my job when I'm there and also on my family when I'm here." Byron chuckled.

"That makes sense. I'm relieved the move has worked out for the best. Everyone appears to like Las Vegas. I'm looking forward to spending some time with Colleen and getting to know that handsome son of yours."

"Ben—he is something! Grace is like a little Mother to

him, Aria sings to him all day, and Viv showers him with hugs and kisses. He's landed into a cradle full of love, and it shows!"

"How is Colleen?" asked Andrew.

"I'd say today has been one of her best since before Benedict was born. It's been ten days since her final chemo treatment. She appears to be motivated, excited, and looking forward to being as normal as possible. I must say, I'm delighted you brought Heather along; it will be great help to all of us, in fact."

"Heather is very good with Katie and Babs; they're used to her now, and she them. She also keeps my life in order—not only domestically, but she actually helps professionally more than she needs to."

"And she's also very easy on the eyes. It helps to have a little glamour around the place." Byron wiggled his eyebrows up and down, grinning.

"There's no question she is gorgeous; however, it creates more than a few suspicions," Andrew replied.

"What do you mean?"

"My Mother's not too thrilled. It appears everyone assumes two good-looking heterosexual people living together must be bonking like bunnies."

Byron laughed out loud.

Andrew went on, his face serious. "It's true. People don't understand the principles of a Motherless family. The importance of the children's welfare and also the moral working environment, which is necessary for Heather. She not only works for me, but it's her home; she needs to feel safe."

"I never thought about that. What a relevant point.

It's all about the children and also Heather feeling safe and comfortable. You have no choice but to tread carefully, especially as a doctor," said Byron.

"The moment any romantic overtures are made, we'd be opening up quite a Pandora's box. It really doesn't matter how we feel about each other, and believe me, there is a definite attraction. In fact, it's beginning to create sexual tension between us. However, we can't act on those feelings, not as long as she's working for me."

"That puts you in a very difficult situation. What's important right now is that you have a capable nanny. It appears you do, so looks like you'll have to keep your hands off, old boy." Byron raised his glass. "Here's to the celibate life," he said, smiling.

The following morning, Colleen watched Heather prepare breakfast for everyone. She appeared to float about the kitchen as though she were on an invisible cloud. She and Aria were singing a Scottish ditty about Maggie's wedding. Heather appeared to be in her glory, positively blooming.

"I'm so pleased you were able to join Andrew and the girls. Your energy is very welcome here, as we could all use some," Colleen told her.

"Och, I'm only too happy to be here; I was thrilled when Andrew suggested I come out. What a fabulous opportunity for me to see Las Vegas, all expenses covered. Don't ever look a gift horse in the mouth." Heather smiled sweetly at Colleen.

"Quite right."

"Besides, I realize you want some help with five extras. It's a lot on top of all your own family and your troubles. Is your Mom still with you?" asked Heather, staring boldly at Colleen's chest.

"No, she decided to take some time off and headed home for the week during your visit. We felt you could help. Mom has been a lifeline for me and my family; she certainly deserves the rest."

"Well, you just let me know if I can help you when I'm around. I'm more than happy to." Heather moved around Colleen's kitchen as though she were familiar with it.

Grace, Katie, and Babs came running in, excited.

"We are all here to see Benedict, Mom." Grace was the spokesperson.

"He's in the bassinet beside the window." Colleen pointed to where Benedict lay gurgling and kicking in his basket. He could hear Grace's voice.

"Can we please hold him, Aunt Colleen?" Babette asked.

"Yes. Sit in the rocking chair beside the window, and Grace will hand him to you."

When the girls were organized, all charmed by and charming baby Benedict, Heather spoke up. "Well, you're quite a natural at this, Babette. Would you like a new baby brother?" she asked.

The girls all giggled.

Colleen fixed her gaze upon Heather: her perfect peach-like breasts were perched high under her white silk blouse, revealing the silhouette of her white lace bra. Colleen's hands automatically went to her flat childlike chest; it was like that of one of her little daughters. The realization always took her to a dark and lonely place, deep inside the intricate and complex layers of her feminine identity.

She continued to watch the girls loving and interacting with Ben. Colleen began to feel guilty, mentally chastising herself for her indulgent behavior and lack of gratitude for the multitude of gifts bestowed upon her. She knew she needed to change her persona and her attitude to be the confident wife and Mother of this beautiful family she belonged to, instead of feeling sorry for herself.

"Girls, let's get breakfast! Go find your Dads, and tell them to move into high speed. We have things to do, people to see, and places to go—run along!" said Colleen.

She turned to the nanny. "Heather, would you kindly set the table? Aria, help, please. You can show Heather where everything is. When you're finished, start making the pancakes. Thank you. We might just think about a picnic lunch. I'll talk with Byron and let you know." Colleen picked up Benedict and set him on her hip as she smiled sweetly toward Heather. "I'm so pleased to have you with us, helping." She left Heather whisking batter for pancakes in the kitchen.

On the last evening of Andrew's visit, he was sitting alone in the atrium, mesmerized by the beauty surrounding him. He had thoroughly enjoyed his time there, as they all had, reuniting, sharing, and enjoying one another. He was mostly happy to see Colleen becoming stronger day by day; the family's relocation had been a good move. Andrew was considering how quickly time had passed, when Heather walked into the room.

"Hello. We're all packed and ready to leave tomorrow," she said. "Everyone is sleeping. I took the liberty of pouring us a glass of wine." She handed him a glass with a generous amount of wine.

Andrew thought she looked gorgeous in the soft light: her skin was slightly tanned, and her hair was the color of a rippling cornfield in the summertime breeze.

"Cheers." Holding up her glass, she touched his softly. "I'd like to thank you, Andrew; I've had one of the best weeks of my life."

"I'm happy to hear that. You've been a wonderful addition to this family holiday; the girls have loved it. I know Colleen appreciated the extra helping hands," Andrew replied.

"Ochs, it was no bother. Besides, you know I'd do anything for you." She hesitated. "And the girls."

Andrew tugged at his collar and swallowed some more wine, beginning to feel uncomfortable. "This is a great-tasting wine. Hey, what was your favorite part of the trip?" he asked, and then he began to answer his own question, feeling hot and light-headed. "For me, it was the Grand Canyon. I can honestly say it took away not only my breath but all my thoughts and, for a moment, time and space itself. The sheer size of the gorge and the view of the raging rapids of the Colorado River—I've never seen such magnificent, powerful beauty in my life. I'd like to go back and spend a lot more time there."

Andrew drank a good gulp of his wine, grateful to have something to distract him. Heather moved closer to him on the sofa.

Looking up into his eyes, she whispered, "I think this is a brilliant room. Look at the billions of stars shining so brightly. It's because there is no moonlight tonight. I believe I can catch them they feel so close to me."

She tossed her golden hair over her shoulder. Placing her glass on the table beside her, she looked up at him with seductive eyes. "You want to know something canny, Andrew? My favorite part of the trip was you."

Leaning toward her, he felt as though the stars had tumbled down about them. He pulled her perfect body toward him, and their lips came together almost magnetically, softly at first. Placing his hand on her glorious golden mane, he felt himself letting go. He could feel a dangerous yearning from within him, and he called out, "My God, Heather, how I want you!"

— 19 —

On Easter Sunday morning, Gabriel sipped the last of the wine from his golden chalice, finishing Mass at St. Michael the Archangel. The church was packed. He worked his way through the sacred symbolic rituals: finishing the host, placing the body of Christ in his mouth, laying it upon his tongue, allowing it to melt, becoming like grace, washing his hands, cleansing the chalice, and drying it. Everything was in its place physically and spiritually.

He said the familiar words repeated over and over. "The Lord be with you."

"And also with you."

"Go in peace to love and serve the Lord."

"Amen."

The processional hymn began, and the altar boys and chalice bearers descended the steps of the altar toward the back of the church. Gabriel focused with every part of his senses, preventing himself from running past everyone off the altar, along the aisle, and away from the church to escape.

He wanted to be alone with his thoughts and his memories—alone with his Abigail.

Gabriel decided to jog to one of his favorite places: a wooded trail that meandered its way to the town. At the end of the trail lay a perfect babbling brook. Gabriel thought of it as a reward for the hard work of jogging. It was the perfect place to be alone and find rest, peace, and gentle thoughts.

His thoughts were in turmoil because he'd received a letter yesterday from Rosella and Aidan, who were now living in Virginia. The letter was mostly from Rosella. Their news had turned him upside down and inside out. He'd thought he was cured and had recovered to his jocular self. It had taken five years of prayer, retreats, meditations, contrition, counseling, self-doubt, and recrimination. He had been pleased with his progress. He rarely gave Abigail much thought, thinking of her once or maybe twice in a day instead of every second his heart gave a beat. Finally, he was healing, and he was grateful, thanks be to God.

Yesterday's letter had torn into him like a serrated knife, ripping a multitude of stitches from his broken heart and leaving him open and bleeding, shocked, disappointed, and devastated.

He reached his favorite part of the woods, where he and Abby had met by chance many moons ago. The memory was crystal clear to him, as if it had occurred only yesterday. Gabriel remembered how flustered she'd appeared to him that day when they bumped into one another.

"Hi. I was walking, and I don't know the path, so I was heading back to the house, and I'm sorry. Father, I am surprised to see you!" Abby had blurted out.

"Me too. Let's walk," Gabriel had replied.

Together they'd strolled aimlessly, winding their way through the woods, sharing stories. Abby had described her home so beautifully that he'd felt he could hear the sounds and smell of the North Sea as one looked from the top of a broken-down ancient monastery. She'd told of her siblings and her life. He in turn had talked of his family and the farm. They'd laughed freely among the evergreen trees.

Gabriel had fallen in love for the first and last time of his life with Abigail that winter morn in February.

Now, sitting under one of the tall pine trees, Gabriel opened his water flask and took a long pull. He closed his eyes and searched in his memory for the sound of Abby's sweet laughter on the whispering breeze of the tall pines as they reached for the heavens. Reaching into his pocket, he pulled out the letter. He held it between his hands as though clasped in a prayer. After slowly opening it, he read it one more time.

> Dear Father Gabriel,
>
> We are so sorry to have missed you last year when you returned to St. Mike's. We passed one another by only days, as though God had deemed it so. I hope you are well and happy to be back.
>
> I'm writing to let you know we'll be visiting our friends in Tennessee this summer, in May or June. We'd love to take you out for dinner—a spaghetti dinner maybe!

>Father, I wish to give you an update on Abigail. She is aware that you have returned to St. Mike's, as I wrote to her approximately eighteen months ago. She had planned on visiting us in Virginia; however, the airline she was flying for went into bankruptcy. She wrote to me only recently, explaining that she was working three jobs in order to make her way back, although it's going to take some time. She asked only once in the letter if I had seen or heard from you. I told her I have not. I thought that was best and hope you agree.
>
>I keep you in my prayers and hope to see you in the summer.
>
>Blessings,
>Rosella, Aidan, and family

Blessings! What blessings? The letter was an absolute curse. Gabriel sat silently weeping for some time under the evergreen tree. He finally stood up, resolving to go back to the presbytery and compose a much-needed, long-awaited letter to Abigail.

— 20 —

Abby was exhausted. She set down her mop and plopped onto the cement step at the front door on a gray April morning. No daffodils greeted her, only the damp, dreary view of the terraced Victorian house owned by the Newcastle Council. She and Cammie had been given the contract to clean the homes after the workmen had finished renovations, which included new wiring, new windows, central heating, and new bathrooms and kitchens.

The two of them had been working at the new job for several weeks, and so far, they had managed to clean three houses per week. Most of them were the same size: three bedrooms, or sometimes two bedrooms, and one bathroom. They had made thirty pounds per week, with each of them receiving fifteen pounds. Abby had managed to save all of it: sixty pounds.

The work was disgusting. Abby had never seen such filth in her life. She wasn't sure if it was left by the workmen or by homeless people. Drug addicts, alcoholics, and tramps appeared to have used the houses, because there was evidence of broken windows. However, what people left behind was unbelievable to her; she'd seen cleaner pigs in a sty on Sally's family farm up in the mountains in Italy.

The stench that day was beyond gut-wrenching: decaying human waste and rotten, maggot-ridden food, which often attracted vermin, such as mice, cockroaches, and sometimes the odd fat rat. It depended on how long the house had been empty before they were given the key to go in and clean it.

The homes weren't all so bad; often, the cleanup required little effort. It was not always so horrible. No matter how long it took them to clean the house, they received ten pounds.

That day, she was compelled to come outside and breathe in some of the Northeast's damp, soot-filled air on that April spring day. Drab though it was, the air was cleaner outside than inside the house.

What had happened to her life—those privileged, glorious, carefree days when she had flown to New York and stayed in the Plaza Hotel with marble, crystal, and carpets that practically sank up to one's knees? She quickly realized there was no benefit to feeling sorry for herself and decided to think of a more practical side of things. Abby turned her focus to how many houses it would take for her to save enough money to go back to the United States. She would need at least seven hundred pounds. It seemed like a lot, but if she and Cammie continued to clean three houses a week, it wouldn't take that long. However, she wasn't sure if she could keep up this pace while also working her other two jobs.

Standing up on the step, Abby stretched her arms up to the sky. Though her bones were aching, Abby ventured back into the house and, kneeling on the kitchen floor, went back to work. Cammie was cleaning windows.

"This work is almost pleasant compared to the crap we moved out of here today. You okay now?" asked Cammie.

"Yes, fine. I just needed some air. I hope we don't come across too many houses like this one!"

"Me too. Still, think of the money, honey!"

Abby bent down as she used a razor blade to scrape something indescribable from the linoleum kitchen floor. "Believe me, that is all I think about!" she replied.

When Abby and Cammie arrived home, Abby was exhausted, feeling contaminated with the filth and dirt from house cleaning. Cammie opened the front door, bent down to pick up the post from the floor, and tucked it under her spare arm.

"Let's get the cleaning buckets and stuff put away fast. We can put more coal on the fire to heat lots of water—enough for two baths," said Cammie.

"Oh dear God, I can hardly stand myself. Can we toss a coin for who goes first?" asked Abby.

"No, you go. I'll start making the tea. Welsh rarebit and beans sound good?"

"Like champagne and caviar!"

A little while later, Abby came downstairs after her bath.

"I've put some more coal on the fire," Cammie said. "The Welsh rarebit is almost done, and there is tea in the pot. How are you feeling now?"

"Wonderful. I think I envy you going in for your bath now. I'd like to feel that glorious warm water one more time, washing away not only the day's dirt and grime but also some of my inside woes," Abby replied.

"Oh God, Abby, you are so dramatic. Get away with you!" As Cammie moved toward the door, she turned her head. "By the way, there is a letter there for you—airmail from America. It's on the table beside the pot."

"It's probably from Rosella."

"No, it's not. I was nosy and had a look. Gabriel Spencer is the name on the back. Who is that? A secret lover?" Cammie chuckled as she left the kitchen.

Abby held on to the kitchen chair she was standing beside to stop herself from collapsing. Her heart beat so fast she thought she was going to faint. Cammie must have been wrong. Of course it couldn't have been Gabriel Spencer.

Why is he writing now?

She picked up the letter; it was his handwriting. She would have recognized it a mile away in the dark. She was desperate to tear open the flimsy airmail envelope. She longed to see and touch his words formed on the page, his thoughts and feelings.

Abby held the letter close to her heart, trying to find her soul if she could reach it. After some time, she placed the letter in her dressing gown pocket. She would save it and read it in her bed in privacy. She was going to savor the moments before she opened the envelope and enjoy imagining his words, thoughts, and reasons for writing now.

"That was fantastic. I loved that bath! I feel so much better. Tea ready?" Cammie asked a bit later as she came back into the kitchen.

"Almost," Abby replied.

"Good, because I am starving. Did you open your letter?"

"Yes, it's from someone I met in the youth group," Abby lied. "He's thinking of coming to England this summer; he'd like to visit us in Newcastle." She was as casual as she could be with her sacred secret.

"Are you sure about that?"

"What do you mean? Of course I am."

"When I told you his name earlier, you lost all your color and turned as white as a sheet, and you were shaking," Cammie said.

"No, I wasn't. We've had such a hard day; that house was the worst. I hope we never come across another one like that." Abby tried to distract her sister.

"Whatever you say! Let's have our tea, and when we have finished, we can watch the telly. *The Two Ronnies* is on tonight—we can have a good laugh."

"Yes, yes," Abby replied with her thoughts focused only on the unread letter in her pocket.

At midnight, Abby had been lying there for several hours, completely exhausted from the day—not only gutting the dirty house but arriving home to a letter from Gabriel, which had been the last thing she'd expected.

Her mind was filled with ideas and thoughts like a tombola—filled with notes and numbers being spun around. Imagining what might be written was infinitely more enjoyable as she held off the inevitable opening of the flimsy envelope. However, she eventually propped herself up with her pillow, switched on her bedside lamp, and carefully removed the precious letter. There was only one folded page. Placing her free hand on her pendant around her neck, Abby stared at the words.

> My dearest Abby,
>
> I can see you in my mind's eye, surprised to receive a letter from me after my last letter to you. I know I insisted on no contact. It

proves the adage that we should never say *never!*

There is so much I'd like to say to you. Most important, I pray this letter finds you well and in good spirits.

I received an informative letter from our common denominator, your cousin Rosella, just yesterday. I don't mind telling you it shook me to my core.

Abby, my inner soul overflowed, freeing my pocketful of memories, the ones I keep safe and secure and don't bring out. Rosella revealed them to me. I could not, with all my heart, stop myself from scribbling a few lines to you, at least hoping to hear from you that your life is coming back to some semblance of normal after all your trials and tribulations. I'll keep you in my prayers, as I have every day since you and I met so many years ago in the gardens of St. Michael the Archangel. As you know, I've returned to St. Mike's.

This letter is not about myself, only you, my dearest Abby.

As the sun's rays warm your face in the morning and you kneel at your bedside to pray, remember that somewhere in the distance, I'm with you all the way.

With love,
Father Gabriel

Abby reread the letter several times, hoping to see what she could find between the lines. What on earth was he doing? What did he want from her? Was it as simple as "How are you? I'm thinking of you"? Was he asking her for more?

Abby lay her head on her pillow, emotionally weary and spent, and fell into a deep sleep with the letter from Gabriel held against her heart.

— 21 —

Rosella Kennedy's kitchen looked and smelled like an Italian restaurant and an English tearoom. Rosella had been preparing foods for Christmas for several weeks. She had made pasta, homemade sauce, and meatballs, along with English foods, as she liked to keep both her own and Aidan's traditions going for her children. When Helen, her Mother-in-law, had lived with them, she'd taught Rosella how to cook some of the most delicious English foods, especially Christmas foods: sweet mince pies, Christmas fruitcake with marzipan and icing, Scottish butter shortbread, sherry trifles, and much more. Rosella had made every one of them. She loved Christmas; it was her favorite holiday and a special time of year for all the family.

This year, it was going to be extra special.

Taking a break, Rosella dusted herself clean of flour and sugar, wiped her hands on her apron and removed it, and made herself a cup of coffee. After picking up a letter from the mantel, Rosella sat in the window seat to relax. She read the letter for the umpteenth time.

Dear Aidan and Rosella,

I can hardly believe I am writing this letter to you all. I must pinch myself. I have a big favor to ask you.

After twenty-three months of hardship, heartbreak, and turmoil in my life, I believe the angels have stepped in and taken over!

I decided to visit the travel agent yesterday, mostly to inquire about prices of tickets from Newcastle to Virginia. The travel agent was a lovely lady, and we discussed when I wished to depart and return, which affects the price of the ticket. Possibly February, I told her, thinking of my finances.

She smiled at me and told me of an amazing coincidence; I've got goose pimples just thinking of it. She has a client who purchased a ticket to fly to Virginia leaving December 21, as he wanted to spend Christmas with his family, and it's open to May 12. For reasons that aren't relevant, he cannot use the ticket, and it's nonrefundable. He is willing to sell it for 75 pounds instead of 350 pounds to anyone who could use it.

My mouth was dry, my palms were sweating, and my heart was beating fast as I heard the word come out of my mouth before I realized it: "Sold!"

I have three weeks to clear up things. I can stay for up to five months, if you will have me. I feel so happy I could fly to the moon and tap-dance on the stars!

My only sadness and regret is that I'll not be here to celebrate Christmas with my family and all the Amelia traditions. Although I do believe Amelia would tell me to go!

I hope you are all well and everything is wonderful. Please let me know as soon as possible, and I shall enclose the itinerary.

Love to all,
Abby

Rosella put the letter down and wiped away a tear.

When she showed the letter to Aidan, his response was as she expected: he could not contain himself.

"Fantastic! She is coming back to us! What amazing news. I am so delighted for her. You should reply immediately, Rosella."

Rosella replied to the letter the same day.

Abigail,

We'll all be there at the airport, waiting for you with open arms. What a wonderful early Christmas gift for all of us!

Love,
The Kennedys
xxxx

— 22 —

Heather worked diligently in Andrew's kitchen, preparing for Christmas. Andrew was out Christmas shopping with the girls. *I'd rather it be him than me.*

She felt as though she had just recovered from Thanksgiving week, which was the fourth Thursday in November in America, an important holiday. It seemed to Heather it was bigger than Christmas. Americans traveled across the country to be together, and then there was the shopping. The Friday after Thanksgiving was the biggest shopping day of the year. It seemed to her Thanksgiving kicked off the Christmas holiday.

She loved the way all the different countries had their own traditions. She particularly liked this Christmas. The girls were home, as it was Andrew's turn to have them for Christmas, and Byron, Colleen, and the children were all coming back to Virginia for Christmas to be with family. Andrew had invited all of them for Christmas Day dinner. It seemed like a lot of people; however, one of their amazing traditions was a potluck. Everyone who came brought prepared food—casseroles, dessert, and salads—so the host didn't have to work as hard. The host's job was the turkey. Andrew's parents, Colleen and Byron, and Colleen's Mother would all bring something with them; it made for a sumptuous meal.

Andrew and the girls arrived home just as Heather put a casserole in the oven.

Babs was jumping up and down. "We had so much fun shopping! I am excited to see everyone open their gifts tomorrow. My Dad has bought you a beautiful present."

"Shh, Babs." Andrew put a finger to her lips. "Tomorrow."

"Och, that's true. It'll be fun," Heather replied.

Andrew stood beside her, looking tired yet handsome, as always. "I'm more than grateful you decided to stay with us this year to help us celebrate. We are all looking forward to the holidays."

He smiled his Peter Pan grin at her, which she found irresistible. She fancied him in the worst way. He was gorgeous. She wanted to sleep with him and had for a long time now. She realized she had pushed him too fast by coming on to him in Las Vegas. After the passionate kiss they had shared, he had pulled away from her, suggesting they forget anything ever happened.

"We can't do this, Heather," he'd said. "It's wrong for a hundred different reasons. I don't wish to hurt you. Truly, I don't, but I do wish to forget this moment. We have too much responsibility to ourselves, the girls, and each other."

She'd thought he was a bit of a prude. After all, she wasn't looking to marry him, just to have a fling. Never mind.

She had time on her side and many other attributes, and she was using them all.

On December 21, Abby jubilantly stood in the arrival's hall at Virginia International Airport, looking up at the largest decorated Christmas tree she had ever seen. It was unbelievable. It was more than twenty feet tall and awash with colored balls, ribbons, ornaments of all kinds, and faux snow.

She gazed around, searching the crowds at the gate for Aidan, Rosella, and the children. The airport was a maze of people arriving and greeting friends or relatives. Abby felt an overwhelming feeling of joy as she watched Mothers running toward university children home for the holidays with open arms, grandMothers reaching out for little toddlers and covering them with multitudes of kisses, and lovers wrapped up in blissful yuletide kisses.

Abby smiled. Indeed, arrivals at the airport during Christmas was a happy place to be. Then Aidan and Rosella were standing in front of her with the children between them, both attempting to hug her at the same time. Rosella cried tears of joy.

"I can't believe you are here!" Rosella hugged her close.

"Welcome back, Abby," Aidan said. He took her suitcases and gave the small one to his son Greg. "Let's go home and start celebrating. We have much to catch up on."

Abby and Rosella linked arms just like old times. Rosella said, "I can't wait to hear everything you have to share with us. We've missed you so much, and I'm so happy you found your way back to us."

Abby suddenly stopped, looking about her. "Rosella, I can't believe it. It feels as though I'm in a dream. I wonder where this will all take me."

Three evenings later, Abby sat in a pew at All Saints Roman Catholic Church next to Rosella, Aidan, and the children. They had all come to celebrate midnight Mass. What a magical whirlwind she'd experienced the last three days. Besides being reunited with the Kennedys, she was overjoyed to be back in the States at long last. She'd worked hard to get there.

As Abby looked around her, she felt the church was contemporary, the complete opposite of the dark and damp monastery she was used to. This church sparkled with its stained-glass windows, white pine pews, and white marble—almost a little sterile. It had an unusual shape—octagonal, she thought. It was bright and beautiful but not something she was used to.

"How are you feeling? Jet-lagged? Happy? What are you thinking?" Rosella looked at her and smiled.

"How happy I am to be here in this beautiful church. It's very different from our dark old monastery. And yes, I am a little jet-lagged, but I'm used to it from my flying days."

Rosella hesitated before she spoke. "And Gabriel? Are you thinking of him?"

"Yes, always Gabriel."

There was a gentle silence between them as they took in the church's loving atmosphere.

Rosella sighed contentedly. "I love coming to midnight Mass. This is our first Christmas in Virginia, and having you with us makes it very special. We're all so happy to have you with us. We can pray for Gabriel tonight."

Abby was absorbed in her own thoughts of Gabriel, half praying and half studying the parishioners as they came into church. She saw old couples alone, parents, grandparents, and children. The old and the young and everyone in between were all welcome.

One large group moved into the empty pew in front of them. Abby thought they looked like two separate families. She counted them. The group appeared to be a mam, a Dad, and two little girls and then another mam, a Dad, a red-haired older lady, two little girls, and a gorgeous little baby boy. Abby grinned at him; he looked all boy to her. He was a clone of the tall, handsome man holding him. The two little girls sitting beside him were beautiful. The older one was the image of her Dad, and the younger one looked like a little nymph; she was glorious, with long blonde hair. The Dad handed the baby to the older girl. It surprised Abby that he didn't pass the baby to the mam, who appeared to have a fragile beauty about her, mystical, gentle, and sad.

Abby moved her eyes to the other handsome family. She could see the husband and Dad clearly; he was to the left of her. What a dish—he was stop-your-breath good looking. His wife was equally as beautiful as he was handsome—beauty-queen stunning. What a couple. The two little girls didn't look like they belonged to the Mother; one had bright red hair, and the other looked identical to the Dad.

Amazing Grace

The processional started and changed the direction of Abby's thoughts. She felt a pure elation. Finally, she was on the same continent as Gabriel, celebrating midnight Mass on Christmas Eve at the same time as he was. "Only a short time until I come back to you, Gabriel," she whispered like a prayer, deep in thought.

Time passed as Abby enjoyed the music of the season in the contemporary environment. Guitars and trumpets echoed throughout the glass dome as the priest gave a sermon and talked of a letter to Santa Claus from a five-year-old child requesting nothing that year, only world peace. It was a wonderful sermon and most appropriate.

After the consecration of bread and wine and the prayers, the priest held out his open arms and began reciting. "Our Father, who art in heaven …"

He then invited everyone to offer a sign of peace.

The congregation turned toward one another and greeted as many individuals around them as possible, offering the sign of peace, Christmas blessings, and various forms of peace: hugs, kisses, and handshakes.

"Peace be with you." Rosella hugged Abby and then hugged Aidan.

Several of the family members in the pew in front turned to shake hands and offer their signs of peace. The handsome man opposite Abby turned and looked at her, and he offered his hand. Looking into her eyes, he smiled and said, "Peace be with you."

She noticed the tone of his voice; it was smooth and belonged to his handsome face somehow. Abby noticed strength and softness equally in his grip as he held her hand for a fraction of a moment longer than necessary. Releasing it, he smiled. It was a gesture of kindness—nothing more and nothing less—though Abby felt something stir within her that she hadn't felt in a long time. She was relieved when he turned away to face the altar.

Abby closed her eyes and whispered in prayer, "And also with you."

After the service concluded, Abby and the Kennedys piled into the station wagon. It was a beautiful, crisp, and clear morning; the stars were out, and there was a gentle nip in the air. As they drove home, one of the children spoke to Abby.

"Is there any difference between Christmas in England and Christmas in Virginia?"

Abby nodded. "Oh my goodness, where do I start? Believe me, this is like living in a dream, only I am awake. It's so brilliant. Let me see if I can explain the differences in our Christmases."

She gathered her thoughts for a moment. "Well, to start, everything in America is so much bigger—to see colored lights, ornaments, and eight-foot Christmas trees inside homes, standing in the great cathedral-ceilinged rooms. On the outside of people's homes, I've witnessed the most amazing life-size nativity displays in front yards. They're so authentic I want to walk into the stable. Santa Claus is on every street corner, ringing bells and collecting money for charity. Carol singing in the square. I thought I'd be homesick, but I have to tell you a secret: I cannot imagine celebrating Christmas anywhere else in the world. We have nothing like this in our town at Christmastime."

Rosella glanced back at her with a smile. "Sounds like you're enjoying this time."

Abby nodded with enthusiasm. "Indeed, I am! Back

home is special in its way; we have our family traditions. We all come together to celebrate Christmas. We use the same nativity scene that has been in the family for many years, and we celebrate midnight Mass together, as you do. We cook dinner together, using the same recipes our Mother used. We decorate the tree with ornaments that belonged to her grandMother. It's all about traditions. Not as big and beautiful as yours, but though smaller, equally as special."

"We are excited to show you everything we do, Abby—our traditions. I wish it was morning!" said Greg.

Rosella told him, "It is morning! We can all have hot chocolate when we get home, hang our stockings, and then go to bed."

The family started singing Christmas carols, and Abby sat back in her seat, enjoying the camaraderie, the family's love for one another, and the lights on the decorated homes speeding by.

Colleen awoke gently to the sound of the children outside her bedroom door. It was early, not yet sunrise. A brilliant half moon shone through the drapes, throwing bright silver patterns and shadows across the bedroom walls that looked like snowflakes. Sitting up in bed, she called the children in. They tumbled through the door toward her, running and jumping, and then climbed onto the king-size bed. Aria was singing "Santa Claus Is Coming to Town." Next to her, Byron was still in a deep sleep.

Grace held little Ben's hand as he toddled after his sisters.

"Has Santa been here, Mama? Did he find us here in Virginia? What if he got lost? Can we go down and see, please?" Aria stood up on the bed, jumping up and down in excitement.

Colleen smiled, looking at the clock on the bedside table. "It's only six thirty in the morning, although I'm sure he's been and gone." She smelled the enticing aromas of cinnamon rolls and freshly brewed coffee drifting toward her up the stairs. Thank goodness her Mother was up preparing for Christmas morning.

"Come on. Let's all go down. We can leave Dad a few moments to wake slowly."

Byron turned, pulling the bedsheets over his head, groaning.

"Don't be too long, Daddy, please!" Aria said.

"No, I'm on my way," he mumbled from under the covers.

Fifteen minutes later, everyone gathered in the beach room. No crackling fire was required, as the sun was rising slowly over the horizon. Every surface was colored bright red and orange, creating a magnificent sense of warmth and welcoming on this yuletide morning. The Christmas tree stood in the corner, nine feet high and covered from top to bottom with lights and various types of ornaments: homemade, antique glass, and garlands creating an array of colors. A multitude of gifts were scattered below the tree, all wrapped in lovely gift paper—silvers, greens, reds, and golds—with bells and bows. The gifts were all different shapes and sizes and all just waiting to be given to their rightful owners. Colleen gazed about with great satisfaction.

"I'm so happy we decided to come home for Christmas, Byron," said Colleen.

"Me too. I can't imagine not being here with you and the children. I'm also looking forward to dinner with Andrew and his family today."

"I hope they have enough food for everyone." Viv spoke up.

"I was there yesterday, dropping off some casseroles for today. Heather has it all under control, Mom," Colleen said.

"I'll bet she has," Viv whispered under her breath.

Colleen wasn't sure why Heather appeared to bring out a resentful side in some women, including her and Andrew's Mothers. If she were honest, she herself had felt moments of strong resentment toward her, particularly after her chemo. Perhaps the feeling was attributable to Heather's youth, stunning beauty, overwhelming confidence, and lifetime of opportunities ahead of her. Whatever it was, Colleen intended to make the best of the day and be as nice as possible.

Andrew had told her that Heather had canceled her trip home to Aberdeen in order to stay and help him with the girls and host dinner that year. Colleen was grateful to her for that, although she suspected Heather had her own agenda, and she suspected Andrew was aware that Heather had her eye on him. *One never knows. It could do amazing things for Andrew's confidence and overall well-being to be swept off his feet by a beautiful woman.*

"What are you grinning at, Colleen? You have quite the erotic grin on your face." Byron broke into her thoughts.

"That's my secret!" She smiled at Byron. "Hands up—who wants to start opening gifts?"

At Andrew's home that Christmas Day, Andrew sat at the head of the table; it was quite a vision. The table was extended its full length, and all twelve seats were filled with his family and closest friends. The image was festive with Christmas tablecloth, napkins, and china, all matching with bright red-and-green poinsettias. Standing up, he raised his glass.

"I'd like to make a toast and thank you all for being here today to celebrate with us. This is a special day. My love and best wishes to you all. I especially would like to thank Heather, who has worked diligently and forfeited a visit home to Scotland to be with us today. Thank you. Cheers."

"Och, don't you worry; it's my pleasure. Although it's going to cost you, Andrew," Heather replied cheekily.

Smiling, he rolled his eyes as everyone raised his or her glass. "Merry Christmas to all, and blessings!"

Andrew started to carve the large turkey; it looked plump, succulent, and golden.

"The turkey looks excellent, Son." Andrew's Dad spoke up.

"It has nothing to do with me, Dad; it's all Heather's handiwork."

"Well done!" Harold replied. "My mouth is watering, anticipating the taste. You are such a good cook, Heather!"

"Thank you. It was fun preparing it for all of you."

"What did Santa bring you all?" Grandma Maude asked, and the children all answered at the same time.

"Red shoes!"
"A bride doll!"
"Coloring books!"
"A hairbrush!"
"Reading books!"

"Chocolate!"

"You're so lucky to get so much from Santa. We don't get anywhere near as many toys in Scotland," Heather said.

"Why not?" asked Grace.

Harold laughed out loud. "That's too bad, Heather. You poor thing."

"I have never had so many presents in my whole life. Do you know why?" Heather asked.

All the children stared at her, shaking their heads.

"Ochs, just look at the size of your chimney pots! Santa can get a whole lot more in this chimney than he can in my chimney back home. I'm going to make sure I spend every Christmas in Virginia!" She laughed.

Everyone laughed, and Colleen smiled. "That's a lovely story, Heather. This dinner is wonderful. Thank you so much for giving us the day off from cooking."

Heather toyed with her hair. "Something else I love in Virginia that does not happen in Scotland is that the guests do the hard work by bringing all the side dishes. And just look at the dessert table!"

"I know. I was thinking of starting my meal with the desserts," said Byron.

"When are you going back to Las Vegas, Byron?" Maude asked.

"I'll be leaving on the twenty-eighth. Colleen and the children will follow after the Christmas break."

"I'm so happy to be home in Virginia Beach for Christmastime; we all are," Colleen said.

Andrew leaned back in his chair to listen to the chatter, the tinkling of glasses, forks upon dishes, and the hum of happy activity. He heard Christmas music in the background, saw the sparkle of the Christmas tree lights, and smelled the aroma of the enticing food. The children were laughing, and the buzz of warm, comfortable conversation surrounded him. He was content; this had been his first good Christmas in a long time thanks to Heather.

Little Babs climbed up onto his knee, snuggling up to him, and whispered in his ear, "I'm sad, Daddy."

"Whatever for, little one?" Andrew looked at her with surprise.

"I miss my Mommy." She burst into tears.

Heather stood from her chair and came over to them. "Ochs, what's this all about then? I think you are tired—had a wee bit too much of a good thing today. I'll take her upstairs for a wee rest."

Fortunately, Babs took Heather's hand and followed her. Andrew wondered if he should go instead. He hesitated for a moment and then sat down.

Grace spoke up. "Is Babs okay, Uncle Andrew? Can I go play with her?"

"Thank you, Gracie. She's just tired and needs a rest. Come on, everyone. Let's tuck into this dessert table."

Later that evening, when everyone was filled with turkey, pudding, cake, wine, and candy, Byron spoke up. "I cannot tell you, Andrew, how much I appreciate this. What a marvelous and, may I add, memorable day."

"Uncle Byron, I enjoyed the magic tricks; please show me how you did them," Katie said, her eyes wide with wonder.

"No, sorry, but I cannot do that." Byron shook his head and frowned a little.

"Why?" she asked.

"I am part of what is called the magic circle. We learn

from other magicians who come together and teach one another new tricks. Part of the privilege of being in the magic circle is the vow of secrecy. That means we must know how to keep a secret."

"Oh, I see."

"Besides, if I told you how, it wouldn't be magic anymore."

"It seems to me that's a wonderful way to end the day, as it was magic." Colleen stood up. "Thank you, Andrew. Such a special Christmas, one I'll always treasure."

Andrew kissed Colleen on the forehead. He thought she looked weary. It had been a long day for everyone.

Maude and Harold joined everyone in thanking Andrew for the day. Andrew showed them all to the door, shaking hands, kissing, hugging, and waving goodbye. Coming back into the house, he saw that Heather was taking the girls up to bed.

"Let me do that, Heather. You can start clearing up, and I'll come down and help you finish."

He got the girls settled and returned to the kitchen. "They quieted down right away; they're exhausted."

Heather was almost finished clearing the dishes.

"Leave that too, Heather. I'll finish it off. I cannot thank you enough for all your assistance and everything you've done to help me this Christmas. You've gone beyond kindness."

"I loved every minute; it has been a wonderful experience for me. Thank you for these beautiful earrings." She touched her ears, showing them off.

"We thought the blue would look nice. When the girls return to school, please take your time off; my parents will come help me with them." He stepped closer and gave her an envelope.

"Thank you, Andrew. I have something for you too."

As she tossed her beautiful golden mane of hair over her shoulders, he thought she looked like a goddess.

"Look up," Heather said. They were standing together under the mistletoe. "I'm not waiting one bit longer to kiss you, Andrew; you're what I want for Christmas."

As she leaned into him, he could feel every sensational part of this glorious woman. Dormant sensations within him awakened. As he felt her sweet breath upon his face, his hands were on her head, caught in her silken hair. Andrew felt the shape of her breasts and the firmness of her nipples through his shirt as though they were skin upon skin. Every sinew within him craved her. He kissed her with urgency and passion, overflowing with sexual tension. He knew he couldn't wait much longer. Right or wrong, he was about to suggest that he would look in on the girls and then come over to see her.

"Daddy! Daddy!" He heard Katie's cry from upstairs. "I feel sick."

Andrew released Heather, and she took a step back, shaking her head. "I must go to her," he said.

"You know where I am when you want me. Thank you again for the day and the gift." She held the envelope above her head and sauntered away from him back to her lonely rooms.

Although it was only above his garage, he thought as he ran up the stairs to see to his daughter, her apartment might as well have been on the moon.

— 23 —

Abby awoke to a beautiful, bright February morning. She lay on her bed, looking out the window at the sea, which was calm and shimmering under the early morning sunshine. She couldn't see where the sky ended and the sea began; it all blended into one glorious vision. Every moment of every day, it changed, and she never tired of looking at it.

She adored living in Virginia; she couldn't imagine going home. Her emotions were as tumultuous as the sea. At times, she felt guilty because she was so happy to be away from the drudgery of Newcastle. Yet sometimes she was sad and felt homesick for her family, wishing they could share with her the amazing beauty that surrounded her. Her room had a window seat, and she had spent many hours over the past weeks sitting there, looking out and thinking about her future, mostly about Gabriel and how she would approach him.

She heard a knock on her bedroom door.

"Can I come in?" Rosella came in with a tray. "A little breakfast for you."

"You're spoiling me, and I love it! Thank you," Abby replied.

"I am hoping we can go for a walk today on the beach. I have something I'd like to talk to you about." Rosella had a smile on her face from one ear to the other.

"Okay, sounds rather interesting and mysterious."

"I'm so excited I can hardly sit still. Let's get cracking at the day. We can drop the kids off at school and then head out for a walk. I thought I'd take you to visit Chesapeake Bay. We can enter through Seashore State Park. I think you'll like it." Rosella left the room, almost skipping, clearly happy with herself.

Intrigued, Abby hopped into the shower in her bedroom's en suite bathroom. This was something else she found amazing, one of the simple things she appreciated. She didn't want to get too used to the luxury. Whenever she stepped into the shower and felt hot water on her body, she shivered with pleasure and also felt a twinge of guilt in thinking about how Cammie and Sasha would have loved the luxury of endless hot water in the seclusion and privilege of a private shower. It was bliss to have her own bedroom with a queen-size bed facing the window seats, built-in white wardrobes, and a dressing table. The room was painted muted shades of blue, and the bed covering was blue-and-white lace, with matching drapes. The room looked like a picture from a decorating magazine. Abby was thrilled that it was presently her personal oasis.

Closing her eyes, she let her thoughts drift. She had to find a way to get back to Tennessee. She realized the situation was somewhat delicate, and showing up alone there wasn't a good idea. Aidan and the family were going to visit Tennessee in May, but she would have to be back home by then. Her return ticket was for early May, ten more weeks from now. She shuddered, and this time, it was not a reaction to the pleasure of the hot water. She stepped out, dried herself, and then dressed, wearing jeans and a hand-knit Aran jumper. It had been a parting gift from her best friend, Sally.

"Wear it to keep you cozy and warm. And when you do, remember, you're taking me with you," Sally had told her. Abby missed her friend and wished with all her heart she could have brought everyone she was missing to live there in Virginia.

A bit later, Abby helped the children into the back of the station wagon, which was the size of a bus to her. Rosella needed it to carry her kids around and do the grocery shopping. Abby felt nice and warm sitting inside on the tanned leather seat. With its teak dashboard, it seemed less like a car than a posh living room back home. Americans took their extraordinary luxury for granted, like that station wagon.

As they drove to the school, the kids made all kinds of noise in the backseat.

"Abby, how did your Mom drive you to school, when there were so many kids?" Greg asked.

"Greg, you always ask the best questions," Abby replied. "No, we walked, and the big kids looked out for the little ones. We walked in all kinds of different weather, mostly rain and fog."

"Did you have to walk very far?"

"Far enough for little legs. You children are very fortunate to have a Mom who can drive you to school."

"When I get home from school today, will you show me another dance like you did last night? It was fun!"

They'd all had fun last night as she taught Greg to dance and jive in the family room. The room was reminiscent of a ballroom, with a high ceiling, polished cherrywood floors, sliding glass doors looking out onto the Atlantic Ocean, and a ceiling-to-floor stone fireplace. They didn't even have to move the burgundy leather sofas; the room was a perfect size for teaching her younger cousin how to boogie.

"I'd love to, Greg. You do some good work at school today, okay?"

Rosella stopped the car, and the children climbed out from the back, waving as they headed toward the playground in different directions.

Abby was astonished. "That school is beautiful; it looks like a hotel placed in a playground. I love all the swings and slides and bright colors. What a fantastic place."

"We were very lucky to get them into this school. It's a brand-new, state-of-the-art facility. Not just the architecture but academically also. They're all doing very well, though you can imagine we were concerned about moving them. We're grateful they have adapted to the new surroundings, and part of the reason is the excellence of the school," Rosella said with a proud smile.

"They are such great kids. You should be proud."

"I am, just as you will be one day when you have children. You're going to make a special Mom; you have a gift. Children naturally gravitate to you. They have an innate understanding that you love them."

"I'm used to spending time with children; it's part of who I am. I enjoy their free spirits and honesty."

After they dropped off the kids, Abby and Rosella drove to Seashore State Park and started out on their walk around the Chesapeake Bay.

"Oh, what a glorious day it is—so fresh and clear today." Abby put her arms out and lifted her face to the sun's warmth.

"I love that expression of yours. Fresh!" Rosella laughed out loud. She pronounced the word very deliberately, half English and half southern drawl.

Abbey giggled, linking arms with Rosella as she spoke. "This park reminds me of Bamburgh back home. The sand dunes are very similar. The water is calmer, and the color of blue is more intense. You have better shimmering reflections from the sunshine because there are fewer clouds here and more protection with the bay. However, it's missing the castle."

"That's true. Aidan showed me Bamburgh when we first visited Northumberland on our honeymoon. I remember he was so excited to show me and described it as if it were his own. I see the similarities in the beaches."

"What did you want to talk to me about, Rosella?" asked Abby, nudging her shoulder a bit.

"Listen to me. I had a phone call last night from my girlfriend Jane. You remember her?"

"Yes, she lived a few doors away from you in Tennessee. I liked her. She taught me to do some very nice crafts."

"That's her. She has two boys, remember—the same ages as ours. She told me everyone is missing us since we left, and as they won't see us until May, she has invited us to visit this month. Both her school and our school have a spring break for one week starting Friday next week. I understand it's short notice, but you and I could go with the kids. What do you think?"

"Yes, I think so." Abby stopped walking and stood still as she listened. Gentle waves swooshed relentlessly onto the cool sands as the early morning sun shone like a silver beach ball. Squawking seagulls circled above, searching and scavenging for food. A gentle rustling of the breeze whispered its way through the tall bulrushes and the long green grasses.

Her thoughts tangled about in her head. *Gabriel.* Would he be happy to see her? What would she say to him? That she still loved him? What if he left her behind again like the seaweed among the grassy sand dunes?

The feeling of her heart thumping against her ribs gave her a boost. She looked at Rosella. "It gives me a legitimate reason to visit Gabriel, and I can help with the drive and the kids. A perfect solution. It's like an unexpected gift."

Rosella nodded. "I've discussed it with Aidan, and he's happy enough. He told us to have fun. I've not yet told the kids, but we can start getting organized now. I'm so happy to be going back! I miss them all. You and Father Gabriel again—I feel quite emotional when I think about the two of you seeing each other for the first time after so many years. When we get back from the walk, you should telephone him to let him know you are coming to visit. It will help him prepare for you." Rosella seemed breathless with excitement.

Abby was silent, overwhelmed with emotion and concern.

When they arrived home, Abby went into the kitchen and made some hot tea, as she felt she could use a cup. Rosella went into the office to find the telephone number for St. Michael's presbytery.

"Abigail, you go sit in Aidan's office to make the call on your own, where you have some privacy."

"I appreciate that, Rosella. Thank you," said Abby.

Abby sat in the office chair, sipping her hot, sweet tea for several minutes, feeling as though her senses were getting prepared to run from something she was trying to avoid. Her heart raced, and her hands shook. She picked up the telephone several times, then placed it down. Abby stood up and paced around the office for a while.

It's just a phone call. But what if...

Her mind was in disarray. Abby realized she had been given the opportunity she had spent a long time praying for. Should Gabriel not wish to see her, she wouldn't be any worse off than she was now. After lifting the receiver, she dialed the number. She heard the exchange click and ring.

"Hello. St. Michael's. Father Gabriel speaking."

"Father Gabriel?"

"Speaking. Can I help you?"

"This is Abby."

There was a short pause that felt eternal.

"Abby? Abigail. Oh, mercy me!"

24

Colleen looked out the atrium windows, mesmerized by the constantly changing beauty. The Vegas-area mountains were symmetrically perfect as they stretched toward the cloudless, vibrant, bright blue sky. One might have imagined them to be gray and one-dimensional, yet they were a multitude of different colors, a fascinating mosaic of silvers, charcoal gray, and black, with splashes of bright orange red. As her eyes drifted to the top, she discovered that the snowcapped peaks were a soft pink, a reflection from the sun, even though it was 70 degrees down in the desert in the morning.

Her girls had gone to school, and Byron was still sleeping. She and Ben were having a morning playtime. Colleen wished she had his energy. She had not been feeling well lately and had noticed at Christmastime that she had less energy and more aches and pains. Not wanting to be paranoid, she'd put it down to the busy holidays. But it was now late February, and she wasn't feeling better. She decided to discuss it with her doctor tomorrow.

She focused on Ben again. He was toddling all over

and speaking with a wonderful vocabulary for his age, no doubt because of his chattering sisters. He had three Mothers, although Grace was his favorite. Ben followed her everywhere, and if he could not see her, he could sense where she was. They looked and sounded alike. Aria was more of a dreamer, singing and dancing and looking like a beautiful nymph. She was a typical middle child and entertained herself in many ways.

Grace was mature beyond her eight years. It had been a necessity to lean on her and use her skills after Ben had been born and Colleen had become ill. Grace was given a lot of responsibility in taking care of Aria, including helping her in the mornings to prepare for school and get dressed and packing lunches, and helping Grandma with Ben. Grace had witnessed and held Colleen's hand during her worst moments after chemo. Colleen felt guilty for not feeling capable of much love and attention for Grace, although it didn't appear to have caused any harm—quite the opposite.

"Peekaboo, Mama." Ben popped his head around her chair. He wanted to play and be chased around the room.

Colleen jumped up. "I'm coming to get you!"

Ben giggled with delight, standing on the spot with his baby Byron face shining back at her. His feet moved furiously for a split second, and then he shot off like a cartoon character. She loved to catch up with him, stoop, and pick him up. His baby laughter echoed around the room, unabashed with a freedom that only came with childhood. Colleen lifted him up above her head and proceeded to shower him with a thousand kisses.

She felt a wave of pressure in her chest that alarmed her. Placing him back on the floor, she was breathless. She felt dizzy, and she could hardly catch her breath. Sitting in a chair, she attempted to slow her breathing. It was not working; she was terrified as she gasped to regain her breath.

"Mama!" Ben was climbing up onto her lap.

"Sit, Ben," she gasped.

"Mama, peekaboo." His tiny hands went up to his face as he hid behind them.

"Later" was all she could say.

Gradually, her breathing came back slowly. It was labored, but she was not gasping quite as much.

Byron stepped into the atrium with his coffee.

"Hi, Daddy." Ben slipped from her lap.

Colleen felt as though she had set down a baby elephant; the relief was that noticeable.

Byron and Ben participated in their early morning ritual of Byron throwing him as high as he could toward the twelve-foot ceiling, the higher the better. Ben screeched with delight and clearly adored every precious moment, as did Byron. Their laughter blended in harmony.

Colleen's breathing had returned to slightly more normal; she was able to compose herself, thankfully. Byron put Ben down and sent him toddling off. He sat on the arm of the chair and kissed her on the lips gently. "Good news that you have the energy to chase him; maybe we can chase each other sometime soon." He wiggled his thick dark eyebrows up and down at her.

"I'd like that." She smiled.

"Let's do something spectacular today. What do you say?" Byron asked.

"What do you have in mind?"

"Let's collect the girls from school early and drive into the mountains. We can have a family day and eat a late lunch at the cabin up in the mountains. It's a perfect day for it."

"Oh yes, that sounds wonderful." Colleen coughed to camouflage her shortness of breath.

"Are you feeling well, honey?" he asked.

"Yes," she lied. "Why?"

"You look very pale. Are you tired? Have you been doing too much?"

"No, I haven't. I'm fine. It's that time of the month, and also, I've been chasing our son around."

Colleen didn't want to alarm Byron. The times they shared as a family were few and far between and too precious to allow her problems to disturb the day's plans. Plus, she would visit the doctor tomorrow.

"Honey, are you sure you're okay?"

She stood from her chair and kissed Byron on the lips. "Yes, darling. Help me with Ben, and then let's go have some family fun."

Later that afternoon, Colleen sat at a farmhouse table in the rustic log cabin restaurant. Fifteen-feet-high windows showcased the stunning view. As it was nestled high in the mountains, the temperature was noticeably cooler than in the valley below. The view was picture-perfect, as was that moment. The girls were on each side of her, and Ben was sitting in a high chair beside his proud Dad; both looked handsome. Everyone was patiently anticipating their gourmet lunch of pizza, french fries, and chocolate milk. She was grateful to have a distraction from her episode that morning; she was still feeling shaky.

"Can we walk on one of the trails after lunch and let Ben walk?" Grace asked. "I'll hold his hand."

"We should've done that before lunch, but we can take a nice, easy meander." Byron smiled as he answered.

Later, after everyone was fed and satisfied, the family went out onto the large patio deck, which had a panoramic view.

"We should find someone to snap a family photo for us." Byron pulled his camera from a backpack. "This is one spectacular day. Look at the brilliant, cloudless blue skies streaked with vapor trails. And the snow-covered mountains stretching endlessly toward the horizon. Come on, guys. Let's get this photo set up."

Colleen moved toward Byron, as he had requested. She felt the air was noticeably different outside than inside the restaurant, considerably cooler and thinner. Gasping several times and turning away, she began to cough uncontrollably, panicking as she heaved great spasmic breaths. *No breath. Dear God.* She couldn't breathe. She mindlessly looked for Byron, struggling to take in breath. The last thing she heard was Aria's scream: "Mama!"

Falling to the floor, Colleen passed out.

Later that night, at the Hospital of the Sacred Heart, Byron sat in a chair beside his wife's bed. Colleen was sleeping, as doctors had given her oxygen to help her breathe and sedated her to help calm her. He listened to the hospital sounds surrounding him, including the PA endlessly calling out for a doctor or to announce a code blue or a code red signaling troubles for some poor soul. He inhaled the aromas of antiseptic mingled with the smells of old food—fish and cabbage—which were faint yet unbelievably repugnant.

All he could feel was a fear far beyond his ability to detach—the fear of fear itself, a feeling he was all too familiar with. Once again, his soul mate lay in a hospital bed, looking for all the world to him like one of his daughters sleeping peacefully.

He still wasn't sure what had happened that day; his mind was reeling from the shock. Some of her tests weren't complete, but the doctor had mentioned pneumonia and an undetermined shadow on the bottom of her left lung. The doctor's monotone comments had sent shivers through Byron's entire body, leaving him feeling internally paralyzed. He paced around the room, feeling agitated and helpless. His gaze found the phone.

Andrew! He would call Andrew. He grabbed the phone and dialed Andrew's number. As he did, he realized it was midnight in Virginia, but he knew Andrew would answer.

"Dr. Mason speaking."

"Andrew, I'm sorry to disturb you—"

"Byron? Is something wrong?"

"Yes! Yes, it's Colleen. She collapsed today and was rushed to the hospital—suspected pneumonia. Plus, they found a shadow on the bottom of her left lung."

"Byron, I'm shocked and saddened to hear this. As soon as she's stable, bring her home. I'll call Dr. Burke first thing. Where are the kids? Do you want help? I can send Heather out."

"I haven't seen them; I sent them home in a taxi and called someone from work to stay with them. Viv is on her way, thank God. Andrew, I'm—" Byron's throat closed down. "I'm terrified."

"My friend, bring her and your children home as soon as possible. Let me know if there is anything you need."

"Thank you, Andrew. I'll do that just as soon as it can be arranged."

When he realized he was going to take Colleen home, he wept softly as he thought how to get to Andrew and Dr. Burke. His sense of relief was overwhelming. If anyone could help Colleen, it was her Virginia doctors.

— 25 —

The Kennedys and Abby arrived in Tennessee in the early afternoon of their second day of driving. Abby heaved a huge sigh, overwhelmed with emotion, as they drove past some of the familiar homes and sights. It was surprising how the memories came flooding back. She remembered her walks through that beautiful area so long ago. They passed incredible custom-built homes far beyond her English imagination, including a home with two marble lions on either side of the huge front door and a wrought-iron gate surrounding the property. Smiling to herself, she remembered how she'd believed life there was like a dream. Imagining people living and working in such a luxurious setting—she still couldn't.

Abby had a quick flashback of cleaning some of the disgusting houses with Cammie several months ago, but she pushed the unpleasant thought away. Her senses were alive as they passed homes, white fences, and chestnut thoroughbred horses grazing on the short brownish-green grass of winter as the pale February sunshine warmed them. She was fascinated by the variety of magnificent ancient trees. Many of their branches entwined together, creating a feeling of dusk, although it was midday. They reminded her of the long Gothic aisle in Durham Cathedral, re-creating the serenity of the great sacred sanctuary in Durham, England, there in Tennessee. Abby shivered.

Rosella finally stopped the car on the circular tree-lined driveway outside Jane's home; it had been an eleven-hour drive. However, with the kids in the back of the car, it had taken serval more hours. They had stopped last night to break up the journey and give them all some downtime. The hotel had had an indoor swimming pool—what a godsend.

"Finally, here we are! How are you feeling?" asked Rosella.

"Greatly relieved, thankful, and nervous," replied Abby.

Rosella was about to speak, when suddenly, the front door opened, and Jane came out with her boys running behind her toward the car. "Hi, y'all! Welcome to Tennessee!"

The Kennedy kids clambered out from the backseat one by one, stretching, smiling, and jumping up and down. Awkwardly, the five children mingled about until Jane gave them permission to take off.

"Go run and play, you guys. Have fun. I'll call you in for snacks when your Mom and I are organized."

They all took off running as fast as they could for fear of being fastened down somewhere again for another six hours.

Abby followed Rosella and Jane into the house. She had fond memories of visiting Jane's house when she'd stayed there. The ranch-style home with twenty-foot-high vaulted ceilings created a feeling of space and grandeur. The flooring was ceramic, rust-and-gold tiling that gave the entrance and entire home a warm, welcoming feeling.

Amazing Grace

Abby followed Jane past several doors as the ceramic gave way to thick, warm golden carpet. With her feet sinking into the warm, lush pile, she noticed several fireplaces, each one with a warm, welcoming fire burning. She could smell a hint of pine in the air. Eventually, Jane opened a door and placed Abby's suitcase on the floor beside a large bed. Abby watched Jane in admiration: she was tall and elegant, wearing jeans and an exquisite white cashmere sweater, with a warm, hospitable southern drawl Abby loved.

"I hope you'll be comfortable in here," Jane said. "It's private and has an en suite with a separate entrance from the outside. I'll give you a key. Rosella told me you have a friend here you're hoping to spend some time with. Does he know when you arrive?"

"Yes. Well, I told him I'd call him. I don't expect to connect with him for a couple of days," Abby replied.

"Well then, make yourself at home, as Rosella and I'll be out with the kids most of the time. I've organized several different outings. We're so excited to see everyone."

"I can't thank you enough for your hospitality, Jane. This is wonderful. It's so beautiful here; you have an amazing home."

"You're very welcome. I'd like to thank you for sharing the drive with my dear friend, as we wouldn't have been able to get together if you hadn't helped. Enjoy your time here with us. Dinner is at six every night, or we may go out to eat. Please join us if you wish. I'll leave you to unpack and settle in. There is coffee and cake ready in the kitchen."

"Thank you."

Jane left, and at last, Abby was alone with her thoughts. After looking at her luxurious surroundings, she sat on the bed, gazing out a wall of windows facing the east. Numerous trees were scattered across the manicured winter grass, mostly beautiful ones that looked like weeping willows dressed for a ball. At the edge of the grass, a brook twinkled in the sunshine, meandering its way to an unknown river. Abby closed her eyes, offering a prayer of gratitude.

After finding the bathroom, she splashed her face with cold water, changed her sweater, brushed her hair, and applied some lipstick. Feeling a little more revived, she went about unpacking, hearing muffled sounds behind her bedroom door. The kids had come in from outside for snacks, and she could hear lots of different comments, as well as elephant-like footsteps running in and out. A doorbell chime rang; she heard more muffled sounds; and then, suddenly, a knock sounded on her door.

"Come in," said Abby.

One of Jane's boys pushed open the door. Being a little shy, he stayed outside the entrance. "There is someone at the door for you," he told her in his quaint southern drawl.

"For me? Are you quite sure?"

"Yes. Should I ask him to come in?"

"No, thank you. I'll come see to it."

He ran off, and Abby made her way to the grand entrance, perplexed. Opening the front door, for a fraction of a second forgetting where she was, she was astonished. Standing in front of her was Gabriel. His tight golden curls framed his freckled face and his dancing eyes with the amber light. He smiled, flashing his white teeth. He was dressed in blue jeans and a dark green sweater. He had not changed; his persona still could affect her.

As she continued to stare at him, there was a

difference—not tangible, but she understood and felt it. The boy priest she'd met so long ago was gone, replaced by a confident, handsome man.

"Gabriel, what are you doing here? I can't believe my eyes. Good Lord!" Abby threw her arms about him. She could not contain the euphoria she felt. "Come in, please." Her hands shook as she took his and walked him into the entrance.

"Well, hi to you, Abby, and welcome back. How are you?"

"I am fine. In awe and shocked." Abby heard Rosella come up behind her.

"Who is at the door? Father Gabriel, what a wonderful surprise!" Rosella opened her arms, embracing him like the old friend he was. "What are you doing here, Father?"

"I knew you arrived today sometime. Remembering your old address, I decided to come look for you. I knocked on several neighbors' doors until I found y'all!"

"This is wonderful! Abby, look! Please come in, Father." Rosella excitedly beckoned Gabriel farther into the house.

"Thank you. Just for a moment. I came to invite Abigail out for a cup of coffee with me, if that's all right."

"Yes, of course," Rosella replied, somewhat flustered. "Abigail?"

"Thanks, yes. I'd like that. Give me a moment to collect my handbag and coat," she replied before flying to her room as though she had wings on her heels.

Whatever possessed him to show up like this out of the blue? Abby wondered. When she'd called him last week, they had arranged she would phone him when she was settled. They had agreed to meet after Mass. That had been his suggestion. *I guess he couldn't wait.*

She ran back to the front door, where Rosella was waiting with a smile.

"Have you got everything you need? Good. Go have fun." Rosella gently pushed them out the door and waved goodbye.

A mystical stillness surrounded them; the air was cool, but the afternoon sun was warm upon her face. Aware of every sense within her, she could hear the children laughing as they ran and played in the backyard, cars passing on the road, the dog next door barking, and several cardinals singing their boastful tune high above them among the pine trees. The years of yearning, longing, praying, and moving heaven and earth to make her wish come true had come together into this one magical moment. As they stood inches apart, feeling the warmth of his breath and sensing the aroma of mint, she asked, "How are you?"

"I am amazing. Welcome to Tennessee. Mercy me, I can't believe you are here. I can't. Should I rub my eyes? Oh, come here to me," he said in his warm southern drawl, which never failed to touch her. Reaching out and drawing her toward him, he embraced her with a feeling that belonged only to him. Cocooning her and rocking them gently, he held her so close it was as though he were attempting to imprint the moment inside the layers of his soul. Finally releasing her, he smiled softly.

Abby smiled back, feeling tears of joy well in her eyes.

Gabriel said, "Come. Let's go. I want to be with you. I've missed you so!"

As they climbed into his car and drove away, once more, Abby was moved by Gabriel's ability to communicate with her beyond words. She had just experienced the most powerful expression of love she had felt since they last had embraced on the steps of the altar before parting many years ago. Nothing and no one had touched her in the same way, and no one ever could.

Gabriel drove them into the little town of Sweet Hope Lake and parked in the village square. "I've been thinking about where I'd like to take you. This is one of my little respite spots—a great place for a good cup of coffee and a fresh bagel, with several quiet little corners for me to hide in."

"Father, hello!" In the shop, a short, plump middle-aged lady greeted them.

"Hello, Doris. How are you? This is my friend Abby Lavalle, all the way from England. I've been singing your praises. Would you have a quiet table for two?"

"For you, Father, always. Follow me."

Abby followed Doris past shiny pinewood tables and benches. Frilled red-and-white gingham curtains adorned the windows, with place mats on the tables to match. Southern memorabilia were distributed around the walls: old photos, plates, and antique kitchen utensils. Doris sat them in a corner behind an alcove.

"Would you like the usual, Father?" she asked. "Coffee and a bagel?"

"Yes, please. Okay, Abby?"

"Yes, thank you."

After Doris left, Gabriel stared at Abby. "Look at you. Look at us! I'm still trying to process you coming back. I always believed you would. When I returned to St. Mike's last year after my time away, to hear the Kennedys had moved to Virginia, I was saddened. I thought we might not see one another again."

Abby looked at his face, taking in every individual freckle

and the golden flecks in his amber eyes. Doris returned with a thermos of coffee and two bagels. She hesitated before she came in, but Gabriel beckoned to her.

"Abby, you're going to love these. Doris, how is your family?"

"Fine, Father. Thanks for asking. Enjoy!" Doris smiled at them and left.

Gabriel poured out the coffee as Abby buttered the bagels.

"I'd always intended to come back, but it was different for me," Abby said. "Once my brothers were older and could take care of themselves, it allowed me the freedom to start to make plans. It took me a long time. But here I am, miraculously drinking coffee with you in Sweet Hope Lake Café. You should have more faith!"

"It's good to see you. I'd love to sit in this corner with you until we have filled each other with words and stories of joy, sorrow, life, love, and every exquisite moment you're willing to share with me!" Gabriel laughed out loud.

"How long do you have?"

"Not enough time. I have an appointment later, but I'll be finished by seven. I'd love to take you out for dinner tonight if you're not too tired."

"No, I can sleep next week! Now is our time to be here together. You're the only reason for my visit to Tennessee."

"I am pleased. I know a little Italian bistro not too far out of town." He smiled with a satisfied expression.

They sat talking for the next half hour, enjoying each other's company. "We must get going," he said finally, looking at his watch and placing a five-dollar bill on the table. Gabriel pulled out her chair.

Abby felt the moment was surreal. Had time stood still, waiting, hopeful, and patient, until they found each other again?

"Goodbye, Father Gabriel!" Doris called out, and Gabriel waved.

Driving back to Jane's house, they chatted about their siblings, his parents, and the farm. As far as Abby was concerned, he could have talked about watching wet paint dry, and she'd have joyfully listened to every word.

"Here we are. Thank you for the surprise visit, the coffee, and the lovely bagels; I loved it. I'll see you in a bit," Abby said as she got out of his car.

"I love your unexpected English phrases—see you in a bit. I can't wait." His spontaneous laughter rang out. As he drove away, Gabriel raised his hand, making the sign of the cross, blessing her.

A few days later, Abby was in her room, taking special care with how she looked. She had been in Tennessee for six days and had spent almost every moment she could with Gabriel. That night, he was taking her to Nashville to meet some of his friends and to see the town. She heard a knock on the door.

"Come in," Abby said, and Rosella entered.

"Can I sit with you before you go out?"

"Come sit and talk." Abby patted the top of her bed.

"Abby, you look stunning. Where are you going tonight?" Rosella smiled at her.

"Nashville to meet some of Gabriel's friends and then see the town. Rosella, in all the world, I never imagined feeling so fulfilled, happy, and free. This is so perfect! Gabriel and I are so connected we can read each other's thoughts. He's everything I love in a man."

"Abby, he is a wonderful man," Rosella said. "I can see how you two are well suited; it's obvious to anyone who looks. Jane has made comments, and even the children said, 'Father Gabriel could be Abby's boyfriend.' It saddens me to be the one to state the obvious. You're so smitten you've lost sight of the reality of this situation. We leave for Virginia in the morning, and you go back to England within weeks!"

"Please, please don't remind me."

"Abby, has Gabriel spoken of commitment? Of a future with you or leaving the church? Marriage?" asked Rosella.

"No, not yet!" Abby felt her euphoria being snuffed out like damp fingers on a lit candle.

"Abby, this is an impossible situation for him. If he hasn't mentioned anything, this is the time for you to at least discuss it. Believe me, assumptions and indecision are dangerous, especially for Gabriel. You can make your life and start afresh anywhere. Gabriel's vocation is his life, the pillar of his soul, his very essence. His church, his parishioners, and even his family's pride—all woven and fused together, creating Father Gabriel and his vocation."

"I know that. But what am I supposed to do about it, Rosella?" Abby dropped her head, holding back her tears.

"Simply ask him. Has he made any romantic overtures toward you?"

"No, not at all." Abby felt embarrassed at the question. *Unfortunately*, she thought.

"For your own peace of mind, please don't go back to England with an unknown conclusion. Not this time. If Gabriel loves you enough, in time, he will find the courage to leave and make a life with you. If he loves his vocation more, then he must give you up. It makes me sad to have this conversation with you."

"No, please don't fret. Believe me, I've had this discussion with myself every moment I'm with him and without him. I don't want to be the one to make him choose; it's not my decision to make."

"But he won't, not if he can avoid it." Rosella stood up and hugged Abby. "Good luck. I pray for you both."

Later that evening, Abby and Gabriel stood together on the footbridge, looking out on the lights of the city of Nashville reflected in the Cumberland River. He thought the night sky looked like dark purple velvet scattered with stars. A quarter moon hung above, with its gentle, muted silver tones rippling in the water. Both were immersed in their own thoughts. Abby stood in front of Gabriel with him behind, protecting her.

"I love to look at a city from the bridges and the rivers; it gives one a different perspective." She didn't turn when she spoke.

"In what way?" Gabriel asked.

"A peace you won't find inside the city and also a clearer reflection of the lights from the buildings on the water. It's a more romantic—a softer and gentler impression."

"You're right."

Gabriel smelled the scent from her hair and felt the warmth of her body radiating toward him. The tenderness of her heart and the sadness within her touched his soul. She was made for him, and he for her. They blended in harmony like the warm tones of the earth. As they looked at the mystical moon, Gabriel realized that whenever he was in her presence and listened to her voice or even her silence, his torment disappeared. Abby had always had that ability.

That night, he was filled with despair. It was their last night together. They had spent a week of feeling new emotions he hadn't realized existed. They'd been immersed in many precious moments—the simple pleasure of eating dinner and sharing dessert, walking in the woods, and his giving her communion. Ordinary events became extraordinary memories because he was with her.

Tomorrow she would leave him. He'd been unable to bear thinking on it until now. This was the most privacy they had managed all week. He deliberately had contrived a lack of privacy, as he was terrified of the consequences that could affect his eternal soul and Abby's if he were left alone with her.

"Gabriel, what are we going to do?" Abby broke the silence. Still, she didn't turn around; the question hung in the air between them like the muted tones of the winter moon hovering above the Cumberland River. Gabriel, realizing the question was inevitable, answered honestly.

"I don't know," he said, sliding his arms about her waist and nuzzling his face into her warm, soft neck. He spoke softly. "Is it better to have loved, discovering simple sharing with another human being, certain of their comfort and trust? I didn't realize what I was missing. And once more, you have presented me with an unexpected benediction and also a torment. Do I lose you, having tasted life with this mystery I feel whenever I am with you? Or would it have been better never to have met you and not to have experienced such tangible memories and blissful moments?"

Abby turned to look at him, and her sad dark eyes penetrated every fiber within him. "I know of nothing that compares to my feelings for you," she whispered. "I can't fight my true thoughts or feelings any longer for fear of scaring you off. You need to hear me."

"I do hear you, and I see you—every beautiful part of you. Don't you understand?"

"I think it's easier for you to hide from your feelings rather than face the fact that we're in love. I believe that from the very moment I was conceived, I've been making my way toward you, Gabriel, like the gravitational pull of the earth. I long to hold and feel you where angels fear to tread. To have your breath upon my breasts and your lips touching me a thousand kisses deep, as the poets proclaim normal lovers do."

Gabriel pulled back from her, shaking his head. "I cannot give you what you want. Yet I don't want to give you up."

"Are we not mature enough to make a decision? I have. I did when I met you so long ago. I want to live with you—to laugh, cry, dance, fight, and grow with you. I want to feel our freckle-faced babies growing inside me and end my days with you!" She buried her head in Gabriel's shoulder and wept profoundly. The scene was reminiscent of when they last had parted.

"I cannot make this decision, Abby," he said. "Cannot

when it means betraying my life's love for the love of my life. Don't you see? Please don't ask me for a decision, not now. I love you, and you love me—that is all. It's all I can give you."

Tilting her chin toward him and looking into her melancholy eyes and tearstained face, he placed his lips upon hers, yielding to the growing powerless physical need within him, never wanting to stop and never wanting to start. With her body becoming one with his as he blindly trod into unbelievable territory that terrified him, he opened his heart and soul to her. Yet still, he was unable to choose.

— 26 —

Grace awoke to the sound of strange voices. She lay beside her Mom, sleeping with her head resting on her hands. As she slowly sat up, she remembered where she was—the hospital—and looking at her Mother, she remembered more.

A nurse came into the room. "Hello there. It's time for me to look after your Mom. Why don't you go for a walk and find a nice drink of milk? You've been here a long time; you must be tired and thirsty. Don't you worry. I'll take special care of her until you come back. Off you go."

Grace did as she was told; she would like some fresh air, she thought. She felt as if she'd been in a bad dream since her Mom collapsed. Frozen to the spot, she'd held on to Ben and Aria tightly while her Mom lay there looking still and quiet. A kind lady had taken them to the restaurant and sat them down, giving them each a drink. Her Daddy had stayed with her Mom; he had looked as white as Colleen. She had felt like crying as she looked at them. The same kind lady had told them her Daddy was going to stay at the hospital to look after her Mom, so Grace should take a taxi home. He would call her Grandma to come to the house, and Grace was to look after things until help arrived.

"Will Mommy come home with us?" Aria had asked, looking up at Grace.

"No, I don't think so," Grace had told her.

"Grace, is she sick? Will it be like the last time, when she threw up all day? I remember she cried and cried when all her beautiful long hair fell out and stuck to her pillow. That made me cry too."

Now Grace's gentle tears fell. She'd been sitting with her Mom for a long time. Somehow, she did not want to leave her alone—not only because she didn't want her Mom to be lonely but also because she had the worst feeling inside that if she left, her Mom might not get better, wake up, or even come home. Looking up through the atrium's ceiling, she saw the bright blue sky and fluffy white clouds of many different shapes. She decided to go to the café to get herself a drink, when she heard her name being called.

"Grace! Grace!"

Turning around, she saw Uncle Andrew. At the sight of him, she ran toward him and, surprising herself, broke into a flood of heart-wrenching tears. He scooped her up and held on to her.

"Grace, what are you doing here alone, you poor thing? Now, please don't cry. Sit down." Uncle Andrew guided her to a bench near a fountain. He gave her his handkerchief, and Grace poured her heart out as he held on to her hands, listening to her cares, woes, and worries.

"I'm sitting with Mommy, helping Dad and Grandma. I'm so scared. My Mom sounds like she can't breathe. I think if I leave her alone, she won't get better, Uncle Andrew. And

Aria is scared too; she keeps asking me when Mom is coming home. Ben cries a lot too. Daddy looks very sad all the time. Grandma's eyes are very red. It's awful with Mom in the hospital. It's better now that we are home in Virginia with you and Dr. Burke, but I miss her, and I want her to come home. We all do."

"Gracie, bless you," Uncle Andrew said softly. He put one arm around her shoulders and gave her a hug. "Try to understand that anyone would feel the way you do, big or small. Now, you must listen to me. Your Mom is sick; she has an infection in her lungs called pneumonia. She's in the best place; Dr. Burke, the nurses, and I will help make her well. You don't ever need to worry about not being with her. Do you understand?"

Grace nodded.

"You should go home soon," he said.

"Grandma is coming to pick me up; Daddy will sit with Mom tonight. I'll go home and help Grandma look after Ben. He misses Mom and cries, but he behaves for me."

"Gracie, honey, please don't take so much into your little heart. I can't bear it. Your Mom is going to be fine. Come on. We can go visit her together."

"Thank you, Uncle Andrew. I feel much happier now that we have talked. Well, not happy exactly, just not quite as sad. And scared."

Colleen slowly opened her eyes; she could feel loving hands encircling her own. She understood without looking that it was her Mother. She recognized her Mother's desire to hold her close and attempt to carry the pain, struggle, and sadness of her daughter. Colleen visualized herself at the end of the bed with one of her own three children. The ache in her heart was so great and unbearable that she broke down.

"Mom!" Colleen cried out. Her Mom jumped up from her seat, clearly startled.

"Darling! What on earth? You're awake. Are you in pain? I'll call for help."

"No, Mom, sit with me, please," Colleen said in between sobs.

Viv obeyed, sitting as close to her only child as the hospital bed, monitors, and IVs would allow. "My darling, what is making you so sad? Please tell me," she said soothingly while stroking away the wispy new tendrils of curls falling over Colleen's eyes.

"It's selfish of me, Mom; I put myself in your place. Life is a never-ending circle. I am your child; I have my children. God willing, one day they will each have children of their own. The circle of love continues; everything else may change over time, but the love of a Mother is as perennial as the grass. It's a great comfort to me." Colleen calmed down enough to explain how the overwhelming love of her Mother radiated toward her.

"Darling, please don't talk so much. I'm so grateful to see you awake and talking."

"I'm feeling stronger, Mom—a little better."

Her Mom helped Colleen sit up, held a glass of juice for her to quench her thirst, and then fussed around her, plumping her pillow, and straightening the blankets. "What else can I get you?" Viv asked.

Amazing Grace

"Mom, please, I want to talk to you."

"You've been extremely sick, my darling. Dr. Burke diagnosed pneumonia. The good news is, you're responding to treatment. He's a wonder, and Andrew is watching over you like a guardian angel."

"How long have I been here in Virginia?" Colleen asked.

"Oh, several days."

Sensing her Mother did not want to discuss that, she decided to change the subject. "How are the children?"

"Darling, you are the Mother of three of the most amazing little people. What a treasure that Grace is. She is nine going on twenty-five, with a wisdom way beyond her years. To watch her with Benedict is like watching a beautiful sunrise."

Colleen smiled. "And Aria?"

"That child is a cheerful celestial cherub, singing and dancing her way through the days, cheering everyone on her way. She's a beacon of light. Byron has divided his time between you and the children, but this has been hard on him, Colleen."

"I'm aware of that. I have felt his loving magic beside me moment to moment, even in my dreams."

"He'll be overjoyed to see you are sitting up, talking, smiling, and kissing when he visits later."

"I'm so grateful to you for being the Mother I strived to be for my children."

"Oh, fiddle-faddle!" her Mom said.

"Mom, it's important! Do hear me out." Colleen took another drink and continued. "I've been blessed with a wonderful life—loving parents, a perfect husband, a marriage only fairy tales are made of, and three of the most outstanding children any Mother could ask for. Many people in this world don't experience a fraction of the happiness I've been blessed with. More than most, I've known what it is to love and be loved. As I think about my mortality, love is the only thing that matters."

Her Mom sat back a bit and frowned. "Colleen, I don't like the way this conversation is going. You must rest and understand that you are needed in more ways than you can know. I'm with your loved ones, watching them being as brave as they can while pining away for you all the while. Please, my darling, focus on getting well and coming home."

Smiling, Colleen gently lifted their clasped hands to her lips and kissed them as warm tears fell upon their entwined fingers. "I'm sleepy now, Mom."

"You rest easy, my darling. I'll see you tomorrow." Her Mom kissed her forehead with a tenderness only a Mother could give.

"Mom, kiss the children for me just like that when you see them." Colleen's tears slid down her face onto her hospital gown.

Her Mother wiped her tears away. "Of course, darling, just like that."

After her Mother left, Colleen fell into a dreamy haze. She was as warm, safe, and content as if she, Byron, and the children had been together in the beach room. She imagined Benedict sitting on her knee, with Byron beside her and the girls at their feet. They together watched the sunset; the sky was vivid with colors one could not have imagined. The brilliant orange ball slowly slipped away from the day, beyond the clouds, gone forever, never to be repeated in just the same way. Pale shades of pewter and lavender blended, leaving streaks across the sky like the fingers of God. Blue tones, powerful reds, and vivid pinks spread out like a biblical vale, slowly and gently fading into the night, as a brilliant moon appeared from nowhere, spilling its liquid-diamond beams upon the gentle waves. The reflection of the stars in their multitudes created a clear silver path across the ocean toward uncharted horizons.

"There she goes."

Colleen heard voices in the distance.

"Look. She's disappearing. Disappeared."

Into the horizon, Colleen heard more voices—different voices. She thought she recognized the voices of her Father, grandMothers, and grandFathers.

"Here she comes!" the voices cried. "Here she comes!"

Colleen thought, *This must be the way to heaven.* She stopped and turned to look back at Byron and her children, feeling an urge to run back, hold them tightly, and never let go. Yet here and now, she felt embraced by peace and a feeling of freedom and well-being, with no pain or difficulty breathing.

The pull of the eternal moonlight wouldn't release her. She continued to walk backward, looking at Byron and the children, who grew smaller and smaller until she could see them no more. She turned toward the bright light of the silver moon.

Colleen took her last breath as she peacefully slipped away.

Driving back to the hospital, Byron felt relief for the first time since Colleen had collapsed ten days ago. Viv had called him a little while ago with the great news that Colleen was recovering. Her sitting up was a good sign, one they had been waiting for. As he parked the car, he decided to pick up some red roses, her favorite. He knew she would enjoy them, as she was feeling better. When he arrived on her floor, he saw Dr. Burke and Andrew standing together at the nurses' station in conversation.

"Hi, Doctors. Viv tells me there is positive improvement today with Colleen. I cannot tell you how relieved we all are," Byron said as he approached them.

"Byron, please step into the office for a moment," Dr. Burke said as Andrew stood still and quiet. "You come along too, Andrew."

Andrew followed with his head lowered.

"Yes, of course. Is everything all right, Doctor?" Byron asked as he and Andrew followed Dr. Burke into his office.

"Come in, and have a seat," the doctor said as he closed the door.

"No, thanks. I'll stand. I have these flowers aching to be delivered to my beautiful wife; I want to see her."

"Byron, please sit down," Dr. Burke said. The tone of his voice sent chills running through Byron, and he placed the roses on the desk and sat next to Andrew.

"Byron, I'm afraid Colleen passed away about ten minutes before you arrived. I'm very sorry." Dr. Burke's voice was compassionate and concise.

Byron looked at Dr. Burke, shaking his head frantically. "What are you saying? That's ridiculous; I've got roses for her.

Amazing Grace

She is sitting up in bed, waiting for me. Her Mother spent the afternoon talking with her."

"I understand this is difficult to accept; it often occurs in patients with pneumonia. They appear to rally and look like they are recovering long enough to give hope, and then they slip away peacefully. Colleen just couldn't fight the infection; her immune system was too weak."

Byron shook his head. "Don't be ridiculous. When can I see her? She is expecting me." He could see Andrew and hear Dr. Burke, yet he was not part of this catastrophic story. This story belonged to someone else. "No, no, you must be mistaken!" He fell to his knees on the carpeted floor with his head in his hands, rocking back and forth.

"Byron, I realize this is a shock for you—devastating and unexpected news." Dr. Burke tried to console him. "The original breast cancer surgery was radical, as we discussed at the time—the worst kind to contain, even though we took both breasts and all the lymph nodes."

"No, she's recovering." Byron continued to weep as he spoke. "We were doing fine in Las Vegas. She was getting stronger every day. She was happy."

"Byron, all our recent tests confirm that Colleen had a mass on the bottom of the left lung—malignant. I was going to discuss this with you today. This would have been a struggle for her and you. Although this is no consolation, the pneumonia taking her unexpectedly, peacefully, and without pain is better for her. Why don't you go sit with her now?"

"Byron, would you like me to come with you?" Andrew sobbed out the words.

"How do I tell her Mother and our children? They were

all dancing a jig tonight, expecting her to recover and come home."

Byron was met with stone-cold silence. Returning to the desk, Byron plucked one red rose from the bouquet. He walked away, clasping the perfect red petals, crushing them against his shattered heart as they fell upon the floor.

— 27 —

Beautiful children, sad hearts—that is true.
Mama—she loves you, and your Daddy does too.
I am sleeping with angels, dancing on stars, and showering you with love and kisses from Mars.
You are my grace, my blessing, and the song in my heart.
Nothing will ever keep us apart.
Embrace each moment, sweet children of mine, for I will not leave you through life or hard time.
Stay gracious, strong, humble, and kind.
Always remember Mama lives on in your mind.

Several weeks had passed since Colleen's funeral in Virginia Beach.

Andrew was devastated for Byron and the children. He

and his girls spent as much time as possible with the family. They were all broken, particularly Byron. Viv was in silent agony as she witnessed the sorrow in Grace, who went to Benedict night and day when he cried for his mama. Grace was also in pain and sorrow. Aria fell silent, with no songs and no words, only the sound of sobbing. No one could help her as she stood by the front door night after night, waiting for her mama to return. They witnessed her disbelief every time her Mom did not walk through the door. Someone slept with her every night to calm her; it was impossible to help her understand her mama was not coming back.

"Not even for my birthday, Uncle Andrew?" she asked mournfully like a baby whale looking for its Mother.

The sounds coming from her he had never heard before. He felt as if his heart were being strangled with barbed wire. "No, Aria, not even then."

One evening, Byron and Andrew sat in the beach room. Andrew visited whenever possible. Each had a glass of wine as they sat in the comfortable armchairs. A torrential storm was passing over the area, and sheet lightning lit up the room as though strobe lights were flashing. The rain lashed upon the windows, so heavy it looked like a deluge of tears from the heavens. The mammoth ocean waves heaved relentlessly as the powerful winds brought them crashing onto the shore. Thunderclaps rattled across the mud-colored sky; it all seemed appropriate to Andrew, matching the heavy sorrow between them. Byron had informed him he was leaving and going back to work.

"You shouldn't do that; you are needed here," Andrew told him.

"Life goes on," Byron said with a shrug. "They'll only

allow me so long to grieve. It's been torturous. You can't understand. Since Colleen's death and her funeral, I live my life in a complete haze absent of sorrow, fear, and pain, numb. I am reminded of her with every step in this house. My life is an abyss. I am completely incapable of reaching out to our children." Byron bent and put his face in his heads, his shoulders heaving.

Andrew let him weep.

After some moments, Byron looked up at Andrew. Andrew didn't recognize his vital, handsome, gifted friend of so many years. These past weeks had taken so much from him. His powerful, dark, mystical presence had vanished, evaporated, replaced by an older version of himself. His head of magnificent hair was dull and matted; he was bent over, looking as though he had lost many inches from his tall, elegant frame. His face was agonizing, crippled with a pain impossible to describe. His eyes, once stunning and filled with the magic of expectation, had sunk back into sockets of dark gray, surrounded by heavy black bags. Byron was worn out, with a look of catastrophic despair.

Andrew waited, listening and staying as calm as possible.

"Maybe you can help them, Andrew. After all, you are the family doctor." Byron laughed almost hysterically. "I'm leaving Virginia for Las Vegas, running to forget, to hide, to find a way to learn to live without my Colleen." He sounded like a trapped animal howling out his words with no tears to ease the anguish.

"How do you think Viv and the children will manage without you?" Andrew leaned forward and put down his drink. "Rethink this, Byron. It's imperative you stay with them and grieve together. You're angry, shocked, and scared. Give yourself some time. You will start to feel again."

"I can't. I don't want to feel! It's better this way. If you call me a friend, then for God's sake, help me. I beg you—don't ask me again. Why can't you think of something?"

"I've been racking my brain for ideas. You could look for some help—a nanny or a housekeeper. You'll need it. Viv can't cope alone. I hired Heather using an agency. She gives me peace of mind. It would help you all in the initial few months. The other suggestion is to ask Father Tom to announce on Sunday at each mass that you're in urgent need of a capable nanny and housekeeper. Through the church, we might find someone efficient and appropriate within the community."

"Will you help me with this?" Byron fell to his knees and covered his head with his arms, rocking himself back and forth.

"I'll do anything I can to help you, of course."

"All right then, as soon as we find someone, I'm returning to Vegas. I must support my children. The owners of the club are getting restless, dead wife or not. I've been away long enough. Otherwise, I'll be replaced; the show must go on."

Suddenly, standing up and looking about, Byron randomly picked up figurines he had given to Colleen over the years.

"You see memories of Colleen everywhere." Andrew remembered all the special occasions.

Byron placed the precious memories back. He then picked up a crystal vase and hurled it with as much ferocity as he could, shattering it against the wall. It fractured into tiny fragments upon the floor.

Amazing Grace

"Look!" Byron cried out. "You see? This is exactly how I feel—utterly broken. So badly I'll never be the same."

Andrew stood alongside his friend, feeling helpless, as he knew Byron was right.

— 28 —

Abby and Rosella sat together in the kitchen window seat, looking out to sea on that extraordinary spring morning. The aroma of freshly baked bread wafted from the oven. After four months in Virginia Beach, Abby felt she belonged there. The early morning sun shone through the bay window, warming her completely from the inside out. The vast blue sky was scattered with white powder-puff clouds, almost a reflection of the blue sea with numerous white horses skipping on the waves.

"I can't imagine not sitting with you in this peaceful place," Abby said. The aroma of coffee wafted around the kitchen, warm and cozy. "But the reality is that I leave in three weeks. I can't bear to think on it. Unless I find work that can support me here, my visa and health insurance all expire. Gabriel appears to be as far away from deciding as he was six years ago. I believe he's praying I go home—the distance between us helps him with his confusion and guilt. The closer I am to him, the more I wish to stay until he decides. It's an agonizing, impossible decision; here or there really makes no difference."

"Gabriel knows where you are, Abby. Wherever you go, he'll find you, whatever and whenever he decides."

"I feel if I don't visit Gabriel before I go home, we'll never manage to consummate our love. Or have him come to any decision."

"We should put our heads together and help you look for a legitimate job," Rosella said. "You may have to go back to apply for a visa though. We'd sponsor you, which should help; you'll always have a home with us. The United States is very tricky regarding work visas; the jobs allowed are limited. You should focus on looking and applying for work before you go home. You have three weeks to look. Try the evening paper, and also call some agencies. If it's meant to be, you might find the very thing you need." Rosella raised her china mug. "Cheers. Here's to finding the best job!"

Abby smiled gamely. *This will take so much more than cheers.*

The following Sunday morning, Abby joined the family for Mass. She was always content to be on the same continent and hearing Mass as Gabriel celebrated it. It gave her a spiritual connection to him. Sitting in the pew, looking around, she watched the young and the old as they entered the church, walked up the aisle, and genuflected in front of the altar before taking their seats.

She caught her breath as the handsome man walked

in with his daughters. Abby had seen him several times, minus the beautiful wife, which she thought strange. Maybe she was not Catholic. Abby had found herself searching for him in the congregation, along with his gorgeous little girls. She hadn't seen for some time the other family who'd been with them at Christmas: the Father, Mother, two girls, and baby boy.

Rosella had told her the Mother had passed away. Abby felt sad remembering how the Dad had handed the baby to his young daughter and the melancholy expression on the Mother's face. Abby thought of the Mother and felt tears sting her eyes. *Those poor little bairns without their Mother. The youngest one would never remember her.*

Abby whispered a prayer. "Mother Mary, bless this day; keep them safe in every way. Guide them to a peaceful place; fill their hearts and souls with grace. Enfold them in your tender care. Mother Mary, this is my prayer."

After Mass, Father Tom addressed the congregation regarding the usual weekly announcements. When he was finished, he requested everyone pay attention for an important request.

"One of our longtime parishioners, Byron Grant, recently lost his wife and the Mother of his three small children. He has asked me to read the following message out at every mass today."

> Good morning, everyone. I am asking for your help today. As most of you know, my wife, Colleen, passed away recently, succumbing to pneumonia after a short battle with cancer. I am left with three small

children: Grace, age eight; Aria, age six; and Benedict, age eighteen months. Naturally, we are devastated and in a state of disbelief.

My work is of such a nature that it takes me away from home to Las Vegas. It's imperative I return soon, or I'll lose my contract; I am a magician. Considering this, we're looking to you, the community, and asking your assistance. We need a nanny and housekeeper. The job requires being kind and patient, with a lot of stamina, and able to work with my three grieving children. This person would take care of their daily needs, including meals and laundry, and drive them to and from school. If you think you can help or know someone who can, please contact me through Father Tom. Thank you, and God bless you all.

"I believe you've just found your job!" Rosella exclaimed to Abby. "The Lord works in amazing ways. What a perfect opportunity for you—nanny in a Motherless home. There is no one who could help and understand those little ones more than you."

"It seems a little too good to be true," replied Abby.

"Abby, you get up and talk to Father Tom as soon as he comes off the altar. This is sent from heaven. I can feel it in my bones. Now, go!"

Abby talked to Father Tom, explaining her situation, and he arranged to meet with Abby after lunch that day.

Abby sat in Father Tom's office with his oak desk between them. It reminded her of a desk Aunt Helen had in the old house. A large crucifix hung on the wall behind his head; otherwise, the room was quite stark. Abby felt nervous, mostly because it was likely this would be her only opportunity to apply for a job before she went home.

"Now, tell me something about yourself, Abby. What makes you think you're the right person for this job? You understand when I say that you look very young. This position comes with a lot of responsibility. As you are aware, Mr. Grant won't be resident most of the time; he'll be away working."

Abby looked across the desk at Father Tom; he appeared older than he was. His voice and skin were younger than the gray hair flopping into his watery green eyes. "I realize that, Father. However, I can assure you I can help to take care of this grieving little family."

Father Tom sat back in his chair, looking as though he were relaxing, while a slight hint of a smile crossed his lips. "Please go on, Abby."

"I'm twenty-six years old and one of a large family. I am the middle child, and I have triplet brothers three years younger than me. My parents separated when I was eleven, and six years after that, my Mother died very suddenly. My brothers were fourteen years old; I was seventeen. Believe me,

Father, I understand how to take care of grieving children in a Motherless home."

Father Tom nodded. "Go on."

"It seems a coincidence now; however, I sat behind the Grant family at Christmas Eve Mass. I sensed a deep sadness around the Mother. I now understand why. I have three weeks left on my visa; I must leave Virginia on May eighth. But I'd like to stay in Virginia. I heard your announcement today, and here we are!"

"I'm impressed, Abby. You have quite the résumé. It's as though you've been sent to us for this very purpose. I can't promise you anything; however, I'll be in touch with Mr. Grant today. He's looking for someone as soon as possible. You'll hear from me." He stood and opened the office door. "Good luck, Miss Abigail. May the good Lord bless you and keep you safe."

"Thank you, Father Tom. Goodbye, and bless you!"

Abby received a phone call on the same Sunday evening.

"Hello, Abby. This is Father Tom."

"Hello, Father."

"Abby, I spoke with Mr. Grant, and he's interested in meeting you as soon as possible. He has requested that you visit the family home at eleven tomorrow morning so he can interview you and, if everything goes well, introduce you to the children and his Mother-in-law. How do you feel about that?"

"Overwhelmed, excited, grateful, and very nervous."

"I appreciate your honesty. They're a wonderful family; I've known them for many years. If you have a pen and paper, I'll give you the address: 2375 Seaside. It's about a fifteen-minute drive from where you are. Abigail, bless you. Good night."

"Thank you, Father. Good night."

Abby placed the phone down.

Rosella and Aidan were anxiously waiting to hear the news. Rosella was holding her breath, and her fists were clenched. "Well, what did he say? Tell us!"

"I have an interview with Mr. Grant tomorrow!"

Rosella leaped into the air, and the three of them hugged as they danced about the kitchen. "I am thrilled! I'll pray with all my might that you get the job."

Aidan looked at the address. "That's a nice area, Abby—very exclusive—and not too far to drive. It's a beautiful private cove. This is very exciting. I wish you all the luck in the world. You deserve an opportunity like this one. I don't think for one moment it will be easy, but if anyone can do it, I'd say you could." He kissed Abby on the cheek.

"Oh, I can't thank you enough," Abby told them.

"Always remember, you have a home here with us."

"That's so kind of you. I don't know what's going to happen. We shall see."

"Go have a good night's rest, refresh, and be your best impressive self in the morning," Rosella told her.

Abby lay on her bed later that night, wondering what she was about to discover. She was restless. Her mind overflowed with thoughts and questions. What would Gabriel think if she got the job? Would that mean she was destined to wait for him? That God wanted her there? If she did have to go back to England, how would she afford her ticket for her return? If she wasn't offered the job, what would she do? She had so many thoughts and questions.

Finally, exhausted, Abby whispered, "Gabriel, please make your decision soon."

— 29 —

The next morning, Abby stood at the end of the large circular driveway lined with several tall pine trees. She made her way toward the front door of the mansion, climbed the mosaic-tiled steps, and stopped at the large two-door entrance supported by two white pillars. She had a thought she might turn and go home before she pressed the doorbell; however, her fingers were more courageous than she was. The chimes rang out, sounding as exquisite as the home looked.

Eventually, the door opened, and Mr. Grant stood at the entrance. Although he was still handsome, it was evident the last months had aged him way beyond his years. His face was gaunt and haggard, and his eyes were gray and looked tired.

"Hello. You must be Miss Lavalle," Byron said in greeting her.

"Yes, Mr. Grant."

"Welcome, and please come in. I appreciate your coming on such short notice. Please follow me."

They weaved their way through hallways, and every window she passed looked onto the sea. As they passed by, she peeked into a kitchen she thought must have been every woman's dream.

"Please come in, and have a seat. May I get you something to drink?" he said as he opened a door.

"No, thank you." Abby looked about. Once again, a picture window faced the ocean, with two comfortable leather armchairs facing the window. Most of the room was oak-paneled and tan leather. She felt majestic magic in the room, yet somehow, it had lost its sparkle. Various boxes, top hats, magic wands, multicolored silk scarfs, playing cards, numerous awards, and many books lay about.

"This is an interesting room, Mr. Grant." Abby smiled. "Magical."

"Thank you," he said, though he did not return her smile. "I can see you have the dry English sense of humor. I enjoy English television shows."

"Yes, so do I."

"I was most impressed with Father Tom's recommendations. He explained in detail your situation, and you understand ours. My priority is my children; I need someone to take on their full care when I am not around. A good part of the time, my Mother-in-law, Viv, will help you when required. It's a huge task, Miss Lavalle, and on top of that, my children are grieving."

"I understand. I am acutely aware this will require some tender, loving care, along with an ability to help guide the children back to a normal situation—a new normal. As you know, I have firsthand knowledge of this kind of circumstance—not their personal pain and sorrow but certainly my own and my three younger brothers'. Most of us grieve the same way, Mr. Grant: shock, anger, and disbelief.

Maybe not in that exact order. However, it will come as sure as the sun rises. I'd like to think I could be of some help to you with the children, for a short time at least."

"I think you should meet them. They're waiting for us in the beach room."

Abby followed him to a porch-like room with a wall of windows revealing a panoramic view of the Atlantic. She noticed a short woman with bright red hair, and she recognized the girls from church.

"Miss Lavalle, this is my Mother-in-law, Viv, and these are my little girls, Grace and Aria. This is Miss Lavalle."

"You don't have school today?" Abby asked, keeping her eyes on the children.

"Daddy kept us home to meet you," Grace said.

"Where do you go to school? At St. Martin's? My cousins go there—the Kennedys. Do you know any of them?" Abby asked.

"No, none are in my class," answered Grace.

"I think you have a fantastic school—certainly not like any of the schools in England."

"How are they different?" asked Grace curiously.

"My school was at least three hundred years old. We walked down a very steep, windy hill lined on each side with scary old trees. The school was built in a swampy forest—very dark, cold, and creepy," Abby told them.

"I wouldn't like that." Aria spoke up.

"That's why I love your school. Where is your little brother?"

"Sleeping. It's his nap time," Grace said somewhat protectively.

"He's a very lucky little boy to have two big sisters watching over him."

"I sing to him all the time. Would you like to hear what I sing?" Aria moved closer to Abby.

Abby was moved and amazed at the sounds that came from the child's lips. She was like a nightingale singing in the dawn, pure and sweet.

"That is a wonderful song, Aria. You have the most beautiful voice," Abby told her.

"Thank you. Would you like to see my Mrs. Bunny?" Aria ran off down the hall.

Grace hung back while observing Abby with the same dark, exotic, mystical stare as her Father.

"We are all still in shock," Viv said, looking at Abby with pleading eyes. "We need so much help—and soon."

Abby felt the torment and weariness in Viv's persona.

Byron and Viv shared a glance, and then Byron nodded. "I would like you to start working with us as soon as possible, Miss Lavalle. Would you consider starting tomorrow, just to see how we all get along?" he asked.

"I'm free for the next three weeks; however, as I explained to Father Tom, my papers expire May eighth, and I must return to England then."

"I'd like to investigate that over the next three weeks; leave it with me. Would you like to try?"

"Yes, absolutely, I would, Mr. Grant."

Aria arrived back in the room, clutching a worn stuffed rabbit. "Here she is—Mrs. Bunny. She sleeps with me every night. I don't like sleeping alone. Did you know my Mommy has gone away, and she's not coming back, not even for my birthday? I watch the front door for her every night. Daddy says she is dead, and that word means she's not coming home."

"Aria, may I hold Mrs. Bunny?" Lavalle felt she would burst into tears if Aria continued with one more word.

"No," Aria answered softly.

"Okay, would you like to sit on my knee? You can hold Mrs. Bunny, and I'll hold you."

"Yes, that would be okay."

"I like Mrs. Bunny's pink satin ears. She is soft and smells sweet like you, Aria. I have a cuddly toy at my house. I sleep with him every day. I'll bring him tomorrow," Abby told her.

"Are you coming back tomorrow?" Aria sniffed, trying to control her tears.

"Yes, I am. We can have a tea party with Mrs. Bunny and Teddy. Would you like that?"

"Oh yes, please!"

"Thank you, Miss Lavalle. I can't tell you how much I appreciate your efforts. We'll see you tomorrow." Viv stood up, offering Abby her hand. "Come along, Aria. Bring Mrs. Bunny with you."

"Bye-bye, Miss Lavalle. I'll see you tomorrow." Aria waved Mrs. Bunny's arm.

"How are you getting home? Can I give you a ride?" Byron asked.

"I'd like to walk. My family lives close by, only a half hour away along Seaside Road," Abby answered.

As Abby and Byron approached the front door, Grace arrived with Ben in her arms. If the sight hadn't pulled at her heartstrings so much, it would've been comical. Ben looked to be about twenty months old and almost toppled Grace over with his weight. They looked like two peas in a pod, the image of their Dad.

"Hello, Ben," said Abby, bending down.

"Would you like to hold him?" Grace almost whispered.

"Thank you, Grace." Abby opened her arms wide, and Ben reached out for Abby as though it were part of his daily routine. He chuckled and giggled and grabbed her necklace and pulled her hair.

"He's beautiful. Thank you, Grace," said Abby, handing Ben back. "He looks like you, Grace, and that is very special."

"Miss Lavalle, I have a feeling you're going to have a very good effect on this household." Byron started to open the door. The doorbell chimes rang out, and he opened the front door.

Abby was surprised to see who the visitor was: the handsome man from church.

Byron motioned the man inside. "Andrew, good timing. This is Abigail Lavalle."

"Yes, Father Tom's young lady. Hello, and welcome. Do we know each other?" Andrew held out his hand.

"Hello. Yes, sir, from church."

"I remember now. Call me Andrew," he said, smiling at her.

"Andrew is our dearest friend and the family doctor. I don't doubt you'll be seeing a lot of him."

"This sounds very promising, Byron," said Andrew.

"Yes, Miss Lavalle is starting work tomorrow. She has three weeks left on her visa. I'm going to work something out, hopefully, to obtain an extension."

"Good for you, Miss Lavalle. Please let me know if I can help."

Abby thanked everyone and left. Once more, she was standing on the circular driveway. This home was aching, filled with a grief almost unbearable—the weight of the combined sorrow from the family.

Looking up toward the blue sky, Abby whispered, "Lord, I am somewhat overwhelmed. What have you just placed into the palms of my hands?"

— 30 —

Sebastian and Sasha arrived home in a taxi from Central Station. The April showers that night were torrential, with strong northeast winds. The air was damp, and visibility was almost zero as they dashed from the taxi to the house, protecting their heads with their small suitcases. Sebastian opened the door, and together they stood in the vestibule, shaking the water off their coats and drying their shoes on the mat. Sebastian noticed the post and picked it up off the floor.

"Sasha, let's have a hot drink and put the fire on. We can get warm through before I drive you home. I'll make the tea. You start the fire; it just needs a match," Sebastian said, shivering.

Sasha lit the fire, and it was blazing within moments.

"That feels better. It has been a long day, non?" said Sebastian as they warmed their hands.

"Dad, I wish I was still in France! It's such a magnificent location, surrounded by the mountains, the wine region, and the history, but the best gift of all is the old family home.

We've already made fabulous renovations so far. A few more sessions like we had this week, and we'll have one amazing place. I'm so grateful you have brought it back into the family; everyone loves the idea."

Sebastian smiled and warmed his hands by the stove. "Well, I'm more than pleased with the results, and I agree with you—a terrific week with my sons. All except Eugene, of course. Next time, we'll invite everyone, including the girls, now that we have the plumbing fixed." They both laughed as the kettle whistled.

Sebastian made a pot of tea and set up a tray with cups and some biscuits, milk, and sugar. He carried it in to Sasha, and they sat together, feeling the warmth from the hot tea and the heat of the fire. Sebastian felt cozy.

"Sasha, tell me what you like besides Rougemont itself."

"That village next to ours, Colmar. It's so perfectly well preserved; it looks like a picture in a fairy-tale book."

"Oui, this is one of the oldest towns in the region and possibly one of the most beautiful. They call it Little Venice because of all the canals running through the ancient streets." Sebastian thought back fondly to earlier days in the quaint village—days with Amelia.

It was a stunning town nestled in among overgrown vineyards overflowing with grapes waiting to be plucked and made into delicious Alsatian wine. The variations of the homes created a collage of textures and brilliant colors, and the pride of ownership was apparent in each unique house. The white net curtains billowed in the gentle breeze, with aromas of rosemary and garlic and other tantalizing smells wafting out. The window boxes were brimming with the sheer joy of flowers and blossoms. Exquisite shades of red, orange, yellow, and purple tumbled from the boxes, reaching the cobbled streets below.

"It's the ambience of the village itself—not French and not German but a combination of the very best of both countries," Sebastian said.

"It appealed to me in so many ways," Sasha said. "I had to rub my eyes; the beauty that surrounded me was surreal. The dinner we had that night was amazing—incredibly simple foods but so unique and tasty: leek pie, sauerkraut and sausages, crème caramel, and the local wine pouring like water. It was one of the best-tasting meals of my life! When Eugene and Abby come home, we should all go back together. I'd love for them to see it. Have you heard from them, Dad?"

"Not recently. Abby should be coming home soon; her visa runs out in May. We hardly ever see or hear from Eugene now that he has his family, although I agree with you; we should contact him on his next shore leave and try to get everyone together." Sebastian looked across the kitchen table at the post piled high. A red-and-blue-striped airmail envelope stood out among the pile of brown envelopes, enticing him. Sebastian walked over and picked it out.

"This looks like a letter from Abigail. I'll read it now, and we can hear together her news," he said, holding it up.

Sasha poured a second cup of tea for them as Sebastian opened the airmail envelope and removed several pages.

"This looks like one of her chatty ones," Sebastian said, smiling.

"Yes, you're right there, Dad."

April 15

Dear Dad,

It's so long since I last wrote to you. I apologize for the lack of communication. I hope you and all the family are well. How was the holiday and renovation trip in France with my brothers?

I have so much to tell you, Dad, that I don't know where to begin. As you know, I love it here and would like to live here permanently. It's difficult to believe how the time has passed, and my visa runs out in weeks, not months. This past March, I had the opportunity to travel with Rosella to Tennessee and visit Gabriel; it was an unforgettable week. However, there has been no decision, as it's not mine to make. I shall stand by, wait, and pray.

To this end, I've decided to look for employment. Truly, Dad, you could not make this story up if you tried.

I'll try to cut a long story short. There is a family who live in the parish where Aidan and Rosella live. The Father's name is Byron Grant. He is a famous magician, and he lives and works in Las Vegas when he's not at home in Virginia. Tragically, his wife and the Mother of his three children died from complications from cancer, leaving ...

Amazing Grace

Sebastian skimmed over the details of her new job and then started reading aloud again.

> In many ways, it's reminiscent of when Mam died. I have sad memories of standing outside the boys' bedroom door night after night, listening to my brothers crying, not knowing if it was one or all three of them, at a total loss as to what to do.
>
> I have not had much time to think about anything except helping this family get into a routine. I am blessed to be here in Virginia with Aidan and Rosella close by. All the children go to the same school; already I am carpooling with Rosella and Heather. It's good being useful to someone whilst I patiently wait for the great decision.
>
> I'll close now and hope to hear from you soon. Please give my love to everyone; I miss you all, even though I am very happy here. Lots of love.
>
> Abby
> xxxxxooo

Sebastian carefully folded the flimsy airmail pages and placed the letter in the envelope.

"That's some letter, Dad. What a tragedy—so sad for that family. We were only fourteen when our mam died, and that felt impossible. This will be difficult for her, although Abby appears to have a gift for attracting what she needs.

I'm happy she is staying in the States; she's always yearned to go back there. When she lived with us at home, she pined every day, although I suspected it was also for some bloke. I never asked, and she never said. I'll write to her soon, as she certainly has her hands full," Sasha said.

"Abby is a restless soul who longs for the unattainable, I'm afraid." Sebastian sipped his tea, pondering the letter. "However, the Grant family is in desperate need of help, both practical and emotional. I believe, given time, Abigail is just the one to bring some life and a new outlook to the sad magician and his little ones. Come now. I'll drive you home."

As Sebastian drove through the torrential rain, the wipers on his car screeched and groaned, unable to keep up with the force of the rain bouncing off the windshield.

The distance between the two homes was short. Sebastian pulled up outside Amelia's old house. "Dash in, Son."

"Thanks, Dad. *Tara!*" Sasha patted Sebastian's back.

Sebastian watched as Sasha ran through the wild, wet night to the front door. His silhouette looked almost translucent through the fog, like a ghost or a vision. Then Sasha disappeared, as though he did not exist. Sebastian was left with an empty street, empty roads, and a bleak black emptiness within him after a week of feeling fulfilled with life and filled with gratitude. He spent most of his time alone, and the contrast between the week in France with his sons and this moment felt monumental.

He felt the burden of his guilt, the weight of the mistakes made, and the heartache and sorrow he had caused everyone he loved, including himself, many years ago. For a momentary pleasure, he had betrayed his Amelia with their young boarder, Stella. After Amelia had left him, he had lived with

Stella, and she gave birth to their daughter, Jacqueline. But Stella had left him for a male nurse, Brian, whom she met at work, and Sebastian had allowed them to adopt Jacqueline when they married, so if they had another child, they would be a complete family. He thought about Jacqueline every day.

He knew he could have passed her on the street and not recognized her; she would be twenty years old in September. After tearing his marriage and family apart, he would second-guess himself for the rest of his life. Had he made the best decision for his daughter? He had known he was not capable of taking care of a baby, but his punishment was that he would never know her; that was the price for the sin of betraying Amelia and the children. In gratifying himself for one instant, his devastating, life-changing decision had altered the course of his life and everyone else's.

He was excruciatingly aware of that while sitting in the cold, empty car, listening to the sounds of the penetrating rain pounding the roof. The drops sounded like stones, not water, from the heavens—tears for the stolen years. He felt undeserving of the many gifts bestowed on him, especially quality time spent with his children and grandchildren. Amelia had been denied all those precious gifts because of her premature death. Was he to blame?

As Sebastian aged, he felt a fear, believing something would catch up with him. How or when, no one could know. It followed him like a creeping, angry dog. He sensed it all around him, particularly when alone, grasping at his bones like icy fingers.

— 31 —

Six months had passed since Sebastian and his sons visited France together, and Sebastian once more was preparing to return to France. It was a new decade, the 1980s, which amazed him a bit.

He was in Newcastle again, moving around the sparse bedroom consisting of only a wardrobe, a dresser, and a single bed, which made the drab Victorian room look even bigger. It had potential to be an elegant and inviting room, given some tender loving care and restoration, with its twelve-foot ceiling, original marble fireplace, crown molding, and double front bay window. Light spilled into the long-neglected room he and Amelia had shared with their triplet babies so long ago.

He moved between his dresser and the old brown leather suitcase lying open on his bed; it had been his companion for many years, traveling with him since he'd left home in 1934 on the day his Mother waved him off to join the navy. Sebastian placed socks, underwear, a jumper, one shirt, and two pairs of pants inside. Good—he was packed.

Amazingly, everyone had organized a family holiday in

the old home, except for Abby, who was still in Virginia, working wonders with her grieving family. According to the latest letter, she was concerned about the Thanksgiving and Christmas holidays being the first ones the family would celebrate since the children's Mother died. Sebastian was confident she would make sure everything went as smoothly as possible. He missed her and was aware, more by what she did not say, that she was still awaiting the great decision. He wondered how long she was going to wait. He felt there was a strong possibility her soul mate, the priest, might never decide. It was Abby's life; however, he hoped she did not waste too much time on Father Gabriel. She was young and lovely; this should have been one of the most exciting times of her life. It was his experience that men in love moved fast.

The telephone rang, interrupting his thoughts. After moving quickly to the kitchen, he picked up the phone. "Hello?"

"Hello, Dad."

"Eugene! Bonjour, my son! How is the navy, and how is your mission going?"

"Yes, thanks, Dad. We're all great. I don't have long. I only paid for three minutes. I wanted to talk to you before we leave. It's great that we're all meeting this week. Stephan is so excited. We've rented a caravan. I believe Andre and Leah have done the same."

"Oui. Cammie, the boys, and I will all travel together. Now that we've finished the renovations, we can stay in the house."

"I can't believe we managed to pull this off."

"Where there is a will, there is a way, my son," Sebastian answered.

"We're taking the ferry from Dover to Calais tomorrow night. If all goes well, we'll arrive at your place later the next day."

"Perfect, Son. Safe travels. My love to your family."

"Okay, thanks, Dad. *Tara*."

Sebastian put down the phone, feeling happy, a well-being not familiar to him. Going to the bedroom to finish his packing, he decided on an early night instead. He was to meet Sasha, Noah, Nathan, and Cammie at Central Station early tomorrow. They would catch the 7:00 a.m. train to London King's Cross and then the connecting train to Dover, the ferry to Calais, and, finally, the overnight train to Strasburg. It was a long journey but one well worth the effort.

Sebastian lay down, feeling relieved. He was tired, of course, weary after a busy day. He'd noticed off and on a nagging pain in his lower right groin, likely from lifting heavy boxes in the loft and stretching to reach the suitcase. Maybe he'd pulled a muscle. His thoughts drifted to tomorrow morning, and he fell asleep with a smile.

Sebastian awoke with a start, feeling confused and nauseated. He needed to get to the toilet and made a beeline for the closest sink, where he vomited and vomited until the dry heaves stopped. He made a drink of water with baking soda, hoping it would settle his stomach. What was hurting so much?

Sebastian returned to bed, sweating, where he tossed and turned, desperate to find a comfortable spot. He was going to

France tomorrow no matter what! Eventually, he drifted in and out of sleep until the pain became excruciating, radiating across his abdomen. He looked down to see his lower right groin bulging. The veins beneath his skin looked as though they'd tear at any second, and his intestines would spill from his body.

The bulge was the size of grapefruit and translucent. He grew terrified, realizing he must move. Exhausted, he still had the dry heaves. Deciding to roll off the bed onto the floor, he was aware there was no chance of his standing. Slowly, he crawled toward the bedroom door, stopping to vomit and heave, as the pain was so severe. He continued to crawl to find some help before passing out.

Slowly, he crept along the dark passageway. Maybe he could shout for help. One of the lodgers might hear his cry. But everyone was sleeping. He lay on the floor, cold, terrified, breathless, and shivering in the dark.

Sebastian gathered his strength and attempted to call out, but sadly, there was no sound, only the silence. He had to find a way to call attention and awaken one of the lodgers. Panicking, he looked about him through a haze of pain and recognized the silhouette of the hall stand just behind him. Struggling, at a snail's pace, finally, he reached it, exhausted and weeping from an accumulation of pain and fear. Sebastian grasped the umbrellas and rolled over toward the door. Using the wooden handle, he raised an umbrella, and collecting his strength and rising beyond the pain, he bashed at the door. He bashed and then rested, bashed and then rested. He lay on the floor in vomit, urine, and agony.

Sebastian prayed someone would hear him. If not, surely he would die.

Early the next morning, Sasha, Cammie, Nathan, and Noah assembled at Central Station. All were excited and eager to begin their journey on the train to London King's Cross. It was now 6:30, and everyone had agreed to meet on the platform.

"He is late; I thought he would arrive before all of us," Sasha said.

"He still has time," Cammie said. "At least fifteen minutes."

By 6:45, Sasha was pacing. "I'm going to phone him. You stay here."

Sasha found the closest phone, picked up the receiver, and dialed his Dad's home phone number. He listened to it ring, although he did not expect a response; surely his Dad would arrive on the platform at any moment.

Suddenly, the receiver was picked up. "Hullo?"

"Hello? Who is this?" asked Sasha, as he did not recognize the voice.

"I am Larry, the lodger on the first floor."

"Oh! Larry, hello. I'm looking for my Dad."

"I've been trying to call your home all morning, starting at five thirty, but got no answer."

"Why? What's wrong? Is it Dad?" Sasha asked.

"He's in the hospital," Larry replied. "I found him unconscious in the hallway at four thirty in the morning."

"What the hell are you saying?"

"I'm sorry, mate. He is in the Royal Victoria Infirmary, having emergency surgery as we speak. All they would tell me was to find the family, as they were not sure he'd make it. I don't know what's wrong, as they wouldn't say; I'm not family. He was in one hell of a state when I found him."

"My God, Larry. Thanks. I must go." Sasha dropped the phone and ran to the platform. After finding his siblings, he repeated what he had just heard. They decided together to find a taxi to take them straight to the hospital.

They arrived within moments and eventually found a nurse to help them.

"We are looking for Sebastian Lavalle, our Dad." Sasha was the spokesman.

"He is still in surgery," the nurse answered as she skimmed her reports.

"Is he having an operation? He was fine when I saw him yesterday. Is he going to be all right?" Cammie asked.

"I can't say. You'll have to wait for the doctor."

"How much longer will he be in surgery?" asked Sasha.

"I can't tell you; I don't know," replied the nurse. "You are welcome to wait. Someone will come discuss it with you."

They waited, helpless, for what seemed like an endless amount of time. Eventually, a man approached them.

"Are you the Lavalle family?"

"Yes, we are." The family stood up and spoke in unison.

"Hello. I am Dr. Davies."

"How is our Dad?" Sasha asked.

"I'll explain what's happening. Your Dad was brought in by ambulance early this morning with what is known as a strangulated hernia with peritonitis. The team fixed the hernia. Unfortunately, because of the strangulation, they removed part of his bowel."

"What will that mean?" asked Sasha.

"It creates the complication of infection spreading through his body. We inserted a drainage tube in his lower abdomen to drain the poison. He's receiving large doses of antibiotics intravenously and is in an induced coma to help keep him as calm as possible."

"Is he going to recover?" Cammie's voice broke.

"I'm very sorry, but I can't give you any more information at this time. You should expect him to be unconscious and isolated for the next forty-eight hours. You can stay if you wish; however, it's somewhat redundant. If there's any change, we'll call you."

"What can we do, Doctor?" Sasha asked on behalf of everyone.

"At this point, if you believe in God, I suggest you pray," the doctor replied.

— 32 —

The day before Thanksgiving, Heather worked in Andrew's kitchen, preparing a turkey dinner for the family the next day. She could scarcely believe it was the second Thanksgiving she was celebrating in America. The summer had come and gone, and what a summer she had experienced.

Katie ran into the kitchen, interrupting her thoughts. "Heather, can we help you decorate the table for Thanksgiving for tomorrow, please?"

"Ochs, for sure ye can. You just wait for a wee while. I need to finish the turkey dressing."

"Oh yeah! I'll go tell Babette."

They were canny bairns—no bother, really—and she had a fantastic job: great accommodations, use of the family car, an excellent salary, and, since late April, the new perk of reasonably good sex. Smiling to herself, she chopped the onions and sage for the dressing.

Andrew's parents had taken the girls for Easter week to Disney World in Florida, giving Heather the week off. She'd decided to stay and put her time to good use as she was at home with Andrew all to herself. It had been an opportunity too good to miss.

After the girls had left, Heather had waited for Andrew to come out of the house the next morning, timing her movements precisely so as to bump into him.

"Good morning, Heather. You look fresh this morning. Going somewhere special?" he'd asked.

"I'm shopping for supper. I decided to pull out all the stops. Steak and wine, as it's your day off," she'd replied.

"Yours too." He'd smiled at her. "Better yet, let me take you out."

"I would love it. Thank you."

"A fancy new restaurant opened along the beach. Will I make a reservation and pick you up at seven?"

"I'll be here," she'd said, smiling to herself.

Heather had made sure she dressed like a goddess, wearing a fitted off-the-shoulder black dress that showed her neckline to the fullest advantage. She'd piled her long golden tresses high up on her head and dangled a pair of diamanté earrings. High-heeled sandals had completed her outfit. Heather had smiled as she observed Andrew's reaction when he saw her.

"You look stunning. I'll be the envy of every man in that restaurant tonight, Heather!"

She'd smiled at him, thinking to herself, *Yes, I know.*

They'd had a fantastic evening, sitting together in a romantic window cove, looking out at the beach, watching as the sun slowly slipped away from the day. She'd ordered fresh Atlantic salmon, strawberries, and champagne. Andrew had had a light beer, a fillet steak, cheesecake, and coffee. They'd conversed about the girls and about Shannon, their Mother, coming for the summer; his work; and the loss of Colleen. They'd talked about how Byron's family had improved recently, mostly because of Abigail, their nanny. She'd felt that Andrew went on about Abby a bit too much, but she'd decided to let him ramble; he'd needed to vent, so that night had been an exception.

"Heather, I can't tell you how much I appreciate everything you do for me, my girls, and Byron's family, particularly this year."

"I enjoy being useful; it's no trouble. I loved this evening. Thank you, Andrew."

"I'm delighted to hear that. My pleasure."

They both had fallen silent on the short drive home. When they'd arrived, Heather had stepped out of the car and asked, "Would you like a nightcap at my place?"

Andrew had looked at her, hesitating for a moment. "I would," he finally had replied.

Once inside, she'd said, "Come in, and have a seat; I must slip these shoes off, as they are killing my feet. Help yourself. I have a bottle of champagne chilling in the freezer." She'd left Andrew alone, heading for her bedroom, where she'd undressed and draped herself in a blue silk robe. She'd loosened her hair, which tumbled past her shoulders to her waist, the color of corn in the summertime. She'd smiled at her reflection on her way out to greet him. *Finally, this is it*, she'd thought.

"Let's forget champagne. We can share that after," she'd said as she took Andrew by the hand. She'd guided him to the bedroom, slowly undressing him. Heather had enjoyed being in control, maneuvering him and manipulating him, caressing all the places he had tried to deny existed. She'd spent the night helping him rediscover every corner and part of his body, releasing within him an explosion of pent-up passion.

Afterward, Heather had relaxed, lying in Andrew's arms, feeling gratified, like a satisfied cat. She had liked it enough. However, imagining it had seemed more exciting. Andrew was so handsome, with a perfect physique to match, that she'd believed the sex would be beyond compare. It was not. *He must be out of practice*, she'd thought. It would fall upon her shoulders to help resolve such an issue over time.

For some weeks, everything had been satisfactory as far as she was concerned. Then Miss Goody Two-shoes had shown up at Byron's household.

Andrew would not shut up about her. Abby was Superwoman and an angel all in one and had become a fly in the ointment. Distracting Andrew, she was a pest that Heather intended to remove eventually.

She refocused on the turkey dinner as Andrew came in the door.

Andrew arrived home early, feeling weary as he opened the door. He'd delivered two babies that day, one a caesarean. He was grateful he had the next two days off. His children ran to him to greet him.

He picked up Babs, who said, "Hello, Daddy. Did you have a good day saving lives?"

"Yes, I did. I helped a Mommy with her newborn baby—a

little girl. The cutest thing you ever did see yet not quite as cute as my girls," Andrew told her.

Both the girls giggled, and Katie jumped up. "Heather promised that we can help set the table for Thanksgiving!"

"That sounds like fun. Do you think she would let me help?" he asked.

Katie smiled at him. "She will, Daddy. She asked us to wait a wee moment, as she's fixing the turkey."

Andrew took the girls' hands and walked into the kitchen. "Hi. That is a delicious aroma floating about!"

"Och! That's a good thing," Heather replied.

"How is it going?"

"It's good. I can't believe how easy it is when the guests do most of the work, bringing their favorite recipes all prepared."

"I'm relieved to hear that. Your hard work is appreciated. I want to talk with everyone about tomorrow now that we're all together. As you know, Uncle Byron is home for Thanksgiving. I invited him and the girls and Grandma Viv to join us for dinner, along with Grandma and Grandpa. It might be a little difficult for you to understand. It won't be like other times; we need to be thoughtful and kind to them."

"Is that because they don't have a Mom, and it's Thanksgiving?" Katie asked.

"In a way, yes," Andrew told her.

"It's not hard to understand, Daddy. We're the same—celebrating Thanksgiving, and our mama is in Ireland. I know she's not in heaven, but I miss her."

Sweeping up Katie and holding her in his arms, Andrew kissed her on her forehead. "What a wonder. You understand what I'm trying to say. We'll help everyone through the day."

"Is Abby coming, Daddy? I like her. She's funny and very kind," Babs said.

"I'm not sure, Babs."

Heather said, "She told me yesterday when we were grocery shopping she wouldn't be joining us for dinner because she has her own family to spend Thanksgiving with. Now, run along, both of you, and play. Dinner is ready soon. Then we'll set the table together."

They both ran off to play.

"Did Abby tell you she was spending Thanksgiving with her family?" asked Andrew.

"Yes, she made a point of telling me."

"I'm somewhat surprised that she's not staying with Byron."

"No need—he's coming to your house," Heather replied.

"I'm going to wash up." Andrew went upstairs.

Andrew stood under the hot water, which was almost burning the muscles in his back, trying to relax. He had the feeling Heather was a little too territorial regarding him, the girls, and even their home.

And now he was sleeping with her.

His mind drifted to her peach skin and perfect body—caressing her, kissing her, and using his body in ways he hadn't realized existed, experiencing multiple climaxes. The sex was amazing, and she helped him build his confidence.

They kept their interactions up above the garage and only when the girls were away, which seemed to work well. Recently, though, Heather had become somewhat like a wife. The sexual interludes were her idea. Her possessiveness had appeared when Abby arrived at Byron's. She seemed aggravated whenever Abigail was mentioned, though Abby was the perfect fit for that family.

Women. How does one understand how to handle them and their mysterious ways? He had tried with Shannon and failed. He was not going to make the same mistake again.

— 33 —

Grace watched as the sun's rays danced across the blue Atlantic, as if tiny Christmas lights were sprinkled across the waves. It was nearly Christmas Day and was the first day of her Christmas holiday from school.

Abby was making pancakes with chocolate chips and lots of maple syrup to celebrate. Aria was spending the day at a friend's house, and Ben sat in his high chair in the kitchen with Abby, waiting for his favorite treat. He loved chocolate pancakes. Benedict loved everything, in fact; he was always happy, especially when Grace was in the room.

It seemed to Grace that Ben never felt sad, only if he was teething or had a pain in his tummy. He didn't feel sad about Mom or miss her, because he was a baby. Grace wished she was a baby and didn't have a memory. She was only just beginning to not feel like crying all day. Then her birthday and Thanksgiving had come, and now Christmas. She was worse today than when Mom had been dying. Grace let out a loud sob.

"Can I sit with you, Grace, and hold your hands?" Abby stopped making the pancakes and came over to her.

"Okay," Grace answered between sobs.

"I have a good idea. It's a beautiful day. Would you like me to take you to the cemetery? We can bundle up and take Ben along and make it a little outing."

"Why would I want to go there?"

"Grace, it's normal to feel as you do today and for as long as it takes you to feel better. There's no right or wrong time to feel sad, only what works for you. When I felt like you do, I would visit my mam at the cemetery and talk to her."

"Did she talk back?" Grace couldn't believe her ears.

"In a way, she did," Abby told her.

"A voice? Did you hear her voice?"

"It was more of a feeling. When I was talking, sometimes I cried. I always felt better after a visit with Mam. It was like when I hurt myself, and Mam would kiss it better."

"Really? Can we go after breakfast?" asked Grace.

"Yes, we can."

Grace already felt better just thinking about what Abby had told her. If she could talk to her Mom, it would help.

Later that morning, Grace, Abby, and Ben arrived at the cemetery.

"We can find out in here where your Mom is buried; the office keeps records," Abby said.

Grace pushed Ben in his stroller toward the desk. Abby stood back and allowed her to approach the lady at the reception.

"Hello. How can I help you?"

Grace thought the lady's voice was special, kind and soft; it made Grace want to cry. "Hello. My name is Grace, and this is my brother. We've come to see Mom. She's buried here, but we don't know where. Please, can you help us find her?"

"My goodness, what a beautiful boy. Yes, I can help. Is someone with you?" The lady stood up and looked at Ben.

"Abby. She's our nanny," Grace replied.

"What's your Mom's name?"

"Colleen."

"Do you know when she was buried?"

"I don't remember the exact date she died. In March this year?"

"Give me a moment to look at the files."

Abby stayed beside her at the desk. Grace looked around the room and liked what she saw: a big fireplace with a warm fire burning, Christmas garlands on the mantel, and a gold-framed picture of angels hanging above. A tall Christmas tree stood in the corner, with lots of decorations and with gifts underneath. It was strange that a cemetery office would decorate for Christmas, she thought.

"I found her! Let me show you and your brother where to find your Mommy. We can walk from here," the lady said as she came back.

Grace walked with Ben along the pathway as she followed the kind lady. She looked at the gravestones; they weren't scary at all. Some of them had Christmas wreaths with big red flowers. She passed several with little Christmas trees decorated; it seemed to Grace this was a special place.

"Here we are, along this little pathway."

At the end, Grace stopped. She could not believe what she saw as she heard Abby gasp. "She's beautiful!"

"Your Daddy had this made," the lady told them.

Grace walked over to look a little closer at the life-size

white marble statue of her Mother in a flowing dress. On her feet, she wore dancing slippers, and her hands were shaped like a vase, holding a fresh red rose.

"Where did the fresh rose come from?" Abby asked the lady.

"Mr. Grant instructed his lawyers to put money aside. Each week, a long-stemmed red rose is delivered into the hands of the statue, for eternity. It's the most romantic love story!" cried the lady.

Grace read the writing on the plaque below.

Colleen Vivian Grant
Born October 12, 1950. Died March 17, 1980.
My soul mate, love, and Mother of our children,
Grace, Aria, and Benedict.
Sleep now, darling, in blissful peace
until your dear ones come to you.

Abby had been right; visiting her Mom was a sad and happy feeling all rolled up together. Placed opposite the statue was a little marble stool.

"Sit for a moment, Grace. Would you like me to take Ben?" Abby asked.

"No, I want Mom to see him," Grace replied.

Abby nodded and walked away with her head bowed.

Finally, Grace was alone with Ben and the statue of her Mom. She took a deep breath. "Mom, I can't believe I am talking to you. Abby told me that it might help. I feel so horrible every day since you left us. Sometimes I think I can't get out of bed. I'm so sad. Aria sings on the doorstep, holding Mrs. Bunny, waiting for you to come home, just not every night now. Ben's here. Look at him, Mom; he is sleeping. He's the best baby in the world."

She allowed the tears to come. "You would love him to bits, Mom. I do. Grandma Viv doesn't visit quite as much, but when she does, she cries, especially when she looks at us. Dad is sad with a capital S when he is home. He spends most of his time in his office. I can hear him crying through the door and blowing his nose. I feel I want to run in and jump on his knee and tell him, 'Don't cry, Daddy.' I don't know why I don't. I feel a little bit frightened, like he wants to be alone. I miss him. Sometimes it feels like he went with you.

"We have a nanny; her name is Abigail. I like her. She's the one who brought me here today. Sometimes, when I can't sleep, she lets me in her bed. Abby smells nice and clean, and that helps me feel safe, but it's not your smell, Mom. I miss you so much."

"Grace, are you okay?" Abby tiptoed past her.

"Yes, thanks. I don't want to leave."

"We can stay as long as you need." Abby left her alone once more.

"It's so much worse now that it's Christmas. How can we bear to have a Christmas Day without you, Mom? I don't know what to do." Grace wept so loudly she woke Ben, and he reached up to her. She lifted him out of the stroller and held him up to the statue.

"Hi! Hi!" Ben said. Turning to face Grace and smiling at her, Ben was still. Looking directly into her tearstained red eyes, he placed his little hands on each side of Grace's cheeks and kissed her on the tip of her nose. He giggled.

Grace was surprised. Ben loved playing with her, but he'd never done that before. She remembered she had seen her Mom do it with him, especially when he was sad. Placing her arms tightly around Ben, she hugged him with all her love as she looked at the statue.

"Thank you, Mom. I think I might understand."

— 34 —

Abby awoke, remembering that it was Christmas morning and that she was staying with Aidan and Rosella. She had decided after a long discussion with her cousins and Andrew to give the Grant family the privacy she felt they needed. Christmas would be a painful day for them to negotiate. Grandma Viv had arrived on December 23 to spend the holidays.

Abby was relieved to be spending Christmas with her family. It had been a difficult, emotionally challenging year with little or no time for her own thoughts. Fortunately, Aidan and Rosella had suggested they would host Christmas Day dinner for both Byron's and Andrew's families, including parents and nannies. Abby thought that was more than generous. To her surprise, everyone had accepted the invitation. That day would be hectic, and Rosella would require a lot of help in serving dinner.

Rosella had been working in the kitchen for several days, although most of the guests would also bring prepared foods. She was cooking a twenty-five-pound turkey stuffed with

Auntie Amelia's recipe, along with a sumptuous-looking lasagna made from recipes handed down by her ancestors from the hills of Monte Cassino in Italy.

As Abby showered, she felt somewhat nervous and offered a prayer that the events of the day would unfold peacefully. Byron and his family would survive the day with the help, love, and support of those around them. Abby decided on a black outfit with Stewart tartan trim. Pulling her hair up on top of her head, she felt appropriately dressed.

When she arrived downstairs, the family were having breakfast.

"Happy Christmas, and happy anniversary of one year living in Virginia," Aidan said as he stood up, hugging her.

"Happy Christmas, everyone. Did Santa bring you all excellent gifts?"

"Look! Beside the tree!" Greg said, and he, Ryan, and Kelly all pointed.

"I'd say your Santa Claus is most generous; never have I seen so many gifts. You must all have been outstanding children this year," said Abby.

They all laughed, continuing to share stories and the Christmas morning festivities. After the breakfast dishes were cleaned up, Abby sat in her favorite place: the window seat looking out to sea.

"The sea looks cold today—icy gray—and the sky looks the same," she said.

"The forecast is calling for snow flurries later today." Rosella brought Abby a cup of coffee. "It's good to have you with us today." She kissed Abby on the forehead. "Aidan and I are so proud of what you've managed to accomplish. It has been a wonder to behold the changes within that little family."

"Thank you. I'd be lying if I didn't tell you it's been a challenge and slow going. It's still one foot forward and two back most days. I am grateful to you and Aidan for hosting dinner today. It's a kind, brilliant idea to give everyone a new tradition this year. I'd like to help you as much as possible."

"You have enough to do with Byron's children. Besides, many capable hands are surrounding us today. Don't you worry. Heather is joining us, along with the grandparents. I believe there'll be seventeen for dinner."

"The more the merrier! I'd like to call my Dad, if that's possible."

"How is he, Abby?"

"Recovering well. He is several weeks post-op and almost back to his old self. Sasha wrote that he's lost a lot of weight. However, he is regaining his stamina and becoming stronger every day. I'm hoping to talk to him this morning."

"Use the phone in Aidan's office."

"Thank you. That's a good idea. It's two in the afternoon right now in England, and I'd like to catch them. When are you expecting everyone?"

"I thought around three. With that many small children, we don't want to be late."

"I'll be out to help you as soon as I finished talking to my Dad."

Abby sat in Aidan's office and dialed the phone. She listened as it clicked and connected across the miles until she heard the familiar ring tones beyond the seas to Newcastle. Suddenly, she felt a wave of heavy homesickness.

"Hello! Merry Christmas."

"Hello, Sasha. It's Abby."

"Abby! Great timing; everyone is here. Hang on. I'll hold up the phone, and they can all wish you happy Christmas."

Abby heard a chorus of "Happy Christmas!" and she felt tears behind her eyes.

"We're all about to start eating our turkey dinner with Mam's famous recipes," Sasha said. "The Christmas cake looks delicious this year. I'll post you a slice."

"Don't! You're making me homesick!" Abby cried.

"Oh, I doubt that. All the fantastic stories I'm hearing from Dad."

"How's he doing, Sasha?"

"Hang on, and you can speak to him; I know this costs a million dollars per minute. Take care of yourself, pet. See you soon."

"And you," Abby answered.

"*Joyeux* Noel!" Sebastian said as he took the phone.

"Dad, how are you? It's so good to hear your voice. Merry Christmas!"

"I'm very well, Abby—recovering nicely. We won't waste precious time and money talking about me. How are you and all the little children?"

"Everyone's great, Dad. Aidan and Rosella invited everyone—seventeen of us—for Christmas lunch today."

"Abby, I'm so proud of you and all you've accomplished."

"Thanks, Dad."

"Have you heard from your special friend?" Sebastian asked.

"Only a Christmas card with a short letter. To be honest, Dad, I've had very little time to give him much thought—or the great decision. As I've said before, it's not mine to make."

"Good enough."

"Dad, are you feeling stronger?"

"Oui! Don't worry about me. I shall write this week with more detail. Thank you for calling," he said, and then he addressed the others. "Say goodbye to Abby, everyone."

Abby heard everyone call out. Then the phone clicked, and they were all gone. How she missed them!

The Christmas dinner was a tremendous success, even under such exceptional circumstances. Abby had never witnessed so much delicious food; the buffet was overflowing with casseroles of every kind, vegetables, meats, savories, salads, and many desserts. Seventeen people around the table created plenty of conversation and camaraderie, with entertaining antics courtesy of Ben. Christmas songs heralded across the room courtesy of Aria's sweet voice.

Abby sat between Byron and Andrew. Grandma Maude and Grandpa Harold were sitting with Grandma Viv. Heather was in between the two Grandmas, looking disenchanted.

"Abby, you are a miracle worker," Byron said, leaning over Abby. "Look at my children! They're laughing and having fun. I would not have thought that possible today. Thank you."

"How did you manage this morning?" she asked him.

"It went as you would've expected. I was grateful for the invitation to your family's home for Christmas luncheon. I'm thankful for you, Abby; your unique gifts are precious."

"I feel the same way to be trusted and given such an opportunity. It's my privilege and honor."

"I have some good news for you: your paperwork is complete, and your green card is at the consulate." Moving his finger to his lips and whispering, he continued. "Keep it under your hat just now."

"What a wonderful Christmas gift! I can hardly believe it. Thank you so much."

"No one deserves it more than you do. When you get your green card, America will be stronger for it."

"Thank you, Byron."

"It's well deserved!" Byron patted her on the back.

Viv talked with Maude, with Heather between them. She was, as always, looking glorious, in a shiny, low-cut gold blouse and a black velvet pencil skirt. Andrew, next to her, appeared to be uncomfortable.

"Are you enjoying yourself, Andrew?" asked Abby.

"Yes, what a fabulous lunch. It was exactly what was required this year; everyone appreciates the change. Well done, Abby, for helping organize such an event. Your effect on Byron and his family has touched me. How far they've progressed in the short time you've been with them—it's impressive."

"It's a privilege to help," she said sincerely. "I should add I'm not alone; your constant support and the knowledge that you were available gave me the courage to take on the task. I enjoyed getting to know you and your little girls. They're a credit to you."

"You genuinely are a wonder, Abigail. I hope you plan on staying." Andrew reached over, holding her hand in his.

After the meal, Byron performed magic tricks for the children and adults amid hoots of laughter and awe. Abby and Heather cleared the dishes. Abby had a distinct feeling Heather was not in a festive spirit. As they were loading the dishwasher and washing and drying the pots, Abby asked, "Did you enjoy yourself today, Heather?"

"How could I when stuck between two old biddies? They don't like me!"

"That's not true." Abby laughed.

"How would you know, having fun sitting between the two best-looking men in the room, with them whispering in your ear? I'd like to know what they were suggesting," she said nastily.

Abby slammed down the pot she was drying and threw the tea towel over her shoulder. "Heather, it was nothing like that! I resent the comment. They are very decent men, and I have a lot of respect for them."

"Keep your hair on. I believe you, Miss Goody Two-shoes. But if you do get any ideas, remember this: the doctor is mine. Keep your hands off!"

"What!" Abby exclaimed.

"And keep your gob shut. No one knows."

"Are you kidding me?" Abby was incredulous.

"Why would that be?"

"I don't know. I just thought Andrew—"

"What? Would be celibate?" Heather teased.

"No, it doesn't matter. It won't come from my lips." Abby had a fleeting feeling of disappointment in Andrew.

Hours later, the day was ending, and Christmas festivities were over for another year. Everyone was leaving, and the guests were taking home more food than they'd arrived with. Each expressed his or her gratitude to Aidan and Rosella for opening their home and allowing them to come together and share an unforgettable Christmas Day.

Amazing Grace

After all the guests were gone, Rosella and Abby sat beside the warm fire, watching the snowflakes fall.

"This Christmas was an unforgettable one, Rosella."

"I'm happy it went smoothly for everyone. My, Heather is a beauty! She certainly doesn't look like a nanny!"

"She's doing a good job. Heather keeps herself at a distance from the family; she has the advantage of a Mother in the children's life and also a private apartment."

"I was watching Byron and Andrew with you at the dinner table. They seem to admire you for more than your skills as a nanny."

"Rosella, it's nothing like that! Honestly, people and their imaginations," said Abby. "Byron told me something that I must keep a secret. Andrew was expressing his appreciation regarding the progress of Byron's children."

"Whatever you say." Rosella smiled like the Cheshire Cat. "I have a proposition for you. I received a phone call yesterday from our friends in Tennessee. Jane is inviting us all back in February for the week, including you. Would you like to come?"

"I think so." Abby hesitated, surprised at her reaction.

"You think so? I thought you'd jump at the opportunity to see Gabriel."

"So did I." Abby stared into the distance, watching the Christmas tree lights flash off and on, seemingly reflecting her mixed-up emotions about Gabriel.

— 35 —

Gabriel looked up into the eyes of his spiritual director, feeling crushed and as if he were going around in circles.

"Once a priest who has presented himself as a chaste, committed celibate becomes sexually active, he has destroyed one of the pillars of his vocation and mental health," the older man said.

"I've explained, Father; we were not sexually intimate."

"Gabriel, I'd like you to think about that statement. Have you ever fantasized about making love to her? Caressing her body and holding her in your arms as you both slip into the ecstasy of sexual gratification, beyond the realms of celibacy? It's not possible to have it both ways."

"Father, I'm not assuming I can. I struggle with the decision every day, terrified because she's coming back to Tennessee this week. I am insane with thoughts that I should run away before she arrives or wait till she arrives to whisk her away with me. I love her! She wants marriage, a house, and a baby with me. It's her dream, her mission. In my heart, I know she would make a spectacular wife and Mother.

Amazing Grace

However, to fulfill such a goal, I must betray my vocation for her."

Gabriel broke down, holding his head in his hands. "I can't provide her with what she needs or deserves, and I can't make love to her. Most of the time we're together, I'm intimidated. I don't know what to do while battling with the feelings of being inept, inadequate, and guilty. And my insatiable desire. I'm not an experienced lover, and the thought of attempting to perform anything outside a passionate kiss is beyond me. The guilt and anguish are slowly destroying me. I don't know what to do." He bent and wept like a child.

"If it's any consolation to you, Gabriel, you are not the first or the last priest to face this seemingly hopeless situation. The time has come for you to make up your mind to stay with your vocation, for which you are well suited and needed, or to marry this girl you love." The spiritual director sat back in his chair; his demeanor serious. "Remember, Gabriel, you're not trained for the business world. You lack many of the life skills required to support a wife and children. You must pray for wisdom and guidance as you search for your life's path. I can see this is tormenting you spiritually, mentally, and physically. This is a turning point in your life. Whatever you decide will affect you and the young lady for the rest of your lives. I suggest a two-day silent retreat at the monastery before she arrives to rest, pray, and listen to God's voice. Go in peace. God go with you."

Abby had been in Tennessee for three days, and she hadn't yet heard from Gabriel. It was different from last year, when he'd knocked on every door to look for her the same day she arrived. They had spoken on the phone last week, and when she'd told him the opportunity to visit Tennessee had come up, the discussion had turned from friendly to awkward. She was uncomfortable and confused. How could a relationship change from an unquenchable desire for one another every moment of the day to suddenly be so distant? He'd said he'd contact her after she arrived.

It didn't feel right; he was keeping her at arm's length. When honest with herself, she acknowledged her own feelings of uncertainty. Her doubt wasn't about her love for Gabriel; she would have waited for him until the end of time if he'd asked her. The indecision and a fear of choosing the wrong path were holding her back from a world full of opportunity waiting to be discovered.

A knock on her bedroom door interrupted her thoughts.

"Yes, come in. Hi, Rosella."

"The phone is for you. It's Gabriel!"

Abby ran as though she had wings on her heels to take the call. *What bliss it will be to hear his voice!* Picking up the phone, Abby tried to sound casual.

"Hello, Gabriel."

"Welcome. It's good to hear your voice."

"You're a mind reader," Abby said as he chuckled. "I was becoming concerned."

"I'm okay. I apologize for the delay. I was called away to participate in a silent retreat."

"Okay, that would explain things. You must be fit as

a fiddle and raring to go." Abby heard Gabriel's infectious laughter.

"You're back, and I love it! How about dinner tonight?"

"I'd love to," she answered.

"I'll pick you up at seven thirty."

"I'll be waiting."

"Abby?" he said hesitantly. "I'm happy you've returned."

"Thank you. Me too. See you soon." As she placed the receiver down, Abby's knees were shaking at the sound of his voice. Would she ever recover from the effect he had on her? Praying she wouldn't and, at the same time, praying she would, Abby went to her room to prepare for her dinner date.

Gabriel chose a French bistro nestled within the Blue Ridge Mountains, far away from his world, if only for a few hours. After requesting a table for two, they were tucked away in a tiny alcove. It was a clear night with a bright full moon. Hung between the mountains, the moon looked like a painting with its muted tones of silver light.

Gabriel thought anyone looking in on the candlelit table would have smiled at the lovers stealing away for a romantic interlude, locked together in a communion of souls, oblivious to the outside world. How he wished it were that simple.

"What a perfect setting. Thank you, Gabriel." Abby shone from the inside out, with all her love directed toward him.

"I'm happy you like it, Abby; I chose somewhere special tonight, as I wish to discuss something important with you. Please listen to me."

"Okay! Don't sound so serious." She frowned.

Gabriel ordered a bottle of wine and some appetizers and asked the waiter to leave them for a while. Holding Abby's hands in his, Gabriel looked into the eyes of the face he had grown to adore.

"Abby, you've shown me the beauty of love, introducing me to its many splendorous facets. Instead of feeling shame and fear, I was able to benefit and learn. I'll always love you for opening your heart to me and giving me that gift. I pray you'll continue to love me through this challenging time. You've lived in limbo for the past year. I have a seemingly impossible task: choosing between my love for you—which I do not truly understand and which scares me—and my current life, which is safe, organized, and predictable."

"Gabriel, I'm not asking you to choose between me and your life. I want you to take my hands. I support you with those decisions."

"Are you so sure? I don't know how I'll tell my loving, aging, very Catholic parents that I'm leaving the priesthood to marry, in addition to my siblings, who look up to me; the bishop, parishioners, and fellow priests; my church friends; and family. It's no different from a divorce. It's worse, as I'm betraying God himself." Gabriel allowed his tears to fall. "Never in my life have I felt so hopeless."

Abby placed one of her hands upon his cheek across the candlelit table. "Gabriel, please don't you cry too; I can't bear to see you like this. You're breaking my heart." Abby's tears flowed.

"Abigail, I'm afraid I'm going to break it even more. I can't go on like this!"

Abby pulled her hands away from him, placing them on her lap.

The waiter arrived at the table. "Are you ready to order, sir?"

"No, we're not," Gabriel said shortly. "Please leave us."

The waiter scurried off, apparently realizing this intimate dinner for two was not about joy and bonhomie.

"Abby, we can't marry."

Abby placed her hands over her face. "Gabriel, no. No, please!"

"Abby, I won't prolong this; I cannot marry you. Our friendship is as precious to me as breathing, and I'd like to continue that. However, a life together is out of the question. I cannot give you what you want." The sound of his voice changed. Even he did not recognize his detached tone.

"Gabriel, take me home now, please. I'll wait for you outside." Abby stood from the table, taking her purse, keeping her head down.

Gabriel watched in anguish as Abby left the romantic interlude with her head bowed, as though in shame, running from the restaurant. He drove her home in a chilling silence. When they arrived at the house, Abby had her hand on the car's door handle, ready to run.

"So it's over?" Abby cried out to him in between wrenching sobs. "We are no more?"

"In any romantic sense as lovers or to marry, no, never. As friends forever, if you want me."

"Will you kiss me and hold me one more time?" she pleaded.

"I can only hold you as a dear friend would."

"Gabriel, I love you. The pain of losing you is unbearable. Help me." Sobbing and throwing her arms about his neck, Abby buried her face in his shoulder.

"Don't you see? I am helping you by letting you go." Holding Abby in his arms for what seemed like an eternity,

Gabriel felt a sense of urgency to get away. "It's time for me to go, Abigail." He untangled himself as gently as possible, turning to face the steering wheel. "Goodbye, Abigail. May the angels watch over you!"

Abby opened the door of the car and stepped out. She didn't look back. As Gabriel drove away, her sobs tore into his broken soul.

"I hope there is a kingdom!" he cried out.

— 36 —

Sebastian regained his strength and realized how fortunate he was to have survived. The strangled hernia and peritonitis almost had finished him off. He had spent three weeks in the hospital and then several more at a convalescent home, losing a significant amount of weight. However, he felt better. His stamina was returning from taking long walks on the seafront from Tynemouth to Whitley Bay. He looked forward to them, as the trails allowed him to reminisce and to understand how fragile life was, as tender as a rose petal. God had given him more time. It was up to him to find the reason why.

Tynemouth was where Sebastian and Amelia had had their first date, standing inside the ruins of the priory. Sebastian closed his eyes, listening to the North Sea crash against the rocks with lingering whispers from his past.

"Tynemouth Priory is one of my most favorite places," Amelia had told him. "It overlooks the North Sea and the River Tyne, along with a two-thousand-year-old history. Anglo-Saxons settled here first. Eventually, it became a

Benedictine priory. Queens have lived here; kings are buried here. I love to stand inside the ruins of the cathedral. You can still see where the high altar was and the shapes of the windows. I imagine I can hear the monks chanting the Gregorian words as the North Sea pounds the rocks below and the winds howls around the building through the cracks in the walls and windows."

"You paint a beautiful picture, Amelia; I can't think of a more perfect place than this to kiss you," he had said to her. Six days later, they'd married, and he had gone back to fight in the war.

Now, heading home along the seafront, Sebastian noted the waves were powerful that day. The sun was bright; the sky was a wedgewood blue brushed with the odd fluffy white cloud. Sebastian longed for his home in France. Unfortunately, no one had managed the planned reunion; his emergency surgery had stopped that. The opportunity had slipped through his fingers. Attempting to gather his children together again would be no simple task, mainly Eugene, as he was away with the Falklands War raging. Knowing Eugene was involved gave cause for great concern.

Sebastian was weary when he arrived home. As he filled the kettle for his tea, he heard his doorbell. Slowly, he made his way along the hall and opened the door to a tall, handsome young man—a naval officer. Sebastian's heart did cartwheels.

"Good afternoon, sir. My name is Captain Simms. I am looking for Mr. Sebastian Lavalle."

"Yes, I am he. Come in."

"Mr. Lavalle, sir, I am a representative of Her Majesty's Royal Navy."

Sebastian felt weak and leaned against the wall. The young man helped Sebastian, holding his arm.

"May I assist you, sir?" The Captain walked him along the long, dark passage. After supporting Sebastian to a chair, he pulled another one up and sat opposite, looking into Sebastian's eyes with compassion so powerful Sebastian spoke first.

"Is it about my boy Eugene?"

"Yes, sir, it is. On behalf of Her Majesty's Royal Navy, I regret to inform you that on May 4th, Lieutenant Eugene Joseph Lavalle was lost at sea. He is presumed dead."

"Non. Please, God, non, non." Sebastian let out a sharp cry.

"Mr. Lavalle, I assure you it was instant. We don't believe he or his shipmates suffered. Your son was a credit to you, making the ultimate sacrifice for his country and fellow man. Giving his life and performing his duties to the end. Eugene was respected and well liked—not only by his superiors but also by his fellow workers and everyone he encountered."

"What about his wife? They have a young son."

"Provisions are made for widows and children," the Captain told him.

"That poor girl—a young widow before their life had begun. The boy child will never know his Father." Sebastian couldn't find the words. He felt nauseated and light-headed and choked, not able to control his tears.

"Do you have any liquor?" the Captain asked, and Sebastian pointed to his cabinet. The Captain poured a large brandy into a glass and gave it to Sebastian. "Sip it, sir," he said. The young Captain continued to discuss the details of the demise of HMS *Sheffield*.

"On the fourth of May, two days after the sinking of HMS *General Belgrano*, the British lost the destroyer HMS *Sheffield* to fire following a missile strike from the Argentine vessel *Escuadrilla Aeronaval de Caza*. She was struck amidships, and the attack had a devastating effect, ultimately killing twenty crew members and severely injuring twenty-four others. The ship was abandoned several hours later, gutted by the fires that continued to burn. She finally sank."

Sebastian listened, remembering how terrified he had been as a young man in the navy during World War II after his ship, the *Jeanne d'Arc*, had been hit. The thoughts of his son experiencing the same fear in his last moments made him cry out.

"Why not me? I've lived my life. Eugene had a family and so much potential ahead of him." Sebastian looked to the Captain. "I've suffered many knocks in my time, but nothing ever felt as devastating as this news! How in God's name do I move forward?"

"Moment by moment, if you can, sir. We'll organize a memorial service within a few weeks, and I'll be in touch with the details. If there is anything I can do to assist you, please don't hesitate to call me," the Captain said, slipping a card into Sebastian's hand. "Once again, our sincere condolences. Please don't get up; I'll find my way out."

Captain Simms headed toward the door. Turning to face Sebastian, he saluted.

"Thank you, Captain Simms. You're a compassionate young man and a credit to both the navy and your family. My son Eugene is like you—I mean was like you—in many ways." Sebastian broke down, giving in to the torrent of emotions inside him.

— 37 —

Early in May, Abby and Rosella walked along Virginia Beach. As it was low tide, a multitude of shells were scattered across the ocean floor, shimmering in the sunlight like a stunning jeweled carpet. It was glorious; however, Abby did not feel anything. She was numb that day.

"I'm so sorry to hear about Eugene, Abby."

"I know. It's such a big shock to everyone."

"How is your Dad doing?"

"It was so sad. When Dad was telling me, he could barely finish his words. He was crying and told me he would call me later and hung up. I don't have much information, except Eugene is gone! I'm just grateful Andrew contacted Viv to give me some time off. She'll stay until I go back tonight. Byron's coming home for a few days. I can't do anything for Eugene." Abby started to cry.

"Oh, Abby! Let's sit down for a moment."

"I feel so bad for my sister-in-law and my little nephew. And so guilty."

"Why on earth would you feel guilty?" Rosella asked.

"Because not all my sadness is about Eugene. Most of the time, all I can think about is Gabriel. It's been almost three months since our trip to Tennessee, but I wake in the morning thinking about him and fall asleep dreaming of him. I still long to hear his voice or recognize his handwriting on an envelope in the mailbox. I'm praying to get over the feeling that he's dead and that I'm mourning him."

Rosella Jumped up suddenly and raised her voice in anger, placing her hands on her hips. "Abby, why won't you listen to good advice? Gabriel has decided he can't give you what you want. Move on! You surprise me. You are being rather insensitive regarding the sudden death of your brother."

"I realize it looks that way, but you see, I never got the chance to really know Eugene. He was my brother, and I loved him, but he was gone already in the navy before I knew him enough to miss him. My feelings around him are more about my Dad missing him and about Stephanie, my sister-in-law, and the little one."

"I can understand that, but the pining for Gabriel must stop," Rosella said. "Do you realize how blessed you are? Three families in Virginia love you like their own. Byron Grant moved mountains for you to receive your green card in record time. Please don't lose the opportunity and potential being offered to you. Move on! Let Gabriel go!"

Abby returned to the Grant home later the same day. Viv was in the kitchen, making a dinner of back ribs and roast potatoes, everyone's favorite.

"Hello, Abby. I'm surprised to see you back so soon."

"I was restless, Viv. Besides, I miss the children."

"Believe me, it's mutual."

Ben toddled into the kitchen, reaching for her and calling, "Babby!" Abby picked him up and deposited a multitude of tiny kisses about his face as Ben giggled.

"Abby, play with me," the child said.

"What, Ben?"

"Peekaboo, okay?"

"Dad is coming home tonight for a few days. Abby, can we all go on a picnic?" Grace asked as she set the dinner table.

"Grace, what a fantastic idea. I'm sure your Daddy would love to picnic. We could invite Uncle Andrew and the girls."

"Oh yes!"

"Run along, and wash up; we can talk to Daddy when he comes home tonight," Abby told her.

After supper, Abby joined Aria and Mrs. Bunny for the doorstep ritual.

"My Grandma told me your brother has died like my Mommy."

"Yes, darling," Abby replied.

"Are you sad?"

"Yes, I am."

"Is it like when my Mommy left the house?"

"In some ways, though not quite the same. The sad feels a little different maybe."

"You can sit with me and sing, Abby. They might hear us and come home together."

"Thank you, little darling. I like that idea." Abby placed a kiss on Aria's cheek and hugged the little girl.

"Why does everyone die and go away?"

"I'm not sure. Sometimes people can't stay; it's time for them to go. There are many different reasons."

"When you die, can I put you in a glass box like Sleeping Beauty and keep you in my room? I love you, and I'll miss you if you go away," said Aria.

"Aria, things don't work like that. Besides, I'm not going to die," Abby told her.

"That's good. Will you stay and marry my Daddy?"

"Aria, good heavens, where on earth did you get such an idea?"

"It's a secret. I heard my Grandma talking to my Daddy one night when you were on holiday. She said, 'Abby is a jewel; you should marry her and keep her here. She's good for the children.' Daddy told Grandma to mind her own business. He said other things I didn't understand too; he seemed to be cross."

"Oh, Aria, I bet he did. Don't you worry. How about you and I sing a song together and forget all the silly stories?"

"Okay, what would you like to sing?"

Later, Byron and Abby sat together quietly in the beach room; the children were settled down for the night. Viv had left after supper to go home. Byron watched as Abby gazed out to sea as though looking for something or someone. She had been unhappy since her trip to Tennessee; something was troubling her besides the recent loss of her brother. Byron wished he could help her somehow, as she had helped him over the past months.

"Abby, would you like to go home for your brother's memorial? I'd like to help you with the ticket."

"I'm not sure I want to go." Abby didn't look at him when she answered.

"You would be an excellent support to your Father and family."

"I'm very torn. I don't want to leave this family."

"Abby, no one could have done more than you have. I owe you a debt beyond words, but Viv and I can manage for the short time you will be gone," Byron told her.

"I appreciate everything you're trying to do, but I don't want to go, Byron. I'm struggling with other issues."

"Abby, I don't wish to pry, but I'm concerned. You haven't been yourself since you came back from Tennessee. What's troubling you? Can I help you?"

"No." Abby broke down in tears.

Byron sat next to her with a Kleenex box. "This isn't just about your brother, is it?" he asked, placing an arm around her shoulders and drawing her close to him.

"No, but I can't discuss it with you."

"Don't you trust me?"

"Yes, I trust you. I just can't talk about it."

Byron wiped the tears from her cheeks. Looking into her sad eyes, he felt an overwhelming desire to kiss her sweet, inviting mouth and allow their pent-up sorrows to mingle and maybe disappear for a moment. Realizing it was wrong, he let go, preventing himself from making a disastrous mistake, one he knew he would regret. Andrew had discussed that very subject with him regarding Heather.

"I'm tired. I'm going to bed." Abby stood up.

"Please don't. Allow me to help you," he said.

"I'm sorry, Byron."
"Don't be sorry. Sit down and stay. Talk to me."
"I can't. I must go."

Byron sadly looked on as Abby went to her room and closed the door behind her.

Later, Abby lay on her bed, staring at the ceiling, feeling confused. She prayed she was mistaken. Had Byron been about to kiss her? Lord, after the discussion she'd had with Aria. They couldn't fall in love. It was impossible, inappropriate, and much too soon for Byron to feel anything except a rebound effect, and Abby herself was in a similar emotional position.

For the first time in many months, as Abigail fell asleep, her last thought was not of Gabriel.

— 38 —

"Colonial Williamsburg is a living history museum, the historic district of the city of Williamsburg, Virginia. The three-hundred-acre area includes buildings from the seventeenth, eighteenth, and nineteenth centuries. The historic district is an interpretation of a colonial American city, with exhibits of dozens of restored or re-created buildings. Their motto is 'The future may learn from the past.'"

Grace's eyes almost popped out of her head as she stood in the ancient kitchen, listening to a woman dressed as a slave from the early days. The actor invited Grace to help her grind corn in a big barrel to make flour. She then helped make the bread. It had a lovely smell, and Grace looked forward to tasting it. But when it was done, she spat it out and did not like the feeling of it in her mouth. She, Abby, and Ben sat on a hard bed in a one-room shack, although they were told most people had slept on the dirty floor.

"Oh, those poor slaves. I am glad I live in today's time." Grace was breathless with excitement.

Abby nodded. "I am having so much fun. I love Williamsburg. Gracie, how old are you now?"

"I am almost nine and a half."

"I'm surprised this is your first visit. Did you not come with your school?"

"No, I don't remember ever being here."

"I hope we can come back one day."

Abby grasped Ben's straps to keep him from running away; the wide colonial street was inviting him. Just then, Andrew arrived with Babs and Katie.

"This place is fascinating," said Andrew. "We've all just helped several craftspeople make a brick, a wig, and horseshoe!"

Byron and Aria joined the group, and Byron spoke up. "This is a magical place. I've just accompanied Aria, singing one of her beautiful songs, on a harpsichord that was built here many years ago."

Abby nodded. "How can this be our first visit? It won't be the last. Look along this historically reproduced street. It feels as though we have arrived in a time machine like Dr. Who."

As Grace looked about her, she saw everyone was happy and having fun. She sighed with contentment and took her Father's hand.

Grace thought her Daddy was right—the place was magical. She could see and hear horses and buggies as they passed by; the sound of their horseshoes clip-clopped along the cobbled street. She loved that sound.

Everyone joined for a picnic lunch in the gardens of the Governor's Palace, underneath the cherry blossom trees.

"Daddy, can we come back one day?"

"You bet, Gracie, and as soon as possible." Her Daddy winked at her, and Grace was surprised. He hadn't done that since before her Mommy died. She was happy that her Daddy winked at her; it was a good feeling. She had butterflies in her tummy and also held back tears.

What if her Daddy was forgetting her Mommy?

Back at Andrew's home, Heather was relaxing in her apartment, painting her toenails and listening to the radio. Billy Joel was singing his latest hit, "Uptown Girl." She was enjoying part of the day off, as Andrew had taken the girls to Williamsburg along with Byron and his family. Apparently, the outing had been Goody Two-shoes's idea, according to the girls.

Heather had decided not to go with them. Andrew had clearly taken a shine to Abby. Heather hadn't been too concerned at first, mostly because her feelings for Andrew weren't that deep. Yet over time, in spite of herself, she was finding she was more attracted to him—and not just because of his good looks or the great sex they were enjoying. She had come to realize he was a decent man who was kind toward everyone, especially those he loved. She wanted to please him as a nanny, looking after his children, and in his home, with extraspecial touches, meals, little feminine purchases, flowers in vases strategically placed, and soft music playing, creating a warm, welcoming atmosphere for him when he arrived home from work.

She realized Andrew was becoming important to her. When they were together sexually, she looked forward not only to the pleasure of their lovemaking but also to the after-sex connection, snuggling up to him, lying on his warm chest, watching him sleep, and fussing over him with breakfast. When she wasn't with him, she found herself thinking about him.

She had chosen not to go along that day because of Abby. Heather was jealous of any attention Andrew showed her. Right or wrong, whether she liked it or not, it was clear to Heather she was falling in love with Andrew.

A few hours later, Andrew arrived home with his girls after a great day out. He went into the kitchen.

Heather was preparing supper. Her golden hair floated down her back. "Hello. Did you have a fun day?"

Katie walked over to her. "We wish you had come with us. We had so much fun."

Both girls spoke at the same time, trying to explain everything they had done.

"Och, that does sound like it was a great day, but you need to slow down so I can hear you. Run along, and wash up for supper, and then you can tell me all about it." Heather turned to Andrew. "How did you enjoy your day?"

"It was grand! You should have joined us."

"I'm sure there were more than enough people there. Besides, Miss Goody Two-shoes went along, didn't she?"

"Why do you call her that? It isn't very flattering."

"Of course, Abigail is as pure as the driven snow!" Heather chuckled. "Och! Lighten up. She knows precisely what I think of her."

Andrew watched Heather moving around his kitchen. He realized she always managed to stay slightly detached, especially when they made love. He had realized long before now that giving in to his lust and desire for Heather was a mistake. The sex was glorious; Heather was the most beautiful woman he had ever gone to bed with. But he wasn't honoring her or taking care of the girls, his family, or even himself.

It was wrong, precisely as he had suggested to Byron almost two years ago in Vegas. It was time to put things right.

"If you have a night free next week, I'd like to take you out for dinner. The girls are with Shannon part of the week. I have something I'd like to discuss with you."

"Thank you. I would love that," Heather answered.

Later that evening, Andrew lay alone on his lonely king-size bed, reminiscing about the day he had spent watching his girls interact with everyone, especially Abigail. She was as refreshing as a sunrise. She fascinated him with her ability to make everyone feel he or she was individual and important, particularly the children. He'd been watching her for the past year.

She'd rescued Byron and his children from despair. His feelings for Abigail had shifted; they were becoming more than admiration. He was drawn to her. In fact, when honest with himself, he admitted that what he was feeling was love—the kind of love one felt once in a lifetime, the kind that could move mountains and sustain you through adversity. He'd been aware of her inner strength from the moment he first had held her hand. Something in him was sublimely aware this was special. Closing his eyes, he fell into a gentle slumber with thoughts of Abigail.

39

Back at Byron's home after the long day, Abby stepped into the beach room. "The children are in bed. They fell fast asleep as soon as their heads hit the pillow. No story, no song—they just conked out."

"Would you like a drink, Abby? You deserve one." Byron handed her a glass of wine. "Cheers. Here's to you, young lady. What an amazing day."

"Cheers. Thank you," Abby said as she raised her glass.

Byron appeared to be feeling bright and vibrant compared to the first time she had seen him on Christmas Eve in church last year. There was a significant change in him. However, it was a little disconcerting, as it appeared to have happened overnight rather than gradually. Maybe because she didn't live with him full-time, the transformation hadn't been that noticeable to her.

"We must plan another visit to Williamsburg sometime soon," he said.

"I'm told they do an illumination evening the first Sunday

in December. It's a Christmas light show with carols and activities for the children. We need to be sure not to miss it."

"I'd like to talk to you about this Christmas, even though it's only spring." He smiled at her.

He has an endearing grin, she thought as she smiled back at him. "I love to be organized; it's essential in my life. Fire away."

"Have you heard from your Dad recently?" Byron asked.

"Yes, I got a letter about what happened to our Eugene. The short story is that the ship was blown up, along with him and nineteen of his shipmates. No bodies left to find or bury, but Dad writes there'll be a memorial service later in the year, possibly December, at St. Paul's Cathedral in London."

"I'd like to gift you a ticket home this year for Christmas, Abby. I think it would be good for everyone. How does your Dad sound?"

"Sad and lonely. Also trying to hide his true feelings from me about losing Eugene."

Byron suddenly lost his sparkle. Staring into his wineglass, he spoke out loud, though not to her directly. "Dear God, when I lost Colleen, the pain was beyond endurance, not only for myself but for the children. The worst suffering was Viv's in losing her only child. To lose a child is wrong. A parent never comes to terms with such a loss. Parents should never have to bury their children—it's beyond any suffering or sacrifice. The devastation does not bear thinking about."

"Sadly, I think it's true," Abby said. "I believe he's lost a part of himself, a part of his charm. Tragically, it's not the first child he's lost. He and my Mother had a stillborn baby boy. Mam went full-term, but during her labor, the umbilical cord was pulled around his neck, and he couldn't breathe. Although I was a young child, I remember watching my parents grieve, although I didn't understand at the time that's what they were doing. My poor mam was never the same again. I'm sure this is bringing back some very difficult memories for my Father. He also gave up a child for adoption. I don't wish to share the details with you, as it's a long story, other than that my Father had a daughter with another woman. The consequences of his decisions tore their marriage to shreds."

"Good Lord, Abigail, no wonder!"

"My Mother felt utterly betrayed, and she left my Father, taking all of us with her. My Dad paid the ultimate price for his mistakes. He once told me how much he missed his little girl, confiding that he often would park his car at the bottom of the street where she lived and watch her play as she danced, played hopscotch, and chased butterflies. The idea made me feel very sad—not only for him but also for myself and the rest of his children. It seemed we all were touched by the sorrow of his loss."

"I marvel at how insightful you are, Abby—way beyond your years."

"It is likely the circumstances of my life—what they have taught me." Abby was beginning to feel the effects of the long day, the wine, and the churning up of old memories. She felt her face blushing.

Byron gazed at her. "This conversation is giving me a deeper understanding of you. It appears to me that we are benefactors of all the sad adversities you've faced. You have an uncanny ability with my children; it's priceless to me. I can't always understand the reasons we are given our paths in this life; however, whatever brought you to my front door was sacred intervention."

"I don't know about that. Sacred something!" Abby smiled, beginning to feel an attraction to him that she had not recognized before.

Byron chuckled, and she liked his laughter. "We're delighted with you, Abby; you've given me peace of mind when I'm in Las Vegas."

"That's my job. I don't want you to worry when you're away. We miss you, of course, as always. Andrew has been a great source of support. I love this job, and I find myself feeling very grateful for the opportunities and now a green card."

"Abby, a question, please?"

"Okay," she answered.

Byron refilled the glasses of wine before he sat down and spoke to her hesitantly. "Where do you envision this going long-term?"

"I don't know. I take each day as it comes. Don't you?" She realized she wasn't speaking the whole truth. She had daydreams of staying for as long as they needed her.

"Where do you think you would like to go? What would you like from me?" Byron asked.

"Nothing!" she said, feeling her answer was too sharp.

"Are you sure?"

"Yes!" Abby could feel herself becoming uncomfortable. She was hot and was aware she was blushing. Then came startling words from Byron.

"Abby, do you think you're falling in love with me?"

"Of course not. What a suggestion." She was shocked at his question.

"Why is it such an impossible idea?" Byron asked.

"I … It just is. I don't know." Abby blushed and wrung her hands, feeling as if she were making a complete fool of herself.

"Abigail, you and I have a rather unusual set of circumstances. We live together in close proximity, taking care of my children, my home, and indeed my life. We're young, healthy, single, and attractive, working together as though we are a married couple. It's not my intention to upset you; however, I believe communication is the key to harmony. I don't want to lose you. If we should find ourselves falling in love with each other, you must realize I cannot keep you working here. I'll be forced to let you go, and I don't want that to happen. You're the very best thing for my children and me since we lost Colleen."

"Byron, I assure you there are no worries on that score," she said, her voice moving up an octave. She finished off her wine with one swift motion, showing him she was in control. She was not.

"Really, personally, I'm not so sure I can say the same." Byron stood and finished his drink. "Good night, Abigail, and thank you for a memorable day."

It's impossible. What is he thinking? He is a wonderful man—a kind, loving Father and a fabulous boss. She hadn't seen this coming, although he'd made a lot of sense. *No!* She was in love with Gabriel. She was sure of it, although Byron left her with uneasy and confused feelings. Alone and feeling guilty, she looked out into the dark night, reflecting on the sea.

— 40 —

It was midsummer, the longest day of the year. Heather was excited and looking forward to her night out. She finished her makeup with care, choosing a lipstick that matched the strapless red dress she was wearing that night. Andrew was taking her out to the Ocean View restaurant, one of their favorites.

The girls were with their Mom for the week, which gave her and Andrew some time together. They had always kept their work relationship and their sexual relationship separate, getting together only when the girls were away and always in her rooms. When they had first come together last year, she had felt indifferent about him and the girls. She had wanted him because he was a handsome, desirable, sexy man. However, as time had passed, she had grown closer to him. She'd discovered he was a tender and considerate lover, always aiming to please her. Living and working together in such a personal way, she had fallen for him.

She suspected he was going to tell her he was feeling the same way, and she was pleased with herself. After finishing off getting dressed and putting on her earrings, she took one more approving look at herself in the mirror and then left to meet Andrew.

"I love this restaurant." Heather smiled at Andrew. "Thank you for bringing me here."

"My pleasure. It's one of my favorites too," he answered.

They were snuggled together in a cozy corner for two, with no candlelight necessary. They looked out the large window, which faced west into an extraordinary sunset.

"Look at the sky tonight." She gasped as they both looked with wonder. The sea was calm, with no waves, almost like a lake it was so still. The sky was a mosaic, as though someone had used a large paintbrush with all the colors of the rainbow to brush the blue sky and white clouds until they were kissed with colour.

"Andrew, what a perfect sky. On such a glorious night, truly, Virginia is for lovers," she whispered to him.

Andrew said nothing, which surprised Heather.

"Are you tired?" she asked.

"No, not at all. I feel good. I had a few days to myself, caught up on a lot of paperwork, and had some time to think." Andrew sighed and leaned back from her. "I'd like to talk to you about the summer with the girls. Shannon suggested we share the weeks—three days one week and four days the next—and I've agreed. I'd like you to take any time owing to you when the girls are away."

"Och, but I thought I'd reorganize their bedrooms this summer. And I thought we could—"

"Heather, please, I must talk to you," Andrew said, interrupting her.

"What is it? You seem very upset." Heather noticed now how fidgety he was, clenching his hands and taking sips of water every few seconds.

The waiter interrupted to take their order. Heather ordered fresh salmon, and Andrew ordered steak, along with a bottle of red wine, and then dismissed the waiter abruptly.

"Something is dreadfully wrong," she said after the waiter left. "I may not be the most sensitive lassie in the world, but you look like you've lost your best mate."

"Please let me talk. You look more beautiful tonight than ever," he told her.

"Thank you. It's all for you!"

"That's the problem. I don't want it—this. I don't want you!" Andrew dropped his gaze.

"Andrew, you've got to be kidding me." Heather laughed out loud.

"I'm sorry, but I'm not kidding you."

Heather would not take him seriously. "Are you telling me we're not going to be together, or I can't work for you anymore, or both?" she said, laughing at him. "I thought this dinner was about you saying you'd fallen in love with me and asking me to marry you. I must be as thick as a plank."

"No! Please, this is all my fault. I should never have allowed us to give in to our sexual desires."

Throwing her head back, she gave an anguished cry, gazing at him with widened eyes. "It seems you've enjoyed everything up to now. I don't understand how you can tell me this after everything we've done. I feel as though you've just hit me with a brick, for God's sake!"

"I never meant to hurt you; I was wrong when we talked after Las Vegas. I shouldn't have allowed this to get so far out of hand. I wasn't taking care of my family or you. This must stop once and for all today—this moment!"

"Just like that! What about me and how I feel? My job, you, and the girls?"

"Nothing has to change with respect to your job. I have the utmost respect for you as my nanny and housekeeper. There is no reason for you to leave. We can continue to work together. Our relationship never overlapped with our work life or my home; I was always emphatic about that."

"And what brought you to this decision so abruptly?" She felt tears welling, but she didn't want to weep until they had finished this conversation.

"It wasn't sudden; I've been feeling guilty and ashamed—unprofessional—for a long time. I've been selfish, wanting the reliable nanny and housekeeper, the beautiful woman, and the sex. It was never about being in love with you. I never told you I loved you or misled you."

"The things we did together might suggest you were or could be!" Heather could hear the desperate tone in her voice.

"Heather, I am so sorry. I do not wish to hurt you any more than I have. You and I could never fall in love."

"Och, now, that's where you are wrong, because I've fallen in love with you." Heather started to cry.

"I am sorry to hear that, but you can't imagine a future for us as husband and wife," Andrew told her.

Heather continued to weep, attracting some attention

from the other customers. "Why? Why not? We're made for each other."

"I don't love you."

She stopped crying suddenly in realization, as though someone had opened a black curtain, and she could see the light—light around Abby.

"There's someone else. How stupid can I be? Who? At least answer that," she said.

"No, I'm not seeing anyone."

"Andrew, I don't believe you. Most men don't give up such a good thing unless they have someone waiting in the wings. Who is she? I'm not leaving until you tell me."

Andrew was starting to look exhausted and grim. Deciding she didn't want to push him too far, she shut her mouth.

"Heather, let's not do this, please. We must keep our dignity and our friendship if we're to continue to work together."

"Andrew, in this wee moment, the last thing I'm feeling is dignified or friendly."

"Do you think it's possible for us to work through this and salvage something from our relationship in order to move forward?" he asked.

"Andrew, I'm in complete shock. I didn't see this coming. I can't eat with you, and I won't stay here. I'll get a taxi. Please do not contact me. I'll contact you when I'm ready. Don't imagine for one second I'll make it that easy for you," she hissed, and she stood. She walked out of the restaurant with her head held high, aware of all the eyes watching her as she left the restaurant, leaving Andrew alone.

One week later, Andrew called Byron.

"I wanted to thank you for inviting us all to Williamsburg. We had such a great time. And I should have called earlier. I realize it was well over a month ago."

"Yes, I know. Amazing none of us had visited before. It took an English rose to introduce us to it—that Abigail is really something. I just got back from Vegas last night. I'm home for a few days."

"That's great. I'd like to invite you to dinner. I have something to discuss with you when you have time."

"How about tonight? Is everything okay, Andrew?"

"Never better. Eight at the Ocean View?"

"I look forward to it."

Later that evening, Byron and Andrew sat at a quiet table in the restaurant. Byron watched a summer storm brewing beyond the restaurant windows.

"It's not very often the view is so bland from here," Byron said, looking out at the gray water flecked with white.

"That's a good thing. We won't be distracted." Andrew raised his glass. "To you, Byron, and friendship."

"I second that, Andrew. What do you want to discuss with me? I'm intrigued."

"I won't beat about the bush; it's rather an awkward conversation. I'd like to speak with you about Abigail."

"Abigail? What about her?" Byron felt slightly uneasy, though he was not sure why.

"I've developed feelings for her. This is not a flirtation or sudden; it's been gradual. I think about her all the time when I'm not with her."

Byron sat silently sipping his wine, desperately attempting not to show his true feelings. He paused for a while before responding. "This doesn't come as a complete surprise to me, Andrew."

"You're not surprised?"

"I've been watching you two together from the moment you met, the first day I introduced you. I understand how you feel—believe me. Abigail is a wonderful person. I know you and Abby have spent time together. She often comments on your kind support and her comfort in the knowledge that you're close to her and the children when I'm away. Does she have any idea of your feelings toward her?"

"God, no, I only realized myself how serious my feelings are. I wish to tread very carefully. I'd like your blessing and permission to pursue this further. And there's another issue that I haven't been completely honest about with you. For the past year, Heather and I have been having a relationship."

Byron raised his eyebrows. "Now, that does surprise me after our discussion in Vegas. I thought there was tremendous logic in what we discussed; it's helped me keep everything on track at my own home with Abigail. What changed your mind?"

"Heather's glorious, sexy body and my weak will. My confidence was destroyed when Shannon left me and the kids; I felt inadequate in every way. Heather showed me the way back in a million ways. I'm grateful she was around for the girls and me, but it's become awkward, creating a lot of problems."

"In what way?" Byron asked.

"I told her we must put a stop to our relationship, as it was causing me a lot of anxiety and guilt. She was angry, of course, and also very unhappy. I feel I've been selfish and insensitive. I wish I could erase everything and start over!"

"Andrew, we all have episodes in our lives we'd like to erase. Will she continue to work for you?"

"Well, that's one of the many problems. She left me a very curt note saying she's gone away for a few days to consider her options. That was a week ago. Fortunately, Shannon has the girls right now."

"You don't need my permission to ask Abigail out; she's free to come and go as she pleases. Plus, she has a green card now. She's not obliged to stay with me over and above loyalty and commitment to the children." Byron was about to say he would be devastated and lost without her, as would the children, but he decided to keep the thought to himself.

"I can't do anything until I resolve the issue with Heather. I need to pour oil on troubled waters and be cautious. I'm a family doctor; patients need to believe they can trust me. If Heather decided to cause trouble for me, she could, even though we are consenting adults. I need to keep calm. If she decides to leave, I'll have to look for another nanny. I can't manage without one."

"I wouldn't worry too much, Andrew. Cross that bridge when you come to it."

"Thanks, my friend. These things usually have a way of working themselves out. Now, how about we choose a nice steak off the menu and have an enjoyable meal?"

— 41 —

Heather arrived home to her little apartment in Virginia after a week in Naples, Florida, at a health spa. The trip had been just what she needed and had given her time to think clearly and precisely about how she was going to get Andrew back. She was in the kitchen, cleaning up Andrew's breakfast dishes, when the girls arrived home from their Mother's.

"Hello, girls. Och, I think you have grown at least two inches since you went to visit your Mam. Did you have fun?"

"Yes, we did." Katie smiled. "It was nice to be with our Mom again for the week. We miss her when she's in Ireland. Did you know our Grandma was with us too? She is the best. She gives us Irish chocolate and candy and sneaks it to us when Mom isn't looking." She giggled.

"And she took us to the fair and the movies. I hope summer never, ever ends!" Babs jumped up and down with joy.

"What have you been doing, Heather?" Katie asked.

"I went to visit Florida."

"Did you see Mickey Mouse?"

"Not this time."

Katie spoke quietly. Mickey Mouse was serious business. "Daddy said he'd take us back to Disney World one day. You can come with us."

Andrew came in from the garage, carrying suitcases. "Hello, my girls," he said as he hugged and kissed them. "I missed you so much."

"How much?" Babs asked as Andrew opened his arms and grabbed her, squeezing and tickling her, in a bear hug.

"This much!" he said as she giggled.

"Hello, Andrew. I ordered pizza for dinner, as I had no time to make it," Heather told him.

"That's great, Heather. Thank you. I missed seeing you. Have you been away?"

"She's been to Naples in Florida, but she didn't see Mickey Mouse because he lives in Orlando," said Babs as the doorbell rang.

"That will be the pizza. I'll get it," Andrew said as he left.

Heather felt they had all been saved by the bell.

***

After supper, when the girls were settled down for the night, before Heather went back to her apartment, she knocked on Andrew's office door.

"Come in," he said.

Heather thought Andrew looked exhausted. Secretly, she was glad, as she hoped he had fretted all week.

"I'm relieved to see you back. I was concerned," he told her.

"I suspect for your own selfish reasons."

"I wouldn't put it quite so bluntly. Have you come to a decision?"

Heather deliberately hesitated. "Yes, I have. For my own selfish reasons, I'll stay at least for the rest of this year, with a few conditions."

"What conditions are those?"

"I'd like a raise," Heather said.

"We can discuss that, certainly," Andrew replied.

"When the girls are with their Mother this summer, I'd like to take that week to myself and have the time off."

"I'm always happy to see you take the time owing to you. Anything else?" Andrew looked so relieved she thought he would jump out of his chair.

"No, not now. Let's just see how we get along."

"I am grateful you decided to stay, Heather. After all, we are adults; we can put all this behind us and start afresh. Thank you."

"Okay," she said, tossing her long hair over her shoulder and smiling at him as she turned away, closing his office door behind her. Heather wanted him back. She missed their relationship, and she loved him. Her plan was at least started—to stick around.

With most things in her life, Heather was used to getting what she wanted.

— 42 —

Sebastian sat on the plastic chair in the small doctor's office waiting room, looking about him. Nothing in the room had changed in twenty years. He noticed the same holes in the walls and the strange smell of antiseptic and mildew mingled together. It was a dark room with a small opaque window giving no natural light. That day, he felt as depressed as the room looked.

"Sebastian, hello. How are you feeling?" Dr. O'Malley asked as he entered the room and sat down opposite him, smiling with his Irish eyes and warm, jocular approach.

"I've been better," Sebastian answered glumly.

"Well, let's see if we can help you."

"I'm feeling rather helpless, and I'm concerned, as I only want to sleep. I find myself sobbing like a baby spontaneously for no reason—a grown man. I'm ashamed of myself."

"I'm sure you're well within your grieving rights; it's only months since you lost your child. No matter the circumstances, there's nothing on this earth that will ever feel as painful or difficult to recover from. Let me assure you this is the early stage of grieving. Almost anything you think and feel over the next two years is normal for you."

"I don't like feeling this way. I have the children to think about, but there is nothing within me. I feel so empty, as if I am standing beside myself, watching. They're all concerned about me, and there's nothing I can do. They believe I'm not recovering from my surgery last year."

"That was a close shave. If you think about all you've endured in the past months, it's no wonder you are struggling. I can give you some tablets to help you with the depression and a tonic to help boost your immune system. Think about a holiday. Go to the seaside or into the country. I can assure you that time heals, though it may not feel like it just now. Be patient."

"There's something else, Doctor. I've been passing blood from my back end."

"What do you mean? How long has this been going on? How much blood are you passing, and what's the color?"

"Oh, for about a week. Quite a bit every time I have a bowel movement, and it's dark red, almost black."

"Sebastian, this does concern me; we must get you into the hospital for tests."

"Do you think it's cancer, Doctor?"

"We don't think; we test to eliminate everything until we discover what it is, but it could be one of numerous things. Let's just cross each bridge as we come to it. I'll be in touch with you as soon as I can with an appointment time for the hospital. Try not to worry." The doctor stood up and extended his hand.

Sebastian thanked him and left the doctor's office, feeling worse than he had when he arrived, although he hadn't thought it possible.

Within a day after the hospital tests, Dr. O'Malley called Sebastian back into his office. His usual cheerful face wore a sympathetic, grim expression. "Sebastian, I have your test results back from the consultant. It appears you have colon cancer. I'm very sorry."

"Cancer? Dear God, did you say cancer?" Sebastian felt weak, as though he might pass out. He swayed in his seat.

Dr. O'Malley continued. "I realize this is hard news to listen to and a shock, but there are many ways to address this diagnosis—surgery, chemotherapy, radiation, medications."

But Sebastian only heard one word: *cancer*. "Why is God doing this to me, Doctor?"

"It's not planned; it's random. I understand the question after the year you've had." Dr. O'Malley nodded. "We're making arrangements to admit you within days, not weeks—the sooner we operate, the better the prognosis. I'm sorry for your troubles. You've been given more than one man should have to bear. If it's any consolation, you are in good hands."

Sebastian went through the motions of smiling, thanking the doctor, and shaking his hand, but he left the office in a trance to walk home alone.

Sebastian was admitted to the Royal Victoria Infirmary, affectionately known to the locals as the R.V.I., feeling as though he were living in a continuous nightmare. Walking through the great doors of the hospital felt like entering a freezer filled with devastating, dark memories. Less than a year ago, he'd been rushed into this hospital with his strangulated hernia.

Shivering, Sebastian continued the walk to the admitting office down the endless corridor. It was an old hospital, an excellent teaching hospital affiliated with the University of Newcastle, one of the best in the country. However, because of the lack of funding from the National Health Service, it was in a critical state of disrepair, reminding him of something out of a Dickens novel. He passed cracked black-and-white-tiled walls reminiscent of public lavatories, stepping on well-worn, cold concrete floors. The hallways were dark and narrow, with tiny windows, as he made his way to the office.

His operation was scheduled for tomorrow morning at eight.

Later that evening, he lay on his narrow hospital bed, on a thin mattress with an even thinner blanket, in the male surgical ward. The man in the bed next to his was an old Italian, a double amputee. Sebastian felt heartsick as the old man screamed all night, "Give me something to help the pain in my legs!" and begged Jesus Christ to take him home.

Sebastian prayed quietly that sunrise would arrive; somehow, the hours between three and five in the morning were the loneliest and hardest to bear. The ticktock of the large clock, with its enormous black hands pointing at the Roman numerals like a witch's fingers, was incessant. Each second felt like an hour. Sebastian continued to watch the clock, silently praying Hail Marys in French.

During his surgery, Sasha, Nathan, Noah, and Cammie stayed at the hospital throughout the day of the operation. Later, Andre arrived, and he and Sasha stayed while the others went home.

Some hours after the operation, Sebastian was moved into an ICU ward. He awoke, hearing whispers. Andre and Sasha were discussing his operation. For Sebastian, the conversation was just a bunch of words floating about his mind; not much of it made sense.

"The doctor told us after the surgery that they removed the tumor and part of his colon. He's lucky he won't need a bag, but he'll need chemotherapy. The prognosis is good; they expect a complete recovery," said Sasha.

"Poor bugger. He has had more than his fair share this year. His road to recovery will be long and arduous; he won't be able to stay alone," Andre said.

"He's welcome to stay with us. We have the room, and he'll be closer to the hospital."

"We can all pitch in to help him get through this ordeal; that's what family is for."

Sebastian lay still, listening; he felt peaceful, with no pain or fear. A sweet relief came over him. At last, he was free from the melancholy cloud he had been under. Feeling warm, safe, and cared for, he gently drifted into a peaceful sleep.

The next time Sebastian awoke, he was disorientated; the room was dark, and he was uncomfortable. His mouth was dry, his lips felt like sandpaper, and he could feel an excruciating pain searing across his lower abdomen. Both his arms ached, along with his legs, and he had a headache. He could not move. He attempted to call out for help, but nothing came out of his mouth. Suddenly, a silhouette appeared beside the bed with a soft light surrounding it.

"Oh, Mr. Lavalle, you're awake. I'm Nurse Banner, your night nurse. I'm here to take special care of you. Are you uncomfortable? Do you feel pain?"

Sebastian nodded.

"We can help you with that."

His eyes followed the silhouetted shape of the nurse. Using a syringe, she injected something into the IV line. "Mr. Lavalle, you will feel some relief very soon. Is your mouth dry?"

Once again, Sebastian nodded.

"I can't give you a drink, as you have a tube inserted to help you breathe, but I can pass an ice cube over your lips." She disappeared and came back with the ice cube. As she gently moved it back and forth across his parched, cracked lips, she asked, "Does that feel good?"

He attempted a smile.

"I think that was evidence of a smile. I'll give you a gentle bath before bed."

Efficiently, the nurse washed his face with a warm, soft washcloth, followed by his arms, hands, chest, legs, and feet, without disturbing him. When she finished, she magically changed his sheets, leaving him feeling as though he were cocooned in his Mother's womb.

"How is your pain? Improved?" she asked.

Sebastian nodded again.

"You rest now, Mr. Lavalle, and I'll be back."

As he slipped into an idyllic slumber, Sebastian was sure he had been visited by an angel.

Several days later, Andre came to visit with a smile and some magazines. Sebastian was still on fluids only.

"When can you start eating, Dad?"

"Soon, apparently, I get gelatin."

"Any word on when you may be transferred to the surgical ward?"

"Not so far. They won't discuss much with me. They're happy with my progress, but there are several signs required before I can go on to the surgical ward. I'm not sure what they all are."

"I am sorry you've had such a difficult year."

Sebastian patted Andre on his hand, and his son looked at him with the melancholy gaze of his Mother. His eyes were filled with beauty and love beyond anything words could have expressed. His likeness to his Mother was uncanny.

"Abby called Sasha last night. She was very upset and looking to come home."

"Non!" Sebastian said as forcefully as he could.

"I know. Sasha told her to wait until December to come home for Eugene's memorial and celebrate Christmas. He told her there was nothing she could do at this time except write you a nice long letter; that seemed to calm her down."

"I'm in good hands. This hospital is amazing. Nurse Brown is my day nurse, a battle-ax if ever there was one. She has a pair of shovels for hands. Always clammy—ugh! However, Nurse Banner looks after me overnight. I believe she is an angel. She moves with serenity, grace, and a gentle kind of healing gift. Her whole persona is gracious. I think she likes me because of my French accent."

"Dad, you must be feeling better; you sound like a dirty old man. Ha-ha!"

"No! Nothing like that. She's a lovely young woman. Something about her reminds me of Leah. I'm happy she is my nurse. She's like a ray of sunshine."

Amazing Grace

"That's good, Dad. You need something to cheer you up. Someone will be in tomorrow for a visit. Rest, and get well." Andre kissed his Dad on the forehead.

"The visits are greatly appreciated, my son, as the days are long."

"I left you a French newspaper and magazine."

"*Savant*, merci."

"See you soon."

That night, Sebastian kept his gaze firmly on the door, waiting for Nurse Banner to arrive on duty. She had been off for the past two days, and for Sebastian, the time seemed endless.

"I've been waiting for you to arrive." He grinned at her as she approached his bed with a thermometer in hand.

"Open up, Mr. Lavalle. I need to take your temperature."

He watched her as she moved the blood pressure cuff onto his arm.

"The doctor is taking your stitches out tomorrow; you will be relieved to hear that."

Sebastian nodded.

Nurse Banner counted seconds on her watch. "I think they'll move you to the surgical ward tomorrow if everything is stable." She removed the thermometer, shook it, and placed it back in the vial. "Perfect, as is your blood pressure."

"It must be your diligent care, Nurse Banner."

"You are charmers, you French men. Now, settle down. I'll bring some juice and a gelatin if you like before you go to sleep."

"I'll look forward to that." The nurse always brought Leah to his thoughts. Leah had visited last week; however, his memory was hazy.

Nurse Banner returned with the gelatin and juice. "They'll start you on real solids tomorrow to build you up.

You're making remarkable progress, and you are such a very good patient," she told him.

"My daughter is a children's nurse at the Great Ormond Street Hospital in London," Sebastian said.

"A children's nurse? That is a wonderful specialty and a terrific hospital. You must be very proud of her."

"I am, as your parents must be of you. Have you always wanted to be a nurse?"

"Yes, always. Both my parents are nurses, so it was inevitable."

Sebastian could not reconcile his thoughts and his feelings. Keeping his voice as calm as possible, he encouraged her to continue talking. "I believe that's why you have such a gift."

"I'm only chatting with you tonight because I'm not too busy; it's not really allowed, you know. However, I do love your French accent. In fact, I love everything French: the food, the wine, the country, and even Charles Aznavour—his voice, not his looks." She giggled.

"Have you visited France?" he asked.

"No, sadly, not yet. One day I hope to. I've only just finished my training."

"You're young. I promise you will have much time to visit France."

"I'm twenty-one on September twelfth," she answered.

Sebastian once again caught his breath. He couldn't believe the coincidence: she had the same birth date as the daughter he'd allowed Stella and her husband to adopt twenty years ago, along with an affinity for the French and France. Plus, she reminded him of his daughter Leah, who was also a nurse.

Could this be Jaqueline? He was almost sure she had to be.

"Mr. Lavalle, are you in pain?" She looked concerned.

"No, not at all. With all this talk of France, you make me miss my country."

"You look a little peaky. You're tired. I suspect too much talk. Let's get you settled for the night. Enough talking for one day." Nurse Banner finished her nightly routine with him.

"Will I ever see you again if they move me tomorrow?" It took everything within his power to control himself and keep from crying.

"I won't be your nurse, but I'll check in on surgical to see how you're getting along."

"My first name is Sebastian," he whispered.

"I know. I read it on your chart." Leaning over, she whispered in his ear, "I'm not supposed to tell you this, but I believe you're special." Placing her finger on her lips, she whispered, "My name is Jacqueline."

"An angel's name. You've saved my life in more ways than you'll ever know." Sebastian sighed.

"That's about the nicest thing you could say to me. Mr. Lavalle, you must keep our conversation secret, or I'll be in big trouble with Sister Brown."

"Your secret is safe with me."

"Sleep. I'll be back later."

Finally, now he understood the reason he had been delivered there as if by the hands of God, though not necessarily in a way he would've chosen. Discovering his daughter Jacqueline alive, well, happy, and successful, with a genuine connection to him, was an unexpected gift. He understood he was in a place where he could now make peace with himself, his life, and his God.

— 43 —

Abby drove up to Andrew's home. It was the first day of school after the summer holiday. It was the second week of August and still blistering hot. She and Heather were going grocery shopping, as they did from time to time, and Abby was driving. She honked the horn and noticed Andrew come out and walk up to the car. Abby rolled down her window.

"Hi. Good morning. What a pleasant surprise," he said in greeting her.

"Hello, Andrew. It's grocery shopping day. Back to school for the kids."

"That must be a relief for you."

"Not really. I miss them when they're not around."

"That's something I'd expect you to say. May I add, you look lovely today. Hope to see you again soon."

"Thank you, Andrew." Abby almost told him he looked gorgeous too; he was wearing navy blue and white, and the colors looked amazing on him.

Heather stepped outside, and Abby noticed as soon as Heather saw Andrew, she sashayed all the way to the car, looking as if she were going to a garden party. She wore a canary-yellow summer dress and a white straw hat with yellow ribbons down her back. The gentle breeze lifted the skirt and the ribbons, giving her a Marilyn Monroe effect. Looking radiant, Heather jumped into the front seat.

"Have a good day," she said gaily to Andrew.

"And you," he said tersely.

As he walked away, Andrew turned and flashed one of his brilliant smiles directly toward Abby.

"You look nice this morning." Abby smiled at Heather.

"Thanks. The truth is, it's all for him."

"You mean Andrew?"

"Yes, he hardly seems to notice me." Heather pouted.

Abby didn't know what to say. "Are you still, you know, together?"

"I am; he's not."

"I don't understand."

"He broke it off with me two months ago."

"I'm sorry."

"I'm in love with him." Heather began to sob.

"Oh, please don't cry. Does he know how you feel?"

"Yes, of course he does! I declared my love for him only to be rejected and told he'd never fall in love with me. He liked my beautiful body, and he appreciated my skills as his nanny and housekeeper, but nothing more." Heather continued to wail.

"Heather, to be honest with you, I'm surprised you're telling me any of this."

"Who else can I talk to? Oh my God, I don't know what to do. I feel so miserable. I'm hopelessly in love with him, but he doesn't want me." Heather's sobs continued.

"I think we should stop at Tea on the Sea tearoom and

have a cup of tea, a cake, and a chat. We can grocery shop later this week," Abby said, trying to console her.

Abby pulled up outside the beautiful tearoom, where she and Heather occasionally stopped after grocery shopping. It gave them a little taste of home.

Abby and Heather followed the waitress past bleached pine tables with aquamarine-and-white napkins held together with Mother-of-pearl seashells and teacups with painted shells and flowers. Vases of various shapes, colors, and sizes of sea glass—creating images of stained-glass windows—adorned the sideboards, and paintings of mermaids, sandpipers, seagulls, and sunrises and sunsets over the ocean hung on the walls. The only music was the sounds of the seashore.

Sitting down, Abby ordered a pot of tea and a crumpet; Heather asked for the same.

"Heather, I'll listen to you only if you understand that I'll be honest. I won't lie to you," Abby said. "Andrew is a good, kind man and a wonderful Father."

"Oh yeah, he's good, but he's finished having great sex with me. Now that he has his confidence back, he only wants my housekeeping skills."

"Heather, that's unfair. Was the sex a mutual decision?"

"Honestly, at first, he didn't have it in him. He was more than reluctant. I took him to bed in the beginning. It was no great passion. He was shy and out of practice. He didn't perform as well as his good looks promised!"

"That is not information I need to hear," Abby said sharply.

"What? Don't tell me you've not slept with the mesmerizing magician."

"Absolutely not!"

"Ochs, you don't even fancy him?" Heather asked incredulously.

Abby was starting to feel embarrassed. "Whether I fancy him or not has nothing to do with it. Byron has recently lost his wife and the Mother of his children; he's still grieving her. It's different with Andrew—his wife is still alive!"

Heather laughed. "Oh, you certainly do live up to your nickname, Miss Goody Two-shoes."

"I resent your comment and the nickname." Abby realized why they weren't great friends: they did not have much in common outside their work. "After all, I'm only trying to help."

"Ochs, you're way too serious, just like Andrew. How can you help me besides lending your ear? Andrew's always got something to chirp about what you've said or done. Byron and Andrew hang off everything you say. Remember the Christmas dinner last year? They were both drooling all over you. I'd like to know what you've got that I don't. It appears to me that all men fall to their knees where you're concerned."

"You would be wrong!" Abby retorted.

"Not from where I sit."

"Why don't you stop trying so hard?"

"What do you mean?"

"If any man told me he didn't love me, I am not sure I would try to change his mind."

"I told you: I've fallen in love with him."

"You're quite sure?"

"What are you talking about?"

Abby sat back in her chair and crossed her legs, taking a sip of her tea. She could see Heather was getting aggravated. Abby wanted to try to explain to her some of what she was feeling.

"Look, you and I are in a most unique situation. Byron explained this to me: the four of us are in a working relationship with one another, like married couples. Especially you and Andrew, seeing as you're sleeping together. That would make it difficult to know where to draw the line."

"I don't need to listen to this." Heather looked as if she were about to leave.

"Please hear me out. I do feel extreme attraction to Byron sometimes. I adore his children. I adore all of them. After a time of working in a rhythm with the family, we begin to believe we're in love with the idea of a loving husband and children. It's understandable, but it's not necessarily acceptable or even real."

"Shit, you think too much. Are you trying to tell me you're in love with Byron?" Heather said.

"No, I'm not telling you any such thing." Abby felt weary. "I'm attempting to explain to you how you've convinced yourself you're in love with Andrew. If I were you, I'd let him go gracefully."

"Easy for you to say."

"Actually, I gave up on someone I was deeply in love with and had been for a very long time. He'll always be a part of me, but he doesn't feel the same for me. Accepting his decision and believing it and not running to him to beg him to love me as I love him is taking every ounce of energy."

"Och, you dark horse. Who is he?"

"That doesn't matter. I'm attempting to enlighten you as to why pining for a man who doesn't want you is hopeless. Move on. Heather, you're very beautiful, and you know how to use your … assets. Be kind to yourself, and let him go."

"You sound like me granny—old and wise," Heather said sulkily.

"Will you keep working for him, or does it complicate things too much?"

"Yes, sure it does, but I love my job."

"Give it some time. I'm sure everything will work out all right."

"Well, thanks for listening. Maybe I should come visit the magician."

"No, you won't!" Abby was surprised at her own reaction.

"Och, I hit a nerve, did I not?"

"No, it's just that Byron is fragile; he needs a lot of tender, loving care."

"That's just what I intend to give him." Heather tossed her head back, laughing.

"This isn't funny. Look for someone without complications."

"You mean leave your men alone!"

"I told you: they're not my men."

"Whatever you say."

Abby jumped up so quickly she knocked her chair onto the floor and spilled her water. "I resent your nasty comments about my life, and I prefer you keep them to yourself from now on. I'm leaving!" She snatched up her purse and threw some bills onto the table. "I must pick Ben up from play group. Are you coming or not?"

"No need to get your knickers in a twist. It's all in good fun."

"Maybe so, but at my expense."

"No, I think I'll walk back. It's a beautiful day, and you've given me much food for thought."

— 44 —

Grace awoke early. She was excited, as it was Abby's birthday. She, Aria, and Ben were going to surprise her with breakfast in bed. In order to do that, they had to get up early. Grace tiptoed to Ben's room. He was almost three years old now and was walking, talking, and going to the pot. She was grateful there were no more diapers to change.

"Hi, Gracie. Me up, and we play?" Ben sat up in bed and rubbed his eyes.

"We are going to surprise Abby and do something special!" she whispered. "It's a secret. Follow me."

Ben followed without question. Grace dressed him, and they quickly tiptoed to the kitchen.

"Do you think Abby knows?" asked Aria, standing at the refrigerator.

"No, she's asleep."

"I have a song to sing her."

Together they quietly moved about the kitchen, making breakfast: toast with butter and jam, cornflakes, and orange juice. When they were all organized, they placed a birthday card on the tray. They tiptoed to Abby's room.

"Abby, can I come in?" Grace called out, knocking on the door.

"Of course you can. Are you all right?" Abby answered as Grace pushed open the door.

"Surprise!" Ben ran past her.

Aria burst into song: "Mary, Mary, quite contrary, how does your garden grow?"

Then they all joined in singing "Happy Birthday" together as Grace placed the breakfast tray on Abby's bed. Abby put her hands over her face.

Grace could see tears in her eyes when she looked at them. "Are your tears happy or sad?" she asked.

"Oh, happy! Happy! You wonderful children. How did you know?"

"Grandma Viv told us last week, and my Dad reminded us yesterday when he called."

"I can't remember when anything so special happened to me. Thank you!" Abby said, kissing the three of them a thousand times.

They all sat together on Abby's bed, sharing her breakfast and reading the birthday card out loud: "To someone very special. We love you. Have a fun day!"

Grace left the house, satisfied with their secret. She knew there were more surprises planned for the rest of the day. Her Dad was away until the weekend, but Uncle Andrew had a plan to surprise Abby.

After the girls left for school, Abby started her morning routine. Ben watched cartoons while Abby took full advantage and started the laundry and then cleaned the bathrooms and tidied up. Later, she and Ben walked to the mailbox to collect the mail. The mailbox was full of envelopes, including some that looked like birthday cards from England and mail for Byron. Abby tucked the mail under her arm and took Ben's hand, and they went back into the house.

Abby was about to put the kettle on for tea and settle down to read her birthday cards, when she heard the doorbell. A young man stood at the door, holding an enormous, beautiful bouquet of pink and white roses. Abby gasped.

"Ms. Abby Lavalle?"

"Yes?" she answered.

"This delivery is for you," he told her.

"Thank you!" Abby could hardly believe her eyes.

"Have a great day, miss."

Abby cradled the roses in her arms like a newborn. Who could have sent her something so wonderful? She placed the flowers in the kitchen sink and looked for a card.

> Dearest Abigail,
>
> I am sad that we will not see each other today, although I think the children have it all planned out. I hope you like the flowers. The girls told me to send you pink and white roses because you are English, and English ladies like roses. Enjoy your special day.
>
> Love,
> Byron, Grace, Aria, and Ben

Pressing the card to her heart, Abby had tears in her eyes. The flowers were glorious. Ben toddled out of the beach room, looking for a drink. Abby gave him a cup of milk and went about finding a vase large enough to hold two dozen roses, when the telephone rang.

"Hello?" she answered.

"Happy birthday."

"Andrew, thank you."

"Are you having a good day?" he asked.

"Yes, although I do believe there is a conspiracy going on."

"You might be right; we've all been planning and plotting for weeks. I'm calling to invite you and the children out for a birthday dinner this evening. Please be ready at five, as we have a drive."

"I can't refuse such a kind offer. Thank you, Andrew. We'll be ready." Abby hung up the phone. She liked Andrew.

She arranged the roses, placing them in the vase one at a time with baby's breath and soft fern. The roses were closed tightly, aching to bloom to their full and total glory.

Andrew had invited her out for dinner several months ago, but she'd refused him immediately, believing he and Heather had a thing. But now that he and Heather had split, she was pleased he had asked her. Although hesitant to go with him, she was aware he was special. Something about him had begged her to notice since the first moment they met in church.

It was all complicated; however, she was excited about the idea of taking all the children out with him that night for dinner. Andrew was thoughtful; the gesture was beyond decent, even though he was and had been her mainstay, always walking beside her throughout this new journey, always there.

After Ben went down for his nap, she put on the kettle, deciding to have quiet time and open some of her birthday cards. She sat in the beach room on a cozy chair with her feet up and a nice cup of tea, facing the ocean, which was twinkling blue, with soft white caps. The Brilliant Blue sky appeared endless, with not a cloud to be seen—what a beautiful day.

Looking at the writing on the first envelope, she knew it was from her Dad. Abby opened the card and read the letter inside.

> Dear Abby,
>
> Happy birthday. Just a quick note to let you know I'm feeling much better. I was released from hospital last week and will start my chemotherapy within the month. The doctors are very positive about a complete recovery, for which I'm deeply grateful and relieved. I am looking forward to you coming home in December, although for a very sad event. Hopefully we'll celebrate Christmas together. More later.
>
> Love,
> Dad

Abby was relieved to receive such a positive note from her Dad; it was a great birthday gift. The next envelope had Sasha's writing.

> Hi, Sis,
>
> I'm starting to save my pennies, preparing to cross the Atlantic to Virginia for a holiday with you next year. See you in December.
>
> Love,
> Sasha

Abby felt that a visit home in December was a mixed blessing. She wanted to be present for Eugene's memorial and to spend some time with her near and dear friends and family, but something inside her didn't want to leave Virginia. She couldn't articulate what it was—maybe the fear of never returning. It was a ridiculous thought, as she had a green card and the job with Byron. She shook her head at her own foolishness.

Abby had a sip of tea as she picked up the next card. Turning it over, she immediately recognized the handwriting: Father Gabriel Spencer.

Abby was shocked. What was he doing to her, sending a birthday card now? The front of the card was adorned with a long-stemmed red velvet rose and the words "To a beautiful person. Happy birthday." Inside, he had written, "Dearest Abby, enjoy the rose. I love you. Gabriel."

Inside the birthday card was a folded letter, but Ben was

awake and calling out to her, so she put the letter back inside the card and placed it in a drawer.

I can't think on him just now. Why now? Just as my gaping wounds are growing a transparent skin. How could you, Gabriel?

Later that afternoon, Abby and the children were dressed and waiting for Andrew and his girls to collect them for their evening out. Abby wore a pale blue satin sundress, and she had her hair piled on top of her head; she felt comfortable. The girls were dressed in yellow-and-white gingham sundresses, and Ben wore yellow shorts and a white shirt. Everyone looked bright and cheery. The girls were excited. Aria was jumping up and down, singing "Happy Birthday," and Grace was playing with Ben.

Eventually, Andrew arrived a few moments before five, bringing the station wagon in order to chauffeur everyone.

"Happy birthday." Andrew smiled at her. She looked at him with admiration. He looked handsome, with a new haircut, a royal-blue shirt, and gray slacks.

"You look beautiful tonight, Abigail." Andrew spoke her very thought of him.

"Uncle Andrew!" Ben called out.

"Hi, Benedict, my favorite boy! Come with me! Hi, girls. Let's all go. I'll put Ben in back; you girls climb in with Katie and Babs. They're waiting for you." Eventually, everyone was settled and buckled in.

"Dad, where are we going?" Katie asked.

"It's a surprise," he responded.

The sound of all the girls and Ben rang out from the backseat; the children were having great fun. Several renditions of "Happy Birthday" rang out, along with hoots of laughter.

"This is very kind of you," Abby told him.

"Nonsense. We are all bursting with excitement! It's beautiful to have them together chattering. They get along so well, like a group of old girls." Andrew and Abby laughed. "They're intricately woven together, as their parents are—closer than cousins because they choose to be together."

"I like the way they've all made room for our boy child." Abby smiled. "They adore him. It's as though he was always with us. We should try to get them together more often. I'll make a better effort."

Andrew sighed and smiled, as if he were about to say something.

"What is it?" asked Abby.

"Oh, nothing—a pleasant thought. We'll be there soon."

She noticed they were heading toward Williamsburg.

"Oh wow, are we eating at a restaurant in Williamsburg?" Grace asked.

"Yes, we are!"

"Does that mean we can help make bread and make horseshoes and play the harpsichord?" she asked. "I love it there."

"Me too!" added Katie. The conversations continued.

Andrew glanced in the rearview mirror at the kids. "We're taking Abby to a tavern for her birthday dinner—a colonial tavern called Christiana Campbell, named after the lady herself. It's very old, and it hasn't changed in three hundred years. Many years ago, President George Washington used to eat in this tavern."

"Wow!" said Katie. "What an amazing surprise, Dad."

"A fabulous idea, Andrew. I've longed to eat there. I'm so delighted the children are with us. It's perfect."

"Can we have pizza, hot dogs, and french fries?" asked Grace.

Everyone shouted out different foods at the same time.

"I think we should all quieten down," Abby said, hushing them all.

At the tavern, when they stepped inside, it was as though they were cast back in time, looking into dark rooms with low beamed ceilings, heavy oak tables and chairs, tiny leaded windows with candles, and oil lamps on the tables. Pewter platters were filled with comfort food, including hearty mutton stew and Welsh rabbit. The aromas of honey mead overflowing in pewter goblets and barbecued meat falling off the bone, along with fresh-baked bread, were reminiscent of days long since past.

The hostess showed them to a large, round oak table with a high chair for Ben. Clambering to find their seats, the girls sat themselves next to their chosen friend. Grace sat beside Ben and patted the seat next to her, beckoning Abby to sit beside her. Abby smiled and sat down. The night overflowed with joy and celebration. Abby watched Andrew with all the children; he was patient, kind, and loving toward all of them.

"You must be very proud parents." The waiter commented on how well behaved the children were.

An outsider looking on would have thought they were a handsome husband, a wife, and a family of beautiful children, like a Norman Rockwell painting.

Abby's thoughts wandered to the letter in her bedside drawer. She shook herself. *Don't allow him to prevent you from enjoying this wonderful birthday celebration.*

Suddenly, a hush embraced the rooms, and seemingly out of nowhere appeared a cake with a multitude of candles.

The waiters led everyone in serenading Abby with "Happy Birthday."

Toward the end of the song, Aria's glorious voice rang out, soaring above and beyond all. Her words stilled all the patrons to listen. At the end of the song, cheers and applause erupted, mostly because of sweet Aria and her gifted voice.

"What a wonderful birthday," Grace said. "I wish my Dad was here."

"I know." Abby affectionately stroked Grace's hair. "He would love this."

"We'll surprise him on his birthday," Andrew said.

"The food, the wine—everything about this birthday has been beyond special. Thank you, everyone!" Abby choked back her emotions. As she looked around the table, her gaze fell upon Andrew. He looked at her in a warm, familiar kind of way—a look she recognized only too well through the eyes of love.

Abby didn't smile or utter a word, staying still and silent in the moment, allowing herself to saturate her mind and body with the genuine aura of love radiating from the handsome man she found herself constantly drawn to.

The next day, the sun was milky white as it struggled to share its warmth through the gathering storm clouds. Abby dropped the children off at school and play group and decided to walk on the beach. She had enjoyed her birthday yesterday with Andrew and the children. He had made it special. He was special.

She held on to her letter from Gabriel. Try as she might not to think on it, it continued to nudge at her. She was holding off on opening it, though she was not sure why. Possibly she was hoping to find something that would lift her to a euphoric state, give her a sense of completion, or help her through the confusion of the complex emotions she was trying to unravel around her unexpected feelings for Byron and Andrew. Maybe she simply feared the inevitable double message of love and rejection that lay within the pages of Gabriel's letters.

Based on their last conversation, she thought, she should have marked it "Return to sender" and avoided any of the double messages, but she would not—could not. Abby sat on a large, flat rock as the storm clouds gathered around her. She opened the letter slowly and read the words out loud to the stormy sea.

Dearest Abby,

Happy birthday! I couldn't allow this day to pass without telling you I'm thinking about you and offering a prayer. I wonder how you're making out with the family you take care of. Like many of us, they are blessed to have found you.

My news is rather sad: my Mother has cancer. She was diagnosed in May with pancreatic cancer, although it has now spread to other organs. She is currently in a hospice, receiving palliative care and not doing very well. I'm running around in circles, desperately trying to process this news while attempting to offer support to my Dad and siblings. My mind and body are utterly exhausted.

I miss you, Abigail. I feel you're one of the few people in my world I can trust. I wish I could lay my head on your shoulder and cry until I stop hurting. I'd like to write more, but I cannot. Please know that although we do not communicate, you are never far away from me.

Gabriel
xxxoo
With you all the way!

Abby wiped her eyes, her nose, and her face with the sleeve of her jacket, weeping uncontrollably. As the storm arrived, the rain fell in heavy, large drops much like her tears. How could there be so many similarities? Gabriel's Mother and her Father—wherever she looked, it appeared someone she knew was suffering with cancer. The disease didn't care if one was young, old, rich, poor, Mother, or Father. At least her Dad had a better prognosis.

She sat on the rock, allowing the rain to saturate her, praying the water would wash away the sorrow and her images of Gabriel.

— 45 —

Heather looked out the window of her apartment. It was late afternoon, and the sun was losing some of its heat as it descended. She enjoyed the autumn light of early September; there was something vital and bright within the sense of shorter days approaching and changing leaves. Surely it was one of the best times of the year in Virginia.

She watched the cars go by, waiting for Andrew. The grandparents were babysitting the girls that night, giving her and Andrew the night off. She was bored, especially with no Andrew to flirt with. Most of her peers had boyfriends or other interests.

Heather heaved a great sigh. Finally, he arrived, stopping the car and moving quickly toward the house. She'd found herself thinking about him less since the lecture and conversation she'd had with Goody Two-shoes a few weeks ago regarding the illusions of love. Heather had to admit there was a lot of logic and truth in what Abigail had said. The idea of being in love was intoxicating, especially when they were all playing house together, and both men and both women were attractive and easy on the eyes. It had been inevitable one or two would become entangled.

Ochs, just like Abby to say something so prissy and wise.

They hadn't been grocery shopping together since the teahouse. Maybe it was for the best. Giving herself a shake, she decided she would go out for the night—dress up to the nines and hit the town. She would go dancing and see if anyone interesting was at the new nightclub.

Thinking about what she would wear, she heard the front door close as Andrew left. She walked back to the window. He looked handsome in a suit and tie.

Is he going out on a date? I wonder who he's chasing. The dark horse?

She wasn't sure how she felt about that; her feelings about Andrew were perplexing. She would get dressed, go out for the night, and forget him and everyone else. That was what she needed—a dance and a good fling!

Byron was relaxing in his office, home for the weekend with his family and grateful to be in his chair, looking out the window at the panoramic Virginia view. The September sun slowly descended into the sea, leaving a golden-orange glow. There was no sight of blue, only a powerful, glowing burnt orange—a unique color for that time of year and his favorite.

It had been almost two years since his darling Colleen died, when he'd believed he would never care if the sun rose or set again. Although he and his children missed her more than words could describe, it was a relief to be working through the grief, learning the new rules of life without her, and moving forward. Colleen would have wanted all of them to let go and live their lives.

He attributed most of that to Abby, including his trust in her and his growing respect for her. When he was away working, she gave him peace of mind. Abby was going out on a date that night, and he found himself struggling with the idea. It was unexpected, yet it shouldn't have been, as she was beautiful, young, and lively, in her prime.

Byron heard the doorbell chime, and Gracie opened the door.

"Uncle Andrew, hi."

"Hi, Gracie."

"Have you come to see my Dad?" she asked. Byron was behind her.

"No, not tonight, Grace. Uncle Andrew has come to take out Abby," Byron told her. "Come in, Andrew. Good move, my friend!"

"Thank you, Byron."

Byron was relieved and grateful for his friendship and happy Andrew at last had found the confidence to invite Abby to dinner. Yet he felt disturbed by something else—a new feeling he did not recognize. He was suffering from envy.

"Gracie, go find Abigail."

"I'm right here," she answered.

"Wow, you are stunning!" Andrew beamed at her.

"Thank you." Abigail smiled back at him.

"Abby, I love your dress! It's the color of the sky!" Gracie exclaimed. "It's so beautiful—and your hair and your shoes. You look like a movie star."

Amazing Grace

Byron cut her off. "You look very smart, Abby—nice dress. Let's go look for Aria. Have a good night, kid."

Byron took Gracie by the hand and left Abby and Andrew staring after him.

Andrew escorted Abby to his car, feeling anxious. As they drove away, he looked at her. "I can't tell you how happy I am that you agreed to come out with me tonight."

"I can't thank you enough for inviting me." She smiled at him.

"You look so beautiful; that shade of turquoise or blue looks radiant on you." He felt nervous, as though his future depended on that night. He was determined to make it a magical evening.

"You realize I've been wanting to ask you out alone and take you somewhere very special for a long time. I have a big crush on you." He grinned at her.

"Bless me, I can't turn that sweet comment away. The last time someone had a crush on me, I believe I was five years old." Abby giggled.

"I doubt that. I want tonight to be memorable—like you."

"Oh, stop. I'm not that special," she said.

"You are to me. I've booked us a table at the Ocean View."

"I like that restaurant," Abby replied. "The food is very good."

"Afterward, I thought we could go uptown to the Beaches, a new nightclub in town. It's getting great reviews."

"Sounds wonderful. You've gone to a lot of trouble."

"I'm not finished yet; I have a big surprise at the end of the evening. You ought to be careful. I'm not used to excitement since we went out to the Christiana Campbell. I live a pretty quiet life." They laughed together with ease.

Andrew and Abby enjoyed a delicious meal at the restaurant, and afterward, they headed to the nightclub.

Like most nightclubs of the time, it had low ceilings, flashing colored strobe lights, and a large area for dancing. Intimate lighting illuminated the tables, and the bar stretched across the length of the entire club. There was an excellent choice and variety of music, enough to enjoy a nice selection of both fast and slow.

Finding a corner table, Andrew sat Abby down and ordered a bottle of champagne. In between drinks, they found time to dance to Olivia Newton-John's "Physical," America's "You Can Do Magic," and Paul McCartney and Stevie Wonder's "Ebony and Ivory." When at last a slow song played—Bertie Higgins's "Key Largo," his favorite—Andrew took Abby's hand, and they walked together to the dance floor. Andrew drew her to him, holding her in his arms close to him. Feeling confident and comfortable, they moved effortlessly, as though they had danced together always. It was like placing his hand into a perfectly fit glove.

Abby studied him.

"This is nice. You are a great dancer. Light as a feather on your feet. It feels so good." Andrew couldn't contain himself; taking a chance, he leaned over, placing a whisper of a kiss upon her lips. "You feel magnetic."

Smiling back at him, Abby reached up and kissed him with more passion and fervor than he expected. Embracing her, never wanting to let her go, he closed his eyes, wishing the night would never end.

Heather arrived at the nightclub, wearing a sexy off-the-shoulder scarlet dress, feeling outstanding. She'd arranged to meet up with a new acquaintance—not a close friend, as Heather didn't have close friends. Goody Two-shoes was as tight as she got with anyone.

She stood still and allowed her eyes to adjust to the dark and the flashing lights of the room. She recognized her acquaintance, Amy, at a table in the far corner. The music was loud, which would make it difficult to talk. Heather waved and walked over. Sitting down, she yelled across to Amy, "Thanks for saving the table!" Amy gave her a thumbs-up.

The waiter arrived, and Heather ordered a bottle of red house wine and two glasses, miming to Amy to ask if that was okay. Amy gave her another thumbs-up. Heather was hardly seated, when a reasonably good-looking man approached her.

"Hi! Would you like to dance?" he yelled.

Heather's policy was never to refuse an invite to dance, as one never knew who was watching. As they approached the dance floor, "Physical" changed to "Key Largo." Her dance partner handled the transition smoothly and impressively. He didn't hold her too close, maintaining a comfortable distance, and he didn't try to converse. He just moved her around the floor, mouthing to her that she was beautiful. Heather was enjoying herself, looking around the dance floor—until she recognized Andrew.

So he was out on a date, having fun. He was kissing someone! She couldn't see clearly at first because of the lights.

Oh my God. It can't be. Abby!

They were so engrossed in one another they did not see her. In the middle of the dance, she ran from her partner to the table. Grabbing her handbag, she yelled, "I have to go, Amy!"

"What? Are you okay? What's wrong?"

"I must get away from here! Don't ask me." Heather ran from the nightclub onto the street, where she hailed a taxi.

Once home, she ran into her bedroom in tears. *How long has this been going on?* They'd looked quite cozy. She was filled with emotions. She was furiously jealous and angry. She tore off her dress and threw her shoes across the room. She was so mad she wanted to break something. She picked up a glass vase off her dresser and hurled it at the wall. It shattered and spewed across the floor, fractured into tiny parts.

Andrew hadn't told her he was going to ask Goody Two-shoes out on a date. This was the last straw; she was sure she would never get him back now.

She went to her living room with shaking hands and poured herself a large whiskey. She sat for some time, crying into her glass. Taking the last swig, she stopped crying.

I'll show them!

After leaving a message with her travel agent to book her on the first flight to Aberdeen, Heather started to pack her things up in boxes and label them. After methodically moving around the apartment and cleaning up, she eventually lay down and fell asleep.

When she awoke to a telephone call, it was the travel agent, who'd managed to get her on an afternoon flight.

Heather packed the last of her clothes into a suitcase and finished cleaning the apartment, leaving it spotless. When she was finished, she showered, dressed, picked up her suitcases, and looked around one more time.

Andrew will regret abandoning me—and for Goody Two-shoes, of all people. Hell hath no fury like a woman scorned.

She closed the apartment door, leaving it with no evidence of her, not even a letter explaining. She climbed into a taxi and rode away.

— 46 —

Andrew awoke early to the fall morning's sunrays spilling through the windows and warming his bed. Stretching his body like a cat, he felt like a new man after the wonderful night he and Abby had experienced. She was an amazing and beautiful woman. After the dinner and dancing, he had taken her on a starlight cruise along Chesapeake Bay. The moonlight had provided the perfect finale to their first date. They'd arrived home in the early hours of the morning, where he'd kissed her good night at Byron's front door.

When he'd asked her if he could call her again, Abigail had smiled at him and answered, "If you don't, I'll call you." Andrew had walked to his car feeling like Gene Kelly in the movie *Singin' in the Rain*.

He didn't hear the girls getting ready for school or Heather moving around in the kitchen. He showered and dressed quickly and went to the girls' bedroom.

"Good morning, girls. Wake up. Time to get ready for school. We've all slept in this morning. I'll put some breakfast on the table, and I'm going to see what's happened to Heather. I have a surgery at nine o'clock; we must hurry."

"Okay, Dad, I'll help," Katie said.

Andrew went into the kitchen to put on a pot of coffee. He placed cereal, dishes, spoons, and milk out for the girls. He then crossed the driveway toward Heather's apartment. The car was parked, as usual; she used it for work and personal errands. After climbing the stairs, he knocked on her door and called her name. He tried the door handle, and the door opened.

"Heather, are you there? Are you okay? Heather, may I come in?" Andrew called out. There was no answer.

He stepped inside the apartment. It was empty—all her personal effects had been removed. The bedroom door was open, and the bed was stripped. The sheets and blankets were folded in a pile on top of the bed. He walked into the bedroom and looked in the drawers and closets, which were open wide and empty. He realized she was gone. Several boxes were in the corner, labeled with her address in Scotland, with a note saying to please forward them on. He saw no other notes or evidence she even existed.

Whatever has prompted her to do such an inconsiderate, unprofessional thing?

He shook his head. He hoped he was not the reason for her leaving. But he had no time to think about it now; he went back to the house to help the girls.

"Where is Heather?" Katie asked.

"She's gone."

"Where has she gone?"

Andrew raised his voice. "I have no idea. I do not know. She has left us without help or notice."

"Why, Dad? Why would she do that? I thought she loved us."

"I am sorry, Katie. I don't know. Now, let's get ready for school. We can work something out. I'll drop you at school today, and I'll call Abby to ask if she can pick you up tonight."

"It's not her week, Dad. It's Rosella's week," Katie told him.

"Okay, that's good. Maybe Rosella can drop you at Abby's, and you can play with the girls until I finish work."

"Yeah!" said the girls. "We'd like that."

"Come along, girls—quickly, or I'm not going to make it to the surgery on time."

Babs whimpered, "We don't have our lunch, Daddy. Heather always makes our lunch and puts it in our backpacks—and our homework and a banana to eat on the way to school. Daddy, please!"

Andrew started to feel annoyed. "We don't have time. Come. Let's get going. I'll ask Abby to pack you a lunch today and bring it to you at school, okay?"

"She doesn't know what we like to eat." Babs sulked.

Andrew spoke sharply. "Enough, Babs. We are doing the best we can. Now, stop complaining, and get in the car."

The girls clambered into the backseat, looking as if they were about to cry. Andrew screeched out of the driveway toward the school.

— 47 —

Abby dropped off the children at school and Ben at his play group and then drove to Rosella's for a walk. They'd arranged the outing last week, as they'd found little time to spend together of late.

"You look beautiful," Rosella told Abby with a hug.

"Thank you. I'm feeling very well," Abby replied.

"Let's go while it's nice. We can go along the beach road to the seaside."

The sun was warm for autumn in Virginia. It was a glimpse of heaven's gate. The beauty never ceased to amaze Abby, especially that time of year. She loved the glorious mornings and evenings, particularly the autumn light, which felt warm and cool at the same time, as if it were preparing you for the impending winter. Everything appeared to be draped in a golden light. The grass on the sand dunes was pale yellow amid flowers, bumblebees, butterflies, and bulrushes bending in the gentle breeze. Golden maple trees lined the streets above the seashore. The leaves' burnt oranges and reds glistened on the ancient trees, creating a cathedral canopy.

Silver sands lay on the beach, and the ocean, as always, called with its tidal rhythm. There was evidence all about them of the constant glory of autumn.

"This is the best time of the year—so vibrant," Abby said.

"As are you, Abigail. What is going on? You must share it with me."

"You're a wonderful cousin and friend to me, walking with me through all the crises of my youth—love, family, and every part of my life—and even giving me a home. I'm blessed to have you in more ways than I can say. I'm not sure why I deserve you, Aidan, and the children. Hopefully one day I will find someone to help in the same way. You've given me love so that I found courage and strength to find my way."

"Abby, it was easy. You're part of us, and we all love you. Come on. Tell me. How was your date last night with the dishy Andrew?"

"Amazing! We had dinner at Ocean View, and after, we went dancing. He is a really great guy—very considerate. With great lips!"

"Oh, Abby." Rosella stopped to hug her. "I'm so happy. Did he ask you out again?"

"Yes, he asked if he could call me, and I told him if he didn't, I would. Byron's home for a few days, so it gave me a chance to relax and get away."

"This sounds exciting!" Rosella said.

"It's really not all it's cracked up to be."

"What are you talking about?"

"I feel confused. I'm not sleeping well. I'm wondering through the night if it's possible to be in love with more than one person at a time."

"Good Lord, Abby, what do you mean? It's not that complicated."

"I mean what I say. I have strong yet different feelings of love for all three men."

"How can that be?" Rosella asked.

"Honestly, I don't know. I've been asking myself that question for several months. I'll always hold Gabriel in a special place in my heart."

"He's not available, Abby; we've been through this."

"That doesn't prevent me from loving him. And now I've also developed intense feelings for Byron. There are nights when I lie alone in my bed, steps away from Byron in his bed, and fantasize about a glorious night of unadulterated passion."

"Oh, Abby!" Rosella sounded exasperated.

"There's Andrew, the constant in my life. Last night was so amazing. He made me feel vibrant. When Andrew came to pick me up, Byron was verging on rude. I suspect he is, like all of us, filled with mixed emotions and confused. I have within me a capacity to love them all in different ways."

"Abby, surely one of them stands out more than the others." Rosella stopped and took Abby's hands.

"No, not currently. That's the dilemma."

"What are you going to do?"

"I don't know. Maybe the decision is not mine to make. I'm kidding myself. I must learn to live with my emotions. Fortunately, it's almost time for me to go back to England for a few weeks; it will give me the opportunity to think and sort out a few of my feelings."

"I'll pray for you, Abby."

"Pray for all of us; I'm not the only one with the dilemma," Abby told her.

"Has Byron expressed feelings for you?"

"Yes, he suggested he could be falling in love with me. It's not easy to explain. Also, Heather and Andrew had a relationship."

Rosella stopped again. "I knew it! She had her eye on him right from the start!"

"Why not? They weren't doing anything illicit. Just two good-looking, healthy heterosexuals enjoying one another. Heather believes she's in love with Andrew; she says he broke her heart. I suggested to her it might be the idea of being in love that she's in love with. Living a family life with a man and helping him raise his children is no Cinderella story."

"What did she say to that?" Rosella asked.

"She said I was like her granny—old and wise."

"This is a dilemma for all of you. I see that now that you've explained it to me. I'm sure it will, in time, work out for the best."

"Maybe so, but not without someone feeling hurt or abandoned. We all need to remember the most important part of this story: there are several children involved. And I love them all." Abby started to weep. "I'm sorry. It's just that when I think about the little ones, I feel helpless."

"Abby, you can't resolve this on your own, and it's not all your responsibility. Do as you have suggested: watch, wait, and pray for guidance. It will come to you."

"Thanks for listening, as well as for a beautiful walk and beneficial talk. I must go collect Ben from play group."

"See you later." They hugged goodbye.

Abby arrived home after picking up Ben and laid him down for his afternoon nap at home. The phone rang.

"Hello?"

"Hi. It's Andrew."

"Hi. How are you?"

"I was feeling like Gene Kelly in *Singin' in the Rain* after our special date."

"Oh, you smooth talker." She giggled.

"My bubble burst this morning when I discovered, to my surprise, Heather left. Up and gone. Disappeared."

"What are you talking about? I don't believe it. What for? Did you say or do something to upset her?"

"No, not to my knowledge. But she's gone, and I need to ask a big favor from you. Please, can you look after the girls for a bit until I can work something out? And I left without packing a lunch. Could you take them a lunch at the school?"

"Don't worry, Andrew," Abby said. "I'll see they're okay. I can keep them here overnight and take them to school tomorrow if that helps."

"Yes, please. I have a surgery, so I am heading to the hospital. I can't thank you enough."

"Glad to help, of course. Drop in later if you have time."

— 48 —

Four weeks later, on Halloween, Abby worked alone in the Grant kitchen, trying to organize all the children, both Byron's and Andrew's, for school and help them dress in their costumes. Each of them was beyond excited.

Gracie, who was dressed as Peter Pan, was helping Bugs Bunny, a.k.a. Ben. Aria, as Snow White, was singing "One Day My Prince Will Come." Babs was dressed as a cute pumpkin, and Katie was a witch, with a big green wart on her nose. The noise level in the kitchen was deafening.

Halloween wasn't something Abby had been raised with in England. Sometimes they had bobbed for apples at Brownies, but that had been the extent of it. In America, the children were almost as excited as if it were Christmas morning. She had to admit, though, they all looked cute. Abby was unsuccessful in trying to get them organized in order to take them all to the school drop-off.

Heather had been gone for more than four weeks after disappearing with not a word or even an explanation to Andrew. He assumed she was safe, as she'd left a note for him to forward her boxes. Abby was making inquiries, trying to find out what had prompted such thoughtless, juvenile behavior; she simply couldn't understand. She thought something traumatic must have occurred that they knew nothing about.

Abby had written to Heather, asking her what had been so urgent to make her leave the way she had, leaving this family high and dry. Was it a boyfriend? Was she frightened? Dealing with all the children was a lot more work for Abby; however, in many ways, it made her job easier—the more the merrier. The children got along well; having their friends around kept all the sisters from arguing with one another and supplied Ben with four little Mamas.

But that day was different.

"Be quiet, all of you!" Abby yelled, picking up Bugs Bunny and hoisting him onto her hip. "I can't hear myself think. Everyone calm down, and collect your lunch boxes and your homework. Put on your coats, and stand at the door quietly, please."

"I don't want to wear a coat today. It will spoil my costume!" Aria cried.

"Me too!" Babs wailed.

"All of you, put on your coats now. Do you hear me? Or I promise you, no trick-or-treating tonight!"

"Come on, everyone. Let's be good for Abby and get off to school. Think of all the fun we will have tonight!" Grace said. Miraculously, her words seemed to work, and everyone was finally in the car and settled down.

Abby was tired and feeling short on patience. She couldn't wait for Grandma Viv to arrive. She was coming later that day, as she wanted to spend Halloween with the children. Byron had a big show in Vegas that night, featuring a new trick he'd been working on. It was a big secret he'd shared with her last time he was home—something about making a helicopter disappear.

Later, after she had dropped off all the children, Abby closed the front door and, leaning against it, heaved a great sigh. After putting on the kettle to make herself some tea, she put the breakfast dishes in the dishwasher and then took her tea to the beach room.

Sitting down and looking out toward the sea, Abby thought the scene had a Halloween look that day: dark gray skies with the odd distorted cloud. One looked distinctly like a witch on a broomstick. Abby chuckled to herself as the wind whisked it away. Some of the leaves swirled around the bottom of the trees and the garden and floated down slowly toward the sandy beach, where colorless waves crashed against the rocks. The wind howled, and the seagulls squawked, circling inland—a sure sign of storms at sea.

Abby shivered as she went into the kitchen to prepare a hearty soup and sandwiches for dinner. She would call it eyeball soup and drop some meatballs into it. Abby had also bought some pumpkin cookies with chocolate spiders on top of bright orange icing.

The telephone rang, and she went to pick it up.

"Hello. It's Andrew. I called to see if you survived the morning."

"Barely. They were beyond themselves. I told them to calm down and be quiet before going off to school. They all scampered out of the car in silence as fast as their little legs would go. Do you think you will make it tonight, Andrew?"

"Try to stop me. I can't begin to thank you for everything

you are doing. I'm going to contact the agency this weekend. We've waited long enough for an answer from Heather."

"Yes, well, that's your decision, Andrew."

"We'll talk more about it tonight," he answered.

"Okay, see you later."

Later in the evening, when all the little goblins were preparing for bed after a fun-filled day of trick-or-treating, Abby flopped onto a chair beside Grace. Grandma Viv was reading a bedtime story to Aria, and Ben was fast asleep.

"Grace, you were magic today. I would not have managed the day without you. I'm so proud of you," Abby told her. Gracie smiled and snuggled up closer to Abby, who pulled her in under her arm and stroked her long black hair.

"Thank you. I feel very sorry for Babs and Katie."

"Why?" asked Abby.

"Because Heather left them and didn't say anything, and their Mama is all the way across the sea in Ireland. Not only that, but they don't know who their new nanny will be. If it was me, I'd be really scared."

"I shouldn't worry, Gracie; Uncle Andrew will choose the very best nanny. Sometimes we must be brave and trust that everything will work out."

"He won't find a nanny like you."

"No, that's true, because we're all different. You won't find a nanny like Heather either."

"That's not what I mean," Grace said.

"What do you mean? What's troubling you, Gracie?" Abby continued to stroke Grace's hair.

Gracie began to cry, and tears fell from her big, round, sad brown eyes. The teardrops hung there, supported by her thick lashes. "When my Mom died, I missed her so much. I still do every day."

"Oh, Gracie, I understand."

"No, you don't!"

Abby sat quietly, shocked, deciding to stay quiet to allow Grace to pour out her thoughts.

"I felt sad every single day, and I did not like how I felt every morning. Even when you came to live with us, I was angry that you were here and not my Mom. But slowly, I felt better. I don't know the words or what to call it—just not so sad or mad." Grace looked up at Abby, smiled at her, and hugged her.

Abby remained silent, allowing Grace to continue with her innermost thoughts.

"Something happened that made me begin to feel different. When I came home from school, I could smell the supper. I was still sad. I felt like I was sort of forgetting my Mom, and I felt bad about that. The sad feelings came back. I missed her, but it was more than that. Something else felt wrong too. You know what I mean, Abby?"

"Yes, I do." Abby, desperately holding on to her own deluge of tears, waited for Grace to continue.

"Then do you remember, Abby? One day you took me and Ben to see Mom at the cemetery, and I sat with her and talked to her. That was the best day because it felt like my Mom touched me and told me it was a good thing to have you beside us. After the visit, I felt different. I think we all do. Abby, please don't leave us!"

Gracie began to sob again as Abby took her in her arms, unable to hold back her own tears. They wept together.

"Oh, Gracie, what makes you think I'm leaving you?"

Amazing Grace

"Because Heather left Uncle Andrew and the girls."

She hadn't realized the effect Heather's leaving had had on Byron's children.

"Grace, you look at me, and listen to what I'm saying. I'll never leave you and not prepare you or not return. I can't promise to never leave you, because we don't know what the future holds."

Grace interrupted her. "I think Uncle Andrew likes you. I look at him watching you when we're all together; he has a smile on his face all the time. I think he might take you away to his house to look after his girls." Grace broke down again.

"Please don't worry about such things. I'm here with you now, and I love you all. Grandma loves you, and your Daddy loves you; we'll always keep you safe and warm. I think you've had a very long day, helping me in so many ways. You need to go to bed and have a good sleep. I'll make you some hot chocolate, and we can talk together tomorrow."

Grace's heavy sobs slowed, and she was calming down as Grandma Viv came into the room.

"I was reading a story to Aria, and would you know? I fell asleep," Viv said. "What a day! Would you like me to tuck you in, Grace?"

"No, thanks, Gran. I'd like Abby to do it."

"Good. I'll make some tea. We had fun tonight—all those little goblins, fairies, witches, and princesses coming to the door for the tricks and treats. Did you have fun today, darling?" Viv asked Grace.

"I did."

"What should we do tomorrow when you come home from school? I'll think of something exciting," Viv said, and Gracie kissed her grandMother. "Good night, princess."

Abby sat quietly on the bed with Grace as she sipped her hot chocolate. When she had finished, Abby took the mug and, tucking her into bed, kissed her on the forehead. "Sleep well, darling Grace. All will be well."

Abby quietly left the room, switching off the light and closing the door.

Gently, she heard Gracie whisper, "I love you."

Viv was waiting for Abby in the beach room with a cup of tea. The fire was burning, and the sound of the wind and rain against the windowpane was strangely comforting.

"Sit, drink, and rest, for you deserve it. I'd like to share some thoughts with you if you're not too tired."

Abby sat in her chair, cupping the warm tea in her hands. "Not at all. It has been a long day—and a very good one, may I add. What's on your mind?"

Viv twisted her hands around her teacup. "When my darling Colleen died, I was plunged into a deep, dark, freezing pit with little desire to climb out. Nothing mattered to me, not even my beautiful grandchildren. They were part of her and a devastating reminder of my loss. For me to die would have been simpler, with less pain. For many moments, days, weeks, and months, I moved through time in a daze. Until miraculously, a sliver of tiny light penetrated the dark pit. Since the day you walked through this front door, slowly, gently, and surely, you've brought healing to this family from the inside out. Speaking for myself, today I see blue sky and green grass once again and dancing light in my grandchildren's eyes." Viv cried as she spoke. "I realize we can never replace our darling Colleen, and we wouldn't want to, but I believe she has sent the next best thing to us. Bless you, Abigail, for all you have done and all you do." Viv dried her eyes with a tissue.

"It's an honor to be part of this family; you all help me grow in ways you'll never know."

"I also believe Byron has feelings for you. I think he's finding it difficult to admit it because of his loyalty and love for Colleen. Dare I ask, Abby—do you have any feelings for Byron?"

Abby put down her cup, closing her eyes and shaking her head. "It's so complicated I'd rather not discuss it with you tonight, if you don't mind."

"I see Andrew has been taking you out from time to time," said Viv.

"Yes, we've been seeing each other, although we've had little time lately since Heather left."

"Oh, that one! Good riddance to bad rubbish, I say to her. Not a peep from her after dropping Andrew and leaving him and the children in the lurch. What does she think she's playing at?"

"I don't know, but she does deserve the benefit of the doubt. If she doesn't answer the letters soon, Andrew will replace her," Abby told her.

"Sooner the better, I say."

Abby felt drained; she didn't wish to discuss any of Viv's issues, not that night. "I think I'll turn in. I'm very tired, if you don't mind. Viv, thank you so much for your help today and everything you do to help me. You make my tasks so much lighter." Abby kissed Viv on the cheek.

"Thank you, my dear. Rest well."

The next morning, when Abby went to pick up the post, finally, a letter had arrived for her from Heather. Abby didn't wait to open it, tearing the envelope while standing in the bright November sunlight. She read the letter.

> Hi, Abby,
>
> I am a fool. I am safe but miserable. I made the biggest mistake in leaving. I miss everyone, and I'm writing to you in the hopes you will get me my job back. I realize you don't owe me anything. But I'd like you to speak to Andrew. I know he trusts you. I am lost. I hate the cold, damp fog; the sleet; and the endless nights here in Aberdeen. I want to come back to the warmth of Virginia. I'll explain my reasons for leaving when we meet again, and I hope that will be very soon.
>
> Your lost friend,
> Heather

Abby pushed the letter into her pocket as she went into the house. She was relieved to hear that Heather was safe, and apparently, she was her normal self-centered self, without any contrition for the upheaval she had caused or even a question as to how the girls were.

Time was pushing on. It was November 1. She would ask Viv to babysit that night and invite Andrew out for dinner.

Abby was confident he would reemploy Heather, especially if Abby pleaded Heather's case.

Abby and Andrew had spent much time together, sharing the day-to-day tasks of rearing children, and they were a perfect team. She had discovered Andrew was a dedicated Father, uncle, and friend. Byron was truly blessed; anyone who was close to Andrew was fortunate to know him; he was the most honorable man she had ever known.

Byron was coming home that weekend, and Abby looked forward to seeing him when he returned. It was strange how she missed him when he was away, although her life was so full. She also realized that day by day, she was finding her thoughts of Gabriel were less frequent. They were not disappearing—that would never happen—but they were not as intense, reverent, or longing. There had been a time when she would have run into his arms if only he had whispered, "I choose you." Now she wasn't sure of anything.

Viv breezed into the kitchen. "Hello, darling. How are you? You look so beautiful this morning. What are your plans for today? Would you like me to help with laundry? Is there anything I can do? How about I prepare supper for tonight? I can also pick up Ben from day care."

"Thank you. Viv, you are a Wonder Woman. I'd like to ask you a favor."

"Anything. What can I help you with?"

"I'd like to invite Andrew out for dinner tonight. A letter has arrived from Heather. She wants to come back, and I want to speak to him about it privately."

"I'm sorry, but that selfish little you-know-what does not deserve you or Andrew. How can you trust her?"

"I realize how you feel, Viv; however, better the devil we

know than the one we don't. I'm going home for three weeks in December for my brother's memorial and Christmas. In some ways, it's a selfish decision, but we do need her back here. I must speak with Andrew. Will you help me?"

"Of course I will. You take the night off with Andrew. If that's how you feel, I support you, but I do not like her."

"Fortunately, you don't have to. Thank you, Viv. It will lift a great weight off my shoulders."

"That's all I need to know, my dear. Off you go, and take some well-earned time to yourself today. I'll hold down the fort."

A few hours later, Andrew sat beside Abigail, feeling the warmth of the burning fire. He felt as warm and glowing as the pumpkins that adorned the hearth. He loved this pub; it wasn't too far out of town, and Abby had been the first person to introduce him to the eclectic flavors of the English menu.

"This is great. What a treat. I can smell all the delicious foods they are preparing for us. Someone was telling me the fish and chips are worth having," Andrew said, smiling at her. "What's on your mind, Abby?" He was somewhat anxious, as he was not sure what to expect. His first thought was that Abby was possibly going to suggest they not date anymore, if one could have called their time together dating. He patiently waited.

"I received the letter we have been waiting for from Heather today. She's fine," Abby told him.

"At last! That's a relief. What does she have to say for herself?"

"She apologized, in her own way, for the abrupt departure. She wants to come back to Virginia and to you and the girls."

Andrew observed Abby's beautiful face. Heather would have begged her to talk to him, he realized, and he didn't wish to prolong the outcome or make the situation more difficult. "Yes, she can but on very different conditions." He could see Abby was relieved.

"That's good news for all of us!"

"Why don't I phone her and make it work to our advantage? Don't worry about it, Abby. I'll take care of it from here on. We'll bring her back before Thanksgiving."

Abby leaned into him and kissed him softly on his lips. "Thank you, Andrew. You are one in a million."

"Believe me, it was worth it just for the kiss. There is method in my madness; I'm hoping you and I can start dating on a more serious level."

"Please be patient with me. We can talk about it when I return from England."

"I can't wait that long, Abby."

"Just a little more time. That is all I ask," Abby said.

Andrew was disappointed; he loved her, and he didn't need any more time. He wanted her more than anything—he was sure of it. However, she, for her own reasons, wasn't ready, and he didn't wish to lose her by putting pressure on her.

"I'll wait for you until the stars go out, Abigail. I am yours until you tell me differently."

"Andrew, I believe you are a prince among men."

— 49 —

Byron was home with his family for Thanksgiving and, with the help of Abby and Viv, was hosting everyone who had helped him since Colleen died. For the first time in years, he felt ready to open his heart and doors to all who had stood by him, including Andrew and his girls and Heather, who was back, to the delight of Babs, Katie, and also Andrew, if Andrew were honest with himself. She appeared to have calmed down and "improved her manners," as Abby referred to the change to Byron. He laughed out loud at her.

"Sometimes you sound like a throwback to the Victorian days, Abigail. This is the eighties, you know—get with it."

"Good manners are never out of style," she said, scolding him.

"Yes, absolutely spot on, especially regarding my children. You keep teaching them good manners. We should get the turkey in the oven. What else do we need to do?" He was anxious to help her.

"Rosella is bringing ham and scalloped potatoes, Heather is doing the veggies, and Andrew's Mom and Dad are bringing jellied salad and cookies. Grandma Viv is making pumpkin pie and pecan pie, and I made a sherry trifle—a little taste of home."

"I'm actually looking forward to Thanksgiving this year. I wouldn't have thought it possible to say such a thing last year."

"The children are so happy you're home, Byron."

"Only the children?" he asked, observing her as she blushed softly. She was about to speak, when Viv rushed into the kitchen.

"I need the kitchen space. Need to make my pies. Shoo, you two!"

"Sorry, Gran, but the turkey needs to be prepped," said Byron. "We'll call you when we're done."

"Don't you dawdle, gossiping on. I need time to prepare the pastry," Viv said as she left the kitchen.

"She's been in a tizzy since she heard Heather was back. She does not like her." Abby laughed.

"You don't say. You surprise me," Byron said.

"It has something to do with Grandma Viv protecting Andrew. She has a soft spot for him, you know."

"Who is taking you to the airport next week? Has Andrew offered?"

"No, but I think he believes he will be, although it will depend on his schedule."

"If you don't mind, Abby, please explain I feel it's my place to take you to the airport. Or do you want him to take you?"

She dropped her gaze, not looking into his eyes. "I don't know," she answered, almost whispering.

"He can pick you up when you return home. I'm driving

you." Standing as close as he could beside her, Byron absorbed every part of her beauty. "Come on, Abby," he whispered. "Let's you and I make magic with this bird!" He smiled at her, gently nudging her.

Byron's home was the perfect venue to celebrate Thanksgiving, and what a feast it was! Byron's dining room table sat twenty-five, with every chair facing a spectacular view. All the food was outstanding. The same group of people had gathered as at the Christmas before, and the healing that had taken place was evident by the laughter, conversation, and camaraderie circulating throughout the dining room.

Byron overflowed with gratitude. He was relieved he and the children were moving through their grief, yet he could still feel the presence of his Colleen. Byron stood up, tapping his glass with his spoon.

"Instead of a standard toast and grace, I thought we might go around the table and give everyone a chance to express what he or she is specifically thankful for," he said. "I'll go first. I am thankful to each of you, my family and friends, for holding my hand and showing me the light until I was able to see my way out of the dark. Colleen will never be far away from me. The pain is fading to a soft ache; the memories are becoming easier to retrieve. We all love you, my darling Colleen, and we miss you. We shall never forget you." Byron raised his glass.

There was a long pause, a potent silence.

Heather spoke up. "I'm thankful for getting me job back with these wee lassies and returning to Virginia."

"I am thankful for Abigail and my family. I'll always be thankful for you, Abby," said Grace.

Byron was moved by the breadth and depth of Grace's statement.

"And I you, my Gracie," Abby replied. "All around this table have given me such a gift: a new understanding about the true meaning of love and the many ways to express it."

"It is I who is grateful to you. Thanksgiving is a great opportunity to thank you for what you mean to me." Andrew hesitated. "I—we all love you and wish you a good visit home with a speedy return."

"We second that!" said Aidan. "Cheers!"

"Turkey and Grandma's pie. Grandma's pie!" Ben shouted, and everyone laughed.

"Yes, let's eat turkey and Grandma's pie." Byron almost kissed Benedict for saving him from a moment when he might have said too much too soon. "Good man, Benedict. Excellent suggestion."

After most of the dinner was eaten, Byron turned to Andrew. "What are your plans for Christmas? We're going to Las Vegas. Would you like to come? The girls will be with their Mother this year, right?"

"Yes, they leave for Ireland at the end of the school break."

"Why not come with us then?"

"Oh yes, please, Uncle Andrew. We love it when you come with us," Grace said.

"I don't want to leave my parents alone," Andrew said.

"Bring them along too. Viv is coming," Byron told him.

"Actually, we'll be on a Caribbean cruise," Maude said.

"You never told me," Andrew responded in surprise.

"We just booked it yesterday—now you know. I'm very excited, and so is Harold. Aren't you, Harold?"

"Yes, dear." Harold smiled.

"Well, good for you two. Now you have no excuse, Andrew; come with us to Vegas. You too, Heather." Byron smiled.

"Och, that's amazing. I adore Vegas. I'm dancing a Scottish jig inside me. Wow, thanks for the invitation," Heather replied.

Byron nodded. "There. Everyone is taken care of for Christmas. Now, let's eat Grandma's pie!"

— 50 —

Early in December, Abby awoke on the day she would go home to England. She slipped into her dressing gown and made her way to the kitchen to get herself some coffee. Viv was taking care of the children to allow Abby the day to prepare and pack. There had been several discussions between Byron and Andrew as to who would drive Abby to the airport. She finally had told them she'd take a taxi, as she'd decided she wanted no one. Andrew was on call, and Byron was needed there to help Viv. She was relieved not to be saying goodbye to anyone.

Abby sipped her coffee and looked out the window, saturating her mind with the image of the ocean, a view she wouldn't see for some time. Byron, looking handsome in a royal-blue sweater, came into the kitchen and poured himself some coffee.

"Good morning, Miss Abby. Today is the big day. How are you feeling?"

"Nervous, excited, and sad to be leaving everyone. I wish I could divide myself up into parts like the pumpkin pie at

Thanksgiving: a piece for home, a piece for you and the girls and my Ben, and a piece for Andrew and the girls." She omitted Gabriel.

"Nice to know we're part of the pie," he said. "I don't know how we're going to manage without you; it just doesn't bear thinking about. That's my main reason for going to Las Vegas. At least Andrew and Heather are coming."

"I'd look out for that one." Abby smiled. "Heather has her eye on you; I'd keep Viv close by."

"Are you jealous, Abigail? I'm flattered." Byron laughed out loud.

"Believe me, she is a force to be reckoned with." Abby paused. "Ask Andrew. I think it's a great idea that he's going with you, Byron. I'm really pleased. I know Andrew will feel lost without the girls."

"And you, I expect," Byron said. "When are we going to stop small talk and speak directly to each other?"

Byron shocked Abby. He had the power to consistently do that to her, or she gave him the power. He approached Abby, standing close. His lips brushed her cheek and then moved gently to her lips. His lips kissed hers as though leaving her with a lingering message. He stirred something within her that was unique—there was no other word for it. She was confused, or maybe he was. As she leaned into him to respond, something stopped her. Dear God, what was she thinking?

Stepping back, Abby gasped. "Byron, please."

"I'm not sorry, Abigail; I would have regretted not kissing you if I thought you weren't coming back. A little competition for Andrew."

"What are you suggesting?"

"It's not a suggestion. I'm showing you what we share."

Abby was about to ask him exactly what they shared, when Viv breezed into the kitchen.

"Hello, everyone. What a beautiful day, bright and frosty. The kids were quiet on the drive this morning—sad you're going home. Especially Gracie. She was very subdued. What can I do to help you, Abby?" she asked.

Abby felt flustered, but fortunately, Viv didn't notice. "Everything is fine. Thank you. Most of my packing is done. We can gather up some laundry."

"Absolutely not. You are officially on holiday. Now, go."

"There. You've been told. I have some errands to run. See you later." Byron winked at Abby, and she felt herself blush. She left the kitchen quickly, keeping her head down, hoping Viv would not notice.

Abby didn't come out of her room until it was almost time for her to go and the taxi had arrived. Realizing the ache in her chest was her heart already pining for the little ones, she kissed them each one by one, hugging them and telling them all to be good.

"I've given your Christmas gifts to Grandma Viv, and she'll make certain you get them on Christmas Day."

"We'll call you, Abby. I know there is an eight-hour difference, but I have all the phone numbers," Byron told her.

"Thank you for everything," Abby responded.

Aria began singing "Have Yourself a Merry Little Christmas." Ben threw his arms about Abby and wouldn't let go. Grace stood quietly, looking at her with sad eyes.

"Come with Grandma," Viv said. "Abby has to go to the taxi."

"I'll see you all very soon," Abby said, closing the front

door behind her. With tears streaming from her eyes, she climbed into the taxi.

"To the airport? Going somewhere nice?"

"Yes, I'm going to England for the holidays. And to make an important decision."

— 51 —

The next afternoon, Abby stood beside her Father; her brother Andre; and her sister-in-law Stephanie, her brother Eugene's widow, who was holding Abby's nephew Stephan in her arms. It was surreal; Abby was joining the nation as it came together in magnificent St. Paul's Cathedral to commemorate those who had died during the Falklands War, including Eugene. The vast basilica, with its famous whispering dome, was filled. The Most Reverend Robert Runcie, archbishop of Canterbury, spoke to the congregation, which included widows, families, and military commanders as well as the nation's leaders.

"War is a sign of human failures, a shared anguish, but can also be a bridge of reconciliation. Our neighbors are indeed like us. Sometimes, with the greatest reluctance, force is necessary in order to hold back the chaos that injustice and the irrational element in man threaten to make of the world. But even in the failure of war, there are springs of hope," the archbishop said, reaching out to comfort those who were there. "There is mourning on both sides of this conflict," he said, referring to all the Argentinian parents with lost sons as well as to the British families. Many stood in the congregation with Abby. Widows cradled babies in their arms.

Prime Minister Margaret Thatcher was there with members of the Cabinet and former prime ministers Edward Heath, James Callaghan, and Sir Alec Douglas-Home. Abby couldn't see her, but Queen Elizabeth II was in attendance, and many people saw her that day as more than their sovereign; she was also a Mother. Her son Andrew, a helicopter pilot, remained in the South Atlantic aboard the aircraft carrier *Invincible*.

It was a sad and memorable service—one Abby would remember for the rest of her life with a heavy heart.

Abby walked slowly along the road. All the stores were closed and shuttered, and the street was quiet, with little to no traffic. She was taking a nostalgic walk to her Dad's house for Christmas Eve supper with him, as everyone else in her family was busy doing other things: wrapping gifts, going out with a boyfriend, or visiting in-laws.

Sasha was preparing Christmas Day dinner alone at his request, and they would all congregate that night at the monastery for midnight Mass. The night was fresh, cool, and not too damp. Abby continued to walk until dusk became night. The final moments of Christmas Eve Day had slipped away. She could smell snow in the air, and the odd star peeked through while a bright quarter moon hung high in the sky.

She walked the street with strong feelings of nostalgia. She noticed Sally's ice cream shop. Things didn't change in that town, and since she had arrived home in England, she constantly had found herself comparing everything to the States. She was happy to be home, looking forward to midnight Mass that night and Christmas with everyone tomorrow.

The street was dark, with occasional lit Christmas trees peeking through the net curtains in the windows. Abby walked under the trellis by the gate, stopped for a moment, and whispered a silent prayer. At the front door, she pressed the doorbell and waited as she heard her Dad's footsteps coming along the hall. He was moving slower these days, and she had been shocked when she saw him for the first time at Eugene's memorial. He looked much older, thinner, and paler; his eyes were not as brilliant blue; and his hair was not as thick.

"Come in. *Ça va bien?*" Sebastian said, opening the door as he smiled at his daughter.

"Yes, Dad, and you?"

"Oui," he answered, closing the door, and they kissed each other on both cheeks twice.

"I have the soup, baguette, and runny brie cheese, just as you like it."

Abby followed her Dad into the kitchen. The first thing she saw was a roaring fire, and the first thing she smelled was bread baking. There was no Christmas finery; however, those two enticing fundamental pleasures in life greeted her.

"Take off your coat. Sit. We have time to be together tonight before we go to Mass, yes? And I have many questions for you."

"I am sure you do, Dad," she said as her Dad brought out the food. "It looks delicious. Can I help?"

"Oui, pour the wine."

Eventually, they were both sitting down, raising their glasses, and toasting one another's good health and happiness at Christmastime and always.

"Dad, you've had a difficult year, and I'm so sorry I've been away," Abby told him.

"Don't be, for I'm pleased you are living a wonderful life filled with purpose. My life has lived its best; it's time for me to slow down, be still, and watch. Age brings with it many changes, and most of them are difficult to bear—loss, illness. It's the price we pay for living to old age; however, the rewards far outweigh the sorrow."

"Oh! Dad, you make me sad."

"Then we change the subject. What is happening with you and your life? I am anxious to hear about your Gabriel."

"This past year, living with Byron and his family, I have learned so much, mostly about life and myself."

"That is good, non? An asset to learn more about how you think; feel; and approach opportunity, sorrow, and joy."

"It's been mostly about my feelings around Gabriel. Without my going into too much detail regarding us, he eventually told me this spring he couldn't give up the church. Needless to say, I was devastated at the time, yet there was so much happening around me and my life. With Byron and his children—and Andrew asked me out."

"The doctor, oui?" Sebastian asked.

"Yes, Dad. He's a wonderful man, Father, doctor, son, and friend. He's divorced; his ex-wife and the Mother of his daughters lives in Ireland. I love his girls; they are the best of him." Abby felt a smile broaden her face, a common occurrence when she talked about Andrew. "He helped make it possible for me to succeed in every way toward helping Byron and those little ones. Not alone, of course. We've had the children's maternal grandMother helping, as well as Aidan and Rosella. All working together, we've become one big family."

"This is an amazing story. It's as though, in some way, you were destined to find your way into their homes and hearts. What is the status with Andrew now?"

"We've been dating. My relationship with him feels upside down. He asked me for a more committed relationship. He's very sure of his feelings toward me; I'm just not as sure as he is. This is one of my dilemmas, Dad. How can I feel the way I do for all three of them?"

"I am listening. Go on, Abby."

"Byron has made comments and suggestions that he's looking for more, although he didn't say what." Abby moved restlessly around the room. She stopped at the fire in the hearth and gave it a shake with the poker. "It really is tearing into me night and day. I almost ran home to England to get away from the feelings. I think about all those little children. I care so much for them, especially Byron's." Tears began to fall from Abby's eyes.

"You must not feel so sad; there is always a resolution. I find if you listen very closely to yourself, you can discover the answer. Find some time to spend alone—think, pray, listen, walk. The solution is within you. It will present itself," Sebastian told her.

"It seemed as though Gabriel had made his decision, but

he sent me a birthday card with a long-stemmed red rose on the front. He also told me his Mother is dying."

"I am so sorry to hear that."

"He's struggling." Abby sighed. "Byron is very successful, handsome, and kind. Our relationship began almost backward. I moved in, and we work together like a married couple, doing the business of running a home and family together. As time moves on, naturally, everything we do brings us closer together around the children."

"As I listen to you, I understand you've become a most insightful young woman. Abby, these are powerful and profound observations and, I would think, accurate."

"In many ways, Byron is like Gabriel; his need is always for something more than just me. Colleen lives within him; he talks about her constantly, and so he should. The children need to know her, and he is grieving still and will for much longer—maybe the rest of his life. I imagine most of his feelings toward me are as a sort of surrogate."

"Abby, you are amazingly objective. What truth you tell."

"Yes, I know. Dad, can we discuss something else, please?"

"Let me say this: I believe the answer lies within you. Let us clear up and go to the monastery to meet the family for midnight Mass."

A few hours later, Abby listened to the choirboys filling the cathedral with the sounds and spirit of Christmas wonder. She felt a mosaic of emotions. She was happy to be honoring family traditions; Amelia, her Mam; and her inner voice that constantly brought her back to her roots. That night, however, she was feeling something else: the need to return to America.

She was grateful to have her green card. She missed everyone, especially the children; Virginia and her life there; and something more. Yes, she was beginning to understand. Feeling lighter and more at peace, she studied the familiar ancient pillars that supported the monastery, a beacon to the community surrounding it that stood the test of time.

"It's bloody freezing in here." Cammie nudged her as she shivered. "What are you daydreaming about? Some bloke you left behind in America?" She giggled, and Abby put her finger up to her lips and shushed her.

Turning back to the altar, Abby thought, *The Truth is, Cammie is not wrong.*

At lunchtime the next day, the Christmas table was set, and the family gathered around it. Sasha had worked tirelessly to prepare the classic Christmas feast of turkey, chestnut dressing, roast potatoes, vegetables, and gravy—everything one had come to expect—unlike in America, where the family members participated by bringing in extras. Sasha had worked for several days, along with Cammie, to organize the Christmas feast for their siblings and family. That year was a good turnout, though Leah and her family were at the in-laws' that year.

Abby observed her Father; his traumatic year was

showing in his once handsome face. The lines were deeply engraved now, and his vibrant eyes were now pale, watery blue and tired. He had experienced hair loss, weight loss, and something less tangible. She had suspicions as to whether he was sharing the whole truth about his recovery, as he looked so forlorn.

Sebastian stood up, holding his glass. "I'd like to thank Sasha and Cammie for hosting such a feast. How the years pass. I look around this table, particularly at my grandchildren, who are going to school and growing strong and smart …" He stopped to collect his thoughts for a moment. "I couldn't let this Christmas Day pass without a thought and prayer for Eugene." He broke down with a heart-wrenching sob.

Andre quickly stood up, helped his Dad to sit down and sip his wine, and then searched in his pocket for a hankie before giving it to his Dad and taking over.

Andre said, "We all understand what a horrendous year you have experienced. The loss of Eugene has been an unbearable cross to bear, not to mention your health issues. I speak for us all when I say to you that although we cannot understand the weight of your grief at the loss of our Eugene, we can and would like to help carry you through."

Sasha said, "Maybe it would be appropriate for us all to recite Amelia's prayer together in honor of our Mam and Eugene."

"I have faith that he is safe in his Mother's arms," said Sebastian.

Everyone recited the familiar prayer together: "Mother Mary, bless this day. Keep us safe in every way. Guide us to a peaceful place. Fill our hearts and souls with grace. Enfold us in your tender care. Mother Mary, this is our prayer."

"I'd like to end with a toast to family," Sebastian said. "Near and far. Blessings, good health, and a happy New Year."

Later on in the day, after the dishes were cleared, the guests went home, and all the chairs and tables were returned to their rightful places, Abby, Sasha, and Cammie sat together for a moment around the fire.

"Our poor Dad. That was tough watching him today," Sasha said.

"Yes, I was thinking as I looked at him how he has aged. Still, he's recovered enough to enjoy his grandchildren and the food," said Cammie.

Sasha jumped up. "Hey, let's all go down to the pub! They are having a Christmas sing-along tonight. Let's go and have a good old 'Knees Up Mother Brown.'"

"No, I don't think so. I'm tired, and I'd like to spend some time looking at the tree and the manger," Abby replied.

"Abby, you can be such a killjoy sometimes," said Cammie.

"It's not my intention; I just need some time alone. You go, and I'll come by later. It's still early."

"Promise?" asked Sasha.

"Yes, I promise."

Abby watched them leave while singing "Rudolph the Red-Nosed Reindeer." Arms linked, they went along the street, sharing a joke together and laughing on the way.

She envied them—not just their relationship or the freedom to laugh together but the contentment within the space they filled. What they had here and now satisfied them.

She realized in the depths of her core this was not enough for her. No matter how much she would have liked it to be different, she needed something more. Having witnessed the sorrow in her Father's persona that day and the realization of how fleeting time was through his eyes, she was resolved to return to America with purpose for the New Year.

There must be more!

She would make a life for herself and meet some new people. She would join the little local theater and volunteer at the local hospital. She stood to put more coal on the dying embers to bring the fire back to life. She would return to the love of a good man, family, and friends. It was time she ran toward them, not away from them.

Restless, she put a record on the stereo: *Bing Sings Christmas*. Heading to the kitchen, she decided she would make some tea and enjoy a slice of Christmas cake, relishing this time on her own. Pouring hot water into her teapot, Abby thought she heard the doorbell ring. *Who could that be on Christmas night? Those silly buggers probably forgot their key, I bet.* Slowly wandering along the hall, she heard the bell ring out once more.

"Hold your horses. I'm coming. Did you forget your key?" She opened the front door with a grand gesture.

Abby stood speechless at the sight of the person standing at her door. With wide eyes, an open mouth, and a feeling that she was seeing things, she felt her legs give in to the shock. He calmly stepped inside, catching her in his arms and preventing her from falling. Looking into her eyes, he kissed her softly.

"I apologize to you for the unexpected arrival. I didn't mean to shock you. I realized after you left that I cannot—will not—live my life without you knowing how I feel. I made the journey across the sea with the intention of coming to tell you that I love you, Abigail."

Crying tears of joy as he held her, she looked at him, feeling the love within her for this amazing man, and whispered, "I realized it was you. Only today did I understand completely how much you mean to me. I love you!"

52

Sebastian was mesmerized as he looked out at the picture-perfect day for his daughter's wedding. She had decided to marry on Virginia Beach at sunset. She'd told him she loved the light in the autumn; it was enchanting. He could see why. It was exquisite, with endless miles of beautiful golden sand and sunlight dancing on the calm ocean waves.

A simple trellis had been erected, much like the one over his gate at home. It overflowed with white flowers he didn't recognize, although there were also some roses and greenery. Several chairs were lined up, with a royal-blue carpet creating an aisle between them.

The wedding would be a sunset ceremony with mostly family, close friends, parents, siblings, and children in attendance. It was to be simple, although Abby had invited all the children to participate in her wedding party: Aidan and Rosella's three children, Byron's three children, and Andrew's two girls. Along with her niece Amelia, there were six flower girls and three page boys. There were almost more in the wedding party than there were guests. Sebastian had chuckled when he saw them all at breakfast that morning. They had been full of the excitement of the day, practicing walking up the aisle while holding their bouquets.

He was impressed not only with the area but also the affection the three families showed toward one another, particularly Abby. Looking up at the view, he saw his daughter approaching. That day she looked more beautiful in his eyes than he had ever seen her. *Amelia*, he thought as he heard whispers from the past across the sea.

"Hi, Dad. You're early."

He embraced her, kissing her on both cheeks. "So are you. I was curious to see the layout. I can see why you chose this venue for such an important ceremony."

"Beautiful, isn't it, Dad?" Abby said, gazing around.

"Oui, *chérie*," he said. "It is. I do have something to say as we're all alone."

"I'm listening, Dad."

"Is this the right one for you? Are you happy? Will your feelings today carry you into the future? Through the ups and downs? It's a big decision."

"I love him, Dad. I always have."

"Abigail, that's all I need to hear."

Sebastian could not specifically describe how his Abby looked as he prepared to escort her down the aisle to meet her groom. She appeared to float, blending with the magnificent harmony of the white sand on the beach and the shimmering orange-gold light as the sun slowly set upon the aquamarine-silver ocean. The folds and layers of her soft gown moved with her, billowing gently in the late-afternoon sunshine and the gentle ocean breeze.

She took his arm. "You ready, Dad?"

"Never mind me. What about you?"

"I've been waiting for him all my life."

Together they slowly approached the little children in front of them. Grace held Ben's hand, Katie held Babs's hand, and Aria held Amelia's hand the three Kennedy children followed. The girls wore white dresses with blue satin sashes, and the boys wore blue pants with a white waistcoat. Sebastian could feel his daughter's strength and love as she approached her groom. Together they arrived under the trellis of flowers.

Gabriel stood at the head of the aisle, ready to perform the ceremony. He smiled at Abby, as did the groom and the best man, who were waiting for her arrival.

"Who gives Abigail to be married?" Gabriel spoke softly.

"I do," Sebastian answered, placing Abby's hand in Andrew's strong, soft hand, which had held hers for the first time two years ago.

Andrew and Abby looked at one another as though they had loved in another time and place.

"You look beautiful," he said.

"So do you." She smiled at him.

Byron looked handsome as the best man but with a melancholy resolve. Sebastian witnessed sad tears hovering behind his eyes. Gabriel's eyes held the same sorrow. This was not easy for either of them. Sebastian admired their love and commitment to the couple.

Gabriel began the ceremony. The little ones all sat at their feet, and the best man stood beside them. Andrew and Abby became not only man and wife but a family. Gabriel asked everyone to sit as he spoke with an eloquent voice.

"I'd like to welcome you all to this very special day. I

am touched to have been invited to officiate this ceremony. I'd like to say a few words to Abigail and Andrew and also the children and the guests. I'm not going to quote from the Bible, nor am I going to recite poetry or sonnets. Simply this: there are many forms of religion in this world, with Christianity being only one of them. We could give many interpretations to the meaning of religion after what we have experienced here today in this cathedral of God, enfolded in the glory of the sunset with the ocean sight and sounds—the waves, birds, plants, and aromas of the earth. The coming together not only of two extraordinary people but also of all of you children, parents, siblings, and friends, an outpouring of love and camaraderie and inclusion of everyone—to my mind, there is no greater definition of love.

"Today you have created your own religion, a mosaic canopy of caring, as you stand together strong and kind. You will comfort one another, support one another, and love one another. You are religion, the greatest of all religions. Blessings upon each one of you. May you forever carry within you the feeling of this very moment." He turned to face the bride and groom, directing his words to Abby. "I shall never forget you; I shall hold you in the palm of my hand."

Sebastian was moved by the power of Gabriel's words as they rippled through the congregation. The intended message was layered with many meanings, the greatest of them being love. Sasha stood on one side of him, and Cammie was on the other side.

"That gets you right there," Sebastian whispered, hitting his chest.

"Wow, he's good. Do you think he has a thing for her?" Cammie asked.

"No, I don't," Sebastian replied.

"Then I think you might be a little blind, Dad."

"Non, Cammie, you're wrong. Not everything is how it looks."

"If you say so!"

Andre, who'd been listening in, said, "I think they all have a unique bond. It's the most extraordinary moment to witness. I won't forget it. Abby looks so happy."

"Talking of happy," said Cammie, "look at our Sasha with the gorgeous Heather hanging off his arm. He looks like the cat that got the crème."

"Good for him, I say," Andre said. "He deserves a nice girl."

"They're young, single, and free. I hope they find something of value in each other." Sebastian sighed. "Come. Let's follow them out for a photo shoot."

"Where is the reception?" Andre asked.

"A restaurant called the Ocean View. They've closed it and taken it over for the evening; it's a favorite. There is a beautiful view out to sea and excellent food."

"That sounds lovely," said Cammie.

"They've provided a bus; we are all to drive together from the beach. It will leave after the photos. They won't be too long, as it's getting dark and cooling down for the little ones."

"That's great. They thought of everything," Cammie said.

Amazing Grace

The Ocean View restaurant was as stunning as its name. The dining room was set up with the tables facing the full picture window. A multitude of stars hung over the dark, still waters.

"Dad, what do you think?" Abby asked as she approached him. She looked radiant.

"I am speechless."

"We're having Virginia ham and scalloped potatoes. This restaurant is famous for the local cuisine."

"That sounds very good."

"Have you seen Sasha? I'm trying to keep my eye out for him; I see Heather has taken a shine to him."

"I would say it is mutual."

"Yes, well, still, he's my little brother and—"

"Don't worry about him anymore; you have your own family to take care of."

"I must go find Gabriel; he's only staying to say the grace. I don't want to miss him. I was so moved today. There he is. I must go." Abby rushed off.

Sebastian observed them together, touched by their affection for one another. It was evident they cherished one another. He wondered just how Gabriel must have struggled with his feelings for her and his vocation.

After talking to Gabriel, Abby moved her hand to her heart and then to her lips and finally placed her hand on his heart. Reaching behind her head, she loosened her necklace. Sebastian couldn't see what it was, although he was sure it was the angel she had worn for years. She placed the necklace in the palm of Gabriel's hand, raised his hand to her lips, and kissed it.

To Sebastian's surprise, Gabriel repeated the ritual and then fastened the necklace about his neck, placing it behind his collar. Sebastian had witnessed a declaration of love the likes of which he had never seen before. Abby and Gabriel had met for a reason, and they were separating not for a season but possibly for a lifetime. Each would keep the other in a corner of his or her heart.

Byron approached Sebastian. He was a fine man, and Sebastian liked him. Abby was correct in her opinion: she believed he was still grieving his wife and maybe always would.

"You must be a proud Father of the bride."

"Oui."

"Your daughter is amazing, sir; she brought the gift of healing into our home. I didn't think it possible. I shall be forever grateful." Byron shook his hand warmly.

"I understand, Byron. Abby shared her time with you with great affection for everyone, especially your children."

"I've decided to take them with me to Las Vegas, at least for the school term. I can't be apart from them any longer."

"That sounds like a good idea. How will you manage now that Abby is married?"

"I'm taking Heather along, Andrew's nanny. He doesn't need her anymore." Byron chuckled. "And my Mother-in-law part of the time and possibly your son Sasha."

Sebastian was surprised. "How can that be?"

"Although he's only spent a short time with us, I find I like him. He's a talented young man, and I could use him in many ways—chef, handyman, driver, gardener. He's a male version of his sister Abby. Grace and Ben have already figured that out by following him around all week. It's endearing to watch; I believe he'll help them adjust."

"My late wife, Amelia, had a great sense of faith. She

used to say that when the Lord closes a door, he always opens a window. I believe I am bearing witness to her wise words, no?"

Byron extended his hand once more. "Thank you, Sebastian, for raising such amazing kids."

"The credit belongs to their Mother, Amelia. She was the best of all!"

Sebastian followed the newlyweds with his eyes; they moved in perfect harmony as one, meeting and greeting the guests.

At the start of the dinner, Gabriel stood to say grace. "Andrew asked me if I would recite a family grace, one his Father and GrandFather recited before him: 'Bless, O Lord, a portion of this food to our use and thus to thy service.' In Christ's name, amen."

The food was extraordinary, and the event was exceptionally well organized. As the evening went on, Byron stood to make his speech as best man.

Sebastian thought him a handsome man with a unique aura and presence that no doubt gave him the ability to make a stirring speech.

"Ladies and gentlemen and all our amazing children, welcome to this marriage of two of the best people I've had the pleasure to come to know. It's as Father Gabriel so eloquently expressed: a community of kind, loving friends and family. Yes, Father, religion is the true meaning of friendship. Please join me in this: I wish you love, good health, and the best that life can shower upon you. I love you both. To the bride and groom!" He raised his glass.

Sebastian believed Byron might not make it to the end of his speech; however, as a professional, he hung on, and everyone adored him for it. The festivities continued with songs, food, wine, games, and singing. Children's laughter was the predominant sound; it was a joyous wedding feast.

The time arrived for the Father of the bride's speech. As Sebastian stood, he felt his lips quivering and prayed he would make it through without a tear.

"Ladies and gentlemen, our children and grandchildren, welcome. If someone had told me two years ago that on this day, I'd be giving my daughter away on Virginia Beach in the United States of America to a handsome doctor, I would've told them it was impossible. Yet here I stand, beside a prince among men. Andrew, welcome to our family!

"I've enjoyed the week and getting to know you all, friends and family. I must tell you I'm grateful, as I could not be leaving my youngest daughter in better love and care. Life is a curious enigma. In many ways, I've had two of the most difficult years of my life. I lost a son, Eugene, in the Falklands War, and I've had struggles with my health. Yet amid this turmoil, I was given this unexpected week—a gift I'll carry with me for all the days of my life. I must thank you all from the bottom of my heart. Today let us all make a commitment to congregate next year in France at Rougemont. Allow me to welcome you to our home, where we can share with you the tremendous beauty of my land and offer you some French hospitality. This is my toast to family and friends. *Je t'aime beaucoup.*"

Sebastian was content, at peace with the world and, most

importantly, himself and his children. The new generation was forging ahead into new worlds with brave ideas and time on their side to reach for the stars.

His glorious Granddaughter, Amelia, approached him; she was the apple of his eye.

"Bonjour, Amelia."

"Hello, Grandpa. I've been looking everywhere for you."

"You look beautiful," he told her. She looked so like her GrandMother and Andre, with her long dark golden curls cascading down to her waist and the beautiful, melancholy gaze of her Father, Andre. "You are so grown—a young lady. Are you having fun?"

"Oh, Grandpa, it's so beautiful. Auntie Abby looks like Cinderella!" Amelia's tender dark eyes flashed. "Would you like to dance with me, Grandpa?" she asked, slipping her tiny hand into his.

With tears in his eyes, Sebastian picked her up and, holding her in his arms, smiled at her. "There is nothing in this world I'd like more than to dance with you, Amelia!"

Epilogue

Rougemont, France, 1984

The apple tree stood strong and steadfast, weighed down with ripe, juicy red apples. It was the very tree where Sebastian had chased his sister and gorged on the apples, giving himself a stomachache. He had danced with his Amelia around the tree until they were dizzy with joy when she told him she was pregnant with Andre. Sebastian had sat under the tree on his return to France. After forty years, it was the one tree left alive and filled with apples throughout the orchard. Sebastian had lived a lifetime of memories, some happy and some sad, carrying images of the tree with him throughout his days.

That day, as the sun quietly slipped between the mountains that protected the village like the arms of the gods, the Lavalle children and grandchildren gathered as promised.

Abigail watched Sasha as he gave the brass urn to Andre.

"This is how Dad would want things to be." Sasha turned to Abby and Andrew. "Thank you for coming all this way with your new little guy. Welcome, Sebastian Andrew."

Abby wiped her tears away with the back of her hand. Her Dad's seven surviving children and four grandchildren encircled the famous apple tree, holding hands. They bowed their heads together.

Andre removed the top from the urn and slowly sprinkled his Father's ashes around the base of the tree. "Bon voyage, Papa, until we meet again."

The brass plaque on the tree read,

Sebastian Joseph Lavalle
June 3, 1916–August 25, 1984
Home at last, Dad.
RIP

Book Club Questions

1. How did you experience the book? Were you immediately drawn into the story, or did it take a while? Did the book intrigue, amuse, disturb, alienate, irritate, or frighten you?
2. Do you find the characters convincing? Are they believable? Are they fully developed as complex human beings, or were they one-dimensional?
3. Which characters do you particularly admire or dislike? What are their primary characteristics?
4. Do any characters grow or change during the course of the novel? If so, in what way?
5. Whom in the book would you like to meet? What would you ask or say?
6. If you could insert yourself as a character in the book, what role would you play?
7. Is the plot well developed? Is it believable? Do you feel manipulated along the way, or do plot events unfold naturally and organically?
8. Consider the ending. Did you expect it, or were you surprised? Was it manipulative or forced? Was it neatly

wrapped up—maybe too neatly? Or was the story unresolved, ending on an ambiguous note?
9. Can you pick out a passage that strikes you as particularly profound or interesting?
10. If you were to talk with the author, what would you want to know? (Many authors enjoy talking with book clubs. Contact the publisher to see if you can set up a phone or Skype chat.)
11. Have you read the author's other books? Can you discern a similarity—in theme or writing style, for example—between them? Or are they completely different?

About the Author

Christiane Banks emigrated from Newcastle, England, to Canada in 1980 where she met and married her husband. Together, they have raised five sons and are now enjoying the arrival of their grandchildren. Christiane and her husband live in Ontario, Canada. *Amazing Grace* is the sequel to her debut novel, *Amelia's Prayer*.

Lightning Source UK Ltd.
Milton Keynes UK
UKHW011345200421
382307UK00002B/587